WHITER
THAN
SNOW

Across Time & Space series

The Eternity Stone
Mountain of Glass
Desert of Fire
Desert of Ice
The Hidden Door
Whiter Than Snow
City of Light

Fairytale Memoirs series
The Mostly Forgotten Memoirs of Rose Red
Viola Sends Her Regrets
Gifted

Standalone books
Breaking the Glass Slipper
Unshakeable
Tyger

For information on new and upcoming books,
go to **mmarinanbooks.com**

WHITER THAN SNOW

ACROSS TIME & SPACE BOOK 6

M. MARINAN

First published in New Zealand in 2021
by Silversmith Publishing

A catalogue record for this book is available from the National Library of New Zealand

ISBN 978-1-99-001405-5

*For Anne-Marie, one of my biggest cheerleaders
and an all-round fabulous person.*

*With thanks to Kate for helping to shape
and polish this book.*

Contents

Prologue		2
1.	Unpledged	8
2.	In the Mirror	22
3.	Abandonment	39
4.	Going Too Far	55
5.	Temples	70
6.	Prince of the Air	86
7.	Secrets	101
8.	Words Have Power	116
9.	Growth	132
10.	No Returns, No Refunds	148
11.	The Present, in the Past	164
12.	Boom	181
13.	Stranded	197
14.	The Eternity Stone	212
15.	A Strange Detour	229
16.	Whiter than Snow	244
17.	A New Pledge	260
18.	Enemies	277
19.	Fire and Flame	296
20.	The Mind Trap	310
21.	Truth from Lies	326
Epilogue		345
Dear Reader		350
About City of Light		354

Prologue

The Mountain of Glass, time irrelevant

Time to go home.

Those four words echoed over and over in Jon's head until they were all he could think about. After these last few months away, he'd felt like a new person, like all of that mess back in Erus Province belonged to someone else. But now he had to go back to the future, and all the mess would be his again.

However, he had to say goodbye to someone first. Bets had become a good friend while he'd been in the Mountain of Glass, and he couldn't leave without seeing her once more – if only he could find her. She'd been missing for hours.

"Hello, Jon! Are you full of excitement to see all your old friends?"

The speaker's voice was young, female and cheerful, and for a moment he straightened, thinking he'd found Bets. But when he turned, he saw Bets' redheaded sister Anne instead. He scowled. "Was that sarcasm?"

"Most certainly not!" Anne replied lightly. "Would I use sarcasm?"

Yes, definitely. But before he could say that, she carried on, "So mayhap there are troublesome elements to your return. But indeed, you *shall* enjoy seeing your old friends, for you are not the same as you were before. Besides, you shall have one of us within reach at all times, even if you do not see us."

For a moment Jon thought of Bets, but immediately dismissed the idea. She was small and sweet and helpless, no matter what she thought of herself, or even though she now had some 'fire' gift that only she could see. Would such a thing help her against even one carrier determined to pull her into a Creature temple? Unlikely.

For her own safety, Bets must *never* go to his time, he swore to himself. But to Anne he replied, "Is that so? Thank you, I guess.

But I'm actually looking for-"

"Elspeth?" Having pronounced Bets' tongue-tangling full name, Anne waved a hand vaguely to her left. "Head to your favourite peach tree, and you shall find her soon enough."

"Thanks." Jon gave the redhead a wary look over his shoulder, then headed over to the spot she'd mentioned. Anne had changed significantly since he'd first met her; even more so than he himself had. He'd changed on the outside, but she'd changed on the inside ever since becoming immortal. For the most part, she was now much, much easier to get along with.

Jon located the peach tree that had unintentionally become his and Bets' 'favourite' to sit under, then plopped down in the grass in its shade, trying to think of the right words to say when he saw her. How did you tell someone that you'd never see them again?

But he'd been there less than a minute when he saw Bets wander into sight as if she didn't have a care in the world. She wore a simple cream-coloured tunic typical of the Mountain, with a loose, full-length skirt similar to her own home time, but somehow it looked wonderful with her long dark brown hair and light green eyes.

"Where have you been?" he asked, his mood dropping even lower at the thought of leaving her forever. "I went looking and finally had to ask your sister. I couldn't find you anywhere."

Bets just blinked at him, her mouth opening as if she wanted to speak, but then closing again. She didn't answer, so he got up and walked over to her. This close, it was clear how small she was – she barely reached his shoulder.

"I have to go home, Bets, and soon," he said, his chest aching a little. "It's…well, I can't say, but I have to go. But I didn't want to go without saying goodbye."

Her face fell. "Simplicity said you'd gone back to where you came from."

"You mean the inner mountain? I went to talk to Amaranthus about something, then when I came back, you weren't here." He'd mostly gone to see if he could get out of returning home (the answer was no) so it had been a wasted trip. "Where did *you* go?"

Bets got this funny look on her face, but Jon couldn't place why. After a long silence she replied, "Oh, here and there. When do you leave?"

"Um…now." Unfortunately.

"Oh." Her eyes glimmered a little as if with unshed tears, and she ducked her head. "Then I wish you luck, my friend. You do not need any…assistance?"

"Amaranthus has that covered. I think there are a few people back home who will help where it's needed." Jon sighed, wishing once more that he didn't have to return, or that he wasn't *him*. "Bets…"

"Yes?" She looked up at him wide-eyed.

What could he say? *You're so sweet, Bets, but if you knew what I was really like, you wouldn't like me at all. You'd be happy I was gone. If you knew where I was really from…*

"Thank you," he said stiltedly. "You've been a good friend."

Should he hug her? He should hug her, right? Jon leaned forward to do just that, but stopped himself at the last moment. He wasn't in the habit of hugging friends, and she'd never indicated that she'd want him to do so. He quickly stood and casually scrubbed a hand through his hair. "So, I guess that's goodbye."

"Goodbye," Bets echoed.

Ugh. So awkward. But with nothing more to say, Jon quickly turned and strode towards the gateway that Amaranthus had specially created to send him home. Something about the original remnant gateway being removed? Who knew. Who *cared*.

He was going back to Erus city-state, 3004 AD, ready or not.

Elspeth watched as Jon disappeared around a corner, feeling as if a piece of her heart was going with him. Her chest physically ached, and she resisted the temptation to hang her head and cry.

He did not see you as a suitor would, she scolded herself. *It matters little.*

But it did matter, because suitor or not, he'd been her friend. As a formerly crippled bastard from Tudar Angland, she'd had very few true friends. If not for the way her legitimate half-sister Anne had defended her, her life would have been very poor indeed.

Very well. Mayhap she would cry a little, after all.

Just as she'd let out a shaky breath to do so, a familiar voice piped up from somewhere to her left. "You humans are so emotional. Don't worry. No separation is permanent."

Elspeth looked up to see 'twas the same Person who'd sent her on that wild goose chase some time earlier today. 'Twas no small detour either, since Elspeth had ended up on a barren island in the Other realm where she'd had to hide from villains, then had travelled to the twenty-sixth century where she'd endured a bloody, fire-filled battle, then had travelled on a flying ship *back* to the Other realm where she'd helped return the Eternity Stone to its true resting place.

Quite a dangerous detour indeed, and it had come from Elspeth's mistaken belief that Jon had already left through a particular gateway.

He's gone back to where he came from, the Person had said so casually.

Humph.

But now the Person smiled at Elspeth pleasantly. At first glance she appeared to be the same sturdy, placid woman as when Elspeth had last seen her, but when she moved, her form shimmered as if revealing someone else hidden beneath those ordinary features…

Elspeth now knew well that the immortal People might wear human forms, but they were most certainly not human. Nevertheless, Elspeth felt a little cross with her, so her reply to the woman's comment was sharp. "Oh? And how long might this separation be, pray tell?"

"Somewhere between three hundred and one thousand years."

One thousand…!

No, Elspeth decided suddenly. That would simply not do! She simply would *not* go for that long without seeing Jon again! So with that in mind, she turned and marched for the Hall of Treasures, or the Tapestry Room, or wherever Amaranthus might be.

They needed to talk.

"Simplicity has a tendency to tell you the facts, but without any surrounding context," Amaranthus said some time later, his dark eyes crinkling with humour. "She has a good friend called Insight, and they do very well together. But on her own..."

Trying to hold back her impatience, Elspeth cut in, "So, I shall *not* have to wait a thousand years to see Jon again? Nor even three hundred?"

"She referred to the time between one of the locations you've visited and his place of origin. But as it happens, we have an assignment available in his home time, if you want it."

She just about leapt with excitement. "I do! I do! What is it?"

"Security detail."

Elspeth blinked at him, then scratched her head. "Uh..." *What in the world was a security detail?*

"I'll explain it to you," Amaranthus said, still smiling. "But there is a catch..."

Ooh, she thought a few minutes later. 'Twas quite a catch indeed, that she should arrive in Jon's time many weeks before he himself left, and therefore before he knew who she was. As a consequence she would need to disguise herself, for Jon certainly had not known who she was when they'd met in the Mountain of Glass, which itself existed outside of time and even any normal part of Earth...

Elspeth? Her host's voice came directly into her mind. *You want to see your friend, but will you still want to see him if he looks at you as a stranger would? Will you still want to go if your assignment is not for Jon, or Jayel as he'll be widely known, but for someone else entirely?*

'Twas the second part that made Elspeth pause. She'd be assigned to look after one of Amaranthus's people who lived in the terribly dangerous, Creature-ruled cities of Jon's time, although of course that person wouldn't know her real goal. She would not even be there for Jon himself. But still she replied, "Of course."

"Then I will call your sister," Amaranthus said aloud, "and we'll get you everything you'll need."

Later, in the Tapestry Room, Amaranthus hummed as he moved along the tapestry's vast length. He touched a thread here, a thread there, with myriad tiny images and text flickering with every movement. But then as he reached the end of the tapestry, near where it came to a decisive finish, he paused.

Here, the thick dark threads that represented the Creatures now wove into the main body of the tapestry itself. They choked out the fine white threads, seeming to turn them charcoal grey until the cloth grew darker and darker, with only the tiniest patches of light…

"Where is your thread, Amaranthus?" an inquisitive voice asked from beside him.

He didn't need to turn to see dear Anne hovering at his side. *I don't have a thread,* he answered simply. *I am the light.*

He felt her surprise and smiled just a little. "Or perhaps the darkness is the absence of me," he said aloud. "You're wondering about the tapestry's ending."

She didn't bother to confirm what they both already knew. "Will these entanglements finally be resolved?" Then her lips curved, and an image of her sister flickered in her mind's eye – along with a particular young man. "Although some entanglements are willingly entered into."

Amaranthus already knew that Elspeth had spoken with Anne, and that both of them wanted a course of action. He smiled. "True enough, Anne. Now, let us begin."

1
Unpledged

Erus city-state, 3004 AD
Six months earlier on Jon's life thread

Jayel spread out his arms and soared over the fluffy white clouds that were spread out like an arctic landscape far below him. To his left was a stunning series of rainbows, and to his right the darkness and scattered stars of the universe – physically impossible, but here in virtual reality the physical possibilities didn't matter.

Hence the flying…because only the specially gifted could fly, and he wasn't one of them. He wasn't specially gifted, or even slightly gifted. And that was why he stayed in virtual reality, or VR as most called it.

Jay-Jon.

Jayel's nickname from his adoptive mother appeared in the air as solid text at the same time as he heard it, then quickly dissolved. He ignored it. First warnings were easy to miss. Besides, if Anni was calling him in VR then it meant that it was almost time to go to Centre, and he *really* didn't want to do that. Not today. He didn't want to go any day, but he especially didn't want to go today.

Stubbornly he turned and dove straight down towards the layer of clouds. If he went through just *here*, then his private VR programme would have a deep underwater area based on a reef system. As he didn't need to breathe underwater (since it was basically all in his head) he could dive right in…

JAYEL JONNAMIN!

This time his full name was accompanied by a flickering image to his right, and then Anni was right there, keeping time with him.

Once she was in the programme she looked as solid as his surroundings, and he pulled out of the dive with a sheepish grin. "Ma. Hi."

"Didn't you hear me call?" A moment later she shook her bright auburn head, the ever-present triangular mark of her Creature clearly visible on her virtual forehead. *He* didn't have one of those. "Of course you did. Jayel, you have to go today. Your tutor told me that if you don't at least show up to this Power Performance, you'll have to repeat the year."

His heart sank. The only thing worse than going to the East Erus Centre for Further Education would be going twice over. "Which tutor said that?"

"Mm…a woman. Myrani? Wirrano? I'm not sure."

Jayel knew who she was talking about. That tutor was new, and her name was just unusual enough that it hadn't stuck in his memory. "Fine. I'll be right out."

Anni's figure vanished, and Jayel sighed heavily. In this fantastical environment, his exhaled air shot out in a shimmering blue and silver rainbow, which ended with the cheer of an invisible crowd and a burst of fireworks. That made him want to smile – then *that* made him cranky, because when he'd installed the comic aspect to this particular VR programme, he hadn't intended its quirks to show up when he was genuinely unhappy.

By Auda, he wanted to sigh without an imaginary audience! Was that too much to ask?

"Evacuate," he snapped, and the beautiful scene around him abruptly vanished. He could once again feel the cool surface of his personal VR set through the thin fabric of his socklets, and his whole body slumped at the reminder of his true reality.

He stood on the smooth, grey metallic circle that marked the personal VR set. Anni would be on the set in the living room, as she always said that having VR in her bedroom was too much of a distraction. But then she'd always been old-fashioned. The living room's set could also connect to the public network, and why would he want to access to *that*? In VR he wanted to escape people, not talk to them even more.

Not two seconds later Anni poked her head around the doorway. In reality she was somewhat older and more faded than her VR image had looked, but her golden-brown forehead was now smooth and symbol-free. VR projected whatever version of yourself you wanted the world to see – even if ten years younger – but laws prevented any significant changes. VR was as good as life, and you had to be recognisable. And then there were the Creature marks…

"Do you want a ride?" she asked. "You'll have to go straight to the performance temple, the tutor said, or you'll be late. Don't try to go to Centre first."

While Jayel's Centre was an enormous building that could fit thousands of students at capacity, Power Performance was always held in the Other realm, the entrance to which wasn't far from here. Jayel had been debating whether to head to the Centre building and 'forget' that Power Performance took place elsewhere, but now that plan was ruined. "No thanks. I'll walk."

"Have you eaten today?" she persisted. "You know you'll feel better if you eat."

Nothing would make him feel better. It was *Power Performance*. Jayel had no alter-power gifts, not even a teeny tiny one, and the twice-yearly entry into the Other realm was just a ritual humiliation for him. "I'm running late," he answered shortly, ignoring the fact that he likely would need a ride. He'd go, but he wasn't in a hurry to get there. "I have work right after, so I'll see you tonight."

"OK," his mother replied, that usual worried furrow creasing her brow when she looked at him. "Maybe you can meet the new neighbours then. You know, the ones across the hall? They have a girl about your age – I think she's seventeen too – and she'll be going to Centre as well, as soon as they settle in."

Jayel just grunted, grabbing his jacket then leaving with a nod of farewell. He hadn't noticed anyone new moving in, not even across the hall, but then he only left his private VR sessions when he had to. Of course the new girl would be going to Centre – it was practically unheard of for anyone in Erus city-state between the ages of sixteen and twenty *not* to go. Most of the boring stuff was learned before the age of sixteen, like reading, writing, history and maths, and most of the 'exciting' stuff was learned at Centre.

It all came down to power and allegiances, and it would determine the course of your adult life. Shame he was good at the boring stuff, and that he had no Otherly allegiances. Not that he hadn't tried to make any – none of the Creatures would accept his pledge. Not even one.

He sighed, and this time, no shimmering rainbow shot out to accompany the sound. Real life just wasn't that pretty.

Jayel had held a little hope that the liftpod he'd chosen would be broken, but instead it smoothly took him forty-two levels down to his building's ground floor in its usual two-point-three seconds. At this time of day everyone would be at work or in VR (or at work *in* VR) and so in spite of the area's high population, his building's halls and the roads were empty.

He'd just made it to the road when a large, shining silver vehicle pulled up in front of him. Hovering the usual two feet off the ground, it was completely enclosed, and its windows were reflective.

Jayel only knew one person who'd choose such an ostentatious vehicle, and it was the same person who'd built a fourth level onto their narrow penthouse apartment, making it noticeably larger than any other in their building, or even on the entire street. Not because they needed the room, but because he liked to show off.

Luca, also known as Father Dearest.

Dun dun duuuuun.

As if coordinated to Jayel's mocking thoughts, the car door slid open to show Luca sitting inside, his long limbs comfortably slouched on the shiny pleather, and that ever-present smirk on his handsome face. "Get in, Jayel," he said pleasantly. "I'll give you a lift to the temple entrance for your performance."

Jayel's glance flickered over his father's newly pale skin, with vividly contrasting black hair and bright blue-green eyes. Yesterday he'd been blond and golden-skinned. Eighteen months ago, he'd looked much like Jayel himself, with the same olive, easily flushed skin, dark brown hair and mud-brown eyes. But that had been before Luca had become a carrier…and everything had changed.

"Nice colours," Jayel replied. "But I'll walk. I need the exercise." More like he really, really didn't want to be in an enclosed space with this man, shared blood notwithstanding.

Suddenly Luca's hand wrapped tightly around Jayel's wrist. How had he got so close, so fast? "You'll come in the car," he said sharply, even though that hint of mockery never left his eyes. "I wouldn't want you to be late. What will people think, Son?"

People would think that Jayel knew he was pledgeless and therefore that the performance was pointless. They'd think little of him, though what was new? But Jayel felt the manacle-tight grip on his wrist, and glanced at the cold faces of the car's other occupants, and he knew that he'd never win.

He climbed in, and the doors slid shut after him. Luca didn't introduce him to the others in the vehicle. He never did.

"I thought you were meant to be on that diplomatic trip to Dailan for another week," Jayel found himself saying. "Maybe you should tell Anni you're back home already."

Luca shrugged. "Maybe a pledgeless wonder like yourself shouldn't make judgements on what your superiors should do, hmm?"

Jayel flushed with embarrassment, and one of the others snickered. It was a woman, he noted briefly before averting his eyes: one with hair as yellow as a daffodil, and eyes to match. None of it was natural, of course – beauty was rarely natural here in Erus.

But Jayel didn't counter his father's nasty (but true) comment, or even ask why an attractive, fashionably dressed woman was here in his car after a long trip, when Luca hadn't even spoken to his own marriage partner in two weeks. Anni and Luca didn't have a traditional marriage contract, not even here when 'traditional' could mean almost anything.

Luca acted like this because he was a fiend. End of story.

Into the silence Luca said suddenly, "You may think I'm harsh with you for the sake of it, Jayel. But that's not it at all. I want more for you than this pointless, weak life."

Jayel didn't answer that either, even though he'd have loved to counter it. He'd heard it many times, and there were some arguments you just couldn't win. Like, 'can you please just let them kick me out of Centre for incompetence, like they clearly want to?' The answer was always no.

"Before I was a carrier, when I was still called Luke, I was like you," Luca continued. "Unpledged, miserable. One of society's rejects, and aware of it. Like you, I refused to change…until one day my eyes were opened. I was no longer afraid of the Creatures, but instead I understood what they could do for me, who they could make me. Now I'm a city councillor, answering only to our patron Creature Domitian himself."

Argh, not this story again! Luca loved to talk about himself, loved to make it sound like he had so much control over the lives of the ten million other Erusian citizens. But he didn't. There were eleven other councillors, then Chairman Tybalt, *then* Domitian – and even their city-state's patron Creature had to work in conjunction with the ruling Creatures of the city-states around them. No man was an island, and all that. No Creature, either.

So even though Jayel had been determined not to speak, he found his head snapping away from the rapidly passing city scenery, back to his father's unnaturally bright eyes. "You answer to Chairman Tybalt, who answers to Domitian," he retorted. "And Tybalt holds that position for life. Or has that changed in the last two weeks as well?"

Instead of being offended, Luca just smiled. "The future is full of possibilities. But for you, boy, your future is as empty as your present unless you become pledged."

"It's the Creatures' fault," Jayel countered, as he had so many times before. His neck was hot with embarrassment as he fixed his eyes on his father's. "Not mine! Ma took me to every single Creature temple the moment I was old enough to pledge my allegiance, and not one of them wanted me. Not one of them showed up!"

Throughout Erus and its neighbouring city-states there were permanent doorways into the Other realm where the supernatural, immortal Creatures lived. The Creatures were beautiful and powerful beyond human capabilities, and most humans were pledged to one of them from a young age.

Parents would take their child to the temple – the doorway for each individual Creature – in order of preference, and if that Creature appeared to them then it meant that the child had been accepted and could pledge his allegiance. The Creature would then bestow gifts of power, beauty, strength as it chose…physical gifts, but also supernatural ones.

But when Jayel had gone to the temples at age six, they had remained dark and silent for him. Even Domitian, Erus's ruling Creature who *needed* pledges to remain in power, ignored him. None would appear, not even Sarassius, Anni's Creature. *He* wasn't very high ranked, but he still didn't want Jayel. No one did. And now, eleven years on, no one wanted a boy without allegiance…

"You didn't go to *every* temple."

"What do you mean? Of course we did." In desperation Anni had even offered him as a carrier – basically allowing a Creature to share his body so it could access the normal realm – but still he was unwanted.

Luca just smiled at him, his light eyes seeming to change from blue to green and then back again. "Think about it. Who would Anni have been too afraid to go to, but who could have been the one to help you? Perhaps the only one to overlook your mark."

Jayel could only think of one Creature Luca could be referring to. The White Prince. He (it?) was one of the most powerful Creatures in existence, more than Domitian and maybe even equal with Audaline or Gerak, but he was also the most unpredictable. Most people didn't risk going into his temple because far too many never came out again. Or so the stories went.

Just then he realised what Luca had said. "What do you mean, my mark?"

"The one your birth mother left you with when she abandoned you," his father replied silkily. "The one that means you're rejected everywhere you go. But the White Prince wouldn't reject you."

Luca was talking nonsense, Jayel decided. "I'm *not* going to the White Prince," he declared, ignoring the remark about being abandoned since it was probably true. "I'm not suicidal."

Luca shrugged. "The highest risk brings the greatest reward. Perhaps he would even make you a Prince of the Air."

Whether he'd meant to or not, Luca had stated Jayel's greatest desire. Out of all the powers that the Creatures could grant to their pledged, the most powerful and valued gift was that of flight. It was so rare and honoured that only two students in the whole of his Centre had it, and less than a dozen people in the whole of Erus. Those humans who were gifted in such a way were also honoured with the title of 'Prince of the Air' – and the door would open to just about anything they wanted in life.

Jayel desperately wanted that kind of honour, but he knew he'd never get it from the White Prince. "More likely you'd never see me again," he replied flatly. The car pulled to a halt as they reached the outer colonnades of the Power Performance temple entrance, and the door slid open. "Thanks for the ride."

Luca caught his arm as he went to climb out. "Father."

Jayel dipped his head in reluctant acknowledgement. At least Luca didn't want to be called the informal – and affectionate – term 'Da'. "Father."

Luca made the vehicle wait just long enough to ensure his son actually walked inside the temple, then allowed it to pull away. Ten seconds passed and he didn't take his eyes off that building – not until the doorway disappeared from sight. Then he let out a breath he didn't even know he'd been holding.

"If you dislike it so much, then why do you keep offering him rides?" the woman asked coolly, raising one perfectly shaped yellow brow. "You can see he'd happily decline."

"Because *he* dislikes it even more," Luca retorted. "And I will not tremble before anyone, let alone him. You should know that, Mother."

His mother exchanged a meaningful glance with the third occupant of the vehicle, a good-looking young man in his early twenties. "And the part where you tried to send the boy to old Veritas?" she asked Luca. "Was that also to show your disdain, son? Because the timing is fortuitous, to say the least."

"Why's that?" Luca asked idly. He studied the young man briefly, noting that he was dark-eyed and had black hair that had been shaved almost to his scalp. The mark of a convict. He was also extremely handsome, but in this era of genetic engineering, that was no surprise. And because this young man was with Luca's mother...of course he'd be handsome.

The other two exchanged another glance, and this time his mother nodded to the young man. "You tell him, dear Basir. It *is* such an interesting challenge."

Basir, AKA shaved-head-guy, finally met Luca's eyes. His expression held a little something Luca recognised – ruthlessness, and perhaps a complete lack of conscience.

"What my master Lilith allows me to tell you," Basir said in a flat voice, "is that the Tiger has graciously given us terms for your continued occupation of Erus city-state, even in the midst of his upcoming empire."

"The Tiger's empire isn't guaranteed," Luca retorted. "He'll need my support among others', and I will give it. But I need more than just *occupation*. I need to rule in my own right!"

Lilith waved one pale hand dismissively. "Technicalities, my love. Erus will be yours, but only if you meet the Tiger's terms."

"Which are?"

There was a long pause. "Destroy the White Prince," Basir stated finally. "The Tiger allows no competition."

For several moments Luca couldn't speak, and for him, that was saying something. *Destroy the White Prince.* Really?! That explained why Lilith hadn't wanted to give the bad news, and it wasn't that the White Prince was her own father. She always hated for Luca to be unhappy.

"Creatures cannot be destroyed!" Luca burst out. "We know this better than anyone! If the Tiger doesn't want me to have Erus, then tell it to me straight rather than this…foolish, impossible quest! And I shall go to-"

"ENOUGH!" Lilith hissed. Suddenly she was right next to him, her features having morphed briefly into their true, less symmetrical form, and her sharp nails dug into his knee. "Do *not* speak against the Tiger, my son! Or even my love for you will not save you!"

Luca blinked at her for several moments, and finally her nails unlatched from his flesh one by one. He'd spoken in such a way before – worse, really – but her reaction hadn't been so extreme. "Has the Tiger really gained so much strength, then?"

"*Yes.* And the offer to destroy the White Prince wasn't made in jest. Do it. Take out the Tiger's greatest Creature enemy, make it so he's as good as gone from this world, and you will have a high position in the Tiger's empire for life. Is that understood?"

"Understood," Luca answered finally. His mind was ticking away – how did one destroy a Creature? Or failing that, how did one *remove* a Creature? It had never been done before… "But what if I can't do it?"

"Then you get nothing," Lilith's latest boytoy said in that same emotionless tone.

Luca pouted, drumming his fingers on his quickly healing knee. That, he decided, simply wasn't good enough.

There had to be a way.

Tarie's new apartment was in the middle of a suburban neighbourhood; firmly middle-class and close enough to the city limits that from her view on the balcony she could see the green hills edging the urban jungle. It was practically countryside, right? It was all a matter of perspective, and by all things good, she was determined this new life would be good too.

But then compared to where she'd come from, what could possibly be worse?

"Number forty-two-F Eastern Way," she said aloud, setting her palms flat against their high balcony's clear protective barrier. It gave a little under her hands as she studied their surroundings curiously. She'd never lived on the edge of a city like this. Sure, Erus was half the size of Memrys city-state, but she'd never expected to see so much lush life from her own home. It made something inside her tingle with excitement, made her gift spring to life at the back of her tongue. She swallowed and pushed it back. *Not now.* "It's quite nice, right?"

"It's not as big as our last place," her sister Lydia muttered. Younger by five years but considerably taller, the girl had struggled with the move from Memrys where they'd been born and raised. But then it hadn't been Lydia's fault that they'd had to move.

"It's still nice," Tarie said a little defensively. "And completely furnished." Considering that their belongings at their old home had been torched, that was lucky.

"All the furniture is used, and we'll have to clean everything," Lydia contested. But she still wandered off to look through the apartment, her long-haired baby cavy Brownie cuddled in her arms.

"What do you think, Tarie?"

She turned to see her father there, smiling at her a little anxiously. "I haven't seen all of it yet, but I expect it will be fine, Da." But then she would never complain. They hadn't complained at having to move. Well…not *that* much. After what happened to Ma, anything else seemed minor in comparison.

Tarren Filat nodded. He was short and sturdy with deep brown skin and almost-black hair like Tarie's own, and she'd been named after him. "We were blessed to have such a place on short notice, and already furnished," he said, echoing Tarie's earlier words. He held out a shiny blue packet. "I got you something. A little gift to welcome you to our new home."

Tarie took the packet of sweet jelly worms with a wry smile. She'd loved the sweets as a child, and her father had never quite grasped that her tastes had changed. After all, she was eighteen now, and chances were that she'd be graduating from her new Centre and maybe even finding a partner in the next couple of years.

But she wouldn't take that joy from him, and every time he handed her a jelly worm packet she would eat them with the knowledge that her father loved her as best he could. Anyway, they weren't too bad if she ignored the slimy texture. She used to love it, but now it brought to mind memories that she'd rather not have.

"Thanks, Da. I figure it's got to be a good place. After all, it's on the 'Way', isn't it?"

He got her joke. Most people wouldn't have, but then most people weren't followers of the Way, a system of belief that didn't mesh well with the Creature-dominated city-states. It had got them chased from their home in Memrys; that, and what she'd done.

Tarie popped a tangy sweet into her mouth and sucked on it as she wandered through the apartment. It looked very much like the others in the building, three levels with about ten small rooms, and was accessed via the forty-second floor.

That meant they were one of the top apartments, and shared an entry hall with apartment 42-G. She remembered the address specifically because of the fancy metallic plating on 42-G's door. It had looked like Rhodium, and that was *expensive*. Probably too good for the neighbourhood, to be honest.

But Tarie did note that her new apartment was smaller than the one back home. Back there, they'd been on the eightieth floor, and they certainly hadn't had any decent view from their windows. Their garden had been restricted to their balcony, just like it would be here, she supposed. But what a garden it had been.

She wandered through the apartment, noting the slight wear and tear of the appliances and the wall-coverings, and debated what they needed to make it feel like home. More plants, of course. Updated wall-coverings, or some fluffy blankets for their beds...

"Brownie needs a new enclosure," Lydia announced, walking back into the room with her little pet tucked under one arm.

"What's wrong with the one we brought with us?"

"It's too small, and Brownie doesn't like it." Lydia looked down at her pet, tousling his long, silky brown fur. "Isn't that right, Brownie?"

Tarie thought that the cavy didn't have an opinion on anything besides his next meal, and that Lydia was trying to take some control over her new, unstable environment. Also... "You know that's his butt you're stroking, right?"

Her sister glanced down at her pet, then scowled. "Of course I know." But she still turned the animal around, then resumed petting his fluffy head instead.

Just then their father walked in.

"Brownie needs a new enclosure," Lydia told him. "The one we have is broken."

Tarie raised her eyebrows – in less than a minute the thing had been upgraded from too small to broken – but Tarren nodded, seeming unbothered. "You can order another one through VR. You've got your own login."

"VR's broken too."

Tarren glanced at Tarie, and she just shrugged. "I haven't checked it yet. But didn't the relocation agent say VR could take a couple of days to update?"

That turned out to be the case. Half an hour later Tarie had tried everything to get the worn-looking VR circle to switch on, and it still seemed as dead as a piece of concrete. "You could go to the local shops and use their public VR," she suggested. "Isn't there meant to be something close by?"

Tarren shrugged. "Or you go to the local depo, Tarie. You're eighteen, you keep telling me, so you can take your vehicle."

She'd been taking her self-driving vehicle out alone ever since she was twelve, and it was a perfectly normal thing to do. Still, she hesitated just a moment. Going out in public could be safer than VR since in real life, her allegiance wasn't written on her forehead...but it could be more dangerous, too. If she was hurt in real life, she was really hurt.

But Tarie wasn't the type to let fear hold her back for long. She decided it would also be a good chance to see her new city, or at least this tiny corner of it. "Alright."

"Would you get me a new book too?" Lydia asked, sounding a bit less cranky. "One of the Bridie series."

Tarie cringed. Bridie was a romantic series for younger teens, which of course meant it was hated by *older* teens. She'd glanced through a story or two, and while they hadn't been badly written, she'd found them mushy, idealistic and silly. "Can't you wait 'til the VR's up here, then order it in your name?"

"Come on, Tar'," her father teased. "Are you afraid someone's going to hack into your public VR session, then make fun of you for your reading choices?"

"Yes!"

"Really?" Tarren raised an eyebrow.

Tarie sighed, her shoulders slumping. She knew she was being silly, because the chances of a VR hack were incredibly low. "Fine. Bridie it is."

She grabbed her light jacket – specially tailored for her petite size – then took the nearest liftpod down to the large foyer that they shared with twenty or so other apartments. It was empty except for a green-wall covering one side of the room: the sort with dozens of tiny plants growing from dozens of tiny pots. It was a touch of life in this urban jungle, and it made her smile. Although, the plants did look a bit wilted. She wondered if she could water them or if it would be done automatically.

The wall opposite the liftpods was covered in old-fashioned apartment dropboxes. They were the sort that people could post small items to, and which were meant to send an alert when something was delivered. They didn't always, though. Tarie's family had had one in their old home too, but after the third time someone had left a bag of turds in their box, they'd just stopped using it.

Tarie located box 42-F right next to the green-wall. Like the others around it, it was faded and its metal surface slightly dented, a reminder of the building's age. It would be locked, she mused, and they'd need to have their DNA keyed to it on the low chance that someone actually wanted to send them something worthwhile.

She pressed at the release hatch curiously, not really expecting any result, then let out a soft cry of surprise when the box's door suddenly swung open. The interior was packed with rubbish – ancient, empty drink containers, crumpled plexi-paper, and what looked like fast-food drone cartons. They must be broken, she decided in disgust, else they'd have returned to their respective restaurants.

"Great," she muttered. "The lock must be broken, so someone's using it as a dumping ground."

Tarie emptied armfuls of the waste into the foyer's nearby rubbish compactor, trying to be grateful that at least it wasn't smelly. It was all dry rubbish, the sort that looked unpleasant but didn't actually do any damage.

But just then she spotted a little blue velvet bag, right on the bottom of the box. It was about the length of her hand, narrow and flat, and when she picked it up it was light enough that at first she thought it was empty.

But it *wasn't* empty. She tipped the contents into her hand, revealing a decorative knife that she studied in confusion. It was pretty, she decided, with ornate swirls carved into its surface and a squiggly starfish-like shape on its hilt. But who would have left it here?

The same person who rushed off and left their apartment furnished, and their mailbox full of rubbish, she concluded. She brushed her thumb curiously over the starfish shape, wondering at its spiralling legs that in hindsight reminded her more of a spider, and-

…then everything changed around her.

2
In the Mirror

One moment Tarie was standing in front of the old mailbox in her new building's foyer, brushing her hand over this odd little knife, and the next, everything around her had changed.

She was now standing in a vast, dark space, like a huge room with no walls. The only light shone over where she was standing, showing a plain pale floor…and a mirror.

The mirror stood right in front of her, as tall and wide as a double door, with fabulously ornate trim in that same spider/starfish pattern she'd seen on the knife's hilt. And like time was moving too slowly, she saw a figure form in that mirror, like someone staring at her through the haze of a waterfall. Too large to be human, and with mismatched eyes shining blue and yellow…

"Hello," the figure in the mirror said. Their voice was deep and beautiful, yet with a horrible rasping echo, like several people were speaking at once, just out of time with each other. *"Who might you be, little girl?"*

Tarie abruptly realised that she'd been pulled into virtual reality, surely touch-activated through that knife; that there was someone else here just visible in the corner of her eye…and that she really, really shouldn't be in this VR session. The most immense sense of dismay came over her, even though VR always muted her emotions, and she tried desperately to lift her hand off the knife, to quickly return to the foyer.

But she couldn't see a knife anymore, and her virtual hand wouldn't respond to her mind's instructions. Whoever was just out of sight behind her seemed to be moving closer, but she couldn't even turn to look at them. All her attention was glued on whatever was in that mirror.

Evacuate, she tried to say. That was the code that should get her out of any VR programme, anywhere. *EVACUATE!*

"You'll leave when I tell you to leave," the figure in the mirror said. It was almost fully visible now, humanoid and with faintly striped skin, and when it smiled…she saw fangs. *"What is your name, girl?"*

Other people weren't meant to be able to control you in VR, but this felt like an order. Her dismay now having turned into fully-fledged terror, Tarie opened her mouth to respond, but something very different came out instead. The Words rushed out like water from a burst pipe, her gift bypassing her brain and coming out high-speed in the form of nonsensical, strange sounds, like someone had uploaded a foreign language to her tongue and ordered it to 'speak'.

Oh, how she spoke. She babbled away until the thing in the mirror hissed and flickered, and whoever was in the corner of her eye shrieked like a banshee, and suddenly-

…Suddenly she was back in the foyer, trembling from head to toe, and with her mouth still forming those same unknown Words.

Tarie's speech petered into silence as she realised she was free from that horrible VR session. She didn't need the Words anymore. She looked around, still trembling with fright, and saw the knife on the floor, half hidden under the lowest mailboxes. Her own mailbox, 42-F, was now almost hidden behind the most enormous, glossy green plants. In the few seconds that she'd been using her gift, the entire wall of plants had quadrupled in size.

Her gift always made things grow, whether she wanted it to or not.

I hadn't meant to use the Words, she thought in dismay. Not after what had happened back in Memrys. But here, in that unexpected VR session with what had almost looked like a Creature, they'd been her salvation.

"Creatures can't get into VR," Tarie told herself quietly, as if saying it aloud would make it true. "It was probably just some thickhead playing a prank."

Yeah. That had to be right. Someone had been playing a prank on whoever used to live in 42-F, maybe. Just a prank with creepy shadow-people and whatever had been in that mirror…because with VR, you could do almost anything.

But still she found herself wrapping her jacket sleeve tight around her bare hand, then gingerly picking up the knife by its blade and dropping it in the automatic waste compactor.

Crunch.

The Mountain of Glass, time irrelevant

Security detail. That means a guard, does it not? I could be a guard. I could be a marvellous guard, never mind my lack of height. 'Tis gifts and attitude that truly matters in such things.

Having reminded herself of that truth, Elspeth nodded decisively and once again launched a ball of silvery flame at her distant target. But although carefully shaped and carefully thrown, it didn't quite hit the target, instead dissolving into nothing a foot to one side.

"Oooh!" She slumped in disappointment, allowing the next ball of flame to fizzle out in her palms. "How can I possibly protect anyone if I cannot even defeat this feeble target?" And *that* was only an outline marked on stone. It did not even move!

She did not even have the distraction of Jon here talking to her, as she had in previous days, she reminded herself. But that thought merely made her sad.

"What are you still doing here, Bethie?"

Elspeth jolted just a little at the sudden intrusion, even though her sister's voice had been at once recognisable. "I am polishing my skills," she replied defensively, then sighed, laying down her pride. 'Twas not as though she had much of it anyhow. "Anne, I fear that I shall not be up to the task," she admitted. "How can I protect someone else when I feel so out of my depth in all of this? Surely one mightn't be able to protect someone entirely, merely with the use of flame? What if 'tis a physical enemy that I face; one with a sword or arrows? My flame will not burn *those.* And what if-"

"Bethie." Suddenly Anne was at her side, one hand pressed comfortingly against her own. "Amaranthus quite literally already knows what is going to happen. You have seen the Tapestry Room, and 'tis no small thing. If he chose you to go, then 'tis because you have the means to complete the work required. And if you do fail, then he will have prepared alternatives for that, too."

"Oh." Elspeth slumped with relief, her anxiety rushing out from her much like the flame had. "But…surely an extra day or two of training will do no harm? I will be sent to the same time, the same location nevertheless?"

"Of course." Anne shrugged. "But 'tis not the one you will protect that I fear for. 'Tis you, Bethie. 'Tis not good for you to be here, your mind only on dreadful imaginations, and alone."

Elspeth wanted to say that she was not alone, because her sister was here, but 'twas not really the truth. Anne was not the same as she had been, and while Elspeth loved her very much, she was not sufficient company. Indeed, she was not often *here*. And this place…'twas tremendously lovely and peaceful, but somehow not enough either.

"'Tis because you are still mortal. During your mortal life, you will still long for things to please your mortal needs. Out of habit, more than anything else. But later, when you *see* so much more, you shall also appreciate so much more."

Elspeth turned to stare at her sister with narrowed eyes, for it seemed that Anne had responded to Elspeth's thoughts rather than her words. Was such a thing possible now that Anne was immortal? And what exactly had happened to make her change so? "Is there aught you wish to tell me?" she asked a little testily.

Anne blinked her large dark eyes innocently. "No. Whyever would there be?"

"Oh, I don't know…mayhap that you *died* in 1558, sister? Mayhap that you have changed beyond belief because all of your worst habits died with you, and you gained an awful lot of wisdom and discretion accordingly?"

Anne's jaw dropped, and Elspeth was pleased to see that her sister could still be surprised. But not for long.

"You did not know," Anne accused. "You are merely guessing." There was a pause, and a familiar, slightly amused expression came over her face. "And yet I have now confirmed this guess of yours. I thought you would be distressed if you knew, Bethie. Are you not?"

Was she? Elspeth sat herself down on a nearby bench, pondering the question. "It distresses me to think of you suffering. But 'tis over, is it not? And you cannot be harmed again?"

Anne shook her head, then sat next to her. "I still have my challenges, but I shall never be harmed like that again."

"Then I cannot be too distressed, can I?" Elspeth put her arm around her sister's narrow back. They were very much alike in build and in features, but yet so very unlike in colouring and manner. But still, they were blood – mortal or not. "And in truth, most anything might have happened to you at any time," she admitted. "Back home in Tudar Angland, you might have died in childbirth, or of childbed fever *after* giving birth, or of an infection, or from the pox – the worst one, I mean, not the itchy one – or from the plague, or from eating bad meat-"

"Or from being pushed off the castle wall, or from being hung as a witch," Anne added nostalgically. "That I was merely burned as a heretic is almost disappointing, don't you agree?"

The thoughtful moment was gone. Elspeth scowled at her. "No, 'tis not at all disappointing! Would you not have rather died in your sleep?"

But Anne only laughed, showing that she had been jesting the whole time. "Forsooth, I care very little. But you, my dear sister, are stalling. Will you go, or will you not?"

Elspeth slumped her shoulders again, then let out a heavy sigh. She *was* stalling. "Will you vow that I won't ruin everything? That I won't fail?"

Anne looked thoughtful. "No. But I will vow that you won't be alone. And in the end 'tis not your reputation on the line, Bethie. 'Tis Amaranthus's…and he always keeps his word."

Elspeth sighed again. "Very well. I shall go now, if I must."

"Excellent!" Anne clapped her hands excitedly. "Now come with me, and I will show you a few rather clever tricks…"

Erus city-state, 3004 AD

Jayel tucked his hands into his pockets and ambled into the outer temple. Once he was sure he was out of Luca's sight, he breathed a sigh of relief. But only a little sigh, because he still had the stupid 'performance' in front of him.

The one good thing about Power Performance, Jayel told himself, was that it only lasted an hour at most. Normal days at Centre lasted six, but today he just had to suffer through this single hour and then he was free to go to work. His new boss might be a bit of a thickhead, but at least he wouldn't let Jayel be insulted or abused when he was behind the counter, and it took his mind off things.

Plus, it brought in money. Since Jayel's non-existent Creature allegiances wouldn't get him steady income after Centre, and Luca only funded the bare essentials in spite of his high position, Jayel knew he'd have to do things the old-fashioned way. Actually work.

He stepped into the main colonnade, a wide hallway that circled this side of the building, but which had open walls and elegant metal pillars keeping up its roof. This was by far the most impressive part of the building. The inner temple itself was made up of two ancient stone doorways about twenty feet apart. There appeared to be nothing between them…but when you stepped through the first and found yourself in the Other realm, you might never find the second doorway to get out again. The Other was a strange place, and didn't follow the usual rules of time and space.

Even now Jayel could see a couple of his classmates being ushered through the entry doorway by his new tutor, the one with the fluffy blonde hair and the mysterious, forgettable name. Something starting with…M? F?

"Jayel DeLuca! Is that you hiding behind a pillar?" the tutor called out across the largely empty temple, but he still heard someone giggle. "Come on, you're already late."

Jayel stepped out from next to the pillar he *hadn't* been hiding behind and walked up to her. Once he was close enough for his lowered voice to be heard, he murmured, "Look, you and I both know that I don't have any chance of actually performing. I'll walk in, I'll walk out, and will do nothing worth noticing." Ha, it sounded like his whole life plan in one sentence. "Please, can we just skip this whole farce? I'm sure we can work something out with my…father."

The tutor raised a blonde brow. "Councilman Luca is the one who specifically wanted you to perform. Now get in there, or you'll have to repeat the year. Is that understood?"

Jayel's mouth tightened, but he nodded. Chaos, he hated Luca's guts. Luke had been so much more understanding, and even though he had been bitter over some secret pain from his past, at least he hadn't been a complete horse's rear. But then when he'd become a carrier all the mercy seemed to have drained out of him, hence his promotion from being a quiet nobody to being one of Erus's best-known carriers in less than two years – according to him, at least.

Up head the stone doorway into the inner temple was dark, even though the rest of the building was open and well-lit.

It's not actually a temple, Jayel reminded himself even as his pulse picked up. *It's just an entry to the Other realm. Get in, get out, get a pass mark.*

Just then he saw out of the corner of his eye someone seem to fall from the sky. He just made out dark blue hair, symmetrical features and a white flight suit, then heard the tutor say, "Rokal DeWyet! Welcome."

Argh, Rokal! Besides Luca, Rokal and his friends were the people Jayel hated most in the world. Rokal was the son of another councilman. As one of Gerak's carriers, he was also a Prince of the Air – and females couldn't seem to see past his pretty face to realise how toxic he really was. *He* didn't get told off for being late, Jayel noted. But Jayel didn't want to get caught out here with him, or even worse, caught *in there* with him, so he quickly made his way to the doorway and stepped through.

Jayel's skin tingled as he moved from the normal realm to the Other, and for a brief moment he almost felt like he could float. Then suddenly he could feel the ground under his feet. Couldn't see anything though; it was pitch-black in here.

He'd heard others say that they saw beautiful scenes or fantastical feats during their time in Power Performance. But for Jayel there was only ever darkness, the cold, and the occasional distant, creepy noise. His senses always seemed to be dulled, like he was wrapped in a gigantic fluffy blanket that stopped him from experiencing anything properly. No one else seemed to have a similar experience…but then no one else was pledgeless, either.

But Jayel did have one superpower. No matter what happened, he could always find the exit door. Maybe it was because he had no allegiances and therefore no power that he was blind here in the Other, except to see how to get *out*.

He squinted at a tiny speck of white light in the distance which he knew to be the exit doorway. The ever-present firepit of doom (as he called it) shone faintly orange next to it; both lights clear beacons of which way to go. He quickly moved forward, taking one careful step at a time across the unseen ground, his shoulders hunched with discomfort and his arms wrapped tightly around himself.

Jayel walked for what felt like an hour, but might have been far less. Every now and then he'd catch a glimpse of someone else moving – maybe a white-clad form skimming through the air, only just visible to his near-blind eyes. It had to be Rokal, he knew; either Rokal or his equally gorgeous, equally awful girlfriend Orla, who was the Centre's only other Prince of the Air.

He kept waiting for one of them to dive-bomb him; to knock him down and then pretend it hadn't happened at all, or that it had been some fun joke between friends instead of just a way to give him a bloodied nose. They'd done it enough times outside.

But by some miracle Jayel was left untouched. He figured Rokal must have lost him inside the Other, or had found something else more interesting.

Or maybe you're somehow protected.

Jayel scoffed at that ridiculous thought and pushed it aside. The exit doorway drew closer and closer across that vast darkness, and it truly seemed like he'd reach it unharmed. But just as it seemed within reach, a hint of orange caught his eye.

It was a faint line on the ground, like someone had grabbed a paintbrush and made a thin stripe with luminous paint. It stretched up ahead of Jayel, past the exit, and seemed to grow thicker and brighter as it went along. Fascinated, he followed it for a few paces and quickly realised that it wasn't a line at all. It was a crack, one that led straight to the fire pit of doom.

Ah. Probably a good idea to stop, then. The fire pit was the only supernatural thing he'd ever seen here in this temple: a rocky-edged hole about five feet wide that he'd never dared to get close to. Not after the stories he'd heard about how fire would rush up and envelop anyone foolish enough to do so, or how you could trip and fall into yet another realm, a deadly one that would end you in seconds.

It figured that Jayel's only experience with alter-power

would be something trying to kill him.

But then a light breeze stirred the chilly air, bringing a rush of warmth with it, and the scent of…flowers?

Jayel stopped right next to the exit door, the fire pit just metres to his left. That lovely scent tickled his nose again, and he couldn't help shuffling a few steps closer. He wouldn't get too close, he told himself. He'd just check from a distance to see if there was something inside.

Maybe it's not a fire pit at all. You should find out.

Maybe he should, he agreed. He shuffled closer with the exit at his back, craning his neck forward to see over the pit's edge. It felt warm, sure, but the warmth of a sunny day rather than of boiling lava. And it really did seem like that lovely scent was coming from the pit. Was that fruit he smelled?

Jayel leaned forward just a little further…and suddenly felt like he was hit by a truck.

One moment he was about to see inside the fire pit of doom, and the next something hit him in the gut and sent him flying backwards, all the air forced out of his lungs in one painful huff. He felt hard ground under his back and his head hit it with a crack. And abruptly it was daylight again, almost painfully bright against his watering eyes.

"Arghh…." he groaned. "What happened?"

A familiar male face popped into view, almost perfectly symmetrical and looking terribly bored under a corona of dark blue hair, then a second, female face as perfect as the first – this time with purple and pink hair, and smirking at him from a different angle.

Jayel blinked, finally realising what had happened. Someone – probably Rokal – had spear-tackled him right out of the exit door. Now he and Orla were taking full advantage of his embarrassment.

So much for being unnoticed.

"Poor little Jail," Rokal said in his typical apathetic tone, mispronouncing his name as usual. "You really were going to walk into that fire pit, weren't you?"

Jayel scowled, but that only made his head hurt. "I was just looking." He tried to sit up, but a pointy-heeled shoe hit his chest hard, forcing him back and making him hit his head again.

"Shhhh," Orla told him in a mock-soothing tone, pressing

her shoe harder into his chest. It felt like she had spikes in her soles…and knowing her, she probably did. "You've had a nasty fall. You need to rest for a bit, get your strength back."

"I wasn't going to walk into the fire pit," Jayel argued, but his tone came out much weaker and less forceful than he'd intended, as it always did with this lot. It was like they took his sense of self and screwed it up into a tiny little ball, then stepped on it over and over. Like they carried with them this incredible sense of confidence and authority, which seemed to drain the strength from anyone else in their presence.

But he still tried to push Orla's shoe off his chest. "Get off me!"

"You should be thanking us for helping you," Rokal said. "I saved your life."

Yeah, that wasn't going to happen. "Get off me-" Jayel tried again, but then suddenly Rokal bent down and grabbed him by the shoulders, lifting him to his feet in one smooth move. Jayel swayed at the sudden shift, his head thumping in pain, and he felt so very small in the taller boy's presence. Just like he always did.

Well, Rokal *was* half a head taller, and mostly made of muscle. That'd make anyone feel small, right?

"Let me help you up," Rokal said, a few seconds too late.

Jayel blinked again, feeling woozy and startled by the sudden change of tone.

"Jayel DeLuca!" the tutor's voice came from just behind him. "What happened in there?"

Ah. That explained the sudden 'kindness', Jayel realised in dismay. He set a hand to his thumping head, feeling an egg-sized lump on the back of his skull. "Rok-"

"He was about to fall into a fire pit," Orla cut in sweetly. She smiled at the tutor. "Rokal knocked him out at the last moment. Lucky, don't you think?"

"I wasn't-"

"Lucky indeed," the tutor agreed. She gave Jayel a stern glare. "You know as well as anyone that there are dangers in the Other. I'm tempted to fail you for this one, even though you did exit within a reasonable timeframe."

Jayel just stared at her. Either she hadn't seen what happened, or she didn't care. Probably both. Here, people like Rokal and Orla ruled. Chaos, Rokal even had a city councillor for a parent too…but unlike Jayel, Rokal and Orla were pledged.

"I have to go now," he blurted out. "I've got to work."

Oh, he hadn't meant to say that. No one was meant to know he had a job…especially not these two.

Rokal cocked his head to the side, and Orla looked delighted. "You've got a job, Jail?" she said sweetly. "That's great! Where is it?"

"We'll come show support," Rokal added.

"That won't be necessary," Jayel snapped. "I have to go now."

Argh, he was like a broken VR session, saying the same thing over and over. He managed to make his escape, checking in the reflection of a nearby window that they didn't follow him. They didn't…but he could still see Rokal's flat, cruel gaze following him right up till he was out of sight.

They mustn't find out he worked at a nearby local goods depo, Jayel thought, urgency speeding up his pace. He'd got off lightly today, since their friend Gavriel hadn't been there, and Gavriel was even worse than the other two. Rokal and Orla were nasty, but Gavriel was *vicious*. Jayel had heard a rumour he was finishing at Centre, but that was probably too good to be true.

Jayel's head was still throbbing, but he knew he could pick up some painkiller at the depo. That was one of the good things about his new workplace: it sold everything. At work he'd just shift goods and deal with the occasional customer. In a city of this size, most customers were strangers, and they didn't need to know he was unpledged. In contrast, in VR *everyone* knew he was unpledged. Here in the Centre, too. They didn't need to see his blank forehead; they just needed to listen to the gossip.

Jayel had a fantasy that one day he'd wake up to find that everyone else had been stripped of their powers and were all unpledged like him. And then he'd find that he'd gained every single one of their powers…

That would never happen, of course. His second fantasy, the slightly more possible one, was that one day he'd simply leave and never come back again, and he would find somewhere he'd be accepted for who he was and not who he was pledged to.

Sigh.

Up ahead the depo's familiar entrance came into sight: two pink pillars marking a narrow doorway, set in the base of an apartment building. He was late…just.

Forget the fantasy, he told himself. *This is what you've got. Make it work.*

Tarie made her way out through the foyer to the shared garage. She located her apartment's section, then quickly unlocked the door by swiping her finger across the lockpad. That at least was working.

Inside the garage were piles of the larger goods they'd brought with them this morning, but were yet to unpack. She knew some of them wouldn't fit in their new apartment anyway. She located her violet-purple vehicle neatly folded underneath a smallish table, then tugged on the handle, pulling it out into the open before pressing the 'unlock' button. With a few clicks and groans the vehicle unfolded to its full, unimpressive size…minus the front bumper. Tarie scowled then hit it with a fist, and with an unhappy creak the last piece finally popped out.

"What a piece of junk," she muttered. "I can't wait until I can buy a replacement."

"Old but solid!" came her father's voice through the garage's small speaker, which she hadn't noticed up 'til then. "Just like me." He chuckled.

Tarie wanted to roll her eyes at the often-repeated joke, but she figured there might be video too, hidden somewhere in the small dark space. *Old vehicles do the job,* Tarren had told her many times. *You don't need a new one.*

Or they couldn't afford it after putting all their funds into coming here, more like. As for her, she thought she didn't *need* to stand out in any way whatsoever, least of all because she had a too-old vehicle. Even her section's violet colour was faded and scratched well past its former vividness. It was hard enough being strange because her family followed the Way rather than a Creature like everyone else; that and her 'gift'. She didn't need anything else to make her seem even more odd.

Tarie climbed into the vehicle, and once her presence was registered the clear protective cover slipped over her head, creating a bubble of safety. She set the autodrive to the nearest public VR access point, then noticed an odd marking on the windshield as the vehicle picked up speed. It looked like…some kind of code?

A few moments later she realised what it was. Someone had scratched 'WAY-FOLLOWER' into the thick, clear casing, but of course to her it was now back-to-front. Her lips tightened. She'd need to fold the vehicle down quickly, she decided, before anyone could see it.

Goodbye Memrys Province, she told herself. *I won't miss you.*

Old as it was, the vehicle took her straight to the nearest public VR point without any trouble. It was located at the base of an apartment building, between a couple of small food shops, and not far from the Centre she'd be attending the following day. The shop's sign read *Timm's Depo - we sell everything*. That usually meant she could order anything there, and they'd get it sent to her house from the suppliers within the day.

This part of the city was quiet, with plenty of grass and trees and even edged by appealing hills, but even so the streets were noticeably empty. Back home- back in busy Memrys, most people spent their time in VR, so this would be normal. But Erus was half the size of Memrys, wasn't it? Even though it had more Creature temples…

Hmm.

The parking lot was nearly empty, so Tarie quickly folded her vehicle down and locked it into a parking slot on the building's side. Inside, Timm's Depo proved to be much like those shops back in Memrys. There was a row of worn-looking VR circles just inside the door, then shelves and shelves of everyday goods, all visible behind well-lit plastiglass. A young man sat behind the nearby counter, barely looking up as she walked in.

Tarie stepped onto the nearest VR circle, feeling the slight tingle as her mind was pulled into a new, artificial place. Now she stood across from a high desk, its front covered in flickering images. Behind the desk stood an orange-haired woman, a bright smile plastered on her artificial face. "G-g-greetings," she stuttered. "How m-m-may I hp you?"

How may you hp me? Stupid VR programme was on the blink. Ah, well. As long as it still worked. "I need a small animal pen," Tarie began. She listed off the requirements, adding a couple of her favourite foods while she was at it, then reluctantly added

Lydia's book request.

The woman, who'd been nodding eagerly at each added request, seemed to go into a spasm with that last query. Her form flickered rapidly, her chin bobbing at high-speed. "Brrbbbbrrrbbbrrbbbrrrbbbrr-"

Argh! Tarie waited a few moments longer, then gave up, deciding the set's VR connection must be damaged. She stepped off the circle, blinking a little as her surroundings changed back to the shop. She had a brief flashback to the surprise VR session in her building's foyer, but pushed the memory away as she stepped onto the next VR plate.

"It's broken."

She paused with one foot on the floor, one on the VR plate, and glanced over her shoulder at the young man behind the counter.

He shrugged apologetically. "Sorry. I would have said something when you walked in, but I was too slow, then I thought maybe it was working after all. We were supposed to get it fixed yesterday, but that never happened. It needed new parts."

"And you don't sell them yourselves?" Tarie said dryly.

He looked startled, then seemed to get the joke. "Now that would be too easy, wouldn't it? Can I take your order directly? If we can't send it with you now, we can get it to you within an hour."

They chatted for a bit and Tarie recounted the same order she'd given in the VR booth, but she hesitated a little on the last part. "You wouldn't have the Bridie series, would you?" she said in a lower voice. "My little sister loves them."

The boy, whose nametag read 'Jon', didn't raise an eyebrow. Clearly he'd never heard of the books – probably because people just ordered them at home, without coming to a place like this. "If they exist, we can get them for you." But then he went quiet, his eyes widening as he looked at something over her shoulder. "Ah...I'll just get my boss to help you with that."

Then he quickly slipped through a nearby door to a back room, out of sight.

For one confused moment Tarie thought he'd been fleeing the Bridie order, for which she couldn't really blame him. Then she glanced behind her – and upwards – to see new customers had come into the store. With that odd, delayed thought process she sometimes had, she saw a young couple in their late teens. They were both tall and powerfully built, dressed in fashionable white clothing made up of sheer fabric panels divided by thick opaque straps over the important bits, and plain white trousers. They both had colour-streaked dark hair, and she might have thought them related if not for their very different facial features.

Good-looking, she thought. Ooh, *very* good-looking, in the boy's case.

He sneered at her. "See something you like, Shorty?"

Tarie blinked and a wash of warmth rushed up her neck. She hadn't realised she was staring. "I didn't realise coloured hair was in fashion here," she found herself saying. "I've just moved in from Memrys." She would have added 'it looks great' except that the boy had been rude, and she suddenly disliked him as much as she'd found him appealing.

"Clearly," the boy said, his tone suggesting that the effort of speaking was terribly difficult...and yet he was doing it anyway. "You're barely understandable."

Right. Thank you for noticing my accent, thickhead.

The gorgeous girl squealed in mock dismay. "Oh Rokky, don't be so mean to the little girl! Look at her! Of course she doesn't know anything about fashion."

Tarie stared at the girl, finally connecting her white, fantastically clean outfit with something she'd read about Erus Province – the white suit meant she was some kind of big deal. Wonderful. But Tarie wasn't interested in being insulted by big deals, no matter how gorgeous, so she turned back to the counter.

The young guy, Jon, had been replaced by a shortish middle-aged man with such perfect hair and eyebrows that they must be fake. His nametag read 'Timm'. He smiled at her expectantly. "I hear we have an order to complete, hmm? Those Bridie books really do sell like chocolate for you young folk. My twelve-year-old daughter loves them too."

Tarie closed her eyes just briefly as she heard a giggle from behind her. "Thank you," she said a little sharply. "It's for my little sister. Let's finish, shall we?"

"Little sister, eh?" Timm winked, seeming unbothered by her tone. "Let's hope she enjoys her book, then."

And this was why Tarie preferred to buy in VR – no judgement. And she was never, ever, *ever* going to buy a Bridie book again, whether in VR or real life. Lydia could Chaos-well do it herself. It took what, ten seconds in VR?

Tarie's eye twitched – but she took the bag anyway. One pop-up enclosure for Brownie, a range of ingredients for the nutri-dispenser…and the code to one teeny, tiny digital book file.

Outside, she found her vehicle was parked in by a trio of others, all connected together to form one very long, shiny vehicle. Sitting on the multi-vehicle's gleaming front bumper was another young man, probably in his late teens or early twenties. He looked up when she approached, and she quickly took in his fashionable clothing and handsome face. He wore green rather than white, but what was the bet he was connected to that couple?

"You've parked me in," Tarie said politely, pointing at her own folded-up, faded little vehicle where it was locked into the nearby rack.

"Oh, the antique?" the boy asked. Even sitting, his lean build was apparent. He had short, wavy blond hair and excellent cheekbones, and Tarie quickly decided she disliked him as much as the other two inside.

Was that fair? Probably not, but she hadn't had the best ten minutes. "Yeah, that's right," she responded flatly. "The antique. Would you move your vehicle, please?"

"Nope."

"What?!"

"We're not parking you in," the blond guy countered. "You've got plenty of room to get out, see?" He pointed to the narrow gap between her folded vehicle and their outstretched, multicoloured one.

Tarie just stared at it in disgust. "Sure, I'll pull my vehicle out. But when I scratch both vehicles, whose do you think will look worse?" Hint: it wouldn't be her old clunker.

The blond just smiled. "Try it. But if you scratch any of our vehicles…you'll pay."

Right.

Tarie looked at her folded-up vehicle, then at the lengthy, rather gorgeous multi-vehicle connected in front of her. Then because she'd travelled a long way to get here, hadn't even unpacked, had just been mildly insulted by several strangers and she was CRANKY, she squared her shoulders, turned sideways then slipped into the gap. She shuffled over to her vehicle, then pressed her back against the blond guy's shiny vehicle and pushed hard.

There was a creak and a gasp, and the entire multi-vehicle skidded several feet back across the ground. No longer parked in, Tarie calmly unclipped her own car from the parking slot, moved it out to an open space, then unfolded it to its full, unimpressive size. She didn't even have to whack it this time to make it open entirely.

As she climbed into her old car, she met the blond's eyes. He was now standing in front of his vehicle, probably having been knocked off the bumper when she'd moved it. He was smiling, but his eyes weren't friendly.

Yes, I'm stronger than I look, Tarie thought with a smirk. *Filats might be short – well, especially me – but we're sturdy.* And she hadn't even scratched their vehicle.

"What's a Way-Follower?" the boy called suddenly. He'd clearly read her graffitied windscreen.

Tarie tapped in directions for home, then smiled right back at him. Her smile didn't reach her eyes either. "I have no idea."

Then she left, thinking: *thank the Timeless One I'll never have to see* them *again.*

3
Abandonment

Jayel hid in the warehouse part of the depo for an hour, supposedly checking orders as they were automatically packed then shipped off to hundreds of different destinations, but actually just…hiding.

Finally Timm came out to find him. "Jon, where have you been? Surely you weren't in the toilet that whole time?!"

Oh yeah. Jayel had claimed he was about to throw up as his excuse for fleeing the front shop, then had simply failed to return until he was sure the Terrible Two had left. He'd told Timm that he'd fallen while at Centre, and Timm had seen the lump on his head and accepted the explanation for his slight lateness today.

"No, only a few minutes," Jayel replied, trying to sound surprised. "I feel better now the pain meds have kicked in. I don't want to be sick anymore. Then I saw you were serving people, so I stayed out here and watched the machines. Was that not right?"

Timm looked a little deflated, then lifted his chin again. "A couple of your friends came to see you, and they waited a good twenty minutes before finally leaving."

"Oh?" Jayel wanted to say 'I must have just missed them' but couldn't force out such a blatant lie. He'd fled the moment he'd seen Rokal and Orla come in. He'd wondered how they'd found out where he worked, but like allegiances, employment was a matter of public record. Going by part of his middle name clearly hadn't saved him for long.

"Mm. They were asking for Jayel, but of course I knew who they were after. Anyhow, they were both Princes of the Air, would you believe it? I asked them which Creatures they were pledged to, but they didn't say." Timm looked disgruntled at that. "It wasn't a difficult question since only three Creatures can gift flight, and they weren't buying anything."

There was a pause.

"I don't have any friends in those circles," Jayel said finally, when it became clear Timm wanted a response.

"But your father..."

Jayel shrugged. "Is a carrier, and I'm unpledged. You did know that when you hired me."

"Oh."

But feeling a little sorry for the older man, Jayel added, "I do go to Centre with a couple of Princes of the Air who are both pledged to Gerak, but we're not friends. Barely acquaintances." Bullies-and-victim, more like.

Timm seemed to brighten. "Well, you can always have more friends. Who knows? Maybe they can put a word in for you with their own Creature."

Ah, so kind, and so very clueless. Jayel just nodded. "Shall I keep working out back?"

By the time Jayel got home that evening, the pain in his head had subsided to a dull ache, and his foul mood (typical for post-Power Performance) had softened to mild depression. He sat at the kitchen table with an unopened bottle of mint fizz in one hand and a cold-pack pressed against the back of his head.

Ten minutes later Anni swept through the front door, and he quickly dropped the cold-pack into his lap, wanting to avoid awkward questions.

She didn't notice. "Hi darling," she called from the front room. "Oh, the day I've had. Someone has been stealing medicine from the stock shelves and selling it on the side, would you believe? The higher-ups are looking at my area, and I can't imagine who it could be." She walked into the kitchen and bent down to kiss him on the head.

"Argh!" Jayel jolted away, lifting a hand to his throbbing scalp where she'd touched him.

"Jay-Jon! What happened?"

He ducked his head, not meeting her eyes. "I fell."

There was a heavy silence. "I see. And who helped you to fall? The usual?"

Jayel turned away again, not wanting to broach the subject since it just made him feel angry and helpless all over again – pretty much like every time he ran into those people. "Ma, I'm not a kid, and I don't want to talk about it, OK? I went to Power

Performance, I didn't perform *or* have any power, and then I went to work. That's all."

"I see," Anni said again. There was another silence, but this time she moved briskly to the other side of the room and shuffled around in a drawer. "I'll get you a cold-pack, at least."

Jayel lifted up the one he'd been hiding. "No need."

"Oh." His mother didn't suggest anything else, but her earlier energy had vanished.

He knew that when he was unhappy, she was unhappy too, but didn't know what to do about it. "Luca's back," he said instead. "He took me to Power Performance this morning."

"Really? Then I suppose he'll come by tonight or tomorrow." Anni sounded far less concerned about this than by Jayel's own injury. "It was nice of him to take you."

"Not really," Jayel muttered, "considering that the tutor says he insisted on me 'performing' even though he knew I had nothing to show. Oh, and he spent the whole trip telling me how I should become a carrier like him, because then I'll finally be worth knowing."

"Oh," she said again in quite a different tone. "I wish he'd just leave you be, Jay-Jon. Sure, you'd probably find it easier at Centre if you were a carrier, but…well, you might not be *you* anymore." She sighed, then added quietly, "He sure isn't."

Yep. Anni was saying in her own particular way that yes, Luca was a thickhead, and Luke hadn't been. Anni and Luke had signed a marriage contract when Jayel had been twelve. Before then, Luke had been living outside of Erus for years, in the neighbouring city-state of Dailan, while Jayel had barely known his father's name except for what Maia had told Anni before Jayel had even been born.

Then one day this man had shown up at Anni's house, saying he was Jayel's father and that he was going to marry his mother (Anni) so they could look after him together. Jayel remembered Anni smiling at him reassuringly while this incredibly tall, slightly dishevelled man had stood quietly in the background.

Jayel hadn't been sure what to think of him, but he'd wanted a father. As for Luke, it seemed that he wanted a son. Back then, anyway. Now Luke was Luca, and Luca didn't seem to want anything except to please himself.

Jayel looked up at his adoptive mother and wondered if she regretted signing that marriage contract, even one as loose as theirs seemed to be. "You don't love him, do you Ma?"

She looked down, then busied herself at the nutri-dispenser. "Luca? No. But he is my legal marriage partner, Jayel, and he is your father."

"That doesn't mean much," Jayel said under his breath. Especially not in his parents' odd situation, and the reason they'd contracted in the first place. "You know, if he wanted to abandon us just like my birth mother did, I wouldn't mind at all." It would probably make life easier, because there'd be one less person haranguing him. He knew Luca wasn't kind to Anni either, and he hated seeing her treated that way.

But Anni bolted upright and turned to Jayel, an expression of dismay on her face. "What do you mean, abandon you like your birth mother did?! Maia never abandoned you!"

This was something they hadn't really discussed since he was a kid, because Anni always got upset, and he never felt very good about it either. But it had to be said. "Ma, your estranged younger sister dropped her baby at your place, said she'd be back in a few hours, then never returned. If she didn't choose to leave me with you for the last seventeen years, then what's the alternative?"

Anni's face fell. "Something could have happened to her," she said quietly. "Maia loved you, Jayel. I only saw her with you a couple of times, it's true, but I could see how she loved you fiercely. How could she have walked away from you when she felt that kind of love?"

He wanted to believe her, but… "You said that she was young, and that your mother was unsupportive. You said that she was naïve and really seemed to be struggling. People have walked away for much weaker reasons."

"Yes, but…but Jay-Jon, Maia wanted you so badly that she pretended you were a girl for three months just to keep our mother happy! She was talking about making changes in her life. I really thought things were going to turn around-"

"Wait, wait," he cut in. "Go back to the first part. Did you say she pretended I was a *girl*? Why!?"

"I'm sure I must have told you about this at some point."

"No, no, you didn't," Jayel said emphatically. "I would

definitely remember."

"Oh." Anni's eyebrows shot up, bemused. "Well, what did I tell you?"

"Ah…your mother was a difficult person, and your childhood was unhappy, so you left home young. Maia was your much younger sister, and she would sometimes come to visit you. Then she left me with you when I was a baby and never came back."

"Right." There was a lengthy silence. "Strange, how this could be so much a part of our past, but that I've never spoken of it. Well, let's see if I've got any pictures…"

Anni sat down at the table with him, then pulled up the room's hologram. A shimmering 3D image of a young woman popped up. It was one he'd seen before; a young woman with Anni's red-brown hair, but with skin a few shades lighter, a leaner build, and delicate features. She smiled at whoever had been videoing, and Jayel felt a flash of recognition. Odd, when looking at this unfamiliar girl barely his own age. "She looks like you."

Anni gave him a sceptical stare. "What, the hair? That's about it, because we only share a mother. No, Jay-Jon, she looks like *you*."

Jayel had always figured he looked like Luke (not Luca), but it made sense he could resemble both parents. But then the hologram flickered and changed, and now there was a group of females, ranging in size from childish to middle-aged.

"I haven't looked at these for a long time," Anni said with sadness in her tone. "This is from before I left home, when I was eighteen. See how Maia is only a child here?" She pointed to the smallest figure. "And here's my mother Davinia." She pointed to the oldest figure, who had rather striking deep red hair and very pale skin. "See how much Maia looks like Mother? She was the favourite."

Jayel thought that actually, Anni looked a lot like Davinia herself, just with darker skin and rounder features that must have come from her own father. In spite of their obvious differences, the whole group had a strong resemblance, and he again had that strange sense of familiarity and recognition. Family, but strangers.

"Anyway," Anni said, waving a hand so that the hologram switched back to just Maia's older image. "My mother was a powerful woman with links to all kinds of Creatures, but was pledged to none of them."

"And she was powerful anyway?" Jayel asked in surprise.

Anni shrugged. "As far as I can remember. But we lived outside the cities, in a border town, and she gave up a lot in order to remain unpledged. She was a cold, miserable woman, Jayel, and she hated men. Something to do with her own father, and mine, I think." Anni brushed a hand across the hologram, stroking Maia's shimmering cheek. "After things went badly with my father, my mother had Maia carefully designed and implanted. A lab baby, and a perfect specimen. As I said, Maia looked more like her.

"She was more like her in supernatural giftings, too. That was partly why I left all those years ago. I might have been the firstborn, but I wasn't the one Mother was proud of. That was Maia, see? She could do no wrong, even though she could also be very flighty. Mother was...so unhappy when she got pregnant young. She was...harsh with Maia."

Anni shrugged again, then continued, "But then Maia left you here with me and disappeared, and I didn't hear from anyone for weeks. I thought Maia was just being Maia. But then finally Mother showed up here, and she was terribly upset. She said Maia had been caught up in something Creature-related before she went missing, and that something must have happened to her. Doesn't that sound suspicious to you, Jay-Jon?"

"Yeah, I suppose it does." Jayel frowned, considering that new information. "Do you think that my grandmother... Davinia...might have been imagining things? You said she wasn't pledged herself, so maybe she was one of those conspiracy theorists who always imagined the worst."

Anni gave him a sharp look. "No. No, I don't think that at all. It wouldn't be in character for either my mother *or* Maia."

Jayel still wasn't convinced. But he changed the subject. "So what happened to my grandmother? Is she still alive?"

His adoptive mother's expression closed immediately. "She passed away suddenly not long after this all happened."

"Oh." Perhaps he had known that fact, and it was obviously a touchy subject for Anni. But she'd basically just described how her whole immediate family had died or disappeared in a short space of time. Now she told the story, it *did* sound suspicious how

Maia had vanished. Maybe…maybe she hadn't abandoned him after all.

Jayel frowned. "Luca said my birth mother left some kind of mark on me when she left me, something that makes the Creatures reject me. Do you think it might have had something to do with all of this?"

"Chaos-damned Luca," Anni muttered under her breath. Then more loudly she said, "I don't know. But you do know that the things Luca says…"

Just then the door from one of the side parlours slid open and Jayel's father leaned through, a quizzical expression on his face. "And what do I say, dear?"

Anni's eyes widened, and both she and Jayel stared at Luca. "How long have you been here?" she asked, her voice choked.

"Only half an hour or so. Why?"

So he'd probably heard more than he was letting on, Jayel figured, feeling a growing sense of dismay. He saw answering dismay on his mother's face, then pushed back any sense of guilt. Anything they'd said that insulted Luca was true…although to be fair, they hadn't intended for the man to hear it.

Jayel went on the offensive. "Did you see my Power Performance today?"

"I had the details sent to me. You were abysmal, of course."

"Then why did you insist I participate if you knew I was going to be so terrible?" Jayel snapped suddenly. "All it does is embarrass me, and you by extension. Everyone knows I'm your son – so your failure."

There was a long silence as his parents stared at him in shock. Luca would say all sorts of things, though it took a lot to make Jayel respond in such a way. But he wouldn't take it back, Jayel thought fiercely. It was true!

Then Luca laughed. "You're right. You *are* a failure, but I don't get embarrassed anymore. I don't need you to like me, son. Not you, nor my somewhat faded, very ordinary marriage partner." Ignoring the others' shouts of outrage, he continued, "I like myself now, and others respect me. And because you *are* my son, I want to see better for you."

He stepped out into the room, and Jayel saw he was dressed to go out. "I'll be staying at the council apartments tonight because I have a very important meeting about access rights to the

Reamas River, although I don't expect you two to understand it. But you heard me this morning. You're marked in a way that means all the ordinary Creatures will reject you. All except one, and I'll happily humiliate you until you're brave enough to take the risk that will get you that reward. Don't be like I was for so many years. Take the risk, or you'll always be a loser, plain and simple."

And with that kind goodbye he finally left.

They both waited in silence until they heard the outer door click shut, and then Anni swore in a way Jayel had never heard her do in his entire seventeen years. "Jayel, what Creature was he trying to get you to pledge to? And what mark was he talking about?"

Jayel was silent a moment before answering. "He wants me to go to the White Prince."

"WHAT?" she exploded. "That's madness! Tell me you won't do it!"

"Of course I won't do it," he agreed with a half-laugh. "I'm not suicidal. I can't name one living person pledged to the White Prince. Not in Erus, anyway." Rumour had it that the Creature killed anyone who approached him – and maybe even ate them.

Anni seemed placated by that, and Jayel quickly made his excuses and fled before she could question him any longer. He had a lot to think about. Sure, his father was odious. Sure, his birth mother had probably abandoned him…or was dead, at least.

But what if Luca had been right about that mark Maia had supposedly left on him? What if Luca's mysterious Creature *had* given him a tip that the White Prince would accept Jayel when everyone else rejected him?

What if you go back to the Power Performance temple and check out that fire pit? It smelled like fruit and flowers…

Uh, nope, Jayel thought definitively. If his choices were between suicide by fire pit or suicide by Creature, he might just choose the second. Because he realised in that moment that while he couldn't name one single living person who was pledged to the White Prince…he couldn't name one single person who'd been killed by that Creature, either.

Tarie was determined to be early for her first day at the East Erus Centre for Higher Learning. She'd carefully dressed in her most fashionable clothing – a snug, pretty yellow top over loose grey troushoes that were good for walking – and had tamed her longish mane of curly black hair into a slightly tidier version of itself. The ends were faded ginger from a long-ago dye job, and she wondered if she should have some new colour put through it to celebrate her new start in Erus. Maybe a nice bold pink…

A moment later Tarie realised that she was copying that gorgeous/awful couple from yesterday, so she rejected the whole idea and set off. As she stepped out of the liftpod in the foyer for the healthy half-hour walk to the Centre, she saw a lanky young man leaving the building just ahead of her. She caught a glimpse of dark brown hair and long limbs, then he was gone. He must be a neighbour, she figured as she trotted after him.

Tarie caught glimpses of him again as she wound her way through the tight, multileveled streets of the suburb, usually as he turned a corner just ahead of her. It was almost as if he was going to the same place, but of course with that extra height he could walk much faster than she could.

But even with her headpiece giving her directions along the way, Tarie arrived within a few minutes of her start time. The Centre was just another large building on yet another street in this densely populated city, but it had a nice tiled area leading into its wide entrance, with a couple of sturdy trees on either side of the doors. Students were filing in, looking anywhere from mid-teens to early twenties, and not paying her any attention at all.

Good, she thought. It was better to be ignored than targeted.

Tarie made her way to the reception, which was a signposted area just to the side of the entrance. There was a wide grey VR strip on the floor, big enough for several people to stand on at once, but still she found herself stopping just short of it.

She'd thought this place focused on real-world learning. It was part of why they'd chosen to settle here rather than the other options available. But there was no hidden door, no pop-out office where she could speak to a real live person. Finally Tarie sighed, then stepped onto the strip.

The virtual reception area popped up around her, almost identical to the real world except for the brighter walls and reception desk now in front of her. A middle-aged man sat behind the desk, a sharp green triangle marking his virtual forehead. Chances were he was in some cubicle across the city, doing the same job for a dozen different Centres. "New student? Your face isn't on our records."

"Tariana Filat. I just moved from-"

"Memrys, yes I see. A relocation programme participant, are we?" He squinted up at her. "I don't recognise your Creature symbol."

Tarie lifted a hand to brush her forehead where she knew her Way symbol would be. It looked something like a splotchy, smudgy gold thumbprint, not at all lovely. "Uh...it's not that common."

"And..." the man prompted. "Who's your Creature? We require all basic details as part of your student profile."

"Um..." She'd hoped they wouldn't ask this, but it was probably expecting too much. She searched for a way to say who she followed without actually saying those words that had been such a trigger back in Memrys – the Way. "He's...um...the Timeless One." It was an old, obscure name that was accurate enough, but hopefully wouldn't make such a connection.

"Hmm. Another mysterious minor Creature, I see. What gifts and abilities do you have? I don't mean are you good at playing the flute; I mean supernatural gifts."

Tarie hesitated again. Back in Memrys, people knew that only the Way followers had the gift of Words.

"Or don't you have any?" he asked flatly.

"I do," she argued, "I just don't know what to call it. I, um, can speak a supernatural language...that makes plants grow."

The receptionist gave her a long look, eyebrows raised. "And can you demonstrate this gifting?"

"Not in VR."

"Very well." The man leaned over his desk, moving his hands over documents or screens that she couldn't see, then smiled at her. "Thank you, Tariana. Here's your class schedule. It'll upload to your wrist comm then wash off. Have a nice day."

The VR reception area vanished, and Tarie found herself standing back on the grey metal strip, with a shimmering piece of virtual paper in her hand. It dissolved into her palm as she watched it, leaving text that read, *Tariana Filat. DOB 12-08-2986, Memrys. Creature: Timeless One. Notable: speech impediment, gardening.*

"Hey!" she said indignantly.

The virtual text on her palm then changed to read, *Next class: history in room 214. Hurry, or you'll be late.*

Tarie scowled down at the text for a moment, displeased with the description the receptionist had chosen. A moment later she shrugged. It was better than 'Way-follower' and everything that would accompany that. It came down to the Creatures influencing their pledges, and the Creatures *hated* her Creature. Well, not that the Timeless One was even a Creature…

You are now late, the nanotext informed her.

Time to go.

Tarie quickly found her classroom by following the map built into the walls. She slipped inside and found herself at the back of a large room, with perhaps thirty or forty students, all facing the wall-sized hologram of that class's tutor – an older man that the schedule had called Senu Pedro. She veered straight for the nearest empty chair, and had barely put her bag down when suddenly, all she could see was light.

"Tariana Filat!" the tutor's projection boomed. "Good of you to join us!"

Tarie froze, literally in the spotlight as most of the class turned to stare at her. She quickly realised that this was how the 'real world' tutor managed to catch an individual's attention. "Uh…hi?" Was she supposed to apologise for being late? Because that was partly the receptionist, surely…

"Everyone, welcome our newest student from the darkest depths of Memrys, right to our front door." Senu smiled as the class gave a lacklustre, inharmonious 'hello'. "Tariana, I see that you're pledged to, er, the Timeless One? And that your gifts are…" His voice petered out. "Sorry, does this say speech impediment?"

Now several people snickered, and Tarie wanted to climb under her chair and hide there. But because she was her, she lifted her chin instead. "I don't know why that was put down as a gift, because I don't have a speech impediment," she countered firmly. "Except for my accent, and that's a matter of opinion. Also, please call me Tarie."

Senu laughed at her weak joke, and it seemed genuine. Tarie decided she liked him – except for the hideous introduction, and the light that was still shining in her eyes. "Tarie it is. I won't bother introducing the rest of the class – they can do it themselves later – but for now, who's got some spare time?" The spotlight finally moved off Tarie…then settled on the person directly to her right. "Ah, Jail DeLuca. You can help our newest student settle in today. Now…back to the lessons."

Senu launched into a spiel about the origins of the modern city-states, and he'd just reached 'twenty-seventh century nations in upheaval over widespread Creature influence' when Tarie finally felt like everyone's eyes were off her, and back on the screen. She glanced at the person next to her, the unlucky second recipient of the spotlight, then did a double take as she recognised him. It was the guy from the goods depo, the one who'd run off when the gorgeous couple had come in.

She leaned over to him. "I thought your name was Jon," she whispered.

His eyebrows shot up, and his olive cheeks flushed red. "It's my middle name. Have we met?"

"Not really. You served me yesterday at, um, Tom's Depo? The VR wasn't working."

Jail/Jon blinked, and a little recognition seemed to come over his face. "Timm's Depo."

"OK, Timm's. So are you Jon or Jail?"

The spotlight swung back around to blind Tarie, and the tutor said cheerfully, "Glad to see you're so interested in the class, Tarie. What do you think about the break away from the old republics and democracies to the city-states of today?"

Tarie sat upright again, her quiet conversation cut short. But luckily she'd been half-listening to the tutor speak, and she'd done well enough in her Memrys classes to answer the question. "I think that the old forms of government never really allowed for the presence of the Other realm," she began, "and once the borderlands opened up and the old technologies began to fail due to all the alter-power in the atmosphere, changing to smaller, more self-sufficient city-states was only logical."

Senu seemed happy enough with that, and Tarie was left feeling quite good – but she also took the time to focus on the rest of the lesson. When it finally finished, she turned back to her neighbour. "So, do you prefer Jail or Jon?"

"Actually it's Jay-*el*," he replied, emphasising the second syllable. "But everyone seems to say it wrong here, so I go by my middle name Jon." He coughed a little, looking sheepish. It seemed to be this boy's default setting. "Or I'd like to, anyway."

"Jon it is," Tarie said cheerfully. She glanced him over, making yet another connection. "Any chance you live around Eastern Way? I think I might have seen you this morning, too."

"Really? Where do you live?"

She told him, and his eyebrows shot right up. "Seriously? We must be neighbours. What a weird coincidence."

"Or maybe she's just stalking you, Jail," a smooth male voice interjected mockingly. "You know how you attract all the ladies."

There was a burst of laughter at what was clearly intended to be a joke at Jon's expense, and Tarie looked up indignantly to see another familiar figure – the gorgeous guy from yesterday. Here he was again, standing in front of her desk, in a different white flight suit with geometric cut-away squares around his shoulders and chest. His longish dark hair was tipped in gold from what must have been nanites – tiny programmable particles – since yesterday it been streaked with blue…

She caught herself just before she could be accused of staring again, but she was stunned at her own bad luck. So much for never seeing this thickhead again. "Who's the stalker?" she retorted. "I saw you yesterday at that shop too, and I'll bet you weren't there to buy hair cleanser or snacks. And his name is pronounced Jay*el*, if you're hard of hearing, or if 'Jon' is too difficult."

The gorgeous – no, *horrible*, he was the horrible guy – narrowed his dark eyes at her. "You have strong opinions for such a stumpy little thing." He turned and called to someone just out of sight behind her. "Hey Gav, Orla, come say hello to our newest little student."

Tarie turned, feeling almost as if she was in a dream, and there they were – the nasty, beautiful girl from the shop, and the blond guy with the great cheekbones who'd parked her in. Right there, staring at her like she was something they'd scraped off the bottoms of their expensive shoes. Perhaps she'd feel upset later, but now everything was just feeling ridiculous. Almost like a repeat of Memrys…

No, she caught herself. It would *not* be a repeat of Memrys, because she wouldn't let it be. So she made herself smile tightly at the two not-so-new people and wondered how in a city of so many millions, she could be so incredibly unlucky. "More of Jon's friends, I see."

"Oh, sweetie, Jail doesn't have any friends," the girl retorted with a thin smile. "It's the curse of being unpledged, you see."

Ah. In that moment Tarie *did* see, and it explained these three's nastiness and apparent targeting of her new neighbour. It even explained Jon/Jayel's timid manner, the way he'd put his head down the moment the gorgeous boy had arrived, as though he literally couldn't even look on the same level.

They weren't targeting Tarie because she was a Way-follower, even though she had no doubt that they would if they knew. No, she realised they were just generally nasty folk, and poor Jon or whatever his name was would always be a target, because he was one of those rare few unpledged. Not a Way-follower. Not even pledged to the lowest, most useless Creature. Just…without allegiance. Even now, she could feel the tension in his body, as though he was waiting for her to reject him too.

But instead Tarie lifted her head and smiled at the other girl. "Well, now he has a friend. Me."

There was a moment of stunned silence, and when the others started their predictable laughter, Jayel completely ignored them. Instead he stared at his new neighbour in amazement.

Even seated it was clear that she was really short, with strong features that didn't quite suit her small stature, but were nothing out of the ordinary. Her Memrys accent was noticeable, and he'd quickly checked her records while their tutor had been droning on about the rise of the Creature-led city-states. She did have a Creature of her own, although not one he'd heard of, and surely she didn't have any significant power or else it would be recorded. But in spite of that, Tarie Filat seemed to be one of the bravest people he'd ever met.

It wouldn't last.

"This is Rokal," Jayel said, gesturing to the nearest boy who stood in front of their desks, looking down at them. "He's one of Gerak's carriers, and a Prince of the Air. So's his girlfriend Orla.

Both of them have councilmen for parents." He nodded towards the third person. "This is Gavriel. He's pledged to Domitian, who as you know is the patron Creature for Erus-"

"Which means I'm extremely fast," Gavriel cut in with his customary smile/smirk. He could seem polite, this guy, but you didn't need to watch for long to see it was all an act. "Plus I have a few other marvellous gifts that Jail is terribly intimidated by. What he's saying, little Tarie Filat, is that we're rather important, and you ought to be polite to us." He smiled directly at her. "Then we can all be friends, hmm?"

There was a brief silence while Jayel waited for Tarie to apologise, to step back. But instead she said, *"Soyez silenso tu'mah, y fev'goh."*

There was a stunned silence, then Rokal said, "Excuse me?"

Orla let out a short laugh, but it lacked any energy.

Tarie blinked, and were her eyes just a little wider than before? "I said, nice to meet you. It's a greeting back in Memrys."

"I see," Rokal said, but he looked baffled.

Uncharacteristically, Gavriel was still silent.

As for Jayel, he was staring at the desktop in front of him in shock. A tiny little red shoot was unfurling from its gleaming surface, rather like the beginnings of a plant.

But it was growing from the desk. He didn't know what it was made of, but it certainly wasn't wood.

Just then Tarie slid her hand across the desk, right over the red shoot, and it disappeared. She looked evenly at Jayel. "Don't we have a VR-based class now? I don't want to be late."

"Um...yes." He stood and left, resisting the urge to check over his shoulder to see if the Terrible Trio was preparing fireballs to throw at their heads, or something.

But he kept thinking of that little red shoot that had so grown so impossibly from that desktop, and which Tarie had so quickly hidden away.

The Timeless One, her records said. *Speech impediment...and gardening.*

What exactly had she been growing?

Every time the Words were spoken in the normal realm, several things happened in the Other realm. Firstly, in the very centre of the Mountain of Glass, a pulse would come from the heart of the spring of the water of life. That pulse would carry power and the knowledge of how the world should be, rather than how it was.

That power would speed along invisible threads that attached the physical and Other realms, and whenever someone gifted by Amaranthus spoke Words they didn't understand…that same power would pulse out into the atmosphere.

A new reality would emerge piece by tiny piece…one thought at a time, one tiny red leaf at a time.

And once planted, even the smallest Word trees were almost impossible to destroy.

4

Going Too Far

Jayel quickly made his way towards the nearest group VR access point. He didn't realise he'd outpaced his shorter-legged companion until he heard her call after him.

"Jayel! Jon, I mean. Wait!"

"Sorry." He stopped, waiting for her to catch up. "It's habit to move as fast as possible," he explained. "Less chance of…running into certain people."

Tarie wrinkled her nose. "I don't blame you. Are they always like that?"

Jayel shrugged dully. "Sure. Maybe they've been around more lately though. They must be bored." He'd think that he'd get more respect now that Luca was on the Erus council, but it didn't seem to have worked that way at all. Luca was far more Jayel's enemy than aimless, bitter, unpledged Luke ever was.

"Oh." But Tarie didn't dwell on that subject. "So we really do have a VR class, right?" She held up her hand, palm outwards. "What's Super-Session?"

Jayel brightened. He hadn't realised what today's theme was, and it was one of the better ones. Just for fun, really, compared to the many educational VR sessions they had. "It's a rec session – a game where everyone joins in. It's based on the old superheroes, you know, before carriers were common? You get given a set of superpowers, and you have to use them to achieve a target. But you don't know what the target is until you're already in the game." He shrugged. "It's pretty harmless if you get yourself knocked out of the game as soon as possible." He always made a point of doing that, since the abilities he was granted were usually rubbish.

"But it's VR," Tarie countered. "Surely it would be harmless to stay in the game, as well? Or is it one of those games where you can feel pain?"

"No, no, there's never any pain. It's just..." Jayel faltered, realising he didn't have a real reason for purposely getting knocked out. He didn't want to catch anyone's attention, was that it? Too late for that. "...Habit, I suppose," he finished.

She didn't say anything further, but he got the feeling she thought it was a silly habit. And for someone like her, who didn't seem to be scared of anything except that tiny red shoot, it probably was.

Jayel pointed her towards the nearest group VR access point. It was a long, clear-walled cubicle with a bar along its length so users wouldn't accidentally wander into each other or fall over (both of which were real dangers). He stepped inside, taking the first available spot, then gestured to the place next to him as Super-Session's usual scenery sprang up around him and Tarie vanished.

A moment later he was fully in VR, feeling the usual slight numbness that such things brought, in spite of their cheerful surroundings. He now stood in the centre of a colosseum, a round space big enough to fit several hundred people. There was bright green grass underfoot, and the distant edges of the ring-shaped building were multicoloured. Just then Tarie's virtual form appeared next to him, and he saw her Creature's symbol like a blurry gold spot on her forehead. She would see his blank forehead, he knew, but at least she'd already been told he was unpledged.

"How does this game work?" she asked.

"You have to catch a raindrop, and that'll hold your superpower for the game."

"What?!"

Had he not explained it clearly? "The rain," Jayel began again, but then suddenly there was a crack of thunder, quickly followed by a speckling of tiny, glowing raindrops. He stuck out his hand, waving it around randomly until one landed on his skin, then felt the warm tingle as it turned into a gold coin. He held it up to the light. *FLIGHT*, it read.

Jayel blinked at it in shock. Just like in real life, Flight was one of the rarest, most highly sought-after superpowers. He'd *never* had it in these games – and obviously not in real life. Instead he'd usually get something pointless like predicting next week's weather, or perhaps changing his eye colour at will. Not so helpful when these games usually ended up in a battle…

"My coin says 'breathing underwater'," Tarie said from beside him. "Do you think that'll be useful?"

"Only if the colosseum fills up with water," Jayel replied absently. "So probably not."

"Oh. What did you get?"

Still trying to take it in himself, he showed her.

Her eyebrows shot up. "Not bad. So will you still try to get yourself removed from the game as soon as possible?"

Jayel blinked down at the gold coin, wishing desperately it was real life, and closed his fist around it till the object shattered into fine, shimmering dust. "Maybe not. Let's have a go at using our powers, then see what the game contains."

Tarie watched as Jayel stretched one hand into the air, then suddenly took off like a rocket. No, actually like a rocket – with a cloud of fire and smoke behind him, so fast she lost sight of him in the sunny virtual environment. She was sure she heard him say "Yippee!" somewhere along the way.

Oh well, at least someone was having fun. For herself, she didn't mind games, but real life was just more…solid. Obviously.

Last man standing, someone whispered in her ear, but when she turned, there was nothing to see.

Tarie looked down at her own useless coin with bemusement, then checked around her as if an ocean would suddenly materialise in this urban VR setting so that she could test if she could actually breathe underwater or not. Her surroundings remained disappointingly dry. "What's the goal of this game again?" she asked herself aloud.

Just then a male appeared right in front of her. Tarie took in his blond hair and sharp cheekbones, plus a stylised image of a horse on his forehead, and added those features together to make 'Gavriel'.

"The goal is last man standing," he said with a grin. "It's for fun, see? Like this."

Then he punched her in the chest, and his hand went right

inside, through her collarbone. Tarie stared down in dismay, noting the lack of gore – and that this wasn't healthy, even for VR. "I guess I lose," she began, then the scene changed around her.

She was suddenly standing back in the group VR booth, one hand on the safety rail and both her feet on the metal access plate. Her chest was notably whole, but she couldn't shake the sense of unease at that experience.

Jayel stood next to her, his own expression blank and his eyes glazed. Occasionally he trembled a little as if acting out whatever was taking place in his own mind. The other half-dozen people around them woke up one by one, and she watched as they shook off their own VR sessions, also presumably losers in that particular game.

"Someone dropped a rock on my head," she heard a disgruntled boy say.

"Yeah, well someone picked me up and dropped *me* on my head," his companion countered.

Neither sounded too bothered by it, but Tarie decided that *last man standing* could be translated as *how to creatively kill your classmates…for fun!* "Punched through the chest," she quipped.

Both students looked at her. "Had to be Gavriel," one of them ventured. "He always does that move."

"Let's hope not in real life," Tarie joked. But when neither smiled, she just sighed and headed for the cafeteria. Forget the classes: she'd judge this place by its food.

Jayel raced around the VR environment, giddy with excitement. Who knew Flight would also come with speed and a decent amount of strength? At some point during the game he'd decided to stay, to play the thing out as if he was at home in one of his private VR sessions, then he'd just forgotten where he was.

He'd knocked another player off a wall *here,* or dropped a handy boulder on another player *here,* and crowed in triumph when they vanished from the game. He took great pleasure in moving so fast that no one could seem to get a fix on him, not even whoever had laser vision and was leaving gaping, burning slashes in the VR rock walls.

But then as Jayel flew one last loop high over the colosseum, he couldn't see anyone else. The game was still running, so he knew there must be someone else in here with him. He came to rest on the highest wall of the colosseum, a narrow, arching stone path only just wide enough for his feet. The virtual ground was far below him to his right; the many empty stone seats far below to his left.

Crunch. Suddenly the wall trembled and several pieces fell away as a new figure appeared. It was Rokal, standing not ten feet away from Jayel on the top of the wall. He wore his customary white, but he wasn't flying. No one else was flying – Jayel hadn't seen anyone else do so this whole game.

"Jump off the wall," Rokal ordered. His figure shimmered in and out of sight – he must have been gifted with invisibility rather than any decent fighting skill. "Leave the game."

The wall trembled a little again, and around them Jayel saw the colosseum's other walls were beginning to fall. This must mean the game was near its end, although of course he'd never made it this far before. "I've got Flight," he said, but his voice sounded weak to his own virtual ears. "I won't fall."

The wall shook, and Rokal swayed where he stood. His lips tightened, and his curved-horn Creature mark shimmered on his forehead. "Then make yourself fall, *Jail*. Do it now."

Jayel just stared at him. In that moment he realised that Rokal was actually afraid of something, but also that Rokal was trying to get Jayel out of the game before he himself was ejected.

Everything in him wanted to acquiesce, to fall in line as he'd always done. *Don't make Rokal mad.* But when had that ever helped?

Jayel swallowed, then said softly, "It's just a game."

At that moment the wall beneath them crumbled, and Rokal went with it. Jayel stayed where he was, hovering in the air, until the other boy's figure vanished into the grey dust cloud.

Well, Rokal clearly couldn't fly in this particular game, could he?

Congratulations! a cheery voice rang from around Jayel. *You're today's last man standing!*

He was?!

Right then the VR surroundings melted away, and Jayel once again found himself standing in the group access booth, one hand on the metal support rail. He was alone. He'd won in the game, but in real life…?

"It was just a game," Jayel told himself. "No one will care that I won." Hey, maybe someone would even be impressed.

But on the off-chance that Rokal and co weren't impressed, but were actually after revenge, perhaps Jayel would make his way to his next class quickly and quietly. He didn't need lunch, right?

Trying not to creep too obviously, he cautiously walked out of the booth then out of a side door that led across a courtyard to the other side of the Centre. It was a shortcut, and no one was in sight. What luck!

But Jayel hadn't taken three steps into the courtyard when Rokal landed in front of him hard enough to dent the ground. "If it isn't the last man standing," he sneered. "Did you enjoy being a winner for once in your life?"

Jayel turned and dashed for the door, but was abruptly caught short by a grip on the back of his jacket. Then suddenly his feet were leaving the ground: the tiles of the courtyard growing smaller and smaller as Rokal shot up into the air, dragging Jayel along with him.

They were still going up. Up and up, higher than the Centre's first few levels, then as high as the building's roof, then right up to the top of the crows-nest type structure that marked the building's highest point. Rokal came to a halt in the air, then slammed Jayel back against something hard and narrow.

"Why don't we play that game again?" Rokal hissed into Jayel's ear. His voice was rough and fury-filled, more so than any other time Jayel had ever heard him. "Last man standing, here in the real world. Do you give in, Jail?"

Terror consumed Jayel so strongly he couldn't even struggle, because struggling would mean falling. And while heights didn't scare him at all in VR, here in real life his body obviously knew that falling meant damage or death.

Rokal shook him. "Well? Shall I leave you here on the flagpole a little longer?"

Was that where they were? Rokal suddenly moved away, still hovering in the air, and Jayel let out a terrified cry as he felt himself drop down; heard the fabric of his jacket tear. He'd clearly been hooked on, but his clothing wasn't made to carry his own weight.

"Please," he begged, hearing his own voice thin and high with terror. "I give in! Please, let me down!"

The Prince of the Air looked into Jayel's face, his dark eyes narrowed with disgust, and with beads of sweat pearling on his forehead...perhaps Jayel was heavier than he'd realised...? "I don't think I will. I think it'll be you against the hard ground, and let's see who's still standing."

Jayel whimpered again. His whole world had reduced to fear and their sheer height, and the knowledge of his own extreme mortality. "Pl-please..." he tried again, his eyes scrunched tightly shut.

"*HEY!*" a gruff voice burst out, seemingly right in Jayel's ear, and he almost screamed with fright. But out of nowhere strong hands were grabbing him by his upper arms, and he felt himself lifted down until once again solid ground was under his feet. "Kid, are you alright?"

No. No, Jayel was not alright. He couldn't even open his eyes. He couldn't stop himself from shaking. But then that strange, warm fuzzy feeling came over him again; the one he so often had in the Other realm.

Maybe it was panic overload.

Finally he calmed down enough to look around and see he was now standing on the tall building's solid roof, edged with forcefields that would prevent anyone from accidentally falling off. The same forcefields were meant to keep anyone from climbing up the flag tower – but wouldn't stop a flight-gifted Prince of the Air from doing anything at all.

Rokal was nowhere in sight.

In front of Jayel was a grizzled old man who had apparently been his saviour. He didn't look like much, being a little shorter than Jayel with a significant hunch and a mass of shaggy white hair that blended in with his beard. He had bright eyes under hairy white eyebrows, and wore a severe scowl as he finished climbing down the flagpole structure, faster than any elderly person should have been able to do. Maybe he had cybernetic limbs like some old folk got – making them stronger than when they'd been young. "You need a drink, kid?"

"Just...just the lift downstairs, please." Jayel's voice came out small and hoarse, but all he could think of was to escape. Home would be best.

The old man pointed him to a nearby doorway, and Jayel ran for it. His own cries still seemed to be echoing in his ears, and he couldn't shake off how dreadful that moment had felt, being up so high. That was the worst Rokal had ever been. Jayel had never before thought Rokal would kill him – but in that moment, he'd really been afraid that he would.

But then Jayel came out of the liftpod to the ground floor, and he realised that he wasn't imagining cries echoing in his ears. They were all around him – these huge, hideous images of some guy sobbing, the videos plastered up over the Centre's high walls. Jayel stared in shock as other students stopped what they were doing and stared along with him.

Chaos, that guy looked terrible crying. He looked *terrified*. "*Pl-please…pl-please…pl-please…*" he was begging over and over…

Oh…*no*. The hideous realisation dawned too late, even as the other students turned to stare at Jayel. He could hear them whispering, *"That's him! Isn't he the pledgeless one?"*

No. No, no, no, no, no, no, no! This couldn't be happening!

Jayel turned and ran for the nearest exit even as the staring faces and whispers seemed to come from every direction, overlaid by that horrible repeating video of his own crying face. He made his way outside the Centre, straight out into the city streets, and stumbled as a low-speed multibus almost hit him full-on. But then he shook himself and kept running. He'd go anywhere, it didn't matter, as long as he was away from there.

Because one thing was for certain – he was never going back.

Tarie was in the nearest cafeteria when the awful video came onto the walls. And not just one wall; all of them. It played over and over for three minutes straight before finally reverting to the original forest and bird scenery.

By the time it had been shut off, it had gained the whole cafeteria's attention. At least a hundred students were whispering or even laughing about what they'd just seen. But their reaction, and seeing so many widened eyes, suggested it wasn't entirely normal.

As for Tarie, she was utterly horrified to see her new neighbour in such a way, and it brought flashbacks to her worst experiences in Memrys.

It's not like that here in Erus, she reminded herself. *There are laws against harassment here. Erus is meant to be safer.* But she still found herself gripping her chopsticks in a white-knuckled fist, her appetite suddenly gone.

Across from her sat a trio of younger students: a couple of boys to one side, and a young, wide-eyed girl to the other, her hair and face mostly covered by a fashionable hood. The boys were chatting noisily, while the girl didn't say anything at all.

"Is that normal?" Tarie blurted out to them. "That kind of cruelty?"

"Of course not," one of the boys retorted as if surprised. "Whoever did that was a fool to let it get recorded. It'll be traced soon enough. They might even get suspended." Then he added in a lower tone, "Even if it *was* only the Pledgeless Wonder."

"Hey!" Tarie snapped, just as the other girl jolted to attention, her face twisted in a matching indignant scowl. "Don't be rude," Tarie continued in a more normal tone, feeling a little cheered by the other girl's implied support. "Do you really think someone chooses to be unpledged?"

Privately, she thought it was better to be unpledged than with most of those Creatures. But she didn't voice that idea.

The boys exchanged glances that seemed to say Tarie was an oddball, then moved away from the table. She turned to the other girl instead. "But seriously, I'm new here and that – that was really concerning, don't you think?"

The girl just stared at her.

"Or perhaps you're not concerned," Tarie added, feeling disconcerted by the lack of response. "Perhaps you always look like that."

The girl lifted one hand to her face, her wide eyes widening even further, then abruptly stood up and moved away, following after the boys. She glanced once at Tarie over her shoulder, looked appalled to see Tarie was still watching her, then pulled her hood over her face and ducked out of sight.

Tarie looked back down at her tray of half-eaten food, which up till now she'd have rated as pretty decent. The company? Well, it could improve.

By the time Tarie began her walk home at the end of the day, she had changed her opinion just a little. She didn't see Jayel again, and didn't know whether it was because he'd left entirely, or because they just didn't share any more classes. Luckily she didn't repeat her earlier little lapse with the Words, which tended to spill out whenever she was feeling strong emotion, including anger.

Up until Tarie's early teens the Words *had* seemed like a gift, as her small group of Way followers had called it. She had only ever used her power in their presence, and it had always been greatly encouraged.

She wasn't the only one with that power amongst them. One of the old men within the group had it as well, and he'd said that if Tarie kept using it, the Word trees the gift brought could grow taller than a house and have incredible fruit that was said to heal. He'd had an orchard in his backyard that was the results of many years of the Words being spoken. Tarie had thought that was very impressive, and she'd looked forward to having one of her own.

But she'd been home-schooled in their rather cloistered community while she was very young, because in Memrys openly admitting you followed the Way was asking for trouble, and she hadn't known what other people would think of her ability. What other *children* would think of it.

Then Tarie had gone to study at a public Centre. And the first time someone had laughed at the Words, she'd merely shaken it off. And the second, third and fourth time. But after that, she'd begun to hide it, since it seemed easier than having to constantly defend herself. She liked to think that she'd grown very thick skin, and that if people didn't like her (and her gift) then that was their problem. But the truth was that she was ashamed.

Ironically, that was when she stopped growing as well. Before the age of twelve she'd been of average height, but after that she was quickly surpassed by others her age. Now, at the age of eighteen, she was easily half a head shorter than other girls.

But Tarie didn't really care about her height. It was what her 'gift' had once brought that was the problem.

It had been eighteen months earlier in Memrys. Tarie's father had been visiting the hospital, waiting to hear the results of her mother's surgery for an upgrade to her cybernetic lungs – not an unusual procedure for those who'd grown up in polluted industrial cities. Their parents had tried to keep things as normal as possible for the girls, so Tarie and Lydia had gone to Centre and school as usual.

Tarie had come home to find the nutri-dispenser's stock cupboard had broken in the kitchen and had sent ingredients and flavoured liquids everywhere. Worst of all were the dehydrated clams. They were Ma's favourite, a bit rubbery when cooked, and expensive enough to call them a delicacy. But now they lay scattered throughout the rainbow-coloured puddle on the floor, puffing up as they absorbed the liquids around them. They were unnaturally bright; translucent and shining with a coat of slime and a faint fishy stench.

Tarie had begun to clean them up, grimacing a little at the texture that reminded her of her favourite sweets, when her wrist comm went off. Then the apartment video-wall flicked on to display her father's sobbing face. Sobbing open-mouthed, like Tarie had never seen him before.

"*She's dead,*" he'd said. "*There was an accident and the machine used the wrong amount of sedative. It was lethal. She's…she's dead.*"

And Tarie had stood there with a slimy, colourful clam in each hand as she'd realised that her mother, her beloved Ma, would not be coming home.

Worse was still to come. Tarie had heard one of their friends in the background. The woman had snapped, "*A Way-follower suffers an accident in Memrys? I don't think so. The carriers found out what she believed, who she was pledged to, and they took the chance to get rid of her.*"

Someone had hushed the woman, but the words had stuck in Tarie's mind. "*How would they have known?*" she'd asked in disbelief as the vid had flashed and flickered over the apartment walls.

And someone – she didn't remember who, but their words stuck in her mind – answered, "They joined the dots. Only followers of the Way can speak the Words."

And out of the family, only Tarie was known to speak the Words.

It had been her fault.

Things had got bad after that. Tarren's business had gone downhill when customers went elsewhere, and then an end was put to it when the office was burned down. The culprits were never caught. Centre for Tarie had gone from bad to terrible, and Lydia had come home from school with a black eye and her clothing ripped. She'd been rescued just in time, but it had become clear that they had to leave.

The Filats weren't the only ones to go, even though they were the only family to move to Erus Province. Over the next six months their entire small Way community moved out of Memrys, presumably to start over somewhere that was kinder to those who didn't follow the Creatures. Her father had said that it wasn't her fault; that the world was wicked and that the Words were only ever good, that she should never hide them, and that things would be better in Erus.

Ah...not so much. Judging by today's experience, Tarie was unlikely to be chased out of town, but she certainly wasn't going to be accepted. Whatever she did, she *must not use the Words in public*. Maybe she should just stop using them at all for a while. That way, she'd train herself not to use them except when she really wanted to.

For the first time, that idea seemed to hold some real merit.

Letting out a deep sigh of resigned disappointment, Tarie carried on down the road, reversing the instructions that had brought her to Centre this morning. The area was quiet considering its population, but was still filled with city sounds of people and vehicles and even music somewhere nearby. She watched where she was walking, trying to ensure she didn't step on an annoying pop-up VR ad or stumble over the curb. In fact, she was so focused that she didn't see the shadow until it was right upon her.

She screamed more from reflex than any real fear. "Ahhh!"

Gavriel jumped back, a quizzical expression on his face. "What? Surely you saw me coming."

"No, I didn't!" Tarie snapped. She was shaken, although she tried to hide it. Her mind flashed back to that terrible scene with Jayel, and she resolved that she'd start kicking before anyone ever lifted *her* into the air like that. "How fast do you move?!"

He shrugged, grinning. "Fast enough to blur your

vision…but only in short bursts. What were you thinking about to make you frown like that?"

She wasn't going to tell that story, and certainly not to *him*. She started walking again as fast as she could, and he moved backwards, keeping pace. "What happened to Jayel today," she said. "Was it Rokal who did that?"

"Of course. Orla wouldn't be able to lift a person, and no one at the Centre has strong enough telekinesis." There was a pause, and Gavriel added, "Rok will probably be suspended. He's an entitled thickhead, but that was going too far."

Tarie gave him a sceptical stare. "You're calling your own friend a thickhead?"

"Born and bred. Hey, it doesn't mean I don't *like* him. But since he became a carrier, his rough edges have become… rougher." Gavriel shrugged again, grinning. "I'm not that easy to offend, in case you're worried about what you did to my car yesterday."

She finally stopped in her tracks. She was still quite far away from her own home, but she certainly wasn't happy at leading him there, no matter how much he smiled. "I didn't do anything to your car. *You* parked me in! Now is there a reason you're following me right now? 'Cos I don't think you just like making new friends."

"Then you don't know me at all," he retorted mockingly. But then he leaned in, close enough that she wanted to shiver and move back. In a low voice he said, "There's someone following you. I might like to play games, little Tarie, but I'm not a monster."

Gavriel stepped back, still grinning as if they'd had a friendly conversation after all. "Keep well. I'll see you tomorrow."

Then there was a blur of colour, almost like a damaged VR scene, and he was gone.

Tarie stood where she was in the middle of that busy street, baffled by his manner and unsure of whether to believe him. But when she turned to look around for this mysterious stalker, she glimpsed a slim, hooded figure in dark grey. She couldn't quite make out their face, but they seemed familiar.

But when she blinked, the figure was gone too.

By the time Jayel's run slowed down to a walk, he found himself in the temple district. Here, the buildings weren't as close together, so they didn't fully block out the sun and wind. The streets were old, their surfaces worn by many feet and the occasional vehicle, but there was a steady stream of people moving about.

Some were visiting the Creature temples, with the biggest queues outside Audaline's iron palace, Domitian's glass dome, or Gerak's forbidding stone fortress. The Big Three also had VR projectors over the entrances, the sort that would light people up as they stepped through, clearly showing their allegiances in the colour of their clothing or briefly, the symbols on their foreheads.

Feeling weary and depressed, Jayel just sat on a low stone wall edging a garden, under the shelter of a tree in full leaf, and watched.

He watched as people moved in and out of the massive temple doorways, speaking to the assistants to be allowed in, or in some cases, marching right through to the inner doorways that led to the Other realm. Even the Creatures had their favourites amongst those pledged to them.

Some of those people were good-looking, some were probably smarter or stronger than average (not that he could tell), but so many pledged just looked ordinary. What made them special enough to be chosen, he wondered, but not him?

Jayel knew he wasn't ugly. He was fairly bright, acceptably athletic, and had basic social skills that he'd happily use if anyone cared to talk to him. So why was he rejected?

He looked up again at the three main temples, each within a stone's throw of each other. It was hard to believe that this area had once been a small town with a river running through it. The Other entrances had still existed, but in the form of free-standing doorframes. In time, after the Creatures and their carriers had arisen and changed the government, those doorframes had been covered over by the existing buildings, complete with glorious statues and dramatic holograms covering their outsides.

He studied the metal statue of Audaline: an ancient Creature portrayed as an elegant woman holding a tall staff, with her long robes swirling around her almost like enormous wings. A veil covered her face, which he'd always found unnerving.

Along from that was the statue of Gerak, who resembled a

hulking man with massive shoulders and curving tusks like a wild boar – which Jayel also found unnerving. Their symbols were a star and a horn respectively, which he'd seen on Orla and Rokal enough times to remember.

Besides the White Prince, those were the two Creatures who could grant true flight. He'd been to see them as a child and had been decisively rejected. They hadn't even shown up. He didn't dare try again now.

Perhaps his problem was that he just wasn't very brave, Jayel mused. He got up and wandered along the road, then paused in front of a tall, glass-framed building. The whole glass wall shimmered white for a moment, then flickered as a vaguely horse-like form skimmed across its surface. As Erus's patron Creature, Domitian was definitely respected, but the queue here wasn't as big as Audaline's, for example.

Maybe he should go inside, he wondered. Try again. The last time he'd been here was what, six years ago? Sure, Domitian had refused to appear for him, but now his father was a carrier and a councilman. Maybe, just maybe now he'd look like a better bet.

Jayel took a hesitant step forward towards those glass doors, and that usual odd sense came over him, like he was surrounded by a huge, fluffy barrier. A thought came to him clearly: *you won't find anything good in here. Go talk to Tarie.*

Tarie, the shorty with the mysterious Creature and 'speech impediment'?

Jayel dismissed the thought, then resolutely stepped inside.

5
Temples

Inside, Domitian's temple was bright from the natural light streaming through all that glass, and Jayel could see a small queue of people waiting to petition the Creature. There was an old man, a teenage girl, and at the end of the queue, a couple with a small boy who was practically dancing in place with boredom.

A thin layer of VR covered everything, which Jayel only knew because he could now see the markings on each person's forehead. The old man was already pledged to Domitian. The girl, pledged to someone else. The parents were both pledged to Domitian – and the child, to no one at all. The parents must be trying to pledge him, Jayel realised, and silently wished him luck.

An attractive temple assistant stood next to the curtain, speaking quietly with each petitioner before allowing them through one at a time. Their visits were never long, though. The old man came back with a scowl, the girl with a blank expression he couldn't read, and the family? It was obvious what response they'd had by the glowing smiles on all three faces. The boy had been accepted.

"Show us what you can do now," the father crowed.

The boy smiled widely and then sprinted straight at the wall, running so fast that he made it halfway up before backflipping and landing on his feet.

"Chaos," the mother said with what sounded like both awe and fear. "I thought he was hard to control before..."

"Momma! He looked like a horse!" the boy shouted, and then they were out of the door and gone.

"Your turn," the temple assistant said to Jayel. This close up she was even more attractive than he'd thought, with an unusual contrast of curly, deep red hair, rich brown skin and light blue eyes. "What brought you here today?" She gave him a quick glance-over. "I see you're not pledged…?"

"Long story," he replied, although really it wasn't. "I just wanted to see…if I would have a different outcome today."

She studied him again, and a flicker of distaste twisted her features before they returned to that friendly mask. "I don't know what kind of luck you'll have. There's usually a reason why someone wouldn't be pledged at your age." But with that final, depressing statement, she pulled open the curtain to reveal a worn stone archway, with grey fog hiding whatever was on the other side.

Jayel felt prickles of unease run down his back and neck, but that odd, blanketed feeling persisted as he stepped through into a completely dark landscape. Just like all the other times he'd visited the Other, it was barren, dark and empty, like a desert at night. When he'd come here as a child he remembered it being much the same, even though Anni had said it was a lovely, light-filled meadow.

Nope. No meadow. No Creature, either – not that he'd seen a Creature before.

"Domitian?" he called half-heartedly. "Please come out. I'm here to speak to you."

To his shock, suddenly the darkness was no longer empty. A figure abruptly appeared, glowing slightly as though lit from within. It had the body of a horse, but where the neck should be it melded into the muscular upper body of a man, and the whole of him was about twice the height of a human.

Jayel noted in open-mouthed shock that he shared his assistant's colouring – or rather she shared his. His body, both horse and human, was black and glossy, his hair and tail were that rich red, and his eyes a warm blue for just half a second before they focused on Jayel and bulged with horror.

"No," Domitian said, and then he vanished.

Jayel stood there, his mouth still half open and his prepared speech forgotten. *No.* The Creature had come, then he'd just said *no…*

"WHY!?" he shouted at the empty space. "You didn't even talk to me!"

The space made his voice sound small and weak, and there wasn't even an echo. He waited a moment longer, then shouted again a little desperately, "Domitian! Come back!"

The centaur flickered back into existence, but still kept his distance. "Go away," he hissed, his voice echoing slightly with each word. "You're not wanted here. I'll never take you, and no sensible Creature will either!"

Stunned by the rebuke, Jayel stepped back. "Why?" he managed to stammer. "Why not me?"

"Because you're fundamentally flawed, that's why. Worthless! If you could see what you look like here in the Other then you would understand, and you'd stop asking. So let me go, and never come back!"

Jayel wanted to leave then. His shoulders slumped, and he felt like he'd been physically beaten. That sense of being blanketed or muffled seemed to increase, but the Creature remained, still scowling at him from a distance. "Luca said I was marked," Jayel said desolately. "By my mother, when I was a baby. He said to go to the White Prince, and that no one else would take me."

That's not true, a whisper came. *Leave the temple. Stay away from the Creatures.*

He ignored it.

Domitian went still, then stared at him for a long, long moment. "Luca...this is your...father?"

"Yes." Jayel shrugged, but he was a little heartened that the Creature still hadn't left. In spite of Domitian's cruel words, his presence seemed to be a good sign. "He's a carrier, but I don't know who for."

Then finally Domitian spoke, his voice a low, gravelly hiss. "Your father was right, because no one but the White Prince will take your pledge. No one else will tell you what happened with your mother, and why you are marked. So go to him, boy, and release me, for you shall get nothing more from me."

"The White Prince," Jayel murmured. So Luca had been right? Maybe he'd finally get the answer he'd wanted for so long.

"Yes, the White Prince!" Domitian snapped. His shiny coat had grown duller and darker as he'd stood there, as though that inner light had been drained from him. "Do you still need me?"

"Uh...no?"

The Creature abruptly disappeared, and Jayel was once again alone in that great dark space. He just stood there, his arms loose at his sides, and his head spinning with new information.

Domitian had called him worthless. Ouch. But it wasn't new information, was it? And what had the Creature meant by 'let me go'?

But Domitian had also confirmed that other, vital point that Luca had earlier raised. It looked like Jayel's birth mother *had* marked him…and only the White Prince knew how or why.

The Other realm

Domitian roared into the underground city at the phenomenal speed he was known for, sending underlings scattering in every direction. He skidded to a halt at the nearest scrying pools, briefly kicking a small Creature into the pool, then hauled it out in disgust. "Where is he?"

"What…?"

Domitian tossed the Creature aside, then turned on the next closest. "The boy called me today. *Me.* I want to know why!" Then without waiting to hear an answer, he leaned forward and stared into the scrying pool. Its surface flickered impossibly fast with a hundred glimpses of a hundred futures, but after a while when he didn't see what he was looking for, his tense shoulders relaxed. "You haven't seen anything to indicate I'll be the target."

"Urgh-"

The centaur Creature huffed in disgust, then tossed that small Creature aside too. (He was known for his speed, not his patience.) "Where is the Tiger?"

Several underlings all pointed in the same direction at once, then stepped back as if to avoid being grabbed themselves.

Domitian kicked up his hooves and sped off in that direction, knocking two more Creatures into the scrying pools anyway to the mocking laughter of others nearby.

Suffering was always funny when it was happening to someone else.

Domitian found the Tiger inside a massive space not far from the scrying pools. He had his back to Domitian and still wore that two-legged form he'd kept for eons. He stood examining something against the wall in the semi-darkness, but his back blocked Domitian from seeing exactly what it was. A large structure sat in the background, made of creaking, sharp yellowed shapes – a throne of bones meant to be intimidating, but Domitian barely spared it a glance.

"Your lackey sent the boy to me!" he burst out indignantly.

"Which boy?" the Tiger answered, but insultingly, didn't even turn around.

Domitian moved closer, fury speeding his movements. "Don't pretend you don't know exactly what I'm talking about. I've heard about your plans for both realms, as well as your promise to that mewling mixed-blood. You promised him Erus! That's *my* territory!"

The Tiger suddenly turned, and his bicoloured eyes were bright with power. Bright enough to shine like lights on the rest of his semi-human face, lighting up its natural speckles and not-so-natural stripes. He held something dark and shrivelled in one hand. Dozens of tiny, colourful strands of power ran straight up from the object, into the roof of the cave they stood in.

"And so you just walk into *my* territory to accuse me of…what? Betrayal?" The Tiger shook his head, his expression barely changing. "If you have Erus now, it's because I have allowed you to retain it. I've made no secret of my intentions, not since the Rift. It was just you – and fools like you – who thought that time would make my plans change."

He stepped away from the wall, and the haze of power that had blanketed this room also receded just a little. Then Domitian saw the figures propped up around the edges of the room, each of them frozen in place and missing a vital body part…

He met the eyes of the closest, and in that moment he realised that the Tiger had held back before. But no longer…

Domitian could feel Creatures moving in from every angle, feel the gathered power rising to turn against him even as the Tiger still casually spun those gathered threads from that stolen heart in his hand. It was fight or run, he realised.

He chose to fight.

The Mountain of Glass

Amaranthus stood in the Tapestry Room. In a sense he was always there – freedom from time meant he could move through all realms simultaneously – but in this very moment, his full attention was on one small thread.

"Stop," he whispered. "Turn around now. This place is dangerous."

From the thread, a tiny image hovered of a dark-haired teenage boy. *This place is dangerous,* his thought bubble agreed. *But if I don't go in, I'll never find out the truth.*

"There are other sources of truth," Amaranthus told him gently. "Go home. Talk to Tarie about who she's pledged to."

There was barely even a pause as the boy dismissed that thought. Like many people, his way of thinking was so entrenched that he quickly rejected anything contrary, even if it was coming from someone who literally could see every moment of his life…and therefore advise the best possible action.

But Amaranthus wasn't surprised or offended, because he knew exactly what the boy was like. He also knew exactly where the boy's life thread could and should lead to, so he turned and moved to the centre of the vast Tapestry Room. There, bright water ran from a shining piece of stone, streaming across the ground and running to touch the life threads. The ones it soaked into turned white, but the others remained dull, darkest grey.

Amaranthus pressed his hand into the water and sent a pulse of power through the water, out into the normal realm where one of his People waited. *Fylax,* he told them. *It's coming. You know what to do.*

The affirmative response came quickly. Then there was nothing to do but wait.

Erus, the normal realm

The White Prince's temple was only a few minutes' ride from the others, so Jayel had picked up a nearby public scooter and had whizzed his way along the distance, then discarded it for the next person to use. Now he stood outside that dark doorway, wondering how it could be so close to the others, yet seem so very different.

Here, there were no glorious buildings surrounding the Other doorway, dedicated to the Creatures' beauty, majesty or wisdom. No, instead there was just the rubble of what might have been here centuries before, an empty space set between looming buildings. A single doorway stood in the middle of the space, built from two straight pillars made of chipped stone. The top of the frame was triangular, with a deeply carved symbol in its centre.

A low metal fence had been built around the doorway. It wouldn't keep anyone out – it wasn't intended for that – but the bright holographic sign took no chances anyone would misunderstand. *TEMPLE OF THE WHITE PRINCE*, it read. *ENTER WITH CAUTION.*

Jayel cautiously shuffled a little closer. Now he could see that the doorway's carved symbol was the shape of a butterfly, with the name 'ALBUS MENDAX' carved above it in worn letters. His wrist comm quickly translated that as 'white butterfly' in an ancient language – not the most ferocious of animals to resemble, even though it made sense if the White Prince could grant flight.

Jayel didn't recall ever seeing that symbol on Luca's head in VR, though, so it didn't answer the question of who Luca was actually pledged to. Luca's symbol was more of a chaotic squiggly shape that seemed to move the more you stared at it.

As for the White Prince, Jayel was going to assume he didn't have an assistant to choose who entered. Chaos, the Creature didn't even have a *roof*. All this place needed to make it completely eerie was a pile of broken bones and a sign saying 'here be monsters'.

He shivered. *This is dangerous*, he thought. *But if I don't go in, I'll never find out the truth.* His mind flashed back once more to the terrible moment he thought he'd fall to his death and the humiliation afterwards, and his resolve hardened. It was better to risk whatever lay in here than to continue living the life he now lived. He'd go home with answers…or not at all.

With that, Jayel stepped through the White Prince's doorway.

On the Other side was pure darkness, and as fear spiked

within him that feeling of being blanketed came back, like all his senses were slightly muffled. But perhaps this time it wasn't as strong as before. He took hope that it meant there wouldn't be the same barrier that had stopped the other Creatures from accepting him, or from even appearing.

But this place was silent, lacking even a breeze, and Jayel shuffled uncomfortably, hearing the faint movement of dust or gravel underfoot. He looked around, his eyes adjusting enough to make out vague shapes in the distance, and saw what appeared to be some kind of structure looming high against the almost-black horizon. Was it a building, he wondered, and how in Hades did the Creatures ever see anything in this place?

It felt utterly desolate, cold and miserable. Behind him, the doorway he'd come through shone like a beacon, and he felt a burst of relief that at least in this temple, you could return the way you'd come in.

Just then there was a faint scraping sound from somewhere nearby, and Jayel froze, the hairs standing up all over his body. "Hello?" he called hesitantly, and his voice trembled. "Is anybody there?"

There was a rustling sound to his left, a rush of moving air, and then it seemed like a light was turned on. In the distance in front of him, shining softly as if lit from within, was the White Prince.

He was as unnatural and inhuman as Domitian had been; both beautiful and horrible. Although it was hard to tell at this distance, the White Prince might have been only as tall as a tall human. He had overlong, very slender snow-white limbs that gleamed in the light, and his oval face was humanish but unbalanced; his black eyes too large in comparison to his small nose and mouth. A tuft of white hair rose almost whimsically from the top of his head.

But most notable were the enormous butterfly wings that rose from the middle of his back and moved gently of their own accord. They looked like intricate stained glass windows transposed into living flesh: their opalescent colours only just visible in the dim light, with striking black struts defining the segments. Finally the butterfly symbol made sense.

The Creature cocked his head to the side and surveyed Jayel like an eagle does a mouse right before it pounces. He stared...

and stared… and stared, until the silence became so uncomfortable that Jayel found himself desperate to fill it.

"I'm here to pledge my allegiance!" he blurted out through the fuzzy haze that seemed to surround him. "If…if you'll accept me." When the Creature still didn't speak, he added nervously, "Domitian said you might, and my father Luca DeMannard – he's a carrier – he said something similar, about…my…mother."

The White Prince's already unreadable expression flared into something distinctly unhappy, and Jayel swallowed, taking a step back. That odd sense of fuzziness seemed to increase, like being blanketed or underwater, and Jayel forced himself to stop moving. No Creature would want to pledge a coward, surely. So Jayel lifted his chin and stood as straight as he could, even though inside he was screaming, *please, please don't eat me.*

Then finally the Creature spoke. ***"Your mother?"*** His – its – voice was smooth and surprisingly soft and considerably more…*solid* than any human voice, even more so than Domitian's. Could such a voice be an indicator of power?

"Ah-" Jayel began, and his voice caught in his throat. "She…might have…marked me? Domitian said that no other Creature would accept my pledge-"

"I heard you the first time. So you wish to pledge to the White Prince, do you? To have beauty and power and my own formidable reputation bolstering your own weakness?" He moved a step closer, although was still a good ten metres away. ***"To become a Prince of the Air, boy?"***

Jayel's eyes widened, and it took everything he had not to tremble or step back. "I wouldn't dare to ask for so much. I only want to be more than what I am now."

The Creature stopped abruptly, his long white fingers flexing at his sides as though he was deciding whether to reach out. ***"And yet I find I wish to help you,"*** he said thoughtfully, his voice almost sing-song. ***"I know what it is like to be slandered, to have rumour after rumour destroy your reputation until you are entirely alone, standing amongst the rubble of what was once yours. So I will take your pledge, boy, if you will swear it to me exactly as I tell you."***

Could he really be so lucky? "Anything," Jayel whispered.

"Swear that you will be my eyes and ears, my hands and feet in the normal realm. Swear that you will further my interests

over your own, and that you will do whatever I ask of you. Swear that you will never turn against me."

"I swear," he whispered. At that point he would have sworn to anything – the adrenaline from coming to this place was making his thoughts swirl around in his head and stopped him from really taking anything in.

"Say it. Swear that you will never turn against me."

"I swear," Jayel stammered. "I'll never turn against you."

Then the White Prince reached out one long-fingered hand, and held up a small dark shape. It gleamed a little in the light, and from this distance Jayel thought it looked like a little plum. He stretched out his hand to take it, but rather than moving closer, the Creature tossed it towards him. Jayel caught it on reflex.

"Eat, and have power beyond your wildest dreams."

Ugh. Now Jayel was holding the thing, it felt rather less fruitlike and more…fleshy. But the promise was enough to overwhelm the strong sense of unease he'd felt since he'd walked through the doorway. He ate it in a gulp, too quickly to really focus on its texture or taste, but the slight tang of metal remained in his mouth. His stomach began to ache, and he felt himself come over in a sudden sweat. "Do I…need to do anything else?"

The Creature stared at him for a long, long moment, his – its – expression unreadable. Then he glanced very deliberately at a spot well above Jayel's head, before returning to look him in the eye. *"No. I'll make sure you keep your word. Now leave, before I change my mind."*

Jayel made his way back through the doorway in a daze. Had that really happened? Had the White Prince, Erus's most feared and wild Creature, *really* just taken his pledge? Sure, he'd had to promise to do anything the Creature wanted, but how bad could that possibly be?

Maybe the White Prince wasn't so bad, he thought as he stepped back into the normal realm. Maybe his reputation far exceeded any truth – maybe he was too much of a competitor for the others. Although he hadn't answered the question about Jayel's mother, had he?

But as Jayel found himself back in that same abandoned lot, with the same looming buildings on either side and that same warning sign on the surrounding fence, a heaviness came over him. He felt as if gravity had suddenly doubled…or like he was carrying something on his back and shoulders. Along with that came a low-level feeling of dread.

"I'm pledged," he said aloud, even though no one was listening. "I'm a carrier! This is a *good* thing."

Now all he had to do was prove it.

The distance home seemed shorter than the trip out, but Tarie found herself hurrying anyway. She hadn't been able to shake the sense of unease she'd felt ever since Gavriel had shown up so suddenly and given her such striking news.

Someone is following you.

Unfortunately, it seemed he was right. Now he'd brought it to her attention, she remembered the slight discomfort she'd felt all day. It wasn't a physical thing, but rather something that made the back of her neck tingle, and made the air around her feel wrong and strangely dry at times. She'd put that down to just being in a new place, but she'd had the same feeling before, when something bad was about to happen. Like before her mother had died, or before Lydia had come home that day with her eye blackened and her backpack in pieces, or before her father's business premises had been set on fire.

Tarie saw the familiar shape of her own building as she rounded the corner, and once again she glanced over her shoulder. Argh! There he was again – that skinny guy in grey, with his hood up over his face, just far enough away not to look suspicious. Except Tarie had seen him twice already, and that *did* look suspicious.

She stopped outside the doors to her building's foyer, but didn't step through. Thirty seconds later the other person turned the corner and trotted into view. Their steps faltered as they met Tarie's eyes, and Tarie realised it wasn't a 'guy'. Instead it was a girl, but a young, slender, pale-skinned one. A kid? Tarie couldn't be sure, but she thought it might even be the same girl who'd been sitting near her at lunch today.

Tarie just stood where she was, watching the hooded girl shuffle nervously in place and avoid her eyes. The girl didn't move closer, nor walk past. She just waited.

That was a sign of guilt, Tarie decided. With a sharp smile, she called out, "Can I help you?"

The hooded girl actually turned and looked behind her as if Tarie could've been talking to someone else, but when it was clear no one else was there, she turned back. Her eyes widened…then she looked behind her again, as if someone would have appeared in the last two seconds.

"I mean you in the grey hood," Tarie said tersely. "You live around here? Because I've seen you behind me for the last six blocks."

The girl's eyes widened even further in an expression of horror. Then she stammered, "I…I am…staying here."

"Here in this building. 42 Eastern Way."

"Er…yes."

"*And* attending the East Erus Centre for Higher Learning," Tarie persisted. "You're saying you have a legitimate reason for being at both of those places, and it's a coincidence that you've been right behind me all the way home."

"Oh, most certainly!" the girl responded in more confident tones. "I do indeed have a truly legitimate and worthwhile reason for my attendance at both."

Tarie's eyebrows shot up at both the girl's odd wording and her familiar accent. She hadn't agreed to the last part, that 'following' Tarie was a coincidence, and that just spiked Tarie's concern over the whole situation. "Are you from Memrys too? Because you sound like you are."

"Ahhh…no?"

That was clearly a lie, and it was enough for Tarie to truly lose patience. She stood tall – or as tall as a petite person could – and lifted her chin. "Really. You got a name, girl who isn't following me and isn't from Memrys and who has a totally legitimate reason for being here, now?"

An expression of distress came over the girl's face, as if she'd been caught out doing something wrong, which of course she had. She muttered something almost unintelligible.

"What? Nesbit?"

The girl sighed. "If you wish."

Nesbit it was. Nesbit, the inept stalker who wanted…what? "Hello, Nesbit. I'm Tarie. Since you live in this area, why don't you go on ahead and go inside?"

Nesbit looked as if she'd rather do anything else. But then her rigid posture slumped, and she sighed again. "Very well. But...be careful!" Then with those equally odd last words, she shuffled her way over to Tarie's building, went into the same foyer, then stepped into a liftpod and vanished.

Huh. If Nesbit had building access herself, then maybe she wasn't a stalker after all, Tarie mused. She hadn't seemed really frightening or devious, just odd, and the world was full of oddballs. Even now, after centuries of genetic engineering, their society hadn't managed to wipe out all sickness and mental disorders – especially since a lot of those seemed to originate in the Other realm. Humanity mostly lived in the normal realm, but everything that happened in the Other had far more impact than many people realised.

"Just an oddball," Tarie said aloud. But even so, she was especially careful to ensure she wasn't followed on her way inside.

Elspeth stood inside the tiny moving room, her arms stiff at her sides and her mouth still frozen in a panicked grimace. She'd been seen. No, more than that: she'd been *noticed* by Tarie, when Anne had sworn most fervently that her new gift of unnoticeability extended to everyone required. *Do not fret,* she'd said right before Elspeth left for her new mission. *Just use this simple gift, for it has saved me many a time.*

"On my oath, I am most displeased!" Elspeth said aloud to herself. "She thinks me a villain. How shall I prove otherwise?"

"Please restate your destination," a pleasant voice said from somewhere near her ear.

She let out a startled shriek which echoed off the narrow room's smooth walls even as the voice continued, *"Floor thirty-three."*

"NO! Forty-two!"

The door, which had just slid open in that slightly magical way to reveal a new environment, slid shut again. *"Forty-two,"* the voice agreed. And off they went again.

Elspeth found it both thrilling and unnerving how in this new time the doors, objects and the very walls of buildings would respond to her voice or mayhap even her desires. It reminded her of a tale from the twenty-first century that Anne had once recounted, of an enchanted castle wherein the servants had all become everyday objects like clocks, boots or teacups.

Anne had much enjoyed the tale, as she'd fancied herself the heroine making use of such objects. But Elspeth had not liked it at all, for she had imagined she might become something dull and overlooked, like a broom or a ladle.

Here, in her new, exciting life, she was still useful...but not a broom at all. No, in this case she was to be a shield. But what kind of shield could she be, when the one who she was to protect had virtually cast her away? By the rood, Elspeth had never been so mortified in her life as when her charge had glared at her in such an accusing manner.

You are following me, Tarie had as good as said. *Stop it.*

Well, YOU are not supposed to notice me, Elspeth had wanted to retort. *And I cannot stop, because 'tis my mission to save your life. So there.*

But Elspeth had been instructed to keep herself and her mission quiet unless it became absolutely essential to speak. She was meant to follow, unnoticed, and use her gifts when needed...also unnoticed.

But then the attempts on her charge's life had also been quiet and so sudden that 'twas a miracle she had seen them at all. They seemed to come from nowhere, like a dark, shadowy mass being shot down from the very skies onto the charge's head, and in the half-dozen times they'd come, Elspeth had barely enough time to shoot her silver flame. And each time, the shadow had vanished as quickly as it had appeared, leaving only a discordant bell sound ringing in her ears. That sound brought to mind a villainess Elspeth had recently faced – but as a time traveller, 'recently' was in truth four centuries earlier.

Tarie never seemed to notice that though, did she, Elspeth thought grumpily. She stepped out of the little moving room, into the hall that led into Tarie's home, then walked straight past her door...and past Jon's door...and into the mostly unseen door at the far end of the hall. It opened at her touch, revealing another tiny room full of what looked to be technological marvels, but were in fact just cleaning equipment.

Elspeth touched her hand to the flat wall on the other side, then stepped right through that as if 'twere mere mist. Now here was her true destination: one room large enough to house two comfortable couch-beds, a small table and a magical, wonderful machine that granted food like wishes. (Fylax called it a 'new-tree dispenser'.) A bathing room sat off to one side, through a final door.

Jon's protector Fylax was kind enough to let her stay here with him, and he swore that the dispenser was not at all supernatural, but merely one of the clever devices of this final age. As one of the immortal People, he did not require food *nor* a couch-bed, but he'd said he enjoyed them anyway.

But he wasn't here, which meant that Jon wasn't either. Mayhap that was a good thing, Elspeth pondered. 'Twas most difficult to see him suffering as he had today; while she was unable to approach him or even to pay him attention. She'd known that she had to watch Tarie instead, and that Jon would not have recognised her even if she did speak to him.

For her part, she'd not recognised him at first when she'd seen him this morning. He'd been sitting in that room with all the other Creature-linked youth, each of them coated in palpable, unclean power. But besides her charge, he'd been the only one not reeking of that same power.

He'd seemed unhappy, though. His whole posture slumped as he sat, as though he expected the worst and always had received it. So different from how she'd met him in the Mountain of Glass; carefree and light.

Jon's colouring had been different today too. His hair had been so dark 'twas nearly black, hanging around his face as though he hoped 'twould conceal his features. Elspeth still found him rather handsome, even though his skin was also slightly darker than she was accustomed to, like one who spent much time in the fields. Odd, when his current form was so very different from what she'd been raised to see as lovely. (Back in Tudar Angland, the most beautiful folk were slender and very pale, with small mouths.)

But then was beauty not found in what one loved?

For now, there was no beauty. Forsooth, there was nothing but an empty room, a lingering sense of disquiet...and free food.

But even the offer of almost-magical food couldn't shake Elspeth out of her unhappy state. So she sat on the smaller of the couch-beds and stretched out her new senses for her third and latest gift – sensing danger.

Then she waited.

85

6

Prince of the Air

Pledged. He was pledged, Jayel thought joyously as he practically skipped back to his scooter. And not just to any Creature, but to a notoriously powerful one who could grant flight!

A moment later he recalled how he'd basically turned that gift down, saying he wouldn't dare to ask for such a thing. His shoulders slumped, and he tried to remember exactly what the White Prince had said in response. *I'll help you – if you do what I want.*

Hmm. Jayel looked around to see if anyone was watching, and when he seemed to be alone, he stretched his hands above his head and thought, *fly.*

Nothing happened.

He tried again, this time jumping off the ground, and pushing his arms up in a forceful movement. *FLY!*

The sudden movement upwards caught him completely by surprise. Unexpectedly the ground was no longer solidly under his feet, and his arms pinwheeled wildly, trying to catch his balance when there was no longer anything to catch. Then when he finally managed to still his panic and looked down, he saw he'd risen at least his own body length in the air.

"Woohooo!" he shouted jubilantly. "I CAN FLY!"

Or float, rather. But it didn't matter. This was by far the best moment of Jayel's life. He was finally somebody! Just wait till the Terrible Trio found out about *this!*

He made himself float a little higher, until he was level with the second floor of the building next to him. While it was as easy as in VR to have the ground now three metres below him, he suddenly came over in a terrible sweat, his body trembling as it tried to tell him to *panic! You're going to fall and die!*

That made Jayel think of what had happened earlier with Rokal, and *that* memory made him want to puke. "Nothing to worry about," he told himself aloud. "I'm a Prince of the Air now. I can't fall." But his voice shook a little as he spoke.

Just then he caught sight of himself in the nearest window. It was one of those huge, bright VR panels that were meant to make depressing areas like this feel less so. But as he watched, it changed from a faint reflection overlaying the cheerful brick, to a full-sized image of…someone.

Someone wearing ordinary clothing much like his own, but with skin and longish hair as white as the White Prince's had been, and with black, black eyes. A stylised butterfly moved about on the person's pale virtual forehead, and around his mouth was smeared a dark reddish substance.

That couldn't be him, surely? It must be the virtual reality filter just showing the White Prince's influence…

A moment later Jayel heard a gasp from behind him. He glanced back to see an elderly woman looking at him through a nearby open window. He only saw her horrified expression for a moment before the window snapped closed, its surface becoming opaque and reflecting that pale, red-stained person. Him. The window's VR layer made it look like he'd been eating raw meat…messily.

Jayel raised a hand to his mouth, then looked down to see white, white fingers stained red. Perhaps the change wasn't just virtual reality after all. "It was just a plum," he said aloud, but even he didn't believe that. Plums didn't usually taste metallic, did they?

Jayel returned to the ground, breathing a sigh of relief at its safe solidity underfoot, then sought out the nearest water fountain. He washed his face and hands repeatedly, swishing water around his mouth then spitting it out in an attempt to remove the lingering taste. He had the brief fear that it would stain, that he'd forever look like an anaemic cannibal, but the water ran pink and then clear, and he gratefully dried his face on his shirt.

But while the red had washed away, his reflection in the fountain's shining metal surface showed clearly that the new dead whiteness remained. His hair and skin were as white as a flight suit, he thought in dismay. As white as fresh snow – no, whiter, because snow at least had blue undertones. He didn't look handsome. He looked…scary.

But then Jayel remembered the horrible scene at Centre today, and he saw his reflection's expression harden. Even if he was uncomfortable with real heights at first, even if people fled his presence rather than sought his approval, he knew he was better off like this.

It was surely better to be feared than scorned.

Besides, Erus's newest Prince of the Air didn't *need* approval. Forget the scooter – he was going to fly home.

Half an hour later, Jayel shakily came to land on the street outside his building's foyer. He'd indeed flown home, but hadn't been able to make himself fly more than one or two levels above the ground because his stomach would twist in fear, like a horrible flashback to this morning's incident. He'd pushed through it, of course, but even now he was covered in sweat from what had eventually been a building-to-building leapfrog effort.

It didn't matter, he told himself. He was a Prince of the Air! *Whoop…!* But he'd probably feel more excited when he saw everyone's faces tomorrow at Centre, because he wasn't going back today. Not till he'd had more practice flying, in the very least.

Hmm. Maybe he'd take a couple of days off; buy a nice white flight suit like Rokal and Orla's. Or not like theirs, he decided quickly – *better*.

Jayel made his way to level forty-two and stepped into the hallway, heading for his front door. But he'd barely taken three steps before he bowled into someone. The small, hooded figure bounced backwards to sprawl on the ground, and Jayel stared at them in surprise for a moment before guilt came rushing in. He'd hit them hard, and they were small. Maybe he'd hurt them.

But that thought was quickly followed by anger, because he hadn't seen them at all until he'd hit them. "What in chaos just happened?" he snapped. "Are you wearing some kind of camouflage clothing? Or were you purposely trying to trip me?"

The person – some wide-eyed kid – stared at him like they'd seen a ghost. Finally they whispered, "'Twas an accident."

Of course it was, Jayel thought, regretting his outburst. But because he still felt guilty and angry, he nodded at them in feeble apology, then quickly went into his apartment, shutting the door behind him. He briefly considered that his anger was out of character, then realised it actually wasn't. He felt angry and miserable most of the time, he just hardly ever acted out like that. The consequences of doing so would be too harsh. Maybe he'd apologise to the kid if he ever saw them again, he mused. But before two minutes had passed, he'd forgotten about them.

Then even though it would be several hours before Anni came home, and even though Jayel could have gone out again to practice flying once more, he found himself fluffing around the house in boredom. He finally just went into VR as normal. He went straight back to his flying game, then discovered to his dismay that he'd somehow retained his new fear of heights, which made the game almost unusable. So instead he headed to the marketplace to show off his new Creature symbol.

Jayel made a point of buying some small, meaningless objects from a stallholder just to see their reaction. Disappointingly they looked curious rather than amazed – or scared – and he realised that most people wouldn't recognise the White Prince's butterfly symbol. It was too rarely displayed.

But they'd recognise power, he decided. He just had to learn how to use it.

Elspeth sat in the small room at the end of the hall, her hands in her lap. *All will be well,* she assured herself – but still she could feel her hands clenching and unclenching, almost involuntarily.

Jon. He'd been so…so *tainted.* Almost unrecognisable. And so *cold…*

Just then, a patch of air shimmered in front of her, almost like a glimmer of a gateway appearing. Then Jon's protector came into sight. In his human form, Fylax – or occasionally 'Phil' – was a sinewy old man with white, slightly wild facial hair and beard. He always looked solemn, but usually his grey-blue eyes would have a twinkle of humour in them. He reminded Elspeth very much of Amaranthus. But today, there was no twinkle.

"This must be Jon's dread secret," Elspeth said without

preamble. "The great shame which he so clearly carried, which was why he did not wish to return to his own home." Her shoulders hunched, and she added in a low voice, "I thought 'twas me. I thought he kept his distance because of *my* history, my birth." Of course he'd not said such a thing, but she'd drawn her own conclusions. In hindsight, she'd been most incorrect.

Fylax's shaggy white eyebrows raised as he sat on the couch, and Elspeth suddenly realised that she'd been telling him of the future – for while she had seen the future Jon, had spoken with him, presumably Fylax had not. "Uh…"

"It's an ugly thing, isn't it?" the protector said gruffly. "For a human to become a carrier. But they don't see it like we do. They can't."

"Clearly not." Elspeth stared down at her feet. In this moment she felt no sign of danger from her now inbuilt 'evil alarm', so she felt safe to remain and chat. She thought again of Jon's new, repulsive appearance. That pure white skin and hair, and those black, black eyes.

Once, she would have found such colouring comely, for in the time she was born, people strove to be pale. Only peasants had suntanned skin. But today, she could only think of the stench of the Creature that covered him so heavily.

Although, it did finally explain why Jon's colouring had darkened throughout the time she'd known him. He was shedding the Creature's influence, day by day.

"What now?" Elspeth asked finally. "Must I watch this new, terrible version of my friend? I suppose you must keep your distance, for it must be even more repulsive for you as a Person than for me as a mere enlightened human. And I am not here for Jon, for all of that he was my true reason for coming."

"People who are shown little kindness have little kindness to show in turn," Fylax said sagely. "Don't think of who Jon appears to be now. Think of him as he will be."

'Twas good advice, Elspeth supposed, although she still struggled to get that dreadful interaction out of her mind. Then suddenly she recalled the interaction with Tarie today.

"Oh no! Fylax, I was seen today! Not once, but twice, and now Tarie thinks I am some sort of scoundrel, following her for some villainous purpose! Am I not meant to be unnoticeable?! Whatever shall I do now?"

Fylax's eyebrows, which had relaxed to their usual position half-covering his eyes, shot up again. She realised she had been blabbering like a drunken fishwife.

"Life rarely goes to plan," he said finally. "Or more like, we don't know what the plan is. But we've been given our tasks, little Bets. We will continue to do them."

"But have *you* ever had a charge notice you?" she persisted.

"A few times." He shrugged his bony shoulders. "If the unnoticeability failed, then I figured they were meant to see me. I just went with it."

"Oh." Elspeth briefly wondered whether people had seen Fylax's humanlike form or his true form, which was certainly difficult to overlook. "Then I shall simply 'go with it' too," she murmured.

"But not till tomorrow, since no one's going out tonight," Fylax said cheerfully. He held out a packet of what smelled like fresh bread. "Dinner?"

"Yes, please."

But as they ate, and Elspeth did her best to distract herself and focus on her mission, she couldn't help wondering if the cost of being here was higher than expected.

When Jayel heard Anni arrive home, he was floating in front of the living room's flashy reflective VR-wall, checking his new appearance from every angle. Luca had added those walls in when he'd become a council member and had decided to make their house bigger and better in every way. At the time, Jayel had thought it was just a reminder of what he *didn't* have, but today, it was actually useful.

He heard Anni bustle around the kitchen for a few minutes, making the usual busy sounds of cupboards sliding open, then the click-whirr-slosh of the nutri-dispenser making a drink, and he couldn't decide whether he wanted her to see him or not. The change was…significant.

But a few minutes later Jayel saw her enter the living room behind him, and their eyes met in the wide VR wall. She simply stared at him blankly for a moment, then he saw the moment she spotted his own symbol. The red butterfly moved across his pure white forehead, looking like an endlessly moving blood stain. The colour was startling against his skin and newly white hair.

"Jay-Jon," Anni breathed. "Is that…is that a costume? Are you…? You're not standing…"

He turned away from the glossy VR reflection to look her in the face. As always, the contrast to her real self was a little startling – in reality she was older, more worn and less shiny than her VR version. "No," he said, feeling an odd mix of pride at his own change and distaste at her inability to see it. "It's real. I'm pledged to the White Prince."

She stared at him for a long moment, her expression unreadable. "Oh, darling…are you alright?"

Jayel turned back to his new reflection in the VR-wall. His facial features were subtly different, perhaps more regular, but they were still recognisably his features. His build was still long and lean, but he seemed to be taller, and had more defined shoulders and muscles. But it was his colouring that had remarkably changed.

He certainly didn't look like a normal person anymore. His skin was about as white as could be without being dead or frozen solid, and his longish hair was a shiny, pale silver-white. His eyebrows and lashes were the same white so that they almost disappeared into his skin, and his irises were as black as the White Prince's had been. If he stared into them in the mirror for too long it seemed he caught a glimpse of butterfly wings – and he wasn't sure if that was just his imagination.

"I had a bad day," Jayel told her flatly. "And I decided that I was sick of having no respect from anyone, so I went to get some."

Anni looked back at him, met those dark eyes, then turned away again. "I see."

"I can fly now. And I can feel that I'm physically stronger than I was. It's a shame I don't have more vivid colouring," he continued. "I'm practically an albino." So much for the promise of good looks, hmm?

"Vivid? Vivid colouring is just a silly fashion, Jayel. You were fine just the way you were. Now – with those eyes against your skin, you're about the most vivid person I've ever met. You're whiter than snow." She shuddered. "I can't say I like the eyes, though. Your own ones were so nice, and these ones…scare me a little."

They scared him too, actually. But then he wasn't the bravest person he knew, and the sudden changes would bother anyone. He would get used to them. "I can't be whiter than snow," he said instead.

"Of course you can. Snow is white with blue shadows. You don't have any shadows – at least they're not blue if you do. You're just plain, pure white now, except for the eyes and your lips, of course. So you are whiter than snow."

Or like a snowman with black coals for eyes. "If you say so."

"It's wonderful that you can fly, but can't you change your colouring like Luca does? Make it a bit more normal? Even if you could get your eyebrows darker again…"

"I can't change them," Jayel replied. "I've tried." He'd spent the last hour trying, in fact, until Anni had walked in. He'd known he might change, but he'd hoped he'd be more handsome. Not just…scary.

"Mm. Perhaps you can dye them."

She still looked anxious and wouldn't meet his eyes, and he found himself growing irritated. "I took a big risk today, do you realise that? I could have died. But I'm here, and now I'm powerful. I'm a Prince of the Air, Ma. Aren't you at all proud of me?"

"I've always been proud of you," she replied softly. "And I know the risk you took, and that you could have died, and that's what bothers me so much. I'm proud of you…just give me a while to get used to it, please?"

Jayel paused for a moment, then nodded. "Of course."

Finally she looked up, meeting his eyes with a faint but noticeable shudder, and smiled crookedly. "I wonder what your father will say."

When Luca finally came home, he just stared at Jayel for a long, long moment, his eyebrows raised. Then he broke into a slow smile, the sort that showed all of his shiny, perfect teeth. "So you finally did it – and you survived. Do you have a new name?"

"He's still Jayel," Anni began to say, but Jayel cut in.

"Jon. It's Jon now." He was feeling flustered over his father's response, perhaps even a little irritated – did the man even care that he was alive? But the question was a good one. While the

White Prince hadn't renamed him, this was the perfect chance to rename himself with something he already liked.

"Jon," Luca mused. "And that's an improvement…how?"

"I think it's a great name," Anni said staunchly. He could see relief in her expression – at least he wasn't going by Zobirax or Hoopsclune now.

But Jayel – *Jon* – felt a sharp pang of anger go through him at the insult, and he straightened his shoulders. "Luke to Luca isn't such a change either. And who is your Creature again?"

Luca just grinned. "Time for dinner, dear family?"

Jon took that as a real sign of approval, since they hardly ever ate together. He sat down at their seldom-used dining table, his eyes fixed on the covered food just delivered by drone. He hadn't eaten anything all day – not since that metallic, suspiciously organic 'plum' the White Prince had given him. His stomach felt like it was caving in on itself.

But when the covers came off to reveal a dark red, lumpy main dish, he recoiled a little. "What's this?"

Anni shrugged, then read the cover description. "Tender morsels of sweetbread in a rich red wine and capsicum sauce. Smells good, yes?"

It did, but it also reminded Jon uncomfortably of the last thing he'd eaten. Fruit. It had been fruit, right? But he took a mouthful of his own portion, intentionally focusing on its rich taste and texture. Ahh, he was *sooo* hungry. He found himself shovelling the food in, trying to fill the aching hole in his gut.

Luca watched him with a spark in his bright blue-green eyes. He'd skewered a piece of meat, but was holding it on the end of his spork rather than eating it. "Such a carnivore, son. Let's hope the White Prince didn't give you his own unnatural hungers as well as his colouring."

Jon froze mid-bite. Suddenly the food tasted ashy and thick, and he swallowed it with difficulty. "What do you mean?"

"Just that the Creature is known for eating its own kind," Luca replied. "That makes it feral even by feral Creature standards." He squinted at his still-loaded spork. "Sweetbreads, hmm? Aren't those organs?"

Jon spat his mouthful out right over the table. Through the ringing in his ears, he heard Anni gasp and Luca laugh, then the faint whirring sound of the table-cleaner getting to work.

"As fun as this is," Luca continued cheerfully, "I've got somewhere to be. You're looking at Erus city-state's next chairman."

"Is Joss Tybalt resigning?" Anni asked weakly.

"Not officially, but anything can happen in this wonderful world of ours. Isn't that right, son?" He patted Jon heavily on the back as he rose to leave. "I used to worry you'd always be a miserable failure. Now, I get to worry that you'll get hit by a drone while flying, eat someone in your sleep, or curse someone by accident."

Now Jon was staring at his father open-mouthed, and across from him he could see Anni wore the same expression.

"Just kidding!" Luca sang. "I don't think about you at all. Enjoy your nice, juicy, meaty dinner."

"Curse anyone...?" Anni mouthed as her husband left. She turned to Jon with a quizzical expression. "What could he mean by that?"

Jon had been more concerned about the 'eat anyone' comment. He couldn't get that bloody plum out of his head, and the more he thought on it, the more convinced he was that it hadn't been fruit at all.

He abruptly stood, his chair sliding back automatically as he did so. "I'm going to be sick."

Anni sat at the table, her slack hands still holding her cutlery. Suddenly she wasn't hungry anymore either. The table-cleaner buzzed around, quickly clearing up Jay-Jon's mess, and after a few minutes she leaned forward and replaced the lids of all three meals.

Another tap of a button, and the containers stacked themselves in a tidy row and hovered off to sit by their delivery window. They'd be picked up overnight, ready to be cleaned out then used again in the next order.

"Both of them," Anni murmured to herself. She couldn't shake the sense of desolation she felt upon seeing her precious son looking so very, very different. Luke had changed so much when he'd become Luca. He might be more successful now, but she couldn't stand to be around him. He was so unkind, and she couldn't trust half of what he said.

Would the same thing happen to Jayel? Or Jon, or whatever he wanted to call himself. Her son wasn't pledged to just any Creature. Luca was right – Jay-Jon was pledged to the most feral of those that had a temple.

Just then, the newly pale version of her son walked back into the room. Jay-Jon now wore a long-sleeved black jacket over a white shirt, and he didn't meet her eyes. "I'm going to practice flying. I'll be back late."

"Do you want a-"

But the door had already slid shut after him.

"Flight-suit," Anni murmured to herself. Her idea of trying to celebrate his change by ordering him a new, distinctive white outfit now seemed foolish.

She sighed, her shoulders slumping, then went to sit on her balcony. From here she could see the outskirts of the city and the green hills in the distance. It was a nondescript day, neither hot nor cold and without much wind, but she felt utterly shaken inside. Lost. She sighed again.

"That sounded serious."

The male voice was kind and even familiar, but Anni found herself jumping a little anyway. She looked across to where her new neighbour stood on his own balcony, leaning against the clear barrier. He smiled at her.

"Oh…Tarren." She fumbled to remember his name, then forced a return smile. She thought he had a friendly sort of face rather than a handsome one, the sort with smile lines worn in at the edges of his mouth and eyes. He was short and sturdy, probably no taller than Anni herself, with a short beard and warm dark colouring that indicated some Afrecan ancestors. Not as handsome as Luca, but still…pleasant. "Hi."

"If you don't mind me asking…is everything alright?"

Anni shrugged, letting out a short laugh. "I suppose so. Luca's career is on the up and up, or so he says, and Jayel finally got pledged to a Creature today. He's become a Prince of the Air."

Tarren didn't look nearly as impressed by that as she'd expected. In fact he looked dismayed. "Oh. Who has he pledged to?"

Feeling a little defensive, she lifted her chin. "The White

Prince."

"I don't know who that is."

Anni's eyebrows rose. She knew Tarren wasn't from here, but weren't Creatures universal? Or perhaps they had different names for them in Memrys. "He's one of the most powerful Creatures in Erus," she explained, telling only half of the truth. "He can grant flight along with Audaline and Gerak. But unlike them, he's very…picky about who he takes on."

"Oh," Tarren said again. "Congratulations, I suppose."

Suddenly all of the stress and confusion she felt about that change coalesced into one angry bundle. "Of course you should congratulate me!" she snapped, feeling her eyes prick with tears. "It's a real achievement! Don't you know there are less than a dozen Princes of the Air in Erus?"

"It is rare anywhere," he allowed.

"And he'll be respected! He'll automatically do well in everything he attempts, he'll be popular…"

"I'm sure he will," Tarren agreed gently.

Strangely, Anni found she was crying. "He'll be happy, won't he?"

Now Tarren was quiet. "I suppose that remains to be seen," he said finally. He sat down on a bench at the end of his balcony closest to her. "If it's so wonderful, why are you upset about it?"

She shrugged tearily, embarrassed, then sat down herself. Except for the balcony wall dividing them, it was almost like they were side by side. "I don't know. It was a long day, I suppose, and a real shock to see Jayel like that…"

"You don't trust the Creature."

"I don't," Anni admitted. "I know I'm not supposed to say that, but come on! The White Prince…?" Belatedly realising she had given only positive information up till now, she explained, "He's considered very dangerous. Crazy, even. I wish that Jayel wasn't tied to him."

"Who's your Creature, Anni?"

"Sarassius. You wouldn't have heard of him; he's got a very small temple on Short Street. Almost has to share with others, that's how small he is."

"And you're pledged to him."

She nodded.

"Would you say it's been worth it?"

Anni shrugged again. "I don't know. I suppose I've got social acceptance, I have a job…"

"What has Sarassius actually given you?" Tarren persisted. "Name one thing."

Suddenly she wondered why he would ask. "You know I can't change allegiances, right? There's no sense in criticising what I have."

"There's no sense lying about what you don't have, either. What has your Creature given you?"

"Nothing," Anni admitted with guilty relief. She'd never said it before, but often thought it. "He's given me nothing."

Even though she'd spoken the blasphemous words aloud, there was no crash of thunder, no sudden heart attack. No consequences at all. And Tarren just *hmmed* and sat there quietly.

"Who's your Creature?" she asked. "I've never seen you in VR, so I haven't seen your sign, and you don't have the markings displayed on your apartment door like some people do."

His cheeks darkened a little, and his eyes flickered down to his lap. For the first time Anni noticed he was carrying what looked like a drinking cup in each hand, with a tiny red plant sticking out of each cup.

"The Timeless One doesn't like to be called a Creature," Tarren replied finally. "He's not at all mortal, but he's not like the others, either."

He held out one of the cups towards her. The clear screen between the two of them shimmered green, and Anni reached up towards him. The screen disappeared, and she took the cup…but she didn't pull her hand back through to her own balcony. "What is it?" she asked curiously.

"A plant," Tarren replied, and the smile lines at the corner of his eyes crinkled even more. "But more specifically, a fruit tree. Keep it long enough, water it and give it sunlight, and the fruit will be as good as medicine. A gift from the Timeless One."

"As I'm a medic supplier, I highly doubt that," Anni countered, but her snooty tone was half-teasing. "I don't know if I can take a gift from someone else's Creature."

"Is, er, Sarassius going to get upset?"

She shrugged resignedly. "Sarassius won't give a damn what I do." Then with sudden decisiveness she pulled the cup through to her own side, and the screen closed over between them. "I always kill plants," she admitted. "But I'll give this one a go."

"You can't kill this one."

"Oh, just watch me." Anni set it on the nearby edge of her balcony, right in the sun. The textured base of the balcony's edge gripped the cup, and she smiled at him teasingly. "I'll water it, same as you do, but I bet it's dead within a month. No, a fortnight."

"Even the most vicious of killers can't kill this plant," Tarren argued, but he was smiling too. "These plants come about through alter-power being used, and they're very, very hard to get rid of."

Anni's smiled faltered. *The most vicious of killers.* It was like…he knew something about her, something that she'd never told a single soul. Something that had been on her mind repeatedly ever since she'd talked to Jay-Jon about his missing mother and aunt, and his deceased grandmother. "Then where did you get these two?"

"Oh…here and there." He paused, then shrugged sheepishly. "Growing in the plant wall in this building's foyer, actually, but they shouldn't have been there. They'll get far too big."

"Oh. Then, thank you."

"You're welcome." Tarren glanced away from her, out into the distance, but he was fidgeting in place. Finally he said, "I know it's none of my business, but I feel like there's something still weighing on you. If you want to talk about it, I'm happy to listen."

Anni turned to stare at him. Did he know…was he taunting her? She should walk away rather than tell anything at all to this stranger. But his pleasant face looked as harmless as ever, and she didn't want to leave. Not yet. "I've…I don't have much family left. Just Jayel- I mean, Jon, and he's actually my sister's son. Maia went missing when he was a baby, apparently after heading into the Other realm. We never found out what happened to her."

She frowned, feeling the weight of that mystery again for the first time in fifteen years. "I stopped thinking about her because I had to. It was driving me mad. The police had nothing, and neither did the Creatures. But my mother…" She shook her head, her vision turning blank as she remembered that terrible time.

"She was convinced that something had happened to Maia in the Other realm, that she was being held by wicked Creatures, and that she could get her back, if only she obeyed their insane instructions."

"What did the Creatures want her to do?"

Ah, now this was half the story. The worst half, almost, that she'd never mention to Jay-Jon. Could she really tell this stranger?

But Anni's hands tightened into fists, and her gaze focussed on that tiny red fruit tree. Everything else seemed to blur, and she found herself saying, "They wanted a sacrifice in exchange for my sister's location. They wanted my mother to kill Jayel."

7
Secrets

Jon had been too optimistic when he'd decided to go 'practice flying'. For someone with a sudden fear of heights, he should have chosen anywhere to start except a forty-three-level building. He'd been flying from balcony to balcony, making his way up and around the building, even as cold sweat soaked his hairline and the back of his neck, and even as his whole body seemed to tremble.

How was he supposed to ever gain anyone's respect, even as a Prince of the Air, if he couldn't even fly? He *had* to learn. He just had to.

But he'd made his way slowly around the building until he was hovering only one level above his own apartment, just above his own balcony. With his back resting against the wall, if he didn't look down, he could almost pretend he liked being up this high.

Then Jon overheard his mother's voice. She was chatting with some guy – Tarie's father, by the sound of it – and he found himself listening in. It wasn't eavesdropping when they were talking about him, right? When he heard Anni sobbing about his new Creature, a stab of anger went through him. He wanted her pride, not her fear...because he wanted to be proud himself too, rather than fearful. Right now he was proud, sure – but he was terrified too.

But then the conversation abruptly changed, and Jon's irritation vanished when she began talking about his birth mother, Maia. They'd had such a brief conversation yesterday that he'd almost forgotten it with everything else that was going on, but now he realised exactly what she hadn't told him. Now, she was telling it all to some stranger instead.

"They wanted a sacrifice in exchange for my sister's

location," Anni was saying, her voice low but audible. "They wanted my mother to kill Jayel."

Ohhhhhhhhhhhhhh…

Kill Jayel?! Er, *why??!!!* Jayel/Jon's eyes bulged, and he stopped breathing. He had to hear what she said next, because it seemed that the Creatures had had it in for him a lot longer than he'd realised.

"That's mad!" he heard the neighbour say, sounding appalled. "She didn't do it, obviously."

"She tried," Anni continued in a whisper. "He was only six months old. Such a sweet baby. Her only grandchild too. I always knew that she didn't care for males, and I knew how much she valued Maia. But I didn't think she'd…"

There was a long silence.

"What happened?" Tarie's father asked in a hushed whisper.

"Mother asked to babysit him for a weekend, to take him back to the town she raised us in, which is on the borderlands between the normal and the Other realms. She said she wanted to use his blood to locate the others. I thought she meant his blood connection, so of course I let her. But then I realised I'd forgotten to pack his medicine. He had breathing issues as a baby, just mild, but enough that I had to give him a shot every day to help strengthen his lungs.

"So a couple of hours after she'd taken him, I followed with the medicine." There was another pause, and the sound of a sucked-in breath. "My mother was not always a good woman, Tarren. She had this place under her house where she'd sacrifice animals to various Creatures in return for power. A temple of sorts that led straight to the Other. She wouldn't pledge to just one Creature, and she considered herself a sorceress.

"I…I found them down there. Jay-Jon was strapped to that filthy altar, crying and naked. She was dressed in full ceremonial regalia, standing on the dais, and she was holding that knife…"

In that moment, Jon could have missed a parade of flying elephants making their way between the nearby buildings, he was so fixated on what Anni was saying.

"I screamed when I saw them. My mother turned to look at me, and she stumbled. She fell off the altar, and she broke her neck."

There was a long, long silence. "That's…anticlimactic," their neighbour said.

"Lucky, more like," Anni murmured. "I don't know if I could have stopped her otherwise. I guess Jay-Jon was always meant to live, even if it meant that Davinia died and we never found my sister."

"It sounds like he was meant to live," Tarren agreed. "He must have some great purpose for his life."

"Well, now he *is* a Prince of the Air," Anni said.

"Yes…but something bigger than that, even. After all, what does a Prince of the Air even do?"

The conversation turned, and Jon found himself moving away from the balcony. He'd begun floating upwards before he even realised what he was doing. Then he clung to the wall, the new revelations spinning around in his mind.

His adoptive mother definitely had secrets. She should have told him yesterday, when she'd revealed all those other secrets about his origins. She should have told him that his grandmother had tried to kill him…that some Creature had tried to have him murdered before he was even a year old.

Maybe he *was* marked, Jon mused in amazement. Marked from birth so that every Creature would hate him. Even the White Prince hadn't seemed to like him at all, and he'd taken him on as a carrier.

Or maybe it was all a coincidence, and the Creatures disliked all kinds of people, and he wasn't anything special at all.

But as Jon caught sight of his new reflection, he recoiled at that white, white face with its too-black eyes, and he couldn't believe that idea. So maybe there was some kind of purpose to his seemingly pointless existence.

But what could it possibly be?

Luca sat in an enormous, comfortable chair in his office. The office was a lavishly decorated hexagonal room, with priceless pieces of art on every wall, a large window and balcony overlooking the council's carefully maintained park, and an enormous desk befitting his position. In front of the desk were two smaller chairs, just nice enough to make visitors know they were 'valued'…but also that they weren't in the position of power. No, the one sitting on the thronelike chair was.

Just then the door opened and another council member walked in. Wyet DeSymon was a burly middle-aged man with the smooth skin and posture of someone twenty years younger, and with the arrogance that came from being in a position of power his entire life. He was pledged to Domitian, just like his son Rokal, who was one of Jayel's chief tormentors at Centre. Luca figured the son would usurp the father sooner or later, a thought he found most entertaining.

Wyet scowled when he saw Luca. "What are you doing here, DeMannard? That's Tybalt's seat."

Joss Tybalt was the chairman of Erus, who'd been personally selected by Domitian twenty-five years earlier. But after the conversation Luca had had with his mother through VR, he knew that Joss wouldn't be needing that seat much longer. Luca didn't hold back the smirk stretching over his face. "Just testing it for size, Councilman Wyet. After all, Joss won't be using it again."

"What do you mean?" Wyet's eyebrows rose in confusion.

"Our beloved chairman had a heart attack an hour ago. Fatal, unfortunately, so our patron Creature will be selecting a new chairman to take his place."

The other man's eyes narrowed. "He seemed fine when I saw him this morning."

Luca shrugged. "What a strange and wonderful world we live in."

"Hmm." Wyet sounded unimpressed, and unconvinced. "And why would you find out about this before me? I'm second in charge."

"Actually, officially all fifteen councilmen are equally ranked," Luca countered. "I have a friend who lets me know this kind of useful information. But who finds out first doesn't matter; it's who's selected next that's important."

"Well, it won't be you with your undeclared Creature and your mere two years in council. So get out of that seat."

Luca just smiled. But he snapped his fingers, and the palatial scene around him faded. Suddenly he was in a much smaller office, reclining in a much smaller chair, at a much smaller desk. The view from his small window was VR, much like that entire scene had been. But this time, he had company.

"Are you finished?" his mother asked, sounding bored. Today, Lilith's daffodil-yellow hair was tinged with green, and her lips were a matching shade. Her outfit was a symphony of delicate drapes and cut-outs. For an ancient Halfling, she really did know how to stay in fashion.

"For now," Luca agreed. "Good morning Mother, how are you? How's your boytoy?"

The third person in the office just glowered. Luca suspected Basir didn't have any other settings. His prison-short hair still gave away his recent background, but he too wore highly fashionable clothing.

"Better this morning for having completed an errand on your behalf," Lilith answered. "The new chairman will be selected in three days, as is custom. But before that happens, there'll be an announcement of a new power in Erus."

"Yes, me." He'd be the new chairman *and* the new power, so he didn't know why she bothered repeating it. "I hope your boy didn't make Tybalt's death too obvious. Even with control of the police, these things can still rear their ugly heads."

"Listen!" Lilith snapped. "The *real* power in Erus will be changing, and in many other places too. The change of ruling Creature will be announced soon, and you need to show you've pledged your allegiance before you'll be announced as the new chairman, family ties or not."

Ugh. Luca slumped in his chair, trying not to pout too obviously as he realised what she meant. The Tiger would become Erus's patron Creature, which was simply unfair since Luca would no doubt be expected to pledge his allegiance along with everyone else. But *he* was almost a Creature himself. He shouldn't be pledging himself to other Creatures, even if said Creatures were phenomenally powerful and tyrannical. "Oh, if it's compulsory, of course I will."

"It is compulsory! The Tiger does not allow any form of dissension in his ranks!"

Luca spread out his hands. "Then of course. I am the Tiger's humble…whatever it needs me to be. Now, did you hear about my dear son and his own allegiance?"

Lilith's eyes narrowed. "I see how you're changing the subject. But tell me."

"Jayel Jonnamin DeLuca," Luca said delicately, "has become the White Prince's newest – and only – Prince of the Air."

There was a silence, and even Basir looked surprised. "This could be a problem," he said to Lilith, showing that he actually had a mind of his own. "The White Prince could use him."

"Or, as most of us have expected from the time we saw his future, he'll most likely be used against any Creature stupid enough to take him on," Luca countered irritably. The two of them had been in the car with him when he'd been goading Jayel to visit the White Prince, and now they so displeased that the boy had actually done it? But then they hadn't thought that he truly would. Neither had Luca, to be honest.

"Does the boy still wear his mark?" Lilith asked.

Luca shrugged. "I can sense its taint under the White Prince's power."

"Hmm." Her neutral expression didn't change.

Why was his mother so bloody difficult to please? "The Tiger gave me an impossible task. Don't criticise me for how I've completed it."

"You haven't completed it yet," Lilith bit out. She stood, gracefully wrapping a white furred stole around her neck. The animal's eyes had been replaced with gleaming blue gems, but it still seemed to focus on Luca with an equally accusing expression. "And if you don't, you'll never get the power you want. Family connections or not."

Tarie drove to Centre the next day. The traffic wasn't too bad – again, for a city this size, the infrastructure was amazing, and most people's lives didn't involve going outside. But she felt disconcerted by her potential stalker, so she'd made a point of buffing the 'way-follower' graffiti from her ancient vehicle's windshield, then swallowing her pride and driving.

She'd parked next to a line-up of brighter, shinier vehicles, then headed inside to her first class. Her nerves were frayed, like she was expecting something terrible to happen at any given moment, but surprisingly the day was uneventful. She was ignored by most people, including the Terrible Trio, and treated with basic friendliness by a few others. Not a bad day, all in all.

However, her new neighbour Jon was nowhere to be seen. She kept her eyes open for her little 'friend' Nesbit too, spotting the girl in the cafeteria for their lunchbreak. Nesbit sat several tables away, and Tarie could swear she felt the girl watching her. But when she turned to stare at her, she was looking away.

Ah, well. Maybe the stalking from yesterday had been a coincidence after all.

But then in the afternoon, at the beginning of Tarie's Relevant History class, an announcement was made. The room's five walls all lit up with projected virtual images, along with the giant screen that was usually the focal point of each class. They all displayed what Tarie recognised as Erus's formal city square – the government centre of the city, and the place where the city was formally repledged to its patron Creature every two years.

A vast statue of Domitian sat in the centre of the square, a centaur-like being with a horse's body and a man's chest and head, rearing up dramatically on its hind legs. Behind the statue loomed the Big Three's temples, complete with their own enormous VR figures – Domitian yet again, then Audaline and Gerak.

Tarie watched the scene with a frown of confusion, glancing around to see the same expressions on other classmates' faces. She could see their Creature symbols on their foreheads too: a sign that the VR had spread right across the room. She accidentally caught Rokal's eye. His symbol was a horn – Gerak – and he sneered at her. She looked away.

A voice echoed through the space. It didn't come from anywhere in particular, and its unnaturally pleasant tones showed it was VR-generated rather than from a real person. *"Good news, citizens of Erus! After negotiations in the Other realm, our patron Creature Domitian has now been replaced by the great Audaline. Audaline, the wise, ancient and flight-giving. All honour to Erus's new patron Creature, Audaline!"*

"ALL HONOUR TO AUDALINE!" a multitude of voices echoed, even as Tarie could hear gasps and murmurs of surprise from those around her.

Then the massive statue of Domitian blurred and changed until it was a tall, angular figure draped in flowing robes. It held a long, claw-tipped staff in one hand, and what showed of that arm under the loose sleeve was marked with stripes. Its face was covered by an opaque veil.

"That's just a VR effect, right?" someone behind Tarie murmured. "They couldn't change a real statue so quickly."

"Nah, I think it's a smart statue," someone else murmured back. "You know, the sort made up of tiny blocks that can be rearranged on command. I bet it's changing in real life."

Tarie idly thought of how such a thing would be easy pickings for a prankster, if only they got hold of the controller. But the VR/possibly real scene around them was still changing. The VR images of Audaline and Domitian flowed and changed on top of their temples, until instead of two moving figures, there was only one enormous form. It was Audaline again, her/its draping robes now red and flowing in the wind, with one foot planted on each temple. The remaining VR image of Gerak now looked small in comparison.

The vast new VR figure faced the matching statue in the middle of the square, but it seemed to look around at the crowds 'filling' the square. Tarie shuddered as its veiled gaze seemed to meet her own. She felt a tingle run across her body, either real or VR she didn't know, and the Words pushed at the back of her throat, wanting to be spoken.

She swallowed them back, ignoring the wave of nausea that came over her as she did so. She knew that now was *not* the time to be speaking alter-power into the atmosphere. Not here.

"Chaos," one of Tarie's classmates murmured from behind. "That makes a statement. I wonder what happened to Domitian?"

"Never mind that," the second one retorted. "What happens to everyone pledged to Domitian?!"

It was a good question, Tarie thought. And as if the VR controller had been listening, that artificial voice said, *"Those pledged to Domitian have now been transferred to Audaline. If you have any questions, please visit your nearest temple representative."*

There was another chorus of gasps, then a wave of muttering that Tarie knew came from her classmates. She looked around, trying to make sense of what was going on. "This isn't normal?" she asked one of the girls standing behind her.

"What, one Creature stealing another's pledges?" the girl replied, her eyebrows raised. "I've heard of it happening once or twice with small Creatures, but nothing like this." She shook her head, her expression baffled. "Nothing like this."

Ah. So this wasn't just some Erusian oddity, then. Compared to Memrys, some of the Creatures here would use different names and images. Tarie had wondered if maybe they acted very differently too, and had hoped so. Then maybe her family would be safer here, just like they'd been promised.

Or maybe they wouldn't. She didn't know what to think.

When finally the VR scenery vanished, and they were finally just back in their classroom, it seemed that everyone else felt the same way. A couple of classmates had abruptly found themselves repledged to Audaline, and the conversation that was set off was so loud that the tutor had to turn his audio up to full volume to bring order back.

"Speak to your representative after class!" the tutor snapped. "Now, I'm going to teach this class its Relevant History, and *you* are going to learn, or else stay behind. Is that clear?"

Clear enough.

As Tarie took her seat in her last class of the day, she found herself sitting behind one person who would certainly have been affected by this change. Gavriel. He was sitting next to her least favourite people, Rokal the Brute and nasty Orla, but her curiosity overcame her dislike.

Ignoring the other two, Tarie leaned forward and tapped Gavriel on the shoulder. When he glanced back, she asked, "Hey, aren't you pledged to Domitian?"

"Don't you mean, *wasn't* he pledged to Domitian," Rokal cut in, his tone as bored and scornful as ever as he twisted back to look at her. "What's it to you, Babbler?"

Tarie felt her cheeks heat. Rokal's black hair had streaks of green and red today, and the colours seemed to reflect in his dark eyes. Anger and unwilling attraction made the Words swell up again at the back of her throat, and she had to pause for a few seconds to avoid speaking them aloud and making herself the fool he thought she was. "I'm not talking to you," she managed to say, biting back the word 'beast'. "I was asking Gavriel."

"Be nice, Rokky," Gavriel scolded his friend, then his golden head turned and he smirked back at her. "Were you wondering if I've lost any of my fabulous abilities? Gained new ones?"

"Yeah, more or less." Tarie shrugged a shoulder, wondering if she'd overstepped by speaking to him. That was always one of her flaws – speaking when she should keep her mouth shut. "You don't sound surprised by any of this."

"I just handle change really, really well," he replied, still wearing that usual smirk that either meant humour or superiority. "But don't worry, little Tariana. Even if I do lose my mind-boggling speed, I can still protect you from ghosties and ghouls."

She blinked at him, then realised he was referring to that odd comment yesterday, about someone apparently following her. "I wasn't...I don't expect you to."

"I know," he said cheerfully. "But I'm just a really good person."

"Modest too," Tarie said dryly, rolling her eyes. She knew he was joking, and even if he did start following her around, she'd consider it the start of a prank rather than any real kindness. But it was better to act friendly, even if she didn't really feel like it.

"Gav, stop flirting with the Babbler," Orla drawled. "Class is starting."

Hmm. Probably better not to sit behind these three again, Tarie thought. It seemed to be asking for trouble, or at least annoyance. And Gavriel hadn't even answered her question about whether he'd kept his abilities since changing Creatures.

She didn't ask again.

After class Tarie made her way back to her vehicle with half her attention elsewhere. After the announcement that afternoon, there'd been a distinctive excitement in the air. Not a happy excitement, more the confused sort where people knew *something* important was happening, but weren't yet sure what it meant for them. The change in patron Creature shouldn't affect her at all – she hoped – but she couldn't shake the feeling of unease.

Maybe it was a shift in the Other realm affecting the normal, she wondered, but she'd had to keep biting back the Words over and over. Even now, as she made her way to her vehicle, her ears seemed to ring with distant music. The air around her seemed oddly dry, and she kept seeing these little flashes of light in the corners of her eyes. But when she turned to see what it was, there was nothing there.

How uncomfortable. Tarie hurriedly climbed into her vehicle, hearing the locks engage with some relief, and set the destination for her new home. But even here, all by herself, she wouldn't speak the Words. A wave of nausea came over her again, along with an ache in her belly.

The moment she got home, she was going to bed.

"Da, Tarie's acting weird and grumpy," Lydia's voice came from the hallway. "I think she's sick."

"Lady issues, is it?" Tarie heard her father call back.

Tarie wanted to bury her head under her pillow, but she could hardly force herself to roll over. Lydia was telling on her because she'd snapped when the younger girl had asked for a hand ordering – wait for it – yet another Bridie book.

Er...*nope.* Even if she hadn't been feeling as sick as a diseased dog, she wasn't going near that cursed series ever again.

"Don't think so," she heard Lydia call back. "See for yourself."

A moment later she heard heavy footsteps, then her father's much closer voice. "Tarie, what's the problem?"

Oh, Chaos. Lydia had gone and got him, even though Tarie had told her not to. "I'm fine," she said tersely, her face buried in her hands. "Just feeling a little off-colour, so I'm having a rest."

With two daughters and until recently, a wife, Tarren had been trained well. He didn't even respond to her harsh tone, looking her over where she lay bundled under a blanket, clearly curled up in misery. "Is it 'that time'? Shall I get you some pain relief?"

"No! No, thank you. I'm fine. Just give me some time to rest."

"If you insist."

Tarie did insist, yes. Her sickness wasn't pain, exactly, or nausea, but it had got a thousand times worse when she'd made her way through the foyer earlier. She'd seen the plant wall and thought it needed a little refreshing, but had resisted the Words again since she was determined to get the habit under control. "*Da.*"

He got the message and left Tarie where she was.

Ohh... The Words pushed again at the back of her throat and once more she pushed them back. She was *not* the Babbler, and she was going to find a better way to deal with stress. Never, never again, she swore, and a harsh cramp shook her body from calves to belly.

"Never again," she said aloud, and this time the cramp was so bad that she almost fainted.

Painkiller, please!

Surely she'd feel better in the morning.

Three days after pledging himself to Erus's most terrifying, feral Creature, Jon was finally ready to return to Centre. He studied his reflection in the VR wall one last time. The flight-suit he'd just had made for himself was classic white, but the cut-out chest and back piece was shaped like a sharp-winged butterfly/bat, and was made of a contrasting blood-red fabric. Very dramatic, he thought, and quite fitting with his new colouring that no longer terrified him.

This was who he was now, he told himself firmly, and he was finally ready to show everyone.

Anni's figure appeared behind Jon in the VR wall. Even through the gloss of VR she had shadows under her eyes, and the hollows under her cheekbones made her look older than when he'd last seen her. Her mediocre Creature's mark sat dully on her forehead. "I'm off to work," she said quietly. "I can give you a lift."

"I don't think that will be necessary," he replied, turning his focus back to his own appearance. Hmm. *His* Creature symbol didn't sit still like hers did; it moved around his forehead like a blade-winged butterfly. Cool. "I'm going to fly."

"Oh. Well…have a good day, then."

"I intend to." Once he overcame the niggling discomfort over the height required to fly, that was. Surely he just needed to practice more. He'd spent the last two days flying, and while he wouldn't say he was over that fear yet, he'd come to terms with it enough to force himself to use his new gift with a fixedly blank expression. Hopefully people would take it for boredom rather than what it really was…and wouldn't notice his trembling limbs.

That appalling fear of heights was Rokal's fault, and if

Jon's *other* new gift worked how he thought it did, Rokal was going to pay.

Jon landed hard in front of the Centre's busy main entrance – hard enough that the shock jolted its way up his legs and almost made him drop his carefully bored expression. As he strode up the stairs to the front door, he heard the chatter around him come to a halt before rapidly rising in volume again.

"Chaos, who's that?"

"I dunno. A new Prince of the Air! D'ya think it's something to do with the Audaline change?"

Ah yes, the Audaline change. Jon found that timing interesting– and he was certainly glad that Domitian hadn't taken his pledge after all. It sounded like Domitian had been overthrown right after Jon had gone to see him. Crazy timing.

But as Jon stepped through the doorway, the security scanner that checked everyone as they entered flashed twice and emitted an alarm. He stopped, turning to stare at the drones that had drawn to either side of him. "What's the problem?"

"Unknown identity," a voice came through the drone's speaker. "Voice verification required."

Ah. Jon had wondered if this might happen. "Jon DeLuca, Prince of the Air," he bit out, fully aware that he had everyone's attention. "Pledged to the White Prince. Is that verification enough for you?"

There was a brief silence from the speaker. "Jayel Jonnamin DeLuca?"

"*Jon* DeLuca," he snapped, hearing the hushed whispers from around him. Jayel was gone – but they didn't know that yet.

Another silence. "Yes…sir. Congratulations on your promotion… and to Chairman DeMannard also."

Luca's own promotion to chairman of the Erus council had only been declared last night. Jon wasn't sure what to think of it, except that if it meant Luca would be out of the house more, then it was a good thing. But he just nodded at whoever was behind the security camera, then walked inside.

With the initial entrance now over, he wasn't sure what do to do with himself. He was a little early, and usually he'd arrive at the last possible moment to avoid awkward times like these. He'd have to check his class schedule, maybe even provide a formal reason for his absence. It had only been three days, but he didn't want to be penalised for his time off. Although, his father's new position and his own new allegiance would surely save him, right?

Just as Jon was walking through the Centre's inner courtyard, a heavy hand landed on his shoulder. He turned to see a broad, white-clad chest, then looked up to see Rokal DeWyet's scornful face.

"Jayel DeLuca," Rokal sneered. "You think white clothes and spray paint are going to convince anyone that you're carrier royalty?"

Rokal surely hadn't seen him fly in, Jon realised. Maybe he didn't even know about Luca's promotion either – or maybe he did, and he was as bitter as his own father Wyet must be at being passed over for chairman. He met Rokal's eyes, seeing his own reflection in Rokal's dark irises. He looked creepy. Good.

"You really struggle with competition, *Max*," Jon said coolly, pushing Rokal's hand off his shoulder. He'd taken the time to look up Rokal's original name, and if Rokal insisted on calling Jon 'Jayel' still, then Jon would call Rokal 'Max'. "Can't handle not being the only male Prince here at Centre anymore?"

"By Auda," Orla murmured as she walked up beside Rokal with Gavriel just behind her. She studied Jon from head to toe. "Is that really you, Jail?"

"Do me a favour," Jon told her coolly. "Call me Jon, and I won't curse you to puke your guts out for the next three weeks."

She laughed. "You can't do that." But her smile fell as she looked hesitantly at her on-off boyfriend. "He can't, right?"

Actually, Jon didn't know if he could curse people. Luca had suggested it, along with some worse comments, but Jon could only hope that the White Prince's reputation would cover over any lack of actual ability beyond flying. But then he'd looked in the mirror last night and had seen the White Prince looking back… That had led to an interesting, if terrifying conversation, and the White Prince had certainly made some bold claims.

Here was hoping that what the Creature had claimed turned out to be true.

Rokal was still fixed on Jon's earlier statement. "I enjoy competition," he said flatly. "But I'm not convinced that you meet that definition. I think you're a scummy poser…just like your father."

Gavriel whistled, a long, low sound. If they hadn't had everyone's attention before, they sure did now. "And you claimed you weren't holding a grudge on your father's behalf," Gavriel said mockingly to his friend, then nodded to Jon. "Well, butterfly man. If you're brave enough to face the White Prince, I'd say you can handle a challenge with Rokky here."

Jon put his hands in his pockets, leaning back in what he thought must be a relaxed manner. But inside he felt anything but relaxed. The last time he'd been here, he was humiliated. He had to regain respect. He *had to.* "What kind of challenge?"

Gavriel glanced at Rokal in an exaggerated sort of way, his eyebrows raised as if waiting for something. "Let's say...a race. First one to reach the top of the flagpole and back wins. Easy, right?"

Chaos. Jon was going to get his arse kicked, because he flew like a bumblebee to Rokal's hornet. And the flagpole!? He didn't exactly have good memories of that thing.

But because he couldn't say no without destroying all the lovely fear and respect he'd just built up, he thought back instead to what the White Prince had told him last night in the mirror. *Let me speak for you.*

And like last night, a tickling pain seemed to lock his jaw and make his throat burn. Rather than fight it, Jon relaxed and felt his mouth open. *"Let's do it,"* the White Prince said through Jon's lips. *"Go on, Rokal. Break a leg."*

8

Words Have Power

Break a leg, the White Prince had said. Jon had felt alter-power rush out into the atmosphere even as that old-fashioned phrase had left his mouth, but no one else seemed to notice. They had everyone's attention now. An impromptu race was nothing unusual; a *flying* race between Rokal and 'the pledgeless wonder' was a whole different story.

"Even if you *are* pledged," Rokal sneered, "you're still second rate."

"And you don't know when to stop talking," Jon retorted, feeling his heart pounding in his chest in spite of his casual words. "Now are you going to talk or fly?"

"Fly," Orla cut in. Her multicoloured eyes were bright with excitement. "*I* don't have anything to prove, *Jon*." She nudged her boyfriend. "To the flagpole and back. Three…two…one…GO!"

Rokal exploded into the air like a rocket, bowling over a nearby junior student from the force of his take off. But Jon hadn't even lifted off – didn't even try to – by the time Rokal reached the flagpole high above their heads. He made a filthy gesture down at them, then came hurtling back towards the ground at high speed.

Nope, Jon realised suddenly. Make that hurtling towards *him* at high speed. Jon gently lifted aside at the last moment, and Rokal landed hard on the polished tile floor instead of breaking Jon's freshly white head.

There was a tremendous *crack*, and Rokal let out a horrible, gasping shriek. He collapsed to the ground, his face turning a pasty whitish-green. *"My legs!"*

Orla swore, and the cheers of the students around them faded into silence broken only by Rokal's whimpers. His legs were now the wrong shape inside his fitted white trousers, and when red began to stain the cloth, Jon almost vomited.

"How ironic," he managed to say, and was glad to hear his shock didn't show in his tone. "Saying break a leg is supposed to mean good luck. I suppose I should be careful what I say now."

When the White Prince had spoken to Jon through the mirror last night, it- *he* had said, *There's life and death in the power of the tongue. Let me shape your words, and shape your world.*

Jon had agreed, because he'd already given his word back in the temple and he couldn't take it back, even though he'd felt sick at the thought of letting the White Prince operate any of his body parts.

But even though Jon had been hesitant, it seemed Luca had been right after all. Jon *could* curse people, and with the White Prince's help he'd dished out a fitting revenge on Rokal.

"I guess you won the race," he told Rokal even as gasps and hushed whispers sounded around them. He reached down and patted the groaning young man on the shoulder. "Good job. May you keep this position of honour for the rest of your life."

"Chaos, he just cursed Rokal again!" someone whispered from the crowd. "Now his legs won't heal!"

That wasn't at all what Jon had said, although he was happy for people to think so.

Orla turned to Jon, her eyes wide and a little fearful. "I guess you really did go to the White Prince."

"Did you think I lied?"

She shrugged. "Maybe."

Jon studied his three worst enemies. One was incapacitated (and should probably see a medic soon), one was watching him with fear…and the last wore his usual grin.

"Are you going to curse us too?" Gavriel asked lightly. "Test your power a bit more?"

"That depends," Jon replied neutrally, but inside he was elated at the show of respect. "Are you going to keep giving me a hard time?"

Gavriel barked out a laugh. "Not if we want to keep our limbs intact, I think." He glanced down at his groaning friend. "What did I say about watching your landings, Rok?"

Rokal just groaned.

The other two stood there looking at Jon, and he didn't know what to say next so he just turned his back on them and walked away.

Weird colouring – yep. Flying – yep. Cursing enemies – yep. Unnatural hungers…?

Jon's stomach rumbled, and even though he'd already eaten a large breakfast that morning, he turned and headed straight for the cafeteria.

He could eat again. And being hungry wasn't the same as being *unnaturally* hungry, right?

Elspeth lay on her back on the floor, her arms spread out above her head. Her hands almost touched either side of her small bedroom. Verily, she was most tremendously bored! She had not thought such a thing was possible, not while here at the edge of time on her very important mission.

But then neither had she supposed that her charge would spend three days lying on her bed like a great big slug. Or a small but sturdy slug, rather. Regardless, Tarie would not leave her boxlike 'apartment' home – and so *Elspeth* could not leave either.

By the rood, Elspeth would almost rather go back to that Centre of dubious learning rather than wait here another hour. The world outside these walls was bizarre and fascinating, full of objects and images that would have left a younger her screaming 'witchcraft!' But in truth, they showed what incredible feats humanity was capable of when building upon the knowledge of previous generations – and with the help of a little alter-power at times.

However, Elspeth dared not go out and leave Tarie behind, not when the girl truly was the target of repeated and nefarious attacks. Attacks at a higher speed than her eye could follow, and with the faintest sound of bells in the distance.

'Twas a true gift from the Mountain of Glass that Elspeth had been able to step in just in time, every time so far. It seemed as though time itself would slow down, and she would feel a most intense tugging in her gut, along with a tremendous sense of urgency. Then she'd turn to see a dark shadow bearing down on Tarie, and fire would shoot almost involuntarily from her palms.

Poof. (Eee!)

Well, Elspeth thought practically, she now knew that her gift of cleansing flame could be used across great distances. On one occasion the flame had even turned a corner. If only it could remove the threat permanently...

The whole situation reminded Elspeth most strongly of a villain she'd chased off mere days earlier (or centuries earlier, depending on how one counted time). Lily...Lilibet? *Lilith!*

She thought back to the conversation she'd had with Jon's protector last night. She'd ventured her opinion that Tarie's attacker shared some abilities with this ancient, hopefully dead Halfling.

But Fylax had told her that firstly, Lilith was still alive. She was not mortal, so would not conveniently die of old age. And secondly, she no longer had the abilities that had made her so dangerous to the little town of Erastus. Instead, she bonded men to her rather like a Creature took a carrier, and gave them a version of her old powers.

Mayhap one of these men was the attacker, Elspeth mused. She'd thought on it all night, and 'twas a logical answer. "Now if only we might locate said attacker," she mused aloud, "we might attack *him* in a self-defensive manner afore he attacked yet again, thus saving time and effort."

You mean kill them?

The thought was very small, but pricked enough that Elspeth paused to consider it. Did she mean to kill someone? No, not some*one*, she scolded herself. Some*thing*. A malignant dark shadow with foul intent, so 'twould not be murder at all, she told herself. Mayhap.

No further thoughts came to mind, but Elspeth now felt uncomfortable pursuing that line of thinking. She sat up, feeling her hair sticking out in every direction from the roughly carpeted floor. "If I do not escape this place I vow I shall go mad," she muttered. She stretched out that special sense that was tied only to Tarie, and when she felt the girl still in the same location as before, she huffed out a sigh of relief then made her way to the exit. "Just a short walk."

After all, this time period was most fascinating. So very different, even though there were more buildings than she could have imagined, in the oddest shapes like blocks piled on top of each other. They stretched up higher than seemed safe, but the locals comfortably lived in their odd box-like buildings and walked across their spindly, winding roads in the air – when they *did* walk, which was not very often.

It seemed to Elspeth that here in this time, one could spend one's entire life inside a tiny house, with food being delivered to the door, and with one's mind caught up inside virtual reality as replacement to real life.

But regardless of the people's hermitic habits, she found them odd and interesting too. They would carry on one-sided conversations as they went about their business, ignoring the real people around them. Elspeth had thought them mad at first till Fylax had explained they spoke through tiny devices implanted in their lips and ears, and might even be in conversation with a friend on the other side of the world.

It still seemed madness to Elspeth, but fascinating madness.

And just as fascinating was the way people of this time looked. Most of them were so very tall (excepting Tarie), and so very colourful.

When Elspeth went to Centre, 'twas like attending a carnival. People wore bright paint on their faces, their hair, their hands – and their clothing was not at all modest, but even that was fascinating too, in a startling way. Their skin came in all different shades, from as fair as her own to the darkest brown, and their features tended to be very regular. Not a bulbous nose or cross-eye among them. Not even the odd hairy mole!

When she'd commented on such, Fylax had said that people would usually choose their children's features afore they were born; choose their heights, weights and features for optimum beauty. 'Twas an odd thing to consider, but mayhap 'twas why Jon had never seen Elspeth as more than just 'friendly little Bets'. She must seem overly short and plain in comparison to the carefully bred people of his own time. Like a miniature donkey next to an Arabian horse.

Her (small, ill-bred) shoulders slumped at that thought, and she glanced across the hall to where the single door marked the home Jon shared with his mother and his carrier father. As to the latter, one could not breed character, could they?

What secrets Jon had been hiding. The more Elspeth saw of his life here, from the horrendous incident several days earlier to him…*Jon*…becoming a carrier himself, the more she understood his secrecy in the Mountain of Glass. After all, what should he have said?

'By the way, Bets, I'm bound to one of Amaranthus's worst enemies'?

Elspeth reached the end of the hall and paused in front of the little moving room that would take her to the ground level. The door opened, and she glanced back to Tarie's nearby door, and Jon's on the other side of the hall. She'd previously considered waiting in the hall so she might 'accidentally' run into him again, but after seeing him so very changed (a carrier!) she didn't dare.

She ought to have kept her distance as agreed, she reminded herself. Then she never would have seen him in such a terrible state.

But Elspeth did dare to venture down to the ground floor, where the building's entrance was lined with little lifting rooms, a wall of closed shiny boxes, and another wall of tiny, lush plants. 'Twas almost as if she was inside a very small, tidy forest, if a forest could be vertical.

And I am very bored indeed, if I'm pondering plants, Elspeth thought wryly. She turned to the wall of shiny boxes, running her hand across their surfaces until she reached the one marked 42F. Her actions came from boredom, but she paused when she felt a tingle of alter-power run through her hand.

Elspeth looked down and saw a crumpled metallic object on the floor. The alter-power emanating from it could be felt even from her standing position, and she'd bent down to touch it before she even considered her actions.

A sudden chill at her fingers was her only warning, and she only just managed to release some of her cleansing flame before the world around her changed.

Tarie had never been so tired in her life. These last few days she'd felt like her whole body had been battered and bruised, and it was all she could do to get herself up for the bathroom and to keep drinking liquids. Da insisted on using the porta-medic when she hadn't felt better by the following evening, but when it tested her blood and vital signs, the reading declared her healthy.

It was mostly the fact that Tarie wasn't talking that worried her family so much. She couldn't explain that the only reason why she wouldn't speak was that every time she opened her mouth the Words tried to come out…and she wouldn't let them.

Nope, she would vow every time she felt the urge. *I need to get control over this, because otherwise we'll never be safe here.*

But when Tarie woke this morning the overwhelming urge to speak the Words had weakened, and when Lydia came in to check on her, Tarie mumbled from under her covers, "Fine. Now go away and let me sleep."

That cranky response must have cheered her family up enough to leave her alone, because Lydia had gone to school and Tarren to work without further comment.

By the afternoon Tarie felt hungry. Ravenous, actually, and because she hadn't eaten properly in about three days (and because she felt well enough to get up) she went to the kitchen to get some food. She diverted to the bathroom first, staggering a little at the movement and noting grumpily that the seat seemed lower. It was just her being off balance, she concluded. But then she went to wash her hands and noticed the same thing – the sink was lower, and she was looking at the middle of the mirror rather than the bottom as usual.

"What in Chaos is going on?" she muttered to herself, then realised Lydia must be playing some sort of trick on her. Of course. She must've changed the height settings, even though Tarren had warned them to leave them be. He said that having furniture constantly move gave him a headache.

Tarie heard the whoosh of air as the apartment door opened, then Lydia's distinctive clomping steps followed by her voice cooing at Brownie in his windowsill enclosure. Tarie made her way to the kitchen/dining area and the nutri-dispenser then pressed the keypad for quick oats with berry coulis. But the screen lit up with 'berry not available'.

"Lyd," Tarie croaked, "did we not get more flavour ingredients? I asked for them after we arrived."

"Hey, you're up!" Lydia glanced over her shoulder, smiling. "Can you get me a drink too?"

"Nothing berry-flavoured. We're out."

"We shouldn't be," Lydia countered, moving to stand next

to Tarie at the dispenser. She poked at the drink order, then frowned. "Huh. It says we're out. Maybe those five cups of ultraberry-tamarind juice were too much for it."

Ya don't think? Tarie raised her eyebrows – not that Lydia saw – but then noticed something. Rather than looking up at her more average-sized sister like usual, she appeared to be at the same level. But Lydia was supposed to be half a head taller. "Lyd, are you squatting?"

Lydia turned to give her a confused look. "No. You're on tiptoes."

They both glanced down at Tarie's bare feet, which were flat on the ground. So were Lydia's for that matter – and the younger girl was wearing shoes. "Weird," Tarie said flatly. "Either you're messing with me, 'cos the toilet was lower too, or else I've had a growth spurt."

"I didn't touch the bathroom settings!" Lydia countered defensively. "Not after Da told me off last time." Her eyes widened. "Let's measure you! Maybe you *did* grow."

So they grabbed the package-sizer for drone deliveries and ran it over Tarie instead.

"Woah," Lydia said upon seeing the readings. "It says you're three units taller. You're almost the same as me now!"

"That's silly. No one grows that much in such a short time." Besides, Tarie was still half-convinced Lydia was playing a prank on her.

"Then let's ask Da," Lydia said staunchly.

"*You* ask," Tarie replied grumpily. She didn't know what to make of any of this, and her whole body still ached as if she'd run a marathon. "I'm going back to bed."

One moment Elspeth had been standing in the building's entry room, her hand stretched out to touch the alter-powered object, and the next she was in a vast, dark space. 'Twas as though she'd stepped through a remnant gateway from one place to another, and she cursed herself a fool. Did she not know that the world was a dangerous place full of unexpected pitfalls? Alter-power was the most dangerous and unexpected of all. Even the crumpled metal object had vanished from her hand.

But then Elspeth realised something odd. While she appeared to be in a place full of darkness, standing upright with empty hands, she could still feel the real ground underfoot. She wiggled her fingers and felt the hard surface of that metal object once again, though she could still see it not at all.

"How curious," she murmured. "The object appears to be a gateway of its own – but an incomplete one, for I do believe I am still in the same building."

Verily, the solution should be simple enough. Elspeth opened her hand to release the object – or tried to. But while the hand she could *see* appeared empty, with her fingers now outstretched like the arms of a starfish, she could still feel her fingers closed around the object.

Hmm. Her eye twitched at the conflict between sight and senses. She tried again, this time closing her eyes and tugging her hand backwards in an abrupt movement. She even added sound effects: "Heeeya!"

No luck. She was still surrounded by darkness, and she could still feel the blighted object under her fingertips even though she could not see it.

Sigh.

Just then a light flickered in the corner of Elspeth's vision. She turned to see a bright rectangle in the distance, like someone had opened a door. "Ooh!" A destination!

She turned to move towards the light, but although it had seemed so far away, suddenly 'twas right in front of her. How odd. She took another step, then she was through the door and inside an entirely new place.

'Twas a city street. Not like the city outside Tarie's home, but rather more like a city of Elspeth's own time period. Tidier, mayhap, and rather less smelly, with narrow streets lined with flat cobbles, stone buildings of only two or three levels high, and a noticeable lack of glass windows.

People moved about purposefully, many of them carrying objects or conversations with other unseen partners. Verily, 'twas a complete contrast to Erus City-state…except for the one-sided conversations, of course.

No one seemed to notice her.

Elspeth stepped back as a man moved past carrying an

enormous flat shape draped in cloth. She'd vow 'twas lighter than it looked, for 'twas far too large to be carried comfortably by one person – and yet there he was, carrying it.

The shape was draped in a solid green cloth that shimmered and changed to a shade of deep red even as she watched. The cloth moved not at all in spite of the man's speed, and a tingle of discomfort moved through her as she realised that this place did not seem to obey the usual laws of time and space.

Could it be the Other realm? Surely not, for she'd never partially entered that realm as she clearly had this one. But there was something here, something that made the hairs on the back of her neck stand up. It felt like…*Creature.*

Elspeth clenched her hands at her side, willing the cleansing flame to burn and remind her of what was real, and what was not. But she could neither see nor feel the flame at all, as though 'twas not there at all.

Another large flat shape was carried past, but this one wasn't completed covered by red/green cloth. She could see a distinctive triangle of shining surface where 'twas exposed.

A mirror. But what for?

Curious, she followed behind the mirror and its carrier as they moved down the street with more ease and speed than they ought to have had. As she followed, she found herself moving with the same unnatural speed. Still, she managed to keep her distance as they turned corner after corner, then walked down a sloping path till they entered the low doorway of what looked to be an enormous room or warehouse, built into the ground.

Elspeth stopped some distance away, looking down on the entrance as many people moved in and out. The odd angle meant she could not see more than a few yards beyond the entrance, so she could not see where they were going or why. The people would go in carrying shapes like the mirror, disappear from her line of sight, then a little later, come out empty-handed.

The people were of all races and ages, but what they had in common was this: a symbol on their foreheads that was as dark as ink, yet seemed to glow a little. 'Twas shaped rather like a sprawling spider-starfish Elspeth had seen once on a visit to the seashore, with long, dangling limbs from a small round body.

Still, nobody seemed to see Elspeth at all. Not until one woman came out. She was short and fair, rather nondescript in fact, but overlaying her form was another sheer one, almost like she wore a spirit-shaped cloak. The sheer form had the ugliest face, with a bulbous forehead and almost no nose at all, and just one googly, red-rimmed eye.

'Twas clearly a Creature…and there was no doubt *it* saw Elspeth.

"ENEMY!" it shrieked, and its voice overlaid that of the woman who carried it. It stretched out a hand to point at Elspeth, and the carrier did the same; the two moving as one.

Elspeth had not been truly concerned before that moment. More curious, if she was to be honest. But in that moment of discovery, true and absolute panic came over her. She felt the cleansing flame shoot from her hands even as the Creature and its carrier shrieked in unison, and the world around her flickered once more.

Then a single eye-blink later, Elspeth found herself again in the real world. She stood in Tarie's building's entryway once more, half bent over and backed up against the wall of plants. Her back ached like she'd been sleeping on rocks.

She had gone nowhere, she realised suddenly. Instead, 'twas her mind that had travelled.

Elspeth looked down to see a crumpled, flaming metal shape in one hand. The item she'd so thoughtlessly bent down to touch was now unrecognisable – not that she'd known what 'twas in the first place.

"Ugh!" She threw the thing away from her. It bounced once then skidded to a stop against the base of the plant wall, almost hidden under the tangled greenery. She clenched her fists, wanting to hide it or destroy it, but she didn't dare touch it again.

The silvery flame continued to burn, although did not touch any of its surroundings. Whatever evil covered that object must go very deep indeed.

Foolish, foolish girl! Elspeth scolded herself. Oh, what consequences had come from her boredom? She knew not what manner of place she had visited, except that it had been neither the normal nor the Other realm. Mayhap not VR either, for surely Creatures could not visit such a place?

She shook herself as though she might shake the Creature's taint from her own memory. What was done could not be undone. But surely, if she was most diligent from this point onwards, then 'twould be as though naught had happened at all.

Hopefully.

So Elspeth quickly entered the nearest lifting room, determined to return to her post. This time she would not fail.

Not long after the Amaranthus-follower had vacated the foyer, someone very different walked casually across to the object half hidden under the green-wall. They wrapped a cloth around their hand, then nonchalantly picked it up and slipped it into their pocket before stepping into a liftpod themselves. Destination: floor forty-two.

The detour had been a little risky, but they considered it worth the risk of being seen. Valuable entry pieces like these shouldn't be left on the ground, even if they did currently look like trash.

"How was Centre today, Jay-Jon?" Anni asked that evening as she unpacked the dinner plates from the delivery drones and onto the table.

Jon shuffled a little in his seat. Chaos, he was starving, and how was he meant to answer that question? *Well, I broke my archenemy's leg. Just one leg, unfortunately. Oh, and I think I can curse people now. Oops!* "It was fine."

"Oh." She paused as if waiting for him to elaborate, but then finally smiled tightly and started to chatter about her own day in that way she would when she was uncomfortable. "We've had a few things go missing in the stockrooms over the last few weeks, and I think it's starting to look suspicious. But my manager says that-"

"Please, woman. No one's interested," Luca interrupted as he entered the room, and Anni subsided into embarrassed silence, her shoulders slumping.

Jon caught her eye and shrugged in apology. Luca had been rude as usual, and while there was no point telling him so – it only made him nastier – Luca had for once been right. Jon couldn't focus on the details of Anni's day, because his own life was so…consuming right now.

"*Jon*, it seems like you're keeping secrets," Luca continued with a smirk. "Councilman Wyet tells me that there was an incident at Centre today. Something to do with a race?" Jon looked up at his father where he leaned against the doorframe. Luca wasn't even trying to hide his amusement, and Jon was reminded yet again of how very much he'd changed. "It was an accident," Jon said defensively. "Rokal isn't pressing charges, is he?"

Anni's head snapped up from the nutri-dispenser, her eyes widening in horror. "What happened?!"

"I believe my son challenged Wyet's to a race," Luca said with some glee. "Flying, of course, but the other boy didn't land well at all."

"He's not…" Anni whispered, one hand moving to her chest.

"No, he's not dead," Luca snapped, rolling his eyes. "He just has two dramatically broken legs. Apparently right after my son wished him good luck the old-fashioned way."

"Wyet's son…" she murmured. "Is that the one who gave you a hard time, Jayel? Russell or something?"

"Rokal," Jon corrected, feeling a warm flush of satisfaction warring with shame. Anni clearly hadn't understood the reference to good luck or she'd be a lot more upset. "And I thought it was only one leg."

"Definitely both," Luca countered. "Wyet is fuming. Ha."

Anni's face fell. "Oh, Jayel. You didn't…*push* him?"

"It's *Jon*, and I didn't touch him," Jon snapped back. "He flew so fast that he was back before I'd even left the ground, and he was aiming to land right on my head. I dodged, he broke his legs on the concrete. If he'd hit me, then I bet he wouldn't be giving me any sympathy while I got my skull plated back together!"

Anni gasped, and Jon added darkly, "Rokal deserved what he got."

She fell silent.

"As much as I'm enjoying this conversation, I have somewhere to be," Luca cut in. "Chairman DeMannard is a busy man." He let out a short laugh, adding, "I just dropped by to congratulate my son on his first day as somebody…and to let you know we're moving house in two days."

"What?!" Jon burst out. They'd lived in this place his entire life. When Jon had been a kid and Luke and Anni had contracted, Luke had moved here. Of course it hadn't looked the same back then…

"But we just renovated," Anni added worriedly, her arms wrapped around herself. "Where are we going?"

"To old Joss Tybalt's place, of course." Luca stretched, then yawned, displaying what looked like gem implants on his molars. "Now that's a proper residence, and you know it's been recently vacated."

As in, the old chairman had just dropped dead of a heart attack two days earlier…and Luca had been sworn in late last night. That made Jon the son of the most powerful man in Erus…and he wasn't sure how he felt about it.

But to move house so quickly, and to what he assumed was a mansion? "Do we have to?"

It was a curious question rather than a complaint, and Luca responded accordingly. "Of course you do. My family lives with me. The packers will be coming tomorrow, so make sure anything fragile is labelled." With that cheery comment, he turned and left.

"This is starting to feel like a familiar routine," Anni muttered, moving away from the table to pour herself a cocktail. "And I don't know why he wants us to live with him when he's never here." There was a pause, then she added under her breath, "Luckily."

Jon ignored her and focused on his meal. He felt as hungry as he had since becoming a carrier. He'd easily doubled his food intake over the last few days, although if anything he just looked leaner. Sometimes his stomach felt like it was caving in. Not a nice side-effect of the change, but a manageable one. "So are you going to move?" he asked through his mouthful.

"Eat, then talk," Anni said absently. "But what do you mean? Of course I'll move. Luca wants us to." She sighed heavily, studying the walls around them and no doubt their expensive coverings.

Jon swallowed. "But you don't want to," he pointed out. "You don't even like Luca, and he treats you like rubbish. Does a big fancy house mean that much to you?" Because if Tybalt's place was what Jon thought it was, then it was fancy indeed. An actual building all on its own not far north of here, where an old national park had been sold to make spacious homes for the rich.

"It's not the house," Anni argued. "It's keeping our family together. And Luca *is* my contracted partner." She sighed again, and her eyes darted to Jon's face before quickly sliding away. "And with everything going on at work, this is a lot to handle."

Or with Jon's new look, he knew she meant. A wave of bitterness washed over him, and he slapped his hand on the table. Somehow it landed in his meal instead, but he didn't even care. "You're always so unhappy," he said flatly. "If Luca makes you so unhappy, then leave him. If your job makes you unhappy, then leave that too. I'd rather you didn't have either than hear you complain about them all the time, yet do nothing."

The silence was broken only by his mother's gasp. When she did speak again, her voice trembled and her face was pale. "Maybe I *do* complain too much. But that doesn't mean that running from my problems is the right answer, or that just because something isn't perfect, it's not worth having at all." She lifted her chin. "And you, Jayel – you sounded just like your father then. In the worst possible way."

Then Anni turned and left.

Jon hadn't meant to say what he'd said. But it was true, wasn't it? A home truth, even if harshly delivered.

So he didn't go after her. Instead he pulled his hand out of his meal, licked the gravy off it, and finished his plate. Then because neither of his parents were eating, he ate theirs too. Then he made himself dessert from the dispenser…then had seconds. But somehow, even though Jon's belly felt distended with his massive meal, the gnawing hunger still remained.

To distract himself, he sent a resignation message to Timm, explaining that he was now a Prince of the Air and wouldn't be coming back to work. (Since who'd ever seen a Prince of the Air working behind a counter?) Then he went to his room and stepped into his favourite VR programme: the endless skies which he'd flown many times, if only in his mind. Here he would feel the freedom to fly fast and high, free from the crippling fear which plagued him in reality-

Oh. No, he was wrong. He was scared here too.

"It's just imaginary!" Jon roared within the safety of VR.

"This isn't really happening, and there's nowhere to fall! There's nothing to be afraid of!"

But the fear remained, and eventually he left the programme. His mind was more difficult to convince than he'd expected, and he felt like such a hypocrite when he thought of the things he'd said to Anni.

He was still miserable, just in different ways.

But was he even fixable?

9
Growth

Tarie slept for the rest of the afternoon, and by the time she dragged herself out of bed to use the bathroom again, she'd convinced herself that the earlier sizing issue had been a prank...or her imagination.

Then through the thin bathroom door, she heard faintly, "Da! Tarie grew!"

Ah. Their father was home...and Lydia had sounded slightly accusing just then.

Tarie ran her hands through the sanitiser, shouting back through the door, "No, I didn't! Lydia's messing with you!"

Except the bathroom settings were still a little too low. Feeling a little defiant, Tarie moved them all up two notches...then three, until her head was at the bottom of the mirror. Just like it was before.

Then she made her way to where Tarren was taking off his jacket, his expression bemused as Lydia waved her hands about, no doubt telling some fabulous, unbelievable story.

Lydia turned to see Tarie, and her eyebrows shot up. She pointed accusingly. "See! See, she's taller!"

"Don't be-" *ridiculous*, Tarie started to argue, but then she realised something odd. Even her father looked shorter today, like he was crouching a bit. She frowned at his legs as she saw he was still wearing shoes, complete with sturdy soles...and she could almost look him in the eye. "Um..."

His eyebrows shot up as he studied her from head to toe. "I think we'll need the scanner."

"See, I *told* you you'd grown," Lydia said smugly. "Four units. Four units, Tarie!"

Not three like they'd thought this morning. If not for the way their father seemed so stunned – and definitely appeared shorter himself – Tarie still wouldn't believe it. But even she had to face facts. "My nightclothes are tighter," she admitted. She'd barely got changed since she'd started feeling ill. "I didn't think much of it, though."

"This says you're just under average height for a girl of your age," Tarren told her, studying the small holographic screen that emanated from the measurer. He shook his head in amazement. "That makes you tall for a Filat, hmm? I suppose...I suppose you've had a growth spurt."

If so, it had been a long time coming. Tarie was so used to being unusually short that the idea of being...average...felt all kinds of wrong. Like it wasn't really her at all. "It's not normal to have a growth spurt in only four days," she said numbly.

"But you don't look stretched," Lydia added. "You're the same shape as before, just taller."

Hooray. She'd gone from extra-short and sturdy, to just shortish and sturdy.

"What have you been doing differently?" her father persisted. "Have you eaten anything strange, taken any medication, been exposed to any alter-power?"

Tarie shook her head even as a bolt of nausea twisted her stomach. The Words bubbled at the back of her throat, and like she had every other time, she swallowed them back. Then a faint, uncomfortable tingle ran down her limbs...and she realised she'd been feeling that too, but had thought it was a side-effect of her sickness.

Oh. "Well..." she said uncomfortably after a short pause, "I've been trying to control when I speak the Words, so I don't blurt them out in public and put a target on us as Way-followers all over again. Maybe that's got something to do with it."

"And you're not speaking them at all?"

Tarie shook her head, waiting for him to explode and tell her that she had a responsibility to use her gift, et cetera. "Not for a few days."

But her father simply looked thoughtful. "I wouldn't have thought you used them that much anyway. Not for a few days to make a difference. But maybe gaining some control would be a good thing, if you need it."

Tarie's eyebrows shot up, and she glanced at Lydia to see she wore the same expression of surprise. She didn't mention that she would often speak the Words under her breath. In the bather, in the liftpod…in her vehicle. Also when she was scared, when she was bored, and when she was angry. Just…really, really quietly.

All the time, really. Maybe her Word silence *was* a big change after all.

"I thought you'd tell Tarie off," the younger girl said bluntly. "Say she's wasting her gift, blah blah blah. Not just say it doesn't matter."

Tarren flushed a little. "It matters. But our lives here matter too." He leaned forward and kissed Tarie on the cheek. For the first time, he barely had to lean down to do so. "Now make sure you start speaking the Words again before you get too tall to fit through doors, alright?"

She nodded. It would be hard enough getting used to her new average height. Being any taller would be a complete disaster.

But for now…time to go clothes shopping in VR.

"Good eve, Fylax," Elspeth said demurely as the protector walked in. She sat on the same couch with an old-fashioned holographic film playing in front of her and a half-empty glass of whatever liquid came from that dispenser. *Why yes, I have been here all day. Thank you for asking.* "How goes things?"

"They go," Fylax replied with a slight crinkle at the edges of his bright eyes.

'Twas the same thing he always said, and Elspeth thought him rather irritatingly close-mouthed when it came to Jon. She wriggled a little in her seat, wanting to ask more, but also aware that she would rather keep silent on the events of her own day in turn.

Fylax sat on his own, extra-large seat. His old man's form seemed to be swallowed up within the seat's velvet frame, but he leaned back, apparently satisfied to sit quietly and peacefully and-

"I went downstairs and became trapped in some evil world full of

mirrors and Creatures and one of them saw me!" Elspeth burst out in a rush. Fylax raised a shaggy eyebrow, and she added as her shoulders slumped, "I was most tremendously bored...but I shall not do it again."

There was a brief silence, then he shrugged. "You know you're not trapped here, little Bets? A protector's role is different for one such as you. You don't have the patience that my kind does."

Elspeth's eyebrows shot up. Then she said carefully, "Are you telling me that I might have left at any time?"

"How you carry out your role is up to you. It would be wise to stay within hearing distance of your charge, but that's not always possible."

"Oh." She thought back to how far her fire gift had stretched when she'd sensed Tarie was in danger. Quite far, indeed. "Oh," she said again.

Fylax stretched one arm far, *far* out to the nutri-dispenser and pressed a couple of buttons. As it whirred into action, he said, "But you ought to be careful when it comes to virtual reality. It can be greatly useful...and it can be a direct route to the Other realm. But like everything, Creatures will twist it in whatever way they can. Even if your body remains safe, your mind can still be badly damaged in those places where Creatures enter VR."

He handed Elspeth a small plate with a soft, flat oval shape on it. It smelled yeasty, but her attention was on his words. A direct route to the Other realm...was that what she had seen? It hadn't felt like any other VR she'd experienced. "What sort of damage?"

The protector took a second serving for himself. "Unwanted or hidden links to Creatures are common. At worst, someone might get trapped inside their mind and not get out without intervention from the Mountain. They might even think that they're dead."

Urgh. Elspeth swallowed, suddenly grateful that her own experience had been so brief. She looked down at the plate in front of her and finally recognised the dish as manchet bread, a luxury food from her home time. Made from expensive white flour, she'd only tasted it when her noble-born half-sister had given her some. It *did* smell delicious, but it ought not to be eaten plain...

Fylax handed her a small bowl of stew.

"Oh. I thank you."

The stew and manchet bread proceeded to be the best she'd ever tasted…verily, *ever*, and it took her attention from what had almost happened. When she finished, she was an inch away from licking out the bowl. "How did you get the recipe so perfect?" she marvelled. "I have never tasted such delicious bread outside-"

"The Mountain of Glass?" Fylax gestured to the small, plain room around them, and his eyes crinkled in a smile. "No one else sees the door to this suite, little Bets. For them, it doesn't exist."

"Oh!" Elspeth said yet again. Verily, it *had* been a day for surprises, and she looked at the room around her with new eyes. Not an odd little house in Jon and Tarie's shared building, but a part of the Mountain of Glass, created in such a way to resemble the world around them.

But such things were now commonplace in the life of a time-travelling, fire-blasting protector such as herself.

She shrugged happily, then returned to her dinner. She was in the mood for seconds.

In a lavishly decorated office-apartment not far from 42 Eastern Way, Luca leaned back in his comfortable chair. He held a blackened piece of metal in one gloved hand, then flipped it to the other, balancing it briefly on the tip of his finger before catching it again.

"These entry pieces to Elsewhise aren't given out lightly," he said. "They're invitation-only. And yet twice, *twice* some random person has used this very piece to enter Elsewhise and have conversations they were never meant to have, or see things they were never meant to see."

From a couch across the room, Basir's dark brows lowered in a scowl. "The knife was meant to be left in your dropbox, not 42-F. It wasn't my fault."

"It wasn't my fault," Luca mimicked Basir's tone, then added an echo so it sounded like a dozen voices were speaking in harmony. "Then why didn't you say something when you couldn't find it?"

"Oh hush, son," Lilith cut in, one hand raised dismissively. She sat down next to Basir, then casually hooked her legs across his lap, linking her other arm around his neck so their bare skin pressed together. The position might look affectionate for anyone who didn't know that there was very little romance between them. It was the price for the power Lilith shared, and it was always paid by the man. "I can't see what difference it makes to you. *I'm* the one in charge of the Elsewhise entry pieces, and you know who I report to."

Luca shrugged, smirking a little. He'd been needling his mother's newest conduit for the fun of it, as she well knew. "What will you do with the two intruders?"

"Take care of them," Basir said grimly.

"What, you'll buy them dinner and a warm coat?" Luca taunted, unimpressed by the young man's attempt to sound powerful, or Hades, even organised. "You'll have to *find* them first."

Basir scowled again, and Luca suddenly felt a sharp flick against his forehead. He rubbed a hand against his temple, then said unrepentantly, "Sorry, Mother." Then he lifted a finger and the VR projection on one wall lit up again. "I've already checked the video from my building's foyer. See?"

The images clearly showed how the first intruder was one of his new neighbours; a clueless, stubby little thing reeking of their enemy.

"We've got it sorted," Basir announced.

Luca rolled his eyes. "*It* looks alive and well. But sure, if you say so. It's the second one that's more of a problem." He skimmed the video forward to earlier today, right before he'd retrieved the entry piece. And even though he'd glimpsed a small figure…

"They're not showing on video," Basir said redundantly. He turned to Lilith. "Maybe it's the same person, Master?"

Luca scoffed aloud. "I liked him better when he didn't talk."

"Hush," Lilith said absentmindedly, but it was clear she wasn't really bothered. "I'm thinking."

Some time later, when Lilith had finished 'thinking' and had left along with her cranky human conduit, Luca was alone in his office. He changed one VR screen to display the view over the Reamas River. A beautiful sight, and one of the few spaces that wasn't packed with buildings. It was because the river was meant to mark the border between Erus and its neighbouring city-state, Dailan.

He'd lived in Dailan for years and years, back when he'd been Luke. It was where Luca had been made, so to speak, but he didn't have good memories of the place, nor good feelings towards it.

But in this particular scene to the north of the city, the Reamas river wound back and forth on its route down the wide, flat valley, occasionally crossing where the borders ought to be. Such movement made it impossible to use the fertile flat land around the river. It would make sense to finally build banks *all* the way down the river, not just where the city was, but that was an expensive task that the Dailans didn't want to share costs for.

The dear deceased Chairman Tybalt had tried to negotiate with them. Something about not wanting to upset their patron Creature, or start a war, or so forth. As for Luca…

He wiggled his fingers at the VR scene, setting off a series of bright white lights that at first looked like flares on the Dailan side of the river. Then within a millisecond they rushed silently outwards until they covered the Dailan land for miles in every direction…but stopped at the river. A few seconds passed, and once the light receded it showed an entirely flattened landscape.

Erus had been building and stockpiling weapons for many centuries. Not to start another highly destructive war between humans, apparently, but just to have them. Or so ex-Chairman Tybalt had insisted. Like keeping a bottle of very expensive liquor unopened on the mantlepiece, just so you could enjoy looking at it once in a while.

But Luca wasn't the sort to leave liquor unopened for no good reason, either literally or metaphorically. He leaned back in his chair again, humming as he studied the image of desolation with raised eyebrows.

He'd love to do it, to really set off those weapons. Doing so wouldn't help Erus pay for the work on the riverbanks – not if the Dailans were wiped out – but if this VR prediction was right, the weapons were indeed impressive. "It would be nice to use them," he acknowledged aloud, "but probably not prudent."

Not yet. Not until he'd fulfilled that impossible request that the Tiger had asked of him. Once that was done – assuming it *could* be done – he'd be free to do whatever he wanted with Erus and its neighbours. And if they didn't like it, they could complain to the Tiger…who'd probably make them into a piece of furniture for daring to waste his time.

Luca swiped aside the VR river scene and pulled up another familiar one, a live view of the interior of 42-G Eastern Way. He turned the automatically recorded footage back to the moment he'd left this evening, and his eyebrows raised again as he listened to the angry words his son had spilled out at Anni. Almost curses, he mused with a smile.

Now *that* was a prime opportunity, and one he wouldn't overlook.

Time to drop some bombs. (Metaphorically speaking.)

The next morning Jon had a hearty breakfast of omelette, two bowls of sweet oats, an array of breakfast meats, half a packet of bonbons and whatever that thing was that had been left in the chiller. He still felt kind of hungry, but decided to listen to his aching, bloated stomach instead of whatever his crazy brain was telling him.

He also decided to take the liftpod to the ground floor rather than fly straight from his forty-second-level balcony. He still had a bit of vertigo – alright, a lot of vertigo – but he'd get past that soon enough if he just kept trying.

Really.

But when Jon stepped out into the corridor wearing his new red-trimmed flight suit, he almost ran into Tarie, who'd just come from the door opposite. He hadn't seen her since that first day at Centre where he'd made the worst possible first impression. She'd obviously missed his grand entrance yesterday too, where he'd somewhat balanced the scales with Rokal.

Now, her eyebrows shot up and she stared at him in what looked like absolute shock. He straightened, puffing out his chest a bit, then waited for her to comment on his impressive change. But she only opened her mouth as if to say something…then clamped it shut again.

"It's Jon," Jon said politely. Perhaps she hadn't recognised him. When she still didn't speak – or move from her spot – he added, "From Centre." *And from Timm's Depo where I sold you a Bridie novel before I ran away from Rokal and Orla. You said you'd be my friend. Remember?*

But Tarie just shuffled uncomfortably. Her mouth opened again, just a little, but then she clamped it shut and gave a little wave instead.

Ah. A pang of dismay shot though him as he realised that she was one of those people who must have preferred him unpledged...and weak. "Right," he said in growing anger. "If you've got a problem with me being a carrier now, then you can just say it. I suppose your offer of friendship doesn't extend this far, huh?"

Tarie shook her head urgently, but still didn't speak.

Jon waited several seconds longer, then let out an unhappy laugh when the supremely awkward silence dragged on. "And here I was willing to be friendly with someone your age who still reads children's books. But you know what? I'm moving house tomorrow, and I don't care if you never speak to me again."

Feeling angry and rejected, he didn't wait for a response. He just left.

Tarie didn't know what the worst part of that conversation had been. That her new neighbour had gone and pledged himself to some Creature that had changed his appearance so dramatically; that she hadn't even been able to say hello since the Words tried to spill out every single freakin' time she opened her mouth; that he'd taken major offense...or that he thought the Bridie book had been for *her*.

Yeah, she'd got that jab about children's books. Thank you, Jon.

And he hadn't even noticed that as of this morning she was *five* units taller than when they'd last spoken. Come on, that wasn't a small change! She'd had to speed-order clothes that would fit, and the drone had barely arrived in time.

Tarie shook off the surprise that had held her captive. Her father had mentioned Jon's change, since he'd heard about it from

Jon's mother Anni, so Tarie had been somewhat prepared for it.

Not prepared enough, though. It was more than a change in appearance. It was the Creature cloud he seemed to carry with him now, like Tarie could feel it there even if she couldn't see it. Or like Jon was now an open door to that Creature's temple.

She'd always avoided Creature temples because they set off the Words. She'd visited one of the lesser ones back in Memrys on a class trip years ago, even though her parents hadn't wanted her to go since they were all Way-followers. But the moment she'd walked in those big, shiny doors she'd felt a wave of sickness. She'd run for the bathroom, uncontrollably spewing out the Words as she did so. She was pretty sure the temple's trash compactor still had a Word tree growing out of it.

The Words were protecting you.

Yeah, maybe, Tarie acknowledged. But it had been humiliating, and the next time there'd been a temple class trip she'd just excused herself.

Anyway, it seemed that the Words were still determined to cause her trouble…or protect her from dangerous Creatures, or whatever. The run-in with Jon had been a bad start to the morning, but she hoped the day would get better.

When Tarie arrived at Centre, she was pulled aside at the entrance for DNA testing.

"Standard process when some physical aspect of testing fails," the bored-sounding man said from behind his VR reception desk. "Facial recognition matches but your height is wrong."

"It's an alter-power thing," she explained. "Surely you have this problem any time someone becomes a carrier or gets more power?" Carriers' faces would sometimes change, taking people from average to beautiful (or scary). She supposed Jon must have had the same issue.

"Standard procedure to avoid identity theft," the man said again. "And there aren't that many carriers in Centres. They tend to leave early." There was a brief pause, then he nodded at her. "Have a nice day, Miz Filat."

The VR scene vanished, and Tarie glanced down at her hand to see her student description had changed a little. Now it read, *Notable: gardening, speech impediment, rapid physical growth.*

"Thanks," she muttered to herself, then set off for her first class before she could be scolded for being late.

Apart from that, the day was incredibly normal. The fact that no one commented on Tarie's change was confirmation that no one noticed her. Even new, freaky pale Jon ignored her all day, so she ignored him right back and focused on her classes instead.

And to make sure that no one noticed her change, she made sure she was the last to leave each class. Watching everyone else file out, she noticed that Jon still had a sizeable gap around him – but she expected the cause was now fear of his apparently crazy Creature rather than any rejection of his unpledged self.

Tarie also noticed that beautiful, nasty Orla was away. Beautiful, nasty Rokal was there – but walking strangely. Floating, actually, with both legs unmoving. Tarie watched him in puzzlement and accidentally caught Gavriel's eye.

He was watching *her*, she realised, and she wondered if she'd have to explain her odd little 'rapid growth'. But he gave her an indecipherable look that she decided not to ponder too deeply.

That was probably a good attitude to fitting in here, Tarie mused. Keep her head down, explain herself only if absolutely necessary…and keep out of other people's business.

It was meant to be their last night at 42 Eastern Way. But Anni couldn't think of that today. She sat on the bench on her outside balcony, overlooking the pleasant, familiar view. Her hands trembled a little in her lap.

It had been a horrible day.

Inside the house, the packers had been and gone. Everything was packed neatly into crates or wrapped in that puffy stuff that would keep antique plastik furniture from being scratched, ready to be transferred to their new house tomorrow. Only her clothes hadn't yet been packed, since she wanted to do it herself – despite Luca's instructions to the contrary.

The balcony door slid open, and Anni didn't have to look around to know it was him. He had a certain presence now, and besides, he moved differently to Jay-Jon who was the only other person who'd be in the house.

"I lost my job today," she said, her gaze still fixed on the distant hills. He'd have to find out sooner or later. "My supervisor accused me of taking those missing goods, but he said that because of your position he'd let me go quietly rather than laying charges."

"Did you steal those goods?" Luca asked. He sounded inquiring and far too calm.

Anni turned to glare at him, outraged. "Of course not! You should know that!"

He stepped out onto the balcony, his expression unchanged, then leaned against the balcony's clear barrier. "I hardly know you, dear contract partner, because you never tell me what you really think." His blue-green eyes slid sideways to meet hers. "You certainly don't know *me*."

True, but that was because Luca was a loose cannon, and Anni didn't want to get to know him. And she never knew how he'd react if she was ever to be truly honest with him.

"Will you speak up for me?" she asked, determinedly ignoring his diversion. "At my job. Will you ask for a proper review into the thefts? Because I really think my supervisor didn't follow the right process when he fired me, and that means whoever really stole the supplies is still there."

"Step in and risk being accused of favouritism?" Luca countered. But his gaze was fixed on the tiny red-leafed plant their neighbour had gifted her the other week. It still sat on the balcony rail, kept safe by the barrier and warmed by the sun. "What's that?"

Anni's shoulders slumped, and she wrapped her arms around herself. Of course he wouldn't step in for her. When he'd become Luca, he'd stopped caring about her in even the smallest of ways – and before that they'd been companionable flatmates rather than spouses. At the start she'd wondered if she and Luke would have a real marriage…but no. She was pretty sure he even had a girlfriend in Dailan, and she didn't care. "Just some plant Tarren gave me. He had a spare."

"Who?"

"You know, the new neighbours from Memrys. A widower with two daughters, one Jon's age? Short, dark, bearded?" *You know, the guy who's a hundred percent nicer than you?*

For a few seconds Luca looked frozen, his expression unreadable. But then he moved forward to open the balcony's clear barrier, and in one smooth move, drew a hand-sized tube from his pocket and pointed it at the plant-in-a-cup. There was a sound like *pfft*, and next thing the entire plant was gone, leaving only a tiny wisp of smoke and shattered pieces of the plastik cup.

"There," Luca said, sounding very satisfied. "You shouldn't be accepting gifts from other men. Not when you're contracted to me."

Anni sat in place, unmoving and with her face slack with shock. *What in Hades are you thinking?* battled with *you shouldn't have that sort of weapon* and *by Auda, it was just a plant!* But in the end she blurted out, "You're crazy."

Oops. But she'd spoken, and she couldn't take it back.

The weapon's sleek barrel raised briefly…then slipped back into Luca's pocket. "And you're weak, timid and dull…and now unemployed," he retorted, with only the slightest bite to his tone in spite of his cruel words. "And you haven't packed your clothes for our move."

Anni's eyes darted to his pocket, but it looked like the weapon was going to stay put. "I don't want to move house," she said in a small voice. She couldn't meet his eyes, because yes, she was weak and timid when it came to people like this carrier. The 'dull' part was a matter of opinion. "Can't we just have two houses? This one's in my name." She'd been living here even before Jay-Jon had entered her life.

There was a long silence where she stared at her feet and waited for the world to explode.

Then Luca said thoughtfully, "There's no reason to continue this farce of a relationship, not now that my son and I have finally achieved our goals. You stay here, I'll go to the new house."

Could she really be so lucky? "What about Jay-Jon?"

Luca shrugged. "He can go wherever he likes."

"OK."

Anni stayed in her seat, watching the distant hills through the gaps in the surrounding buildings, until she heard the door slide shut and she knew she was alone.

Then, she finally let herself smile. She might be weak, timid and unemployed…but the day hadn't been *all* bad after all.

Since Jon had quit his job, he went straight from Centre to one of the shopping and entertainment complexes on this side of the city. It was the sort where people didn't only use VR, but did things in real life too. He killed some time there, watching people's responses to his flight and his colouring, and wondered if they knew who his Creature was.

But they were just strangers in the end, and somehow impressing them didn't leave Jon feeling as good as he'd hoped. Neither did gorging himself on just about every dish available at the market – which was another way of impressing strangers, he supposed. Most of the restos gave him the food for free once they saw him fly.

But feeling empty (yet also incredibly, horrendously full) Jon challenged himself to fly around the city as the sun went down. He forced himself to fly higher and higher until fear-sweat dripped down his neck and forehead, and his whole body trembled…and then he did it again.

After the fifth or sixth time he came to rest in an artificial tree somewhere in the west of his suburb. He must have fallen asleep, because it felt like he blinked and it was suddenly pitch-black except for the lights on the surrounding buildings.

So much for his last day on Eastern Way. Anni would be upset that he hadn't been at home, Jon told himself as he slunk home after 1 AM. Hopefully she hadn't waited up for him. She might've still been grumpy over last night's argument.

But when Jon stepped inside, the apartment's low lights flicked on to reveal a tall, dark-haired figure lounging on one of the long couches that sat in their parlour – now foam-wrapped for moving, of course.

"Oddly, the packaging makes the couch much more comfortable," Luca mused. He sat upright, studying Jon with a gleam in his eye. "Ready to move house in…oh, seven hours?"

The move was meant to happen while Jon was at Centre and his parents were at work. Jon shrugged, because while he wasn't really ready, he couldn't do anything about it.

"I won't ask why you're home so late," Luca continued, still smirking. "A Prince of the Air does as he wants. But I thought you should know that Anni won't be moving house tomorrow. She'll stay here, and I'll move on to the new, far superior place."

Jon felt his eyebrows shoot up. "Oh…well, I suppose I'll stay here too." He shrugged again, although inside he was celebrating. What good luck! Luca was moving out, and it seemed to have come out of nowhere. "I suppose it was too short notice for a big move," he added, trying to sound casual. "Anni's lived here for years." *He* had lived here for his entire life.

Luca was watching him carefully. "I thought you'd be more upset that your parents had separated. But then perhaps you knew our contract was a sham too, hmm? Or perhaps you're more upset at the way Anni lost her job today."

"Whuh…"

"Yes, it was rather strange," his father continued, one hand stroking his chin thoughtfully. "To give faithful service to that rather dull job for year after year…then in one day, to be so cruelly cast out." There was a brief pause, then he jumped to his feet. "Oh, well. Stay with Anni if you want to, or come with me. Princes of the Air do as they like."

Luca continued on, but Jon was no longer listening. He stood in the parlour just inside the closed door, with his hands in tight fists at his side, and his mind full of the argument from last night.

Jon and Anni had been talking about all sorts of things. She'd been complaining about her job and about Luca, of course. But what had Jon said to her? Something like, he'd rather she didn't have either than complain about them and yet do nothing to change things…

And now the very next day, she lost both Luca and the job. No doubt she'd miss one a lot more than the other.

"But it was just an offhand comment," Jon murmured, guilt beginning to prick at him. "It can't be…I wouldn't have…" He shook his head. What if all of this was just Luca playing some trick? "I have to hear it from Anni." Middle of the night or not.

Five minutes later Anni was in the kitchen along with the two of them. Her reddish hair was mussed with sleep, and there were shadows under her dark eyes. "I did lose my job," she confirmed. "And I'm staying here tomorrow while Luca moves." She looked at him sympathetically. "I hope you're not too upset, love."

"Me upset?" Jon exploded. "You're the one who just lost everything! Ma…" He choked a little. "I think I *cursed you*."

Her eyes widened in shock. "Oh, of course you didn't! If

you're talking about that argument – Jay-Jon, these things were underway long before you said anything. We – and my supervisor – made decisions of our own free will. Do *not* blame yourself."

Jon wanted to believe her. He really did, but could it be such a coincidence?

"Hmm, free will," Luca mused. "Wyet's boy flew far too fast and landed far too heavily all of his own free will, and the consequence was two broken legs. Perhaps that was a coincidence too – or perhaps Jon's Creature has been overstepping, and turning casual words into reality. If so, it's not at all Jon's fault." He shrugged, yawning dramatically. "Oh well. Time for bed. Goodnight, don't curse anyone in your sleep, et cetera."

"Jay-Jon," Anni said, but Jon shook his head.

He felt cold and strangely numb. "I have to go."

He had to make this right.

10

No Returns, No Refunds

Jon didn't wait for morning. He locked himself in his bathroom then switched the full-length mirror's light onto dim, trying to recreate how it had been that night when the White Prince had spoken to him through his own reflection.

"White Prince," he whispered. "Are you there?"

But his reflected self just stared back at him, pale and hollow-cheeked and dark-eyed. Then perhaps thirty seconds later, the atmosphere changed; grew cold. Jon felt the hairs prickle on the back of his neck, and then the image in the mirror changed too.

It was like another face overlaid his, one with sharper, inhuman features. *"You called me."*

The thin, raspy voice was in his head – or was it aloud? Jon couldn't tell. Either way, he heard it very, very clearly.

Jon was shaking a little, just like he always did during these interactions. He stared at a spot somewhere on the White Prince's pointed chin, and his voice trembled as he replied. "Yes. Thank you for coming. Um…I've done something. I think I cursed some people that I didn't mean to curse, and-"

"No."

"Pardon?"

"You cannot lay an accidental curse. A careless one, perhaps, but your words reflect what is in your heart. Whatever you said, you meant it at the time."

Jon went to argue, but then his heart sank as he realised the Creature was right. Even though he didn't want Anni to lose her job, at the time of the argument maybe he'd meant what he said.

Just a little. (The Luca thing he wasn't so upset about – in fact he was leaning towards being relieved.) "But I didn't want to curse my mother," he whispered. "How can I undo it?"

There was a long silence where Jon almost thought the White Prince had left, except for the chill in the air. Then the Creature said, *"There is only one way to lift a heart curse already laid."*

Anything, Jon almost said, but managed to keep silent. He didn't want to accidentally make an oath to do something stupid.

"Speak carefully," the Creature continued, *"because this WILL happen again. But if you truly want control over how you change the world, if you want to undo what has already been done, then you need to find me the curse-breaker."*

"What's that?" Jon whispered.

"It's an Otherly object, a metal circlet that blocks and breaks curses. This curse-breaker was taken from me long ago by another Creature…and if you want that control, you need to take it back."

Oh? Jon thought a little hysterically. Retrieve a precious object from a Creature strong enough to rob the White Prince? Was that all?!

"I shall give you my strength," the White Prince carried on. *"Go to the temple used for Power Performance and walk into the Other, then call for Audaline."*

At hearing that name, Jon just about imploded. Audaline was one of the Big Three – the very one who'd just pushed Domitian out of his place as Erus's patron Creature. A striped, veiled, feminine being who scared the wits out of him.

"Then what?" Jon asked, half-joking, because this was sounding like a suicide mission. "Do I just ask for the circlet back?"

The White Prince wasn't smiling, and a pinprick of red seemed to glow in each large black eye. *"No,"* he answered flatly. *"You'll take it."*

Then the Creature vanished from the mirror, and Jon was left staring at his own appalled reflection and choking at the audacity of what he was being asked to do.

Oh, you don't want to curse people accidentally? he thought maniacally. *Just wander into the Other, which is full of Creatures who apparently hate you, and tackle one of the biggest. No problem!*

He did not like that option. Not at all.

"This is impossible," Jon told his reflection desolately. "Ma's just going to have to find a new job."

The next morning – AKA a few hours after the second terrible mirror conversation – Jon stood in front of his mother with a heavy heart. "I'll be staying with Luca for now," he said dully. "Just until I get myself under control."

Anni studied him, her expression thoughtful and a little sad. "You're always welcome here, Jay-Jon. It's your home."

"I know," he agreed, because he really did know that. Then he lowered his voice, even though Luca had left the house long before. "But if I'm going to accidentally curse anyone again, it's definitely not going to be you!"

Anni sighed, then leaned forward to kiss him on the cheek. "Message me a picture of your new room."

Jon shrugged. "Sure."

And even though everything felt like it had changed, at the same time nothing had.

He left the apartment and headed to Centre.

Tarie had grown another two units overnight. That made her a solid seven units taller than she'd been a week ago. She could now look most of the other girls at Centre in the eye...and she was feeling somewhat panicked.

What if she never stopped growing? What if she ended up so tall that she couldn't walk through doorways, and all her clothes had to be custom made, and she looked down on everyone else, and her heart couldn't handle the strain of pushing her blood around her too-long limbs, and-

Or, maybe just start using the Words again, Tarie told herself. That would surely sort things.

Maybe in another couple of days. She really thought she was starting to get control over it this time!

So perhaps she wasn't so panicked after all, she allowed.

But speaking of panicked, Jon had come to Centre today and he'd looked like roadkill. Absolutely wrecked. His longish white hair looked like he'd gone through a wind tunnel, and there were purple shadows under his creepy black eyes.

Tarie felt a surge of pity for him and remembered that he was no longer her neighbour as of today. She hadn't had the chance to even say goodbye, not after their odd interaction yesterday where he'd thought she was refusing to talk to him.

She was going to say something, she decided. Even if they didn't have a true friendship, she wasn't going to leave that misunderstanding in place.

So when they next had a shared class, she sat next to Jon before the lesson started and went to say *good morning*. But the strangest thing happened – nothing came out. Even the Words didn't try to come out this time. That would probably be a good sign, but she wondered if maybe the fact he was a carrier now *did* stop her. She wouldn't have thought so.

Tarie could see Jon looking at her out the corner of her eye. She smiled at him ruefully, then went to say *hi.* (Y'know. Like normal people did!)

…But all that came out was an odd sort of cough-gag.

The boy sitting in front of Tarie jolted, looking back in panic as if he thought she'd thrown up on him.

"Just something stuck in my throat," she explained, waving a hand in the general direction of her neck. "I didn't spit on you or anything."

He nodded, but shuffled sideways with a nervous glance towards Jon.

For goodness sake. "I don't see why you're acting so scared of Jon," Tarie said a little belligerently. "He might look different, but he's still the same person he ever was. What do you think he's going to do to you?"

The boy fled without answering, moving to another seat across the room, and a familiar golden-haired young man took his place. Gavriel grinned back at Tarie. "Maybe you missed all the drama while you were away being stretched, but our newest Prince of the Air takes no prisoners. Just like his Creature, huh?"

Tarie rolled her eyes at the silly comment about 'stretching'. If she'd been stretched she'd be skinnier, but she still had the same solid proportions as before. But it was interesting that Gavriel was the first classmate to comment on her height change. "What did I miss?" She glanced back at Jon, who had his shoulders hunched and his hands in fists on the table in front of him.

Gavriel glanced slyly at Jon, then grinned at Tarie again. "Oh, I think I'll keep my mouth shut. Talking can be dangerous." He nodded towards the front of the room, where Rokal was floating into class again rather than walking. He was alone, and now she could see his oddly thick boots and braces that ran up his legs, almost blending in with his flight suit. He looked cranky – but didn't he always?

She didn't understand what Gavriel was implying. "What?"

"Chaos, I cursed him to break his legs, alright?" Jon snapped suddenly. One fist thumped down on the table, but his face was still set in lines of misery rather than satisfaction. "What Gavriel is refusing to say, is that besides flying, it seems I can now curse people by accident. So maybe you *shouldn't* sit next to me. I'm not safe." Then he stood up and stomped off before she had a chance to argue.

"Oops," Gavriel whispered, his eyebrows raised.

"Is he serious?!"

"As a broken leg. Or two." Gavriel leaned back in his seat. "What, haven't you heard of curses? Humans have been throwing them at each other for as long as they've had speech. It's when you dislike someone enough to want bad things to happen to them."

Tarie glanced across the room to where Rokal had paused. She met his eye...and he curled his lip then sat down near the front of the room. The two girls to his left giggled, and the one behind him immediately started preening and fixing her hair.

Ugh.

"Are you even listening to me?" Gavriel teased. "Or have you got your eye on someone else?"

Tarie felt her cheeks heat, but kept her composure. "I was just thinking that if Jon was going to curse anyone at all, then Rokal probably deserved it the most," she replied evenly. "I haven't been here long, but he's not exactly all sweetness and light, is he?" More like a giant, extremely handsome thickhead, as opposed to the normal sized, fairly handsome thickhead in front of her.

"He's kinder once he trusts you, but he doesn't trust many people. Not after what happened to his mother."

Ooh, now this sounded interesting! Just in a general sense,

Tarie assured herself hastily, not because she was *interested*. "What happened to her?"

Gavriel's voice lowered almost to a whisper, and he leaned in. "She left Rok's father when he was a little kid. Nothing too unusual about that, except she left him for a really nasty piece of work who used to beat her, and Rok too when he was there. She never stood up for him, and it was before he was a Prince of the Air. He couldn't defend himself."

"Oh," Tarie said, wrinkling her nose. "That's..." Really sad, but it also wasn't an excuse for bad behaviour this many years later.

"But that's not the bad part," Gavriel continued quietly. "One day the boyfriend beat them both so badly that she died and Rok was left for dead. Then the fiend took off with their valuables." He shrugged. "No one's seen him since, and it was pure luck that Rokal survived. I know he's always got one eye open, looking for his mother's killer. Always wanting to avenge her – and himself – if only by some miracle he gets the chance. So if he's not sweetness and light, then that's why."

Tarie was stunned into silence. She just blinked at Gavriel, taking in what had been said, then glanced across the room again to where tragically orphaned (half-orphaned) Rokal was slouched between those girls...one of whom was now sitting in his lap.

"That's awful," she said finally, thinking she really *did* feel sorry for him – although it was clear he was doing plenty to cheer himself up. "But I don't know if he'd want you spreading that story."

Gavriel shrugged again, leaning back and spreading his hands outwards. "Everyone knows it except you, it seems. But never mind Rokal. Why have *you* changed? Let me guess, it's something to do with what I told you that second day..." Tarie stared at him blankly, and he added, "You know, your little stalker problem?"

Tarie realised what he was talking about and shook her head, half wanting to laugh. *Little* stalker – compared to her current height, that kid Nesbit certainly was small. "I haven't made myself grow just so I can deal with some probably imaginary problem," she retorted, shaking her head in amusement. "It's just a...delayed alter-power thing. I haven't worked it out yet."

"Oh?" Gavriel cocked his head. "If you're certain you're safe, then I won't push the idea. Maybe I was wrong."

She wanted to argue that he must be wrong, because who wanted to be in that kind of danger? But instead she frowned. "OK, there is one weird thing. Sometimes I can hear distant music, and the atmosphere around me changes. It goes kind of…dry, and sometimes I feel short of breath. Then suddenly it goes back to normal. Have you ever heard of anything like that?"

"A villain with a theme song," he quipped, grinning. "No, sorry. It could just be a faulty setting on your communicator. You could have picked up a VR ad somewhere – the sort that pops up – and it keeps playing. It could be all sorts of things."

"Yeah…" But that didn't explain that weird shortness of breath. Maybe it was all in her head.

Gavriel went to sit with Rokal, and Tarie was left alone but thoughtful near the back of the room. Regardless of his history, Rokal was still someone she wouldn't trust a fraction. He was just…mean. Orla too. Gavriel, she wasn't so sure, because he'd been friendlier to her than almost anyone else here in Erus.

But she still couldn't fully relax, not after how he'd behaved that first time they'd met outside Timm's depo. Not when he was friends with the power couple, who were both so very dangerous and unlikeable, regardless of any tragic backstories.

But there was no sense in making enemies if she didn't have to, Tarie acknowledged. Chaos, she wanted to do the exact opposite here! The more friends, the better. Maybe in this case she could have a friendly acquaintance with Gavriel – the sort she smiled at, but watched carefully until she could trust him completely.

Just then, something reddish caught her attention from the corner of her eye. She turned to see a small red-leafed plant, no taller than her index finger, and very noticeable where it grew up from the gap between the floor and the bench seat.

Tarie carefully checked to see no one was watching, then stealthily leaned over, picked up the Word tree seedling she'd inadvertently planted on her first day and slipped it into her pocket.

Then she let out a slow, relieved breath, trying to relax her tense body. All of her refusing to speak the Words would become pointless if an unmoveable tree appeared in her classroom, and it wouldn't take anyone long to make the connection. She'd have to keep an eye on this spot to make sure it didn't grow back.

Because once Word trees were planted, they were tremendously hard to get rid of.

But finding the seedling wasn't the strangest thing to happen that day. Tarie headed to an outside balcony at afternoon break, looking for some fresh air and quiet. She choose one of the further ones, since the closer ones tended to already be occupied.

But when she stepped outside, she found Jon. He was standing at the edge of the balcony with his hands pressed up against its clear barrier, as if he'd tried to make it drop so he could fly out. Of course he couldn't do that, she thought, because the barriers were locked here. (If students wanted to play games with heights, they could do it at home!)

But then Tarie stepped closer and saw that his hands weren't pressed *against* the barrier – they were inside them. And what she'd taken for red trimming on his wrists was actually blood. The thick plastik, which should have been unbreakable, was shattered in spiderweb-like lines around his wrists, and was breaking and resealing even as she watched.

Jon looked over his shoulder and saw her. His eyes were wide and his mouth tight as he gritted out, "Get me out of here! I think my hands are getting cut off."

Well, that was horrifying! Tarie rushed over, letting out a dismayed hiss as she saw the extent of the damage. *What do you want me to do,* she tried to ask, but the words wouldn't come out. Instead there was just an odd, animalistic groan.

She looked around urgently, trying to find something big enough to rebreak the plastik so she could pull him through, but there was nothing. Finally she took off her jacket, wrapped its thick, smooth fabric around her wrists a few times, then swung at the barrier with all her might.

"Don't!" Jon shouted, but it was too late. Tarie's blow landed, and she gasped as the plastik exploded outwards in tiny shards. They both stumbled, but she had just enough presence of mind to grab the back of Jon's suit and yank him downwards before the plastik could reform.

He stumbled again, then fell heavily onto his backside, his bleeding wrists extended awkwardly in front of him. "Chaos," he muttered. "Didn't think that was 'sposed to happen. You're not supposed to be able to break that stuff."

Tarie wanted to mutter some kind of agreement, but her tongue didn't seem to be working yet again. Instead she gritted her teeth, wrapped her jacket tightly around his wrists, then dragged him off to the medic – privately grateful she'd chosen to wear multiple layers today.

Three minutes later they were sitting in a small, sterile room. Jon's arms were locked into two round cufflike shapes, like a parody of how he'd been injured, while tiny, remotely operated medidrones buzzed around the damaged flesh, stitching it up.

"You're probably wondering what happened," he said dully.

Tarie nodded tersely.

"I was just frustrated," Jon continued. "I slammed my hands against the barrier. I didn't think it would break." He looked up at her. "You were really strong, because it didn't break like that for me. And this is a weird question…but did you get taller?"

She shrugged, rolling her eyes. Finally he noticed! "Fffhggh…" She turned the odd sound into a cough, feeling her cheeks heat. What was wrong with her today?!

There was a long silence. "Your records say you have a speech impediment," Jon said finally. "Is that because sometimes you can't talk? Or is it just *me* you can't talk to right now?"

"*Flesh wounds sorted,*" the remote medic said via their holoscreen. "*Painkiller should last several days, but go easy. Check the bandages daily. When the silver threads turn green, that means you can take them off.*"

The medic switched off the holoscreen without waiting for a reply, but Tarie's attention was on Jon. Well, as much as it could be, anyway, because that was a really good question. She *did* only have trouble speaking to him, and only since yesterday.

She turned to stare at the wall, deliberately not looking at him. Then she said carefully, "My records are wrong. Mostly wrong. Ooh look, I can talk again! Maybe I just-*hhgghurgh.*"

Her last words turned into a snort-cough as she turned to face Jon again. She turned back to the wall and shrieked in frustration. "Argh! What's happening?"

"I'm pretty sure I cursed you too," he said in a low, dull voice.

Her eyebrows shot up.

"Yesterday morning outside our front doors, you wouldn't talk to me, so I said I didn't care if you never spoke to me again. Something like that." Jon huffed out a sigh, pulling his bandaged wrists close to his body. The bandages had camouflaged to blend with his pale skin, except for the thin metallic strands that ran across their surface. They were silver now – when they turned green, the skin underneath would be healed enough to remove them.

Tarie was sure he couldn't curse a person so easily, but when she went to say as much, all that came out was another disturbing cough-choke.

Hmm.

She tried again, this time turning her back on Jon entirely and focusing her attention on the now-still medidrones. They were clever little things, except that they'd been the sort to operate on her mother – and they'd failed in that crucial moment two years ago.

But she pretended to speak to them instead. "I wasn't refusing to talk to y-*Jon*. I was just…it's complicated, OK? But I would happily speak to…*Jon*, whether he's a carrier or not." She scowled. "Can he please remove this curse, if that's what's happened?"

There was a brief silence. "I'm working on it," he replied in a low voice. "But it's not that easy."

"Then I'll wait for…Jon…to figure it out," Tarie said. "And…er, he and I can have these weird conversations until it's sorted."

She could see him shrug out of the corner of her eye. She took that as a yes.

Elspeth watched Jon stride out of the little room, his posture seeming tense and his movements a little jerky. He did not notice her as she stood back against the wall, quiet and unseen as always, and her heart tugged again at the difference between what he had been to her, and what he was now.

A few seconds later Tarie also exited. Forsooth, the much taller girl emanated alter-power, although she did not seem to know it herself. Elspeth shrank back against the wall, anxious that she'd be spotted, but Tarie moved straight past.

Sigh. Verily, 'twas no easy feat being (almost) always unseen and unnoticed. Elspeth would almost catch her attention apurpose again – not that the first time had been apurpose at all – just so she would have someone else to talk to. Someone she could share her purpose with…someone who also knew Jon.

SIGH. Now that most certainly was not going to happen either.

Elspeth silently moved after her charge, keeping a good fifteen-foot distance, but her attention was fixed on Jon. Jon, and whatever ailed him.

She wondered why he had rushed away with Tarie just now. She wondered how deep their friendship went – but hastily told herself 'twas not so very deep, and surely not at all romantic, yes?

And as they stepped out into a large corridor, she wondered long 'twould be afore Jon ended up in the Mountain of Glass. And if he did, how long afore he would return to them as his true and complete self?

She longed for the day.

Tarie turned a corner up ahead, and Elspeth ambled after her. She already knew which class she was going to, so there was little reason to hurry-

The thing came out of nowhere. 'Twas as tall as the corridor, with flat sides, and it moved so fast that Elspeth couldn't react in time. She turned the corner just to see it slam into Tarie then crash into the opposite wall, taking the girl with it.

Tarie didn't even have the chance to scream.

Elspeth did it for her. "Eeeeeeeeeeeeeeee!" She blasted the whole wicked, massive beast with her cleansing fire, lighting it up until the silvery flames roared up to the roof. It had to get off Tarie, it must! Elspeth thought in panic. Oh, she might be *dead* and Elspeth would have failed-

Just then there was a creaking sound, and the huge beast-box-thing shuddered, then suddenly spun away from the wall. A moment later Tarie shuffled her way out of the small gap, wearing an expression of irritation and rubbing her shoulder. "Ow."

"By the rood, you are unharmed!" Elspeth blurted out in amazed relief. She darted forward and wrapped her arms around the taller girl in a tight hug. "I'd have vowed you were dead, and then I would have failed most dreadfully!" She stepped back and looked up at Tarie with wide eyes. "Oh, *are* you unharmed?"

"Nesbit?" Tarie said, one eyebrow raised. "Did I just get hit by a cafeteria cart? And…was that you screaming?"

"Erm…" Abruptly realising how much attention she'd drawn, Elspeth stepped further back and clasped her hands anxiously in front of her. "A…cart. Yes."

Was it a cart? Not an evil thing at all, mayhap, unless one strongly disliked the ever-present toasted breads and dips they provided at such places.

This was certainly not Tarie's shadowy attacker; the one Elspeth had saved her from so many times. That dark thing, covered in Creature influence and alter-power, moved faster than the eye could follow. (And did not have any breads and dip, either.)

Tarie just shook her head and straightened her clothing. "I have to go to class."

She trotted off, but Elspeth waited behind, feeling baffled and a little embarrassed. She moved closer to the 'wicked beast', which now showed itself to be…simply a cart. Even the cleansing flame had long since died back, since clearly there was no evil to cleanse.

"Chaos, that girl was lucky," Elspeth heard someone say from nearby. "That thing looks like it weighs a ton. I thought she was crushed for sure."

"It must have been empty," someone else suggested. "I've never seen one move that fast."

The hall that the cart had come from was entirely empty, and the cause of its movement was unclear.

Elspeth could only be grateful that her charge was unharmed…and dismayed that she'd failed once again in her vow of unnoticeability.

She took one last glance at the broken cart, then made her way after Tarie.

The Power Performance temple looked the same as when Jon had last been there, except for the lack of people. Last time, he'd been humiliated as usual. He also hadn't been a Prince of the Air. But still, as he stood at the colonnaded entrance today, he might have been hiding behind a column…just a little.

Of course, this temple wasn't only for Power Performance. It was one of the city's general entryways to the Other realm, complete with a beautiful stone structure built over it. The Centre used it because it wasn't close to any Creature cities or any particular Creature, so any human who walked through wouldn't bother the Creatures too much.

Yet the White Prince had told Jon to walk straight in and call for Audaline. Here, rather than in Audaline's own temple. Then when she – it – showed up, he was to, erm, 'take the curse-breaker circlet'.

Ha ha. Nope. Jon was here just to look today, not to actually *do* anything.

Even though when he'd pledged to the White Prince, he *had* sworn to do whatever the Creature asked of him…

"I'm not suicidal yet," Jon muttered, as if speaking out the words aloud would free him from the fear and dread of what lay ahead of him.

It didn't work.

Just then his eyes landed on the silvery bandages wrapped around his numb wrists, and he sighed. In spite of appearances, he really hadn't tried to cut his wrists. He still wasn't sure what had happened on that balcony. He'd gone there because he was frustrated and confused and ashamed, and he'd wanted to be alone.

He'd been confused at the way Tarie had refused to talk to him yesterday, then had come and sat down next to him today like she really was the friend she'd claimed to be. She'd even defended him to Ullrys, who'd been sitting in front of him and looking like he'd rather be anywhere else. Jon had wondered if she didn't know what he'd become – what he was capable of.

But then slimy old Gavriel had come over and had spilled the whole story, and Jon hadn't been able to stand the judgement or fear that would surely come his way, never mind that Rokal had deserved everything he'd got. So he'd got up and gone to the balcony, and had paced around thinking about the curses and his parents and his own misery, and he'd become so frustrated he'd just…punched the balcony's barrier.

Those things were meant to be strong enough to withstand an out-of-control air vehicle. It shouldn't have broken around his wrists…and it definitely shouldn't have tried to reform right *through* his wrists.

Jon shuddered at the memory. In spite of what had happened, he felt strangely lucky. He'd really thought he was going to lose his hands, and instead he'd just ended up with flesh wounds and a bunch of stitches.

Oh, and he'd worked out why Tarie had been acting so odd. He'd cursed her too.

He thought back to the other things he'd said, wondering if his loose tongue was behind her sudden growth too. It wouldn't be surprising. Lately it felt like everything was his fault.

The temple's inner door was just ahead. A plain stone archway as always. Jon found himself taking a step closer. He hadn't been inside the Other since becoming a carrier – what if this time he could finally see what everyone else saw?

"But I am *not* calling Audaline," he muttered yet again, then glanced around guiltily as if one of Audaline's followers – or the White Prince himself – might be glaring over his shoulder.

No one was in sight, so in he went.

As Jon stepped through the doorway, he felt that usual sense of fuzziness come over him, like he was surrounded by a huge invisible blanket. Maybe it really was just a part of this realm, he mused. But he still felt the cold of the Other, and like last time, darkness stretched out in every direction. Not too far to his right, the exit doorway glowed like a beacon. He looked behind him, and the entry doorway was gone.

He shivered instinctively and squinted into the darkness, rejecting his imagination's suggestions for everything that could be out there. He could just make out what might be buildings. Ruins, maybe?

Jon stepped closer to the nearest pale outline, but it shimmered in his vision then seemed to disappear entirely. He tried with another, but the same thing happened. "Either they aren't really there, or there's still something wrong with me," he murmured. "Huh. Even my voice sounds dulled."

Jon raised his arms in the air then jumped, putting all his intent into that one move.

"Argh!"

He'd shot up far faster than he could have imagined, straight up into the blackness of the Other sky. Fear rushed over him and he began to sweat, scrunching his eyes shut and spreading his arms out in an attempt to slow.

Then when he opened his eyes, he'd completely lost his bearings. The world around him was black – black horizon, black sky, black ground. An orange speck gleamed far below like an ember from a fire. The exit doorway, he realised.

He'd flown up *very* high.

Jon took much more care coming down than he had going up. As he approached the orange speck, it took the form of a rather larger irregular outline. A faint warmth wafted up at him, and even from this undiscernible distance he could smell the fragrance of flowers.

It was the fire pit he'd seen last Power Performance, he realised. The one he'd tried to take a look at – from a safe distance, of course – but Rokal had instead taken it as a chance to knock him around then claim the beating was for his own good.

Well, today there was no one to stop him looking.

Jon flew closer, squinting down into the bright orange haze. He couldn't make out details of what was inside, but the heat emanating from the pit wasn't that warm. It felt more like a summer's day rather than the inferno people claimed it was.

Could he hear…voices?

Overwhelmed with curiosity, and with his reason for coming here completely forgotten, Jon drifted closer to the pit until he was only two body-lengths over it. "I *can* hear voices!" he whispered to himself excitedly.

What if there were people down there? What if the pit was a portal to another part of the Other, or the normal realm? What if-

Suddenly the orange glow shot out of the pit, straight upwards to envelop him. And like a bug caught by a frog's tongue, Jon felt himself yanked downwards, into the light.

Somewhere in the Other, an infinite distance from that temple, yet also really rather close…the White Prince felt its carrier link to Jon stretch then abruptly and definitively break.

Just outside the fire pit that had enveloped Jon, Fylax waited a few moments, then yawned. Time for a holiday. Perhaps he'd visit early Pictland, before the cities were built. He always did like a good misty day.

And not too far from either of them, in the Mountain of Glass, Amaranthus stood at the end of a vast tapestry. He held one tiny dark thread in his head, and he'd just pulled its end away from the fabric entirely. Then with a smile he gently drew it along the cloth, far…far back, watching the sticky charcoal colour drain out of it as he did so…and placed it in an entirely new spot.

"Frencia, seventeen-ninety," he mused aloud. "A difficult year for some."

But it was the beginning of a very, very good year for Jon.

11

The Present, in the Past

Chateau de Chambord, Frencia, January 1793

In a large formal garden out the back of a large formal chateau bathed in cool winter sun, a young woman stood arm in arm with a young man. She was fabulously clothed, with pale powdered hair pinned up in a gravity-defying style that added about a foot in height. Her silvery blue dress had an enormous bell skirt and a very tightly cinched waist. Her pretty face was powdered as white as snow, with red painted lips and unnaturally pink cheeks, and a tiny velvet heart was glued next to one eye.

"It's my betrothed's fault," the woman said petulantly, fanning her face with an elaborate lace creation that was entirely unnecessary, what with the chill in the air. "Foolish Jean-Louis. Why did he have to die?"

"Nadine, *ma petite choux*, the letter didn't say Jean-Louis died," the young man pointed out reasonably. "It said that due to the current troubles in our dear country-" and yes, there may have been a hint of sarcasm in that phrase, "...his father was not certain if your long-standing betrothal should be fulfilled."

Nadine fanned herself faster, her red lips twisting into a scowl that was quite at odds with her angelic appearance. "Bah. Francois, you know I would rather tell everyone that my betrothed died, than admit the truth. *Me*, the daughter of the Comte de Viguerie, dropped by a mere Prusso child."

Francois shrugged. "It would be humiliating, yes. And worse, your father might try to wed you to someone else in his stead." They'd been very lucky up till now, he and his darling Nadine. He was far too poor to wed someone in her position, so her betrothal at age fifteen to a foreign boy of five had given them ten good years together, with everyone else pretending they didn't notice or care.

But if the match with Jean-Louis was properly broken off, then Nadine *might* have to wed someone else. Never mind that Frencia was currently in an uproar. The Bastille prison had been stormed a mere six months ago, rabble were ruling via the National Assembly, and the rights of the nobility had already been reduced. There had even been talk of abolishing the nobility entirely!

It was no surprise that the Prussos were taking a step back – because soon enough, Nadine might not even have a title, nor any land. Things were so uncertain that she, her family and her fifteen dearest friends had all fled – er, *holidayed* to this remote chateau, far enough from the cities that hopefully they'd be overlooked, if the worst was to happen.

And in spite of all of that, and in spite of the fact Nadine would be able to manage her own money in a mere year when she turned twenty-five, her father still thought that his eldest daughter needed to be married.

"He might be right," Francois said into the silence. "Maybe you *would* be safer wed. Maybe you should go and marry some other Prusso, or maybe even an Anglish lord."

His dear, sweet little Nadine just scowled even more fiercely. "Francois, I bribed the messenger who brought Jean-Louis' letter. He left without telling Papa, and there is no reason that Papa should know we're not still betrothed!"

True. "But the boy was meant to visit this year," Antonine mused. "Your father will figure it out when a pale teenage Prusso *doesn't* arrive."

They both sighed.

"If only we could find someone to take his place," Nadine mused. "Someone mad or desperate enough to keep his silence for a few months – perhaps a year or two. Just until this all plays out and I reach my majority. Once I have my own funds, we shall wed, *mon cher*. Never mind what anyone else says."

Francois blew a heavy breath out through his lips. To find someone who could play the part of a foreign noble, who looked like Jean-Louis enough to pass for him, and who would keep his mouth shut without being paid? It would be a miracle.

He opened his mouth to say as much, when the world

exploded.

One moment they'd been standing alone in this isolated, slightly unkempt part of the garden, near a round ornamental pond empty of even fish. Then the next moment, it was as if Francois was looking at the sun. The light faded, and he was left blinking at the pond, which now contained a very soggy, pale young man…dressed in quite revealing white breeches and fitted shirt trimmed with red…with messy silver-white hair falling around his shoulders.

They gaped at the young man, and he gaped back.

"Francois," Nadine squeaked, fanning herself rapidly. Her eyes were wide enough to show white all around the iris. "I think we have our miracle."

When the orange light had shot up to envelop Jon, he'd been certain that was it. He was dead. And in spite of how difficult and miserable life often was, in that moment he hadn't *wanted* to die.

Then it had felt like he'd been stuck inside a broken VR programme. There'd been overwhelming light and sound and images flashing at him from every direction, until suddenly it had all stopped. He'd barely been able to feel his own body, just this sense that he was being held within something much larger. Like a huge soft blanket, or maybe being immersed in a lake of lukewarm water.

In that moment, he'd felt like someone was there with him. A warm presence, a joyful one…

And then the world had flickered again, and here he was. In…um…a pond?

There was a strangely dressed couple standing not ten feet away. Both of them were quite short, and both wore matching expressions of complete shock. The woman – who was absolutely tiny and dressed like she was from a carnival or a historical VR programme – started babbling excitedly in an unfamiliar language, grabbing the man's arm and shaking it up and down.

"Uh…hi," Jon said with an awkward wave. He turned, water sloshing around his knees as he studied his surroundings. He was in a big flat garden, with weird, precisely shaped plants in every direction. Beyond the shaped plants in one direction was a forest, and in the other direction, a very large, pale, ancient-looking building with more forest visible behind it.

There was no city at all. No vehicles or drones in the sky…no glass.

How *primitive*.

Jon scratched his neck, baffled. It felt like he was in a historical VR programme, except that VR could never fill the senses like this place. VR could never give him the sense of lightness he now felt, like a colossal weight had been taken off his shoulders. Like he couldn't sense the White Prince anywhere. Anywhere at all.

He was still wearing his flight suit, he noticed. His silvery wrist bandages flapped loosely, and as he examined one it fell off entirely, revealing a swathe of clear pale skin with just the faintest scarring.

He huffed out a long, thoughtful breath, trying to make sense of things. So enough time had passed – or he'd been hit with enough alter-power – that his injury had healed when it should have taken weeks. And something had happened with his bond to the White Prince – but while his colouring was no longer the terrifyingly unnatural white, it was still much paler than it should be.

Also, he appeared to have travelled through a portal of some kind. And if he was really, really lucky, he'd have left his problems behind in Erus.

He wondered briefly if he could still fly. He raised his arms up in the air, jumping a little, but only succeeded in splashing muddy water everywhere. That was a loss if he couldn't any longer, he decided, but not as much as it could be.

Ahead of Jon, the couple was still babbling excitedly. The woman in particular seemed to be trying to get his attention. *"Shon loo-eee! Shon loo-ee!"* she was saying, pointing at him.

Was she trying to say his name? Jon tapped his chest, then added a bow that he'd learned during some of his history classes – back before alter-power and allegiances became everything. "Jon," he replied. "Jon DeLuca. Or DeLuke, because Luca's a real fiend, y'know?"

There was a silence, then the couple began cheering. Jon let them take him by the hand and pull him out of the pond. And with every squelching step he took in this strange new place, the lighter his heart became.

These people didn't seem at all afraid of him, and Jon could already tell that he wouldn't be seeing the White Prince if he looked in the mirror.

No Luca insulting him. No Terrible Trio. And best of all, he couldn't go into the Other and challenge Audaline for the curse-breaker if he didn't even know where he was.

Yes!

Erus city-state, 3004 AD

"Me?" Tarie said in surprise. "You've got a museum field trip today for my year's top students, and you want *me* to come?"

The blonde tutor (whose name Tarie couldn't recall) raised an eyebrow. "Your recorded levels of alter-power are unusually high, especially over the last week." She added a little reproachfully, "It would give you a chance to make up extra credits, since you've been away more than you've been here."

That was true. Tarie had only moved in two weeks ago, and she'd spent a week of that off 'sick' – growing to her current taller-than-average size.

"Oh…and both Orla and Jon aren't here, as well as a few other students." The tutor shrugged. "We have spare seats. Do you want the credits or not?"

Tarie did want them, even knowing that she definitely hadn't been first on the list. That was why thirty minutes later she found herself one of about fifteen students, packed into a strange, long, rail-bound vehicle called a 'train' that zoomed far…*far* across the city to a museum in an area she never would have thought to visit.

"The borderlands were created in the late twenty-third century after a highly destructive war," the blonde tutor told them as they drove. "The weapons used were so damaging that they managed to breach the gap between the normal and Other realms. For the first time, people could walk right into the Other, just like you'd walk through a doorway. Then those original, small doorways grew wider until they became the stretches of land that we know today.

"The borderlands remain constantly moving, irregular and dangerous places to enter, if you don't know what you're doing," the tutor continued. "They can have quite an effect on alter-power too. Unlike in the Other proper, where people's powers tend to expand, in the borderlands they can fail entirely. We have the same problem with some technology. Most vehicles' hover functions tend to fail, so that's why we use an earthbound vehicle like this train to reach our destination today."

There were hums of interest from some of the students, but Tarie wasn't one of them. She watched the passing scenery through the train's clear side, feeling wary. Not just because this train moved far faster than any city vehicle she'd been in, but also because she didn't want to go to the borderlands. She vaguely remembered hearing about it from her group of Way followers, back in Memrys. It was meant to be a dangerous place, and what the tutor was now saying just seemed to confirm that fear.

Chaos. Why hadn't she asked where the museum was before agreeing to come?!

Tarie glanced around the train, noting a few familiar faces from Centre. Besides Gavriel and Rokal, of course, she recognised another girl from her year…and there was little Nesbit the stalker/hugger, sitting not two rows from Tarie herself. Tarie was surprised she hadn't noticed Nesbit before now, not when she was sitting so close.

Their eyes met and Nesbit glanced away. Tarie watched her for a moment, still not sure what to make of the girl. Tarie hadn't seen her since the incident with the food cart two days earlier. She hadn't seen Jon, either. But then no one had.

Tarie idly counted the train's occupants, then recounted when her numbers didn't add up. There were meant to be fifteen students plus the tutor, but she'd counted sixteen students, including herself.

Her gaze fell upon Nesbit once again. The other girl was noticeably looking away, but Tarie felt her lips thin. They needed to have a conversation, because she sure wasn't good with unanswered questions.

But then they arrived at their destination, and she turned her full attention on the museum. It was a small building all on its own in the forest; unimpressive-looking considering how long they'd travelled to get here. It was cube-shaped and looked about the size of her own apartment. A bubblelike convex roof was the only variation in its boxy design, and the surrounding trees created a canopy over the roof. It was quiet here, with only the chatter of the students and occasional birdsong to break the silence.

"Remember that size isn't everything," the blonde tutor told them all. "You have one hour to find this museum's secrets and treasures – and trust me, they're worth finding."

"What are we looking for?" one of the other students asked.

"You have to work it out yourself," Rokal said, his flat tone suggesting the other student was an idiot. "That's why they're secrets."

Thanks, Rokal.

But Tarie's curiosity had been piqued. Ignoring her sense of unease, she filed in through the plain front door with all the others, the only security appearing to be a simple VR scanning panel.

Inside, the building was dimly lit. A series of old-fashioned unmoving steps led down to a low, dropped floor, so that the whole space appeared larger than it had from outside. It was filled with what looked like shelves stacked throughout the room, but there was a fog in the air that made any details hard to see.

The whole place also smelled faintly like some kind of spice…mixed with unwashed ass.

Tarie's stomach lurched, and her limbs tingled as she bit back the Words swelling at the back of her tongue. She'd started speaking them again, just a few phrases each morning and night in an attempt to slow her growth, and she thought she might have gained the control she'd so desperately wanted.

But in this moment, it seemed the Words didn't want to come out in a mere trickle. They wanted to be a flood…a big, forceful, messy flood that would be impossible to overlook.

She bit the inside of her mouth hard, taking a step backwards as the atmosphere of the room seemed to thicken, and her unease grew into a sense of dread. She backed into someone and felt them fall backwards with a jolt.

"Hey!" she heard Rokal snarl – because of course it would be him, wouldn't it?

Tarie would normally be surprised that she had managed to

knock him over, but in this moment all she could do was shake her head at him apologetically, then bolt for the door.

Outside, the air seemed fresh and so very clean after the funk inside the museum. She leaned forward with her hands on her knees, gasping in careful breaths and regaining control over her tongue. Out the corner of her eye she saw Gavriel approach.

"What was that about?" he asked.

Pause. Breathe. "I don't feel well," Tarie replied finally. "I didn't want to vomit inside the museum."

"Seriously?"

She shrugged, and he let out a short laugh.

"Well, that's bad luck," he quipped. "There's anti-nausea spray in the train's medic cabinet. I'll show you where it is, then you can have a look in the museum before the hour's up and you miss out."

Tarie wasn't going back in there. "Thanks," she mumbled, "but I'll get the spray myself. You go on in."

There was a brief pause. "You're not planning on going back in, are you?" Gavriel asked.

She looked up to see him watching her sombrely, then she shrugged again, deciding to be honest. "It smells like something died in there. It's awful."

His eyebrows rose. "Or maybe the person in front of you broke wind. *I* couldn't smell anything."

Tarie just shrugged once more, then headed for a low bench under a nearby tree, focusing her attention on brushing off the dead leaves before taking a seat.

"So you're really just going to sit out here and miss the entire point of the trip?" Gavriel asked, as though he already knew the answer and couldn't believe it. "You, Ms Bold, Big-mouthed Memryse?"

At least he hadn't said 'babbling'. Tarie finally looked up to meet his eyes. She couldn't shake the sense he was annoyed...but why? "Why would it matter to you if I did?"

He took a step closer to her, then back again towards the museum's entrance, as if he couldn't decide what to do. He was half-grinning in that way he often did, but now she saw it wasn't humour. "When I heard we'd be short a few students, I asked the tutor to invite you. I thought it would be a good chance for you to catch up your missed time…and I thought you'd find it interesting here."

"Oh." That was surprisingly thoughtful, and didn't seem much like Gavriel. "Why?"

"Why you? Or why would you find it interesting?"

"Either."

"The museum is interesting," Gavriel said casually, but there was a real bite to his words, "because it contains things that I've never seen anywhere else, and some that I've never heard of before. And I asked for *you* because when I first met you, I thought you were either crazy or one of the bravest people I've ever met. You were happy to make friends with the Pledgeless Wonder, and wanted to *stay* friends even when he turned into the freakiest carrier in Erus." He shrugged, spreading his hands out in front of him, palms upwards. "And now you've come all this way into the borderlands, only to be a coward at the last minute?"

His final words hung in the silence, and Tarie found herself feeling surprisingly hurt…and guilty. She hated disappointing anyone, even people who really had no right to be disappointed in her.

Even if Gavriel *had* asked for her to come along.

"I'm going to find that anti-nausea spray," she said instead, rising to her feet. "You'd better go back in before you miss out too."

He gave her one final smirk, looking much more like his usual self, and then turned back towards the museum's entrance.

"Sometimes refusal is braver than action," a small voice came from somewhere to Tarie's left. "Even if others think you foolish."

Tarie turned to see her huggy stalker standing quietly not five feet behind her. "How long have you been there?!" she exclaimed.

Nesbit blinked at her, and her pale cheeks flushed pink. Then she glanced to where Gavriel had paused at the doorway, and she waggled her eyebrows in what might have been a meaningful way.

"Are you talking to me?" Gavriel called.

Tarie looked at Nesbit…then at him…then at Nesbit again. Could he really not see her? "Just talking to myself," she called back finally. But she waited for him to disappear inside before turning back to the other girl.

The two of them were due for a reckoning.

Elspeth hadn't meant to speak. Not truly. And even now she could see Tarie's mouth opening to ask what was no doubt an accusing question…

"No doubt there are objects of interest inside," Elspeth blurted out before her charge could speak. "But along with those, there is such Creature influence that it sits thick as mist. You might find something fantastical, but 'tis just as likely you'd come out with a nasty conduit attached, rather like a dog playing in undergrowth gets a spiky burr stuck to its hide."

"A…what gets a what?"

Elspeth heard that faint, distant melody once again. It reminded her of bells, mayhap playing in the next town over…and of a particular villain she'd met (and fought) once before. "My apologies," she added rapidly. "I must go. Er…farewell."

Then she turned and dashed back inside that low, mist-filled doorway.

This might be her chance to destroy the threat to Tarie's life once and for all.

Frencia, 1793

"Bonshoor, Shon-loo-ee," Nadeen said. "Common tallay voo?"

Or at least that's what it sounded like to Jon. Three days here, and he still hadn't managed to work out more than people's names (ish)…the terrifying date…and that this was all real.

Really real. Not just realistic VR real, or even some kind of Otherly hallucination. Real. He was actually here, in some part of Europa, in the eighteenth century.

He truly wished he'd paid more attention in history class.

"Beeyen," he replied carefully, since that was what one of the other pale, poofy-skirted women had said when Nadeen asked them the same question at the breakfast table just now. They'd clothed him, treated him remarkably well – and he still had no idea what they were saying. "Ey voo?"

Nadeen gave him a beaming, bright-eyed smile, then launched into a string of unintelligible words. He stared at her blankly, and after a while she fell silent, then turned to chatter at the person next to her instead.

It had been a strange three days, Jon mused. He'd come through an Other portal to land in some kind of dirty, deep puddle in the garden, with two of the palest people he'd ever seen (barring himself) standing nearby. They'd pulled him out, had chattered at him excitedly or in Fron-swah's case, warily watched him as though he might bite.

Not an unreasonable concern, based on how things had been. But while Jon knew he was separated from the White Prince – could feel that separation – it wasn't complete. His colouring was still abnormally fair, and…well, it turned out he could still fly a bit.

He'd tested it on the first day. Unlike back home, this time trying *gently* seemed to work better than using force. He'd wobbled his way off the ground about five feet, then had seen the goggle-eyed expressions worn by Nadeen and Fron-swah. He'd quickly realised that flying was just not done here.

Nadeen had started shouting something like, "Un onge! Un onge!" and he'd had to try quite hard to get her to stop bowing at his feet. (That sort of thing was better in theory than in practice.)

Actually, Jon had concluded that the Creatures weren't really known here. Not openly like back in Erus. What a strange thought.

"I suppose they still have carriers," Jon said to the person sitting next to him, an older man with a head of perfectly curled grey hair that quite frankly looked like a wig. "And conduits, probably. But do they have temples here, when the borderlands haven't even been created yet?"

The man smiled at Jon, then pointed to the platter of meat in front of them. "Esker voo voolay?"

"Ah…no, thank you." He didn't want any meat for breakfast. Possibly no meat ever again, especially if it was in any kind of red sauce.

By the end of that week, Jon had figured out that there was meant to be something between him and Nadeen. What, he wasn't sure…but when he walked into a room where she and Fron-swah were snuggling affectionately while some others sat nearby, they'd sprung apart and the others had looked at him nervously, as if he ought to be upset.

Eh. He'd shrugged, then left the room. Who could understand foreigners?

Two days after that, Jon decided he ought to check the water portal. He made his way back through the increasingly straggly garden until he found the round, murky pond. Today it reflected the cloudy grey sky, and the chill in the air was almost enough to make him give up before he'd started.

No excuses, he told himself. He had to at least *try* to get back. After all, he'd left several people cursed, and…and…he just had to try, alright?

Checking that no one was watching, Jon summoned his unused flight ability just enough to hover over the water. He was wobbly, and fear pinged at him as he went. But it was fear of getting wet and cold, rather than the intense dread he'd previously faced when flying.

There didn't seem to be a portal. In fact, the air here seemed just as cool and ordinary as everywhere else around the castle-like structure they were staying in.

But he'd been *in* the water when he'd arrived. Damn it.

Jon looked down at his borrowed clothing, which included lace-trimmed knee-high stockings, strange tight trousers that only went to his knee, and a shirt with a waterfall of lace at its sleeves and collar. He sighed. It was his shoes that would get wet, since no one else's fit him.

Ten minutes later, Jon was much wetter and quite a bit colder too, but he'd made his point.

"I won't be going home anytime soon," he told the empty air. "So I may as well enjoy myself."

Then with his heart a lot lighter and his guilt assuaged, Jon went to find a new pair of socks.

Erus, 3004 AD

Elspeth slipped inside the building full of conduits, each footstep careful and quiet as she moved between the high shelves. She thought it unlikely that she'd be caught as only Tarie had seen her in all this time, but it paid to be careful anyway.

Today she was planning to destroy a villain.

Or capture them, mayhap, for Elspeth was not in the habit of destroying anything at all, she acknowledged. Except for that one time back in childhood when she'd accidentally dropped a large bowl of sugared almonds on the way to the dining table. They'd fallen onto the rush and ash-covered floor of the Great Hall – and even though Cook had made her pick up every single nut, they hadn't been fit for consumption.

She'd been in dreadful trouble about that, she remembered, for almonds and sugar were both expensive foods, and not easily replaced.

Elspeth paused midway between two high shelves, her mood abruptly dropping as the remembered shame of that moment came back over her. By the rood, it had been a good decade since that happened! Or a good fifteen hundred years, depending on how one judged time passing. Why should she care about it now?

There'd been worse, like the time that she'd been cornered outside the market by those dreadful bullies who'd pelted her with horse dung, calling her a bastard and lame. She'd stepped away from her mother only briefly, but 'twas such a painful memory. As her father had acknowledged her as his child, even though she'd been born outside wedlock, she'd had a degree of safety. But not always.

Elspeth hunched her shoulders, the remembered emotions making her feel ill. Ashamed.

'Tis not the time, she scolded herself, trying to shake off the heavy darkness. That was when she noticed the person just to her left. A hollow-eyed, dull-looking person.

Elspeth blinked, realising a moment later that 'twas her own reflection in a tall narrow mirror, set in an alcove directly beside her. The mirror was dark and murky, as if its surface was damaged, and as if the room she stood in was even darker than she'd realised.

She took a step closer, unable to take her eyes away from her own reflection. Had she always been so plain, she wondered? So weak in appearance?

Open your eyes, a quiet voice whispered inside her head.

My eyes are *open,* she thought in confusion, blinking again rapidly. Oh, but she felt so *tired!*

In that moment she saw several things. Firstly, that the haze filling the room seemed particularly dark right here, right over this mirror. Secondly, that 'twas *not* a true reflection – for the eyes in that mirror had not blinked, not even once. And thirdly – that a faint shimmer of blue-grey alter-power was now linked between the dark mirror and her own chest.

She'd been caught by a conduit, and even now it sought to drain her.

Elspeth's mouth firmed into a hard, angry line. Then she lifted one hand, summoning up her silvery flame with some effort, for the link seemed to weaken all of her strength, even within her mind. Then she aimed for the mirror.

Phoof.

The mirror lit up with a most satisfying sound, rather like when one shook out a dirty bedsheet, and Elspeth felt immediate relief. The sense of shame and weariness lifted off her, and she shook her head, watching as her reflection shimmered and brightened in that narrow mirror until 'twas what she'd expected to see.

'Twould pay to be more careful.

She moved more quickly now, unwilling to look at anything long enough to be caught by whatever magic it offered. She kept listening for that distant sound of bells, the one she'd vow she'd heard here today. All was silent, except for the occasional footsteps and quiet voices of others in this room, which certainly had not seemed so large from the outside...

She turned a corner and almost ran into two other students who were staring at a small object on display. She crept up behind them, but this time couldn't help glancing over their shoulders at what looked like a plain brown seashell necklace on a thin black cord. Its dull surface was scored with what looked like some kind of ancient text.

"It's a safekeeper," the shorter boy was saying confidently.

"Like a pocket universe. You can command any object to go into it, and it'll stay safe and sound until you call it out."

"Looks like a soul-drinker to me," the taller boy countered.

"What's that?"

"Same as a safekeeper, only you kill people with it. See, look at the writing on it. I think that's old Assiranian." The boy held up his hand, and a light emitted from his wristband long enough to scan the shell-like object. "See, it translates as 'doomed are those whose spirits reside within'. That *has* to be a soul-drinker."

Both boys let out fascinated *oohs* at the same time.

"We probably shouldn't touch it," the shorter boy said, sounding disappointed. "D'ya think it's one of the treasures?"

"Pick it up and see," the taller boy retorted with a scoff.

Elspeth waited quietly as the two of them wandered away, leaving the soul-drinker mercifully untouched. *Doomed are those whose spirits reside within.* "Rather overblown," she murmured, and hoped 'twas not at all true. But just in case…

Not thirty seconds later, the text was blurred beyond recognition, the previously dull surface of the seashell was as glossy as new glass…and Elspeth would vow that any Creature influence it had held was now gone.

She made her way around the building aisle by aisle, taking the chance to blast any object that looked suspicious, which was most of them. In fact, she used her gift so much that the dark haze around her turned silvery and bright as she walked. If not for the way no one else could see her gift, she'd worry that she drew too much attention to herself.

But she again heard the distant melody in snatches, brief moments, just enough to keep searching.

Then Elspeth came to a wall at the very end of the room. All around her silvery flames leapt higher and higher, but she ignored them as they began to lick across the wall's apparently solid surface. It rippled like water, and she cocked her head, curious. She reached out one hand to touch the wall's surface. It rippled under her hand then parted, feeling rather like thick jelly.

'Twas an entrance, she realised. But where did it lead?

Then those bells sounded again, seeming as if they were on the other side of the wall, and Elspeth steeled herself. Her hands lit up with silvery flame, she took a deep breath…then stepped through.

Tarie had just made her way back from the train, having made use of the anti-nausea spray. It left an unpleasant tingling sensation in her nose and eyes, which spread to her limbs but- oh wait, that was just the Words again, pushing to be spoken.

Ignoring them would only make her feel sick and grow taller, so Tarie quickly checked around to see that no one was watching, then began muttering high speed under her breath. She could actually see the grass growing under her feet as she spoke, with a hint of red Word tree seedlings here and there.

She made her way around the side of the museum building, wanting to avoid judging eyes as she tried to expel the alter-power built up inside her. This ancient building in the middle of nowhere had forest almost right up to its outer walls, so she felt confident that she couldn't get lost.

But this time, no matter how much she spoke, the alter-power tingling in her limbs didn't fade. She felt like strength was pouring into her, like she was changing every time that tingling ache began, and she didn't know what to do. The feeling was now far more intense than it had ever been before.

This was madness.

Tarie huffed out an unhappy breath as she reached the far end of the building. Just then she noticed something strange on the wall. It was made of large blocks, like many older structures were, but she could see faint glowing lines showing in a tall, rectangular shape. Like a silver outline the size of a door-

"ARGGGHHH!"

She heard the scream right before the door burst open – because evidently it was a door – and someone came rushing out. Tarie only caught glimpses of huge shoulders, white clothing and black hair, then the person was throwing themselves on the grass, rolling around and shrieking as if they were on fire.

But…they weren't.

Tarie took a step back, trying not to get rolled on as Rokal shrieked and thrashed about. She wanted to help – really – but she couldn't see what the problem was.

Then finally he stopped moving and lay face-down on the grass, his previously flawless outfit covered in green stains.

Tarie crept closer, muttering the Words under her breath, then tapped him on the shoulder. "Hey. Are you alive?"

For a moment there was no response. Growing increasingly concerned, she grabbed him by the shoulder and flipped him over to his back. He was surprisingly light considering his build. But his eyes were open, wide enough that too much white showed. "Don't touch me," he said.

Sheesh. "You seem hurt," she tried. "Can I get you anything? I can find Gavriel or Miz…um…the tutor-"

But Rokal began climbing to his feet, his movements jerky and stiff. "No. No. No, don't touch me. Don't touch me." He punctuated each word with a jittery shake of his head.

Typical. Random girls could climb in his lap, just 'cos, while Tarie apparently wasn't allowed to touch him to save his life. "I want to help," she said defensively. "Can I-"

"No. No. No," he chanted, moving away from her. He banged once into the museum wall, then shook his head and rose off the ground. His flight was as jerky as his speech, but he seemed determined. Within moments he'd disappeared into the forest of the borderlands.

"I feel this could be a problem," Tarie murmured to herself. She quickly checked her wrist comm to ensure that it had recorded the last few minutes, then she uploaded it to Gavriel's direct comm. *Is this normal?* her message asked.

There was no response, so Tarie just looked once more at the now empty forest, then sighed. She couldn't help someone who didn't want to be helped – and that was assuming Rokal even *needed* to be helped.

Just then there was a creaking, rumbling sound. Tarie stared at the half open door, noticing for the first time how bright the light was from inside. It had been dark when she'd gone inside, right?

Or maybe that was only the front of the building.

But the faint rumbling and that light was her only warning of what came next.

12
Boom

Elspeth stepped through the odd jelly-like barrier to find herself in a hallway. It had high walls seemingly made of the same materials as the shelves inside the main building, and when she turned around, she could see an ordinary curtain marking where she'd stepped through. 'Twas not a gateway, she surmised, but rather just a hidden door.

She cautiously made her way down the hallway until the roof stopped, and it became an open, paved pathway with the corridor's walls continuing off into the distance. She could see the walls of what looked like an old city up ahead, and even from here the air above the distant buildings shimmered as if from the heat of the day. She knew what 'twas, though.

Alter-power.

Elspeth shivered. She had experience with many types of power, and knew well that power was tremendously different depending on its source. This power felt heavy and dangerous. She'd bet her life 'twas not from the Mountain.

She lifted a hand to brace herself against the closest wall, only to stumble and almost fall when her hand went straight through. Not even like jelly; the wall was a mere illusion. She shuddered and threw herself backwards, falling hard on her backside on the path.

But 'twas as though touching the wall broke the illusion, and she now saw what truly lay beside the path. To her left the ground dropped away sharply, revealing a deep, dry valley. The steep brown hillside fell away far, far below her, and then the valley itself was deep and dry and brown and vast...

And to her shock, it was also full of statues. They were half constructed: dozens, mayhap even hundreds of them, each one in the shape of an enormous cat sitting on its hindquarters. Each statue was made of some kind of gleaming gold or copper material that shimmered in the sunlight. Even from here she'd vow there were gems set in the statues' sides.

More amazingly, each statue had to be as large as a fifteen-storey building, as large as the Centre that Elspeth had been trailing Tarie to all these weeks. She could see people there too, moving on their sides, looking like ants. No, wait…those were vehicles, she realised. That was how large these things were.

At the other side of the valley, so dreadfully far away, the sunlight stopped. And that, Elspeth knew, was the Other realm. Home of the Creatures, the real home of everything supernatural. And if there was no greenery in sight? Then 'twas not where anyone should want to be.

She hadn't meant to come here. Not alone. Not at all.

Mayhap 'twas not the time to play hero, she decided.

So very carefully, and with her eyes feeling so wide they almost hurt, she turned and crept back to the doorway.

Tarie stood at the half open back door, squinting to see past the light and fog inside. She stepped inside just a little – she could hear sounds now, almost like…screaming…and finally a few figures became visible.

"Get out get out!" one of them screamed at her.

And then the roof came down.

Tarie wasn't quite sure how it all happened, and the video from her comm was damaged because of all the alter-power. But looking at the few other recordings that had survived, it seemed like a metal pillar had fallen right on top of her…and she'd stuck out an arm to catch it.

Yes, she'd somehow caught a structural metal pillar as thick as her own body, and probably fifty units long. And then as the building had crashed down around them, with a strange, fizzing, shimmery light everywhere, she'd held the pillar up as others had fled.

All she remembered was chaos and screaming – hopefully

not her – and holding this increasingly heavy thing while other people ducked underneath it and fled for the door. Then someone had shouted at her that everyone was out, and she'd somehow managed to shuffle to the nearby doorway while still holding the pillar, then dropped it and escaped high-speed even as it fell.

And now, not five minutes later, she stood with a mob of students and their frazzled-looking tutor as the incredibly valuable, ancient and smelly museum collapsed on itself entirely. The collapse was punctuated with bursts of alter-power so strong they were visible, like multicoloured fireworks.

"We're one short!" the tutor shouted suddenly, as if she'd only just realised. Her mid-length, fluffy fair hair was standing up on end, a testament to whatever had just gone on inside. "Where's Rokal?"

"He's out," Tarie reassured her, raising her voice enough to be heard over the din. "He ran out before the building fell. He…uh, didn't seem like himself, and he took off into the forest."

There was a brief moment where it seemed like everyone was staring at her, and she shrugged helplessly. "I couldn't stop him. He's huge!"

"You held up a half-ton pillar," one of the other students pointed out. "You could have stopped him."

Tarie didn't know what to say to that. *Yes, I appear to have bursts of freakish strength, but it's a new thing?* "I didn't know I was supposed to," she said instead.

Besides, he was a head taller than most people, and he was a Prince of the Air. Tarie was sure that he'd be fine, borderlands or not.

But one other person was still missing. Nesbit had gone in and hadn't come out – and it didn't seem like anyone except Tarie would notice her absence.

"I'll look for him," Gavriel volunteered. "His comm shows he's nearby." He glanced briefly at Tarie, lifting his chin as if in acknowledgement that he'd seen the video she'd sent him.

A couple of others volunteered to go with him, and the tutor sighed. Her shoulders slumped, and her expression was absolutely dismayed. "We mustn't," she said, sounding resigned. "Not here in the borderlands, not us. It's too dangerous to leave these marked areas, and out of everyone here, he's best equipped to handle whatever's out there. We'll get a proper search party sent if he doesn't come back on his own within an hour or two."

With minimal muttering, the students turned to head back to the train. The building's collapse wasn't so much of a spectacle anymore, but Tarie found herself pausing at the edge of the woods. Then *pop* – she saw a single tiny, glowing shape shoot out from the building's silver and coloured burning remains. It flew high into the air then curved its way to fall right at her feet.

Tarie blinked down at the object. It was small and brown, and looked quite a lot like a seashell, oddly enough. She bent down to pick it up, noticing that the sleeves of her new jacket had stretched during her ordeal. They now hung past her hands, and she had to shove them back, tapping at the fabric a few times to encourage it to shrink to fit her once more. Luckily she'd decided to pay extra for smart-fabric on the off-chance she grew further – because it could shrink as well as grow.

Tarie bent down to pick the shell up again, but a small, pale hand darted in and snatched the object, right before Tarie could take hold of it.

"My apologies," Nesbit said, "but I trow 'tis dangerous, and I would prefer you keep your distance."

Tarie sucked in a startled breath. "You're alive."

"Should I not be?"

Tarie looked across at the still fizzling pile of rubble, and Nesbit looked with her.

"Oh. I see." Nesbit's expression seemed pained and almost...guilty? "Unexpectedly, the exit led to a different place than the entrance," she said somewhat nonsensically. "Er...shall we leave?"

Without waiting for an answer she turned to go, but Tarie's hand shot out to grab her wrist. There was so much she wanted to ask in that moment – *why can no one else see you? Are you following me? Are you good or evil?* – but instead she met the girl's eyes and found herself asking, "I'm short again, aren't I?" Nesbit blinked, then her lips curved in a smile. "You are not short," she replied decisively. "'Tis merely that the rest of the world is oversized."

"Sounds like something a short person would say," Tarie muttered. She followed her possibly invisible stalker back to the train, feeling baffled and irritated, yet somehow quite good in spite of everything.

Life made no sense right now. None at all.

But maybe…maybe everything was going to be alright.

Frencia, late 1793 AD

It was the end of mass, and Francois rose to exit the chateau's chapel. Up ahead he could see the nobles getting up to leave, including his *chre* Nadine, with their faux Jean-Louis at her side. As always, the celestial Jon wore a slightly distracted expression as though in his mind he was anywhere but here. Francois would blame that distraction on Jon's terrible Frencine – the worst he'd ever heard, in truth – but the service had been in Laten anyway. That meant no one had understood the priest, but everyone else had at least pretended to pay attention.

Jon had been here for six weeks now. From what Francois heard, Jon spent his time either trailing various people around the chateau or wandering the grounds.

He'd been spotted several times with wet stockings. Nadine thought he'd been trying to return to the celestial realm. Francois thought he might be a little mad – but then perhaps a fallen celestial just had no idea how to relate to human beings.

Francois stepped outside the chapel doors into the frigid December air, moving back well out of sight. Winter was well upon them, although no snow had fallen. He watched as everyone filed out of the building, already distracted by whatever filled the rest of their day.

He saw Nadine step aside, wearing her long redingote jacket trimmed with pale fur that accented her always powdered hair. But while he waited for her to quietly move away from the others, another woman walked up beside him. This one was very tall and stately, with perfectly formed features, unpowdered dark hair and striking green eyes.

Francois resisted the urge to flee, instead shuffling in place. "Madame Roelle. Good morning."

Madame Roelle smiled at him, and as always, that smile made him feel markedly uncomfortable. Who cared how good her teeth were, or that she was rumoured to be a former mistress of the Dauphin? There was something predatory about her, something a little bit…off. Even Nadine wasn't sure who'd invited her.

"Dear Francois," she purred, revealing a hint of some unplaceable accent. "I hear you've been making enquiries as to how you might all make your way to Angland."

Sacré bleu, how had she heard about that? They might be isolated out here in the wilderness, but it was considered treason to flee the country at this unrestful time. As it was, Nadine had been making plans to quietly sell all of the chateau's valuables, including the velvet curtains in the chapel. "Uh…"

Madame Roelle's voice lowered. "I'm on your side, of course, because it's also *my* side. I have some news that will please you and benefit all of us, if you'll give me a moment of your time?"

Had she found a way for them to escape? Francois checked that no one was watching – and they weren't, of course, because he wasn't that interesting – then he slipped away with her, out of sight of the others.

2 weeks later

Jon sat back on the low padded bench, leaning as far back as he could without falling on his head. The stone floors of this little building weren't at all forgiving – he'd discovered that when they'd all knelt…then stood…then knelt again throughout this interesting ritual.

The one time he hadn't knelt, trying to preserve his bony knees, everyone had stared at him as if he'd urinated in public. Even the man up the front with the really long white robes had looked appalled (Jon was pretty sure he wasn't a Prince of the Air, white clothing or not). So Jon had quickly learned his lesson – just do what everyone else did, or else.

But hard floors or not, the room really was beautiful. It reminded him very much of some of the older Creature temples, or some historical VR programmes. Built of the same pale stone as the rest of the shattoh-building, it had a high arching ceiling with gracefully curved lines, an altar of sorts, and a high wall full of small glass windows in a simple pattern. The benches all faced towards the altar, and there weren't enough seats for everyone.

Jon had noticed that when they came in here several times per week, the most richly dressed people would sit up the front on these padded seats. The plainly dressed ones would sit or kneel near the back – even Fron-swah, who Jon hadn't seen in some time. Jon would have thought that Nadeen had sent him away, except that she seemed distressed and he'd heard the man's name spoken several times.

Jon didn't know what to make of that. He felt terribly out of his depth.

But as he was sitting here now, he saw from the corner of his eye a man come to sit on the end of his bench. The man was elderly, small-boned and plainly dressed – no doubt one of the servants who if they'd been in Jon's own time, would have been either unpledged or pledged to some lowly Creature. Jon thought that maybe the servant shouldn't be here up the front – but then neither should Jon, really.

The man closed his eyes and began muttering in whatever language they spoke here.

Jon huffed out a low sigh, then tried doing the same. "I swear there's a conduit to the Other realm in here somewhere," he told the empty room, focusing on the darkness behind his eyelids. "I can sense it, but I can't see it."

He hadn't sensed the conduit at first, and he'd been coming here for weeks. Then he'd started to get past the oddities of this time period and its people, and he'd noticed that the locals were trying to connect with something – something Otherly – here in this building.

Well, some of them were. Others looked like they were trying to catch up on sleep with their eyes open. But once Jon had realised the possibility, he'd paid enough attention to see that there was something more here...somewhere.

What will you do if you find the conduit?

Jon sighed again at the thought. "I don't even know," he

admitted glumly. "If I connect with some Creature who's able to get me home – it's not like I was even happy in Erus. But I can't stay here either."

What do you really *want?*

What did he want? Ooh, that was a hard question. Back in Erus he'd wanted to be pledged more than anything. He'd wanted to be so respected that even his worst enemies would see his value – that *he* would see his own value. He'd had the first part, at least briefly.

"I don't know," he whispered. "Every time I go after what I want, either I fail or it doesn't turn out the way I expect. Wanting anything just seems…pointless."

"You need purpose."

It took Jon a moment to realise that the man to his right really had spoken, and it wasn't just his imagination supplying the words. He turned in surprise to see the servant was smiling at him, the expression creasing fine lines around his warm, dark eyes.

"Did you just speak Mesianth?" Jon asked.

"Yes."

There was another silence as Jon pondered whether to question his good luck at having someone speak his language over a thousand years before his language even existed…or was it bad luck, if this was a set up? He decided to go with the first option. "Er…yes. I need purpose." He paused. "Can you help me with that?"

The man stood, revealing that he was a full head shorter than Jon, and bald with it. Back home in Erus, people were only bald when they wanted to be, but this man's shiny head seemed to come from nature rather than fashion. The bald man walked out of the main area into a nearby hall, then to a door set in the far wall. He opened it, then with a brief nod to Jon, stepped through.

Jon paused, unsure whether that was an invitation to follow. He hadn't even realised that door was there.

The man stuck his head back through. *Do you need a written invitation?*

So Jon followed the man through the door without even really seeing what lay on the other side.

And it wasn't until he'd stepped through that he realised the man hadn't asked the question out loud.

Erus, 3004 AD

The train ride home was silent and uneventful, but Tarie didn't mind. She was caught up in her thoughts, because so much had happened that if she didn't make sense of things she felt like her brain would implode.

OK, so she'd grown. Really tall; so tall that she had to prove her identity. She now realised how unnaturally strong she'd been too – there'd been multiple occasions recently where she ought to have been injured or weak, but hadn't been. Take getting hit by the cafeteria cart the other day as an example, or how she'd accidentally knocked Rokal over, even though he was twice her size.

But then she'd used that strength quite dramatically today, and suddenly she was short again. So very, very suddenly. It was the weirdest thing that had ever happened to her, and her life was already weirder than most.

Tarie looked down at her wrists where her new jacket's fabric was noticeably thicker to cover a much shorter distance. She'd just come to terms with being tall, and now she'd gone back to normal! They'd have to move the bathroom fittings again, which would be a pain after the fuss she'd made last time.

But that was only one of today's oddities. The thing with Rokal still bothered her. He'd been so out of sorts, so distressed, even though he'd also been as rude as normal. If Gavriel hadn't told them Rokal had contacted him, she'd probably still be worried about him. Even thickheads didn't deserve to be lost in the borderlands.

And then the way their visit to this 'museum' had ended in an explosion – she didn't know what to think about that either. That was bizarre and incredible, and Tarie knew it had already gone public. She could see messages lined up on her comm from her family and the Centre, but she hadn't bothered to check them yet.

The top theory for the explosion was 'gas leak'. Tarie had to look that up and found out it was a flammable, sometimes smelly substance that ancient folk would use for heating. It sounded dangerous to her, but it also made sense. The building had reeked.

Tarie glanced to the girl sitting silently beside her. Speaking of oddities, Nesbit was watching the passing scenery intently, and she hadn't said a word since getting on the train. Tarie was pretty sure no one else could see her, and that was just as weird as anything else that had happened today.

But when they arrived back at Centre and were told their classes were cancelled for the day, Tarie turned to Nesbit. Luckily today she'd chosen to drive rather than walk. "You want a lift home?"

Elspeth blinked at the other girl in shock, then when she realised the offer was genuine, beamed. "Indeed I would!"

"I've never ridden in this sort of vehicle before," she admitted as they walked towards Tarie's tiny purple hovercart. Vehicle. Thing. 'Twas tied against a wall almost like one tethered a horse, along with dozens and dozens of others. Compared to self-driving vehicles from other times she'd visited, these ones were remarkably, amusingly tiny.

"You mean because it's old?"

Elspeth paused, for that was not at all what she'd meant. But it occurred to her that admitting such would not be the wisest way to keep her true identity hidden. "We mostly walk where I'm from," she replied cagily instead.

"Hmm." Tarie set up the vehicle in a fascinating series of lever-pushing and the occasional hand slap against the metal frame, then was silent as they climbed in. But once they were inside with the doors closed, Tarie turned to stare solemnly at Elspeth. "Nesbit, I think you have something to tell me."

Elspeth's pulse leapt. She had no instructions on how to face such a situation – for to lie outright would be wrong, but surely 'twas not immoral merely to answer part of a question? The silence dragged out painfully until she found herself saying, "Verily…I believe I have saved you from death many times, Tarie, yet I also feel I have failed you. I did not find the source of the music today, and thus failed to find your attacker. Forsooth, I may have even caused the disaster that sent everyone fleeing."

She sighed, then continued, "And I cannot overly regret that, since that building was a dreadful place. But what must you think of me? I vow I am not usually an arsonist. Nor the destructive type, at the very least." She turned to look at Tarie, waiting for a shocked response.

Indeed the other girl's mouth was hanging open, her dark eyes round. "Uh…Can you say that again, but in Mesianth?"

"Oh." Elspeth paused. Her gift of languages smoothly adjusted to match those around her, and she hadn't even realised she'd been speaking Anglish. But mayhap 'twas for the best. She *had* said quite a lot, had she not? No doubt too much. "My name is not Nesbit," she said finally. "'Tis Elspeth, but you may call me Beth, or Bethie, or even Bets, if you cannot pronounce the 'th' sound."

"Es…speff?"

Elspeth sighed again. "Bets."

"Ah…Bets." Tarie frowned. "Was that really all you wanted to say? Because I've noticed you hanging around me a lot, and no one else seems to see you…"

Elspeth looked away, watching the strange, multileveled city whiz by out of the clear windows. She marvelled at how the vehicle did not even require directions – one merely told it where to go, and off it went. But she answered as truthfully as she could. "I'm staying in the same building as you, and remaining unnoticed is one of my giftings. That, and another type of…strong defence."

"No offence, but you don't look very strong."

"Neither do you," Elspeth retorted, raising her eyebrows. "And yet I heard about your own feat of strength today."

"Yeah." Tarie sighed softly, staring down at her wrists for some reason.

"Jon did not think me strong either," Elspeth admitted. "Not even when he left at the end. People cannot see past my appearance."

"You know Jon?"

Should she not have said that? "I used to," Elspeth replied carefully. "Before he was…pledged. He used to be different." Back in the Mountain of Glass, which was confusingly, both before and after this very moment. "Happier." And he never looked past her in the Mountain, that was for certain.

Tarie drummed her fingers on the driver's panel as the

vehicle turned in towards their street, then came down to rest at the base of their building. "So…does Jon know that you're fond of him?"

Elspeth caught the insinuation in her tone, and felt her face heat. "Not currently." That was true, more was the pity. If Jon were to visit today, he'd look straight through her.

"Hmm. You spend a lot of time being hidden, don't you?"

Elspeth turned to look at her, red cheeks bedamned. "You think I'm a stoaker, do you not?"

"A what?!" Tarie laughed.

"A stoaker. One who follows or harasses someone obsessively."

"I haven't decided if you're a *stalker*," Tarie corrected as she climbed out of the vehicle, "but I don't think you're scary."

Elspeth brightened just a little. That almost sounded like a declaration of friendship.

Somewhere, sometime

Jon followed the little old man through the door from the temple-room. On the other side he found himself in a dimly lit space. He didn't take in how big it might be, or what was in it, because right in front of him was a pool of water. About a body-length wide, the shining surface of the water flickered with bright images like an old viewing screen.

"Watch this," the man said.

Jon could have asked *why* or *who are you* or even *I'm sensing a water theme,* but the moment he looked into the pool properly, he was enthralled. "Hey, that's my mother!"

Not Anni, but his birth mother, Maia. He saw her young face, probably younger than he was now, as she clutched at her rounded stomach and watched longingly as person after person turned away from her.

He saw a teenage Luke, with swarthy skin, messy hair and a depressed slump to his posture. Luke had left pregnant Maia far behind along with all his other connections, not even looking back long enough to see her situation. To see *his* baby.

Then there were what looked like friends and fellow students and tutors and family members, each turning away from Maia or shaking their heads in disapproval.

He was seeing more than just images, Jon realised. Somehow, the full situation was funnelling its way into his mind, and it was clear that no one had wanted Maia to have him. Not even Anni, at the start. She'd thought Maia was too young and flighty. Only seventeen, the age Jon was now.

But Maia had clutched her increasingly round belly and had set her jaw, her determination seeming to grow with every rejection. *I love my baby. She's going to be amazing.* The words drifted out across the surface of the water as she spoke.

By the way, Jon thought with raised eyebrows, he was a boy! At least Anni had warned him about this.

Then Jon saw Maia out in the middle of nowhere as she bent down to pick up a thin round shape, like a loop or a circlet, the sort of simple crown that ancient princes would wear on their heads. It bent a little, sending a puff of shimmering alter-power into the air as she read out the word written on the narrow band. *Amaranthus.*

Jon watched in fascination as Maia took to wearing the item wrapped twice around her wrist, and occasionally on her head – as was probably intended. And oh, how she used it. She'd say something, then say the magic word that would send alter-power into the air.

But she always used it for *him*. He saw when she found out he was a boy, since her words changed from *Amaranthus, my baby will be safe and well* to *Amaranthus, my son will be loved and valued. Amaranthus, my son will make a difference in Erus. Amaranthus, my son will be a world-changer.*

"She'd be disappointed to see me now," Jon muttered to himself. A world-changer, really? He *had* started accidentally cursing people, which he supposed changed the world in various ways, but he wasn't exactly proud of it.

Hush. Watch the story.

So Jon kept watching. He saw the change from baby bump to child-in-arms, saw Maia live in a tiny boxlike apartment in the middle of the city, well away from her own mother Davinia. Saw Maia choose a gender-neutral name like Jayel in an attempt to hide his true nature from his grandmother, who really, *really* seemed to dislike males.

And still, he saw Maia using that Amaranthus circlet over and over, almost always for *him*, and almost always for the most ludicrous requests.

A world-changer. Vitally important. A history-maker.

A little time passed and Jon saw Maia anxious over something he couldn't see, saw her give his chubby infant self to a much younger Anni with instructions that she'd be back that afternoon.

Then he saw her step through a doorway in a random part of the sprawling, chaotic, multileveled city. And…like a fish being suddenly caught in a net, she vanished. Anni was left there holding baby Jayel, confusion and dismay clear on her young face. But when she looked down at him, she smiled.

Chaos. That was depressing. Jon wasn't sure if it explained what happen to Maia. It kind of implied something bad had happened, right?

But then the pool showed something new. It was like the colours and lights all changed, and he could suddenly see the same scenes as if he was in VR or the Other. Creature symbols began appearing on people's foreheads, and more than that, he now saw sticky strings leading from people's heads or hearts or from various objects, right through to the Other realm where they attached to these…*Creatures*.

Ugh. Jon recoiled at the images in the water, since these depictions of Creatures didn't look at all like the fantastical inhuman figures he was used to seeing. They were definitely uglier and somehow damaged-looking, kind of like when a nice new toy was dropped on the ground…then rolled in the mud…then kicked a few times…and maybe inhabited by an evil spirit or two.

They looked malevolent.

Jon didn't know what to think of that. Maybe the pool images were biased – wherever they came from. You couldn't just claim that all Creatures were…well, *evil*.

But he kept watching as the scenes replayed, showing Maia covered in sticky colourful strands that he now knew represented Creature influence. And as she used the circlet, and as she spoke that word of power *Amaranthus*, the strands weakened and one by one, fell away.

Then Jon saw something appear on his infant self's forehead. It looked like a bold fingerprint, but it glowed, sending a faint light all over his baby form.

"I *am* marked," Jon breathed aloud. And if he understood this right, then the mark…was because of this 'Amaranthus' circlet which somehow broke connections with every other Creature. "What is Amaranthus?" he mused.

I am.

Jon had almost forgotten the old man was in the room. But when he turned to look at him, the man didn't seem so plain, or so…human…anymore. "Are you…a Creature?"

No, but the Creatures were once a little like me. The man – person – pointed at the pool. *Now they cannot even stand the sound of my name. Watch.*

Jon obeyed automatically and saw that the images in the pool had skipped several years, although they still showed the second type of image with all the alter-power and Creature connections and symbols. Now he saw his six-year-old self walking into a temple in Erus, his hand held by a nervous-looking Anni. The scene was much darker than Jon remembered but he could still see a faint, fuzzy *something* come over him the moment he stepped into the Other realm. Even through that fuzzy whatsit, the mark on his childish head glowed like a beacon.

The Creature – whose name Jon couldn't recall – flickered into sight then vanished immediately, leaving Anni, his younger self and the temple assistants looking baffled.

Then it happened again…and again…and again. It would be ridiculous if it wasn't also answering a question that had plagued Jon his entire life – that had made him feel worthless and fundamentally flawed.

Not flawed. Chosen.

Right. Sure. "But what about the White Prince?" Jon persisted. "*He* accepted me."

The pool's image changed again. This time it was Jon as he knew himself – lanky and brown-haired. His slouched posture told of deep unhappiness, and perhaps desperation. But maybe he was just projecting his current feelings.

As Jon watched himself step into the temple, the fuzzy blanket-thing came to cover him again. Then this Creature appeared. It was almost skeletal, as white as bone with large black eyes and sharp clawed hands and teeth barely hidden behind a small, thin-lipped mouth. And its wings…

Shaped like butterfly wings, they were just struts with empty space between them. A mere framework; there was no way anyone or anything could use them to fly.

That realisation was striking enough, but then Jon saw the White Prince's true expression. It was feral, and the Creature looked like its whole body was poised to strike. In that moment Jon realised that the White Prince wasn't misunderstood at all. In fact, Jon felt lucky to still be alive.

"Why didn't it attack?" he murmured. "Why did it make me a carrier instead?"

The image changed a little until the fuzziness became more solid – but still impossible to define. *You have protection that kept the Creature back. As for the second question, the Creature recognised you.*

Jon turned to stare at his companion. "Protection? What sort?"

Amaranthus didn't answer, and Jon persisted, "And how could the White Prince recognise me if it never saw me before? And what happened to Maia – to my birth mother? What does my mark mean? Who are *you*?"

The man smiled at him, and his form seemed to blur until all Jon could focus on were those deep, dark eyes. "All secrets come to light eventually," he replied aloud.

Then the darkness surrounding them receded, and like a light being turned on in a dark room, Jon finally saw where he was.

13
Stranded

Erus 3004 AD

"Look at this," Tarren announced. "You've grown another unit since this morning."

Tarie shook out her stiff limbs once the package measurer lifted away, feeling a little irritated. She'd arrived home yesterday after the dramatic day in the borderlands, back to her original, very petite height. It seemed like she'd used up all her unnatural strength during the building collapse, and her extra units with it.

Then she'd woken up this morning and although she'd felt the same, she'd checked her height anyway. Yep, she'd grown another unit. Now, at the end of the day, she'd grown two. "And the yoyo begins again," she said grumpily. "Maybe I need to start serious weightlifting whenever I feel myself growing. Use up the alter-power."

"That's not a bad idea," her father agreed.

"I was joking!" She was already short and sturdy. Building muscle would turn her into a cartoon character.

"I wasn't." Tarren looked up at her, finally seeming to take note of her foul mood. "What's the problem?"

Tarie shrugged. She'd told them about the borderlands drama, such as it was, but not about her own sense of guilt over letting Rokal run off when he was out of his head. Now she knew about his background and the way his mother had been killed, she pitied him as much as she disliked him. He hadn't been at Centre today either, even though yesterday he'd told Gavriel on his comm that he was coming straight back. But then it seemed some people only attended this Centre when they felt like it. "I just want some certainty. Is that too much to ask?"

Her father stared at her with one eyebrow raised. Then he

197

said in an even tone, "Just so you can be *certain* about dinner tonight, it'll be just you and Lydia. I'm eating with Anni."

"Jon's mother?" Now Tarie was the one staring. "Why?"

He shrugged, but she could see his discomfort in the way he shuffled in place and glanced away. "She's lonely what with Jon staying with Luca these past few days till he gets control over his power. That's all...and I think you'd understand."

Tarie watched him with narrowed eyes. That sounded suspiciously like a date. "At her house?"

"Ah...no, I'm meeting her in the restaurant."

"You're going on a date with Jon's mother, even though she's still contracted to someone?" Tarie exclaimed, appalled.

"It's not a date! It's just a friendly dinner," Tarren argued, his eyes darting from side to side. "And even if it wasn't – which it is! – Anni and Luca have never had a traditional contract. They've always been platonic partners only."

"Really?!"

"Anyway," he continued hastily, "I'd better go. Uh...have a nice evening."

Tarren fled from his own daughter, something Tarie hadn't seen him do...well, ever. Feeling somewhat deflated, she checked their balcony garden. She'd planted a few flowers since arriving, plus a Word tree in a large container. All looked fine, but she quietly spoke the Words over them anyway. The small tree grew another leaf, and the tight flower buds bloomed. Now *that* was what was supposed to happen.

Then Tarie stepped into their now-working VR, deciding she'd spend the evening distracting herself in an environment where she *wasn't* growing randomly.

Tarie.

Tarie immediately jolted awake. But even though her eyes were open in the darkened room, her brain definitely wasn't engaged. "Whuh?"

There was no one in her bedroom. The door was shut too, which ruled out either Lydia or her father sticking their head in and waking her up for some reason.

Next to her bed her comm lit up, sensing movement. The display showed 4:16 am.

Tarie huffed out a sigh and slumped back into her bed. Some

people might get up before five, but she wasn't one of them. If it was dark, it was night, and she ought to be sleeping. Maybe she'd dreamed someone calling her name. That had happened before-

"*TARIE!*"

Her eyes shot to her window. Her one-way window ran up one narrow wall, and it was completely blacked out, as you'd expect when someone was trying to sleep. She had it set to show the view once she was up for the day. But it sounded like someone was outside the window...on the forty-second level.

She climbed out of bed, straightening her loose sleepshirt and trousers, then stumbled over to the window. A light tap of the hand turned it transparent from her side only – and revealed a massive, looming figure plastered to the other side.

Tarie jumped, unable to make out more than a male outline and tousled hair lit up blue by the soft outdoor lights meant to guide vehicles and flyers away from buildings. Then she connected the figure with the familiar, definitely anxious tone and came up with one person who might be up this high. "Jon!" she hissed through the window. "What in the darkest Other are you doing outside my window at this time of night?"

There was a pause, then the figure shifted a little. He appeared to be clinging to the handles that served as a truly awful fire escape, and she could see his limbs trembling even through the buffer provided by the window. "*Can you let me in?! I'm...something is wrong.*"

His voice sounded strange for starters. Husky and distorted. That was probably the window too, but Tarie rolled her eyes. He'd no doubt been looking for his own home and had arrived at the wrong window...except he'd known it was her room. Maybe there was something wrong with the building access since he'd moved, she wondered.

"Go to the balcony to your left," she ordered him. "I'll let you in. But keep it down!" She didn't want to have to explain this to her father.

Tarie didn't wait for Jon to respond, instead moving quickly and quietly from her room and through to the living room which led to the balcony. She could see him out there, clinging onto the clear barrier that kept out dust, drones, pigeons and apparently Princes of the Air, so she opened the barrier even as she stepped onto the balcony and closed the door behind her.

He stumbled into the small space, landing on his hands and knees and with his dark hair tumbling over his face. And in the dim light of the balcony she could clearly see…

…it wasn't Jon.

"*Rokal!*" Tarie burst out in dismay. "What are *you* doing here? Why did you let me think you were Jon?!" She'd spoken directly to him, she realised. That should have been a solid clue it wasn't Jon, since she was pretty sure the speaking curse was still in place.

The big figure slumped sideways, then almost fell into a seated position. It was definitely Rokal, although he looked dreadful. Even so, Tarie fought with the urge to straighten her hair…or kick him right off the balcony again.

He mumbled something she couldn't make out.

"What was that?"

"Didn't know you thought I was Jon. I just…needed to come inside. I couldn't stand the height." Rokal pushed his tangled hair back off his face, revealing shadows under his dark eyes and sallow, sweat-covered skin.

Ugh. He looked horribly unwell. And a Prince of the Air, afraid of heights? "I see," Tarie said carefully. "Look…I'm going to get someone to pick you up. Shall I contact Gavriel or Orla?" Not that she'd ever contacted that girl before, but if there was a time for it, it would be now. "Or your father?"

He shrugged, so Tarie quickly messaged Gavriel, then sent a request through to message Orla and Rokal's father Wyet. The average person couldn't just message someone directly without permission. But she didn't open the door between the balcony and the living room. Rokal was acting so unpredictably that she didn't want to risk him getting inside her house, if he wasn't in his right mind.

He was awful enough when he *was* in his right mind.

Tarie pushed aside the anxiety that sprang up, then as she felt a tingle of alter-power run down her limbs, she knew she must be growing again. But she sat carefully, crossing her legs on the balcony floor across from Rokal.

"When they get here, I'll walk you down to the ground floor," she said, trying to sound as calm as possible. "So…why did you come to my apartment instead of your own or your friends'? And how do you know where I live?"

He shrugged again. "It's not hard to find out where you live. Orla and Gav know too."

"Oh." That was…uncomfortable.

"And Orla's dating my father now, not me," Rokal continued dully. "Has been for a while."

"Oh…" Tarie fidgeted in place. Yuck. That was even more uncomfortable.

"And Gav's not my friend," he added. "He's a fiend. I don't have any real friends."

Tarie blinked at him, her jaw dropping. Rokal had reached a level of honesty that meant he was either drunk, high, brain-damaged or plain lying, and she didn't know what to make of it. "Ahhhh…"

He huffed out a sigh. "But you tried to help me yesterday. I remember that. And you always look at me as if you like me. So I thought you might help."

She felt her cheeks heating, grateful for her dark skin tone largely hiding the blush. "Rokal…"

"And that's another thing!" he burst out suddenly, finally showing emotion. "Why is everyone calling me Rokal? I don't remember changing my name. I'm *Max*."

In the dead silence after that pronouncement Tarie could hear faint sounds from down on the street, and what might have even been a cricket chirping. She very carefully lifted her comm and switched it to VR scan, then looked at him through the viewer. She'd been half expecting to see someone else vaguely disguised as Erus Centre's biggest brute, but instead she just saw Rokal, still bedraggled in appearance and with that slight shimmer that VR always lent.

Except for one thing. His forehead was bare – his Creature symbol was nowhere to be seen.

Somewhere, sometime

The light switched on in that dark room where Jon stood watching highlights of his own history. Then he saw he wasn't in a room at all. Instead he was on the top of a…city? A gleaming, steeply shaped hill surrounded by a vast garden?

The pool in front of Jon now reflected blue sky. Bright water trickled over the edges of the round shape to run in narrow channels around his feet, then disappeared off down the shining surface of whatever he was standing on. "Whaaa…?"

"Welcome to the Mountain of Glass," Amaranthus said cheerfully. "A city within a garden within a mountain which also happens to be within the Other realm…but quite outside of time. Just a stopover for you, but an excellent one."

"Whaaaa…." Jon clicked shut his hanging jaw, trying to take in the scenery around him. Now he looked up he could see a faint shining barrier in every direction, with the blue sky visible through it. He followed the line of the barrier back down to the green expanse of the garden, noting that it solidified and seemed to turn into a rock wall where it hit the ground in the distance.

This whole place had to be easily as big as Erus city. Now the light was switched on – or maybe the darkness had been switched off – Jon noticed a slight, familiar fragrance in the air. He sniffed – was that the scent of flowers? Or fruit? "Is this…are we…in the temple fire pit?"

He'd stuttered out the question, but Amaranthus seemed to understand immediately that he was referring to the fire pit in the Power Performance temple. "That's one way *you* can enter."

"Oh. And did…did…"

"Yes. I brought you here."

"Oh." Jon craned his head to take in more of his surroundings, then found himself turning full-circle. He couldn't work out if this place was simply enormous, or actually much smaller than he'd thought but with a lot packed into it. And the shining, somehow not-slippery surface he was standing on – it looked like a water fountain. Weird. Wonderful. "Is this a Creature city?"

Oops. Amaranthus had said he wasn't a Creature, hadn't he? But even as Jon thought that, a little thought came clearly into his head.

They wish.

It was a familiar mental voice, quieter than before, but this time Jon immediately connected it with the person who stood before him. "That was you, wasn't it?"

Yes.

"And…you've talked to me before. In the Other…maybe outside too."

Yes.

"And you've been protecting me because of something my birth mother did," Jon continued, gaining enthusiasm as he spoke. "And because I'm meant to be – ha – significant!"

Yes.

"Is this when you tell me I had to go through all that pain to end up where I am now?" Jon asked in amazement. "That I had to be miserable for years, and go to the White Prince, then that place with Nadeen and Fron-swah just so I could achieve whatever it is I'm meant to achieve?"

"Of course not," Amaranthus replied aloud. "The Creatures would have always rejected you, but that makes you lucky, not miserable. You could have come straight here from the temple in Power Performance, if you hadn't delayed the first time you saw the firepit." He smiled, and Jon didn't see one speck of gloating or judgement in that expression. "But we can make good use of your past. And I brought you here regardless of that past."

Oh. Jon wasn't sure how to feel about that – if it was worse for his misery to be somehow orchestrated by others, or to be partly his own doing. "Thank you…I think."

"As for your friends in Frencia – would you like to know a little of what's going on there?"

"Yes, please!"

So Amaranthus directed him back to the pool, whose surface again stirred with images and scenes, but this time of Jon's arrival directly from the Other temple.

And this time, he finally understood what everyone was saying.

Erus, 3004 AD

"Rokal…er, *Max*," Tarie asked carefully, "are you still pledged to Gerak?" Because the VR setting on her comm should immediately show anyone's Creature symbol on their forehead, plus any VR that was being used anywhere around them. People didn't have to be fully in VR to change faces or clothing, or to have one of those damn pop-up ads...

"Dunno. I can still fly, can't I? But..." He shuddered, his expression going vacant. "Something happened at the borderlands museum, I don't know what. I feel so...empty. And my head's been spinning this whole time. I feel like I've forgotten years of my life, or like they were happening to someone else because what I *do* remember just...doesn't seem like me."

It was easily the most emotion Tarie had ever seen Rokal display. The most she'd ever heard him speak, too. He seemed genuine, without a hint of a sneer on his face, but she'd had too many problems with people like him to take him at his word. "Do you remember your mother?" she asked carefully.

He frowned. "Of course. I saw her last week."

Tarie paused. That either meant he *had* lost years of his life, or Gavriel hadn't told the truth about his mother's murder. She tried again. "Do you remember what happened with Jon the other week?"

"Jon?"

"You call him Jayel. Or Jail, or something. You flew him up to the top of the flagpole at Centre and left him there, and you filmed the whole thing." Tarie almost felt mean bringing it up, but it was one of the cruellest things she'd ever witnessed.

Rokal was quiet for a while. "I remember that."

It didn't seem like he'd elaborate, but just then her comm went off.

This happens to carriers sometimes, Gavriel's message read. *It's not easy sharing a head with an immortal Creature. I'll come as soon as I can.*

"Gavriel says he's coming." There was no response from the other two, but it was in the middle of the night. She pushed away the thought that they might be – ugh – together.

"I don't want to see Gavriel."

"Well, you can't stay on my balcony for the rest of your life," Tarie replied lightly. "He can take you home-"

"I don't want to see my father either-"

"Then you can go straight to your room and shut the door." She spoke over him, feeling like the world's worst parent, and of someone literally twice her size. "Come on."

The only problem with her plan was that it involved actually taking Rokal through her apartment. She was half waiting for him to show his true self again and do something really terrible, but they passed through the small space without incident and soon enough were in the liftpods heading down.

In the quietness of the small space, Tarie couldn't shake the thought that something was really wrong. It *felt* wrong. And if Rokal really had been disconnected from his Creature, then shouldn't she be…uh, talking up the Timeless One or something?

Except that trying to poach someone from their Creature was a criminal offence…and Rokal could still fly, she reminded herself. Regardless of what the VR scanner had showed, he must still be connected to Gerak. And regardless of his dishevelment and confusion, he was surely still the same dangerous, unlikeable person he'd always been.

So Tarie ignored that quiet voice that argued otherwise and stepped out the door into the foyer. "We can wait here."

But they didn't have to wait long at all, in the end. Gavriel showed up, looking bright-eyed and annoyingly well-groomed for someone who'd been woken up far too early, and it made Tarie feel even more uncomfortable in her rough sleep suit.

"Nice hair," he told her as a faint melody played in the background – no doubt his personal music settings were up too high. "Have you shrunk again?"

It wasn't his words that made her stiffen; it was his mocking tone. "Nice music," she retorted. "Do you have your own theme song?"

Gavriel's eyebrows shot up, and the faint music silenced. "What?"

She sighed. "Never mind. Just…look after Rokal, alright?"

"It's Max!"

Both Tarie and Gavriel stared at Rokal, and Gavriel finally raised his hands placatingly. "Of course…Max. Let's get home, shall we?"

So off they went in Gavriel's gleaming multivehicle. Tarie watched them disappear around the corner, still feeling that same sense of unease.

But what was she meant to do about it? she argued with herself.

She went back to bed.

"Well?" Lilith rarely raised her voice, but she could make a normal speaking tone sound as harsh as a shout. And she wasn't even in the room – just in VR.

"No, I have not found the boy yet," Luca bit out. It was just after dawn, he wished he was still in bed, and the last few days had been…oh, just the *worst*. "It's like he's vanished from the face of the Earth."

"Then he's in the Other," his mother retorted. "What are your plans to find him?"

"I didn't say he was in the *Other*, I said I can't find a trace of him anywhere in the Other *or* the normal realm. If the White Prince has got him, or if the idiot has run off somewhere in the Other, then he's in there very, very deep." Luca scuffed his foot against the floor of his VR office, rumpling the plush virtual carpet. "And I don't have *plans* to find him. I'm looking. Either I find him or-"

"If you don't do what the Tiger asked of you, you don't get what he promised," Lilith cut in coldly.

No Erus. No little Luca empire within the greater Tiger empire. "I'm well aware," Luca gritted out. His jaw was so tight that he could feel the ache even here in the virtual world. It wasn't as if he wanted to manage the boy, not like he'd been asked to. But the Creatures all knew Jayel Jonnamin DeLuca's face, even if Jon had no idea of his own significance. The scrying pools in their cities only showed snatches of the future, but it was more than enough in Jon's case.

Just then a light touch on one shoulder indicated another incoming VR call. Luca scanned it quickly, noting it was his estranged contract partner. He muted Lilith then allowed the second call through. "Yes, Anni? Why are you calling so early?"

It wasn't really that early, but his attempt to throw her off-guard worked. Anni's virtual figure appeared, only slightly younger and shinier than her actual dull self. Her slightly hunched shoulders and darting eyes clearly showed her discomfort at dealing with him even through this message. "I saw you were up, and I- I haven't heard from Jay-Jon at all," she said defensively. "Not through his comm or VR, and I wanted to make sure he's OK."

Luca already knew this, because she'd sent him three comm messages in the last two days, which he'd purposely been ignoring. Why? Because it was funny. "Woman, it's been four days," he said in exasperation. "He's almost grown. If he doesn't want to check in with his mother, let him be!"

Her cheeks flushed and he practically saw her deflate. "So…he *is* alright?"

"He's sullen, hungry and spends most of his time in VR or out flying, so he's the same as always. If you consider that alright."

"Oh. Alright then…"

"Have a nice day, Anni." Having won the upper hand – not that it was hard – Luca decisively ended the call. Her figure disappeared, then Lilith's transparent image solidified.

"Was there a good reason you muted me?" she asked coolly. A shadowy figure moved behind her, indicating that she was no longer alone in her room across the city. "I was about to give you some good news."

"Keeping up appearances with the boy's mother," Luca replied briefly. He slumped into a nearby couch, leaning back as if exhausted. "And if you've got good news, give it to me. I need something decent to happen today."

Lilith paused for several seconds. "You still need to deal with the White Prince," she said. "But you can make the Tiger…less unhappy with your failure if you do a little task. Deliver Gerak's three Erus Princes of the Air to Elsewhise, without anyone making a fuss."

Luca's eyebrows rose. "When?"

"The sooner the better."

The Mountain of Glass, time irrelevant

After watching scenes in the pool for what might have been hours, Jon was clear about one thing. While he didn't know why he'd come here via Frencia in the late eighteenth century, he could now see that his detour there wasn't really about him. It was about *them*.

Francois and Nadine, he thought, mentally replaying the names he'd heard so perfectly pronounced this time. But of course when he tried to say them aloud…well, there was a reason he'd hadn't studied languages at Centre. Some people's tongues just couldn't twist the right way around any language except their own.

The next few…days? Weeks?…moved strangely. Jon was shown around the Garden and the City by Amaranthus as well as a string of locals who managed to look both completely ordinary and completely odd. They looked human at first glance or even second, but sometimes when they moved, he'd see the shimmering outline of someone else quite inhuman, as if they were wearing an illusion.

Jon privately thought they were actually Creatures – or pre-Creatures; what the Creatures had once been. The more he saw of this place and its treasures, and the more he saw in the viewing pool, the more solidly he believed what he'd been told.

And Chaos, the more scared he was to go back to Erus!

You won't be alone.

Unless you're coming with me along with an army and a suit of alter-powered armour, I'll feel alone, Jon argued from where he sat under a spreading fruit tree. He couldn't see Amaranthus right now, but he knew that didn't mean that he wasn't there. *The Creatures hate me. You still won't tell me why, and I know it's something to do with you, but I'll be a target the moment I go back.*

You were always a target, and yet you're still here. I'll look after you.

Yeah, but he was planning to go back, while using the power initially gifted by the White Prince, and then reject said Creature. No one ever rejected their Creature once pledged. It might have even been illegal. And it turned out that all true gifts originated here at the Mountain, in the most fascinating treasure hall Jon had never known existed.

He'd found out that the Creatures had stolen some of the gifts once upon a time, including flight. But stolen gifts became tainted, and could never be used properly by the ones who stole them. So the Creatures who could gift flight – Audaline, Gerak and the White Prince – could *only* gift flight to others, but not truly use it themselves. Because the gifts were, well, gifted, they worked as intended. But any gifts that came via the Creatures also came with a terrible taint of their own.

Fear.

Jon shuddered again. He'd tested flying just enough to know he could still do it, albeit shakily, but he didn't want to fly properly. It made him think of the White Prince, and it made that horrible fear of falling and heights and death and – *fear* come over him even at the thought.

He remembered the awful day when Rokal had grabbed him and flown him high up to the tower on the top of the Erus Centre. Jon vaguely remembered sweat dripping down Rokal's face, and how his expression was so cold, so *bored* whenever he flew. (And most of the time, really.)

Jon now knew that was a cover for the extreme fear that was always gifted along with flight.

But Amaranthus, who'd no doubt been following along with Jon's thoughts, didn't explain again about how to use the gift yet reject the fear. He'd done that more than once since Jon had arrived. Instead he said, *Have some joyfruit. You need it.*

Which one was that again? There had to be hundreds of fruit trees and bushes in the garden, and-

Just then something fell *plop* into Jon's lap from the tree above. It was a little cluster of golden fruit, looking a bit like a mini bunch of grapes, except caramel-coloured.

He looked at the tree above him to see that yes, it was some kind of stone fruit rather than whatever this was, then shrugged. This place didn't follow any natural laws. *Thanks.*

Then he tasted the fruit.

Ahhhhhhh. Sooooo happyyyyyyyy…

Jon flung himself back on the soft dry grass, grinning up at the blue sky where it glimmered through the Mountain of Glass's transparent barrier. Never mind the world's problems – it was good to be alive! He felt so happy, so joyful that he wanted to laugh out loud, to run to the top of the city (which he'd already done) and to swim in the streams that ran from the spring at the top of the city…which was also the viewing pool. He'd done that, too.

This joyfruit was better than any of the energy shots he

could take back in Erus. Those just helped you get through the day or stay awake at night, but they couldn't truly change your mood. It hadn't hurt that the fruit tasted as delectable as it looked.

Just then Jon heard a scream. Not a scream of excitement, or even one of those creepy bird calls, but like a distant, high-pitched scream of…fear…that seemed to get louder and closer…

He sat up, then stood as he noticed a hole appear in the nearby rock wall that marked the edge of the Garden. It was just about knee height, the size of a dinner plate, and as he watched, it grew larger until it was so big he would have been able to climb inside.

The screaming seemed to be coming from inside *there*.

Jon crept closer, fascinated, and he only just stepped aside in time as a shrieking pile of red and green cloth came shooting out of the hole. It landed on the grass, revealing tangled, dishevelled pale limbs. As Jon tried to take that in, another bundle came shooting out after it, but this one was all in shades of brown.

A moment later all the shapes and textures finally made sense. It was two girls – small enough to be children maybe – with enormous, full-skirted dresses like Nadine had worn back in Frencia, although without any curled white wigs. One girl had the fieriest ginger hair he'd ever seen in real life, the other's was dark brown, and both wore expressions of shock with wide-open mouths and eyes.

At least they'd stopped screaming.

Jon could have helped them up, or welcomed them, or…anything really. But instead he found himself with his hand over his mouth, trying to stifle laughter as the two girls righted themselves, muttering to each other about…flying?

The brown-haired girl got up, brushing off those enormously uncomfortable-looking skirts, and revealing herself to be only about as tall as Jon's chest. She looked around her with an awed expression, then her gaze landed on him. Her green eyes widened even further.

That was enough to set Jon off. Well, that, and the joyfruit no doubt. He wrapped his arms around his middle and grinned, feeling his face almost ache from it. When the girls didn't speak, he felt he had to explain. "You should have seen yourselves," he told them. "When you came shooting out of that hole, the looks on your faces – they reminded me of a stunned mullet. Two stunned mullets, rather."

The red-haired girl got to her feet, a scowl on her face, then she noticeably turned her back on Jon and studied the now-smooth rock wall. The hole they'd come in through had vanished.

But the brown-haired girl beamed up at Jon, seeming unoffended. "I do not even know what a mullet looks like," she said breathlessly. Her voice wasn't as young as her appearance first indicated, and he revised his opinion of her age. Fifteen maybe, rather than thirteen?

But because *he* apparently turned into a six-year-old when he felt this cheerful, he did an impression of how they'd looked, with bulging eyes and a dropped jaw. "Like that."

The brown-haired girl's eyes widened further, and she laughed along with him. The redhead…well, she didn't seem to find it so funny.

And that was how Jon met two Tudar sisters, Lady Anne of Covington and the rather less snooty Issbits. Bessie?

Bets.

14

The Eternity Stone

Jon sat at the top of the Mountain of Glass, right in front of the viewing pool as usual. It had become his favourite place – not because he *wanted* to stare into that pool, but because he couldn't stop himself from watching over and over. Images of his mother, or his home, of the deeper levels of his own life that he hadn't even known about. Trying to see if just once the pool would show him exactly *why* he was meant to be so significant... but it never did.

He had to be grateful that he'd met Bets back when he'd been high on joyfruit. It seemed to have made a good impression that lasted all these weeks they'd both been here on the Mountain of Glass. But he definitely hadn't been that happy since. The high had faded as he'd seen more and more in the viewing pools, and as he'd thought about the future that awaited him.

Literally, Erus 3004 AD was the future, and he had to go there.

It had been an interesting few weeks, though. He'd spent a lot of time with Bets – and occasionally her less friendly sister Anne – and just when he'd thought he'd seen everything the Mountain had to offer, something new and fantastic would appear. Compared to the many, many VR programmes he'd dabbled in, it shouldn't have been that interesting, but there was something about this place that made even the ordinary extraordinary.

It also helped that the other new arrivals seemed just as startled by all this place's secrets. More so, even. But then Jon was pretty sure their time of origin was somewhere in the fifteen-

"

hundreds – 1500 years before he was born. (Wait…*would be* born? Time travel was confusing!)

There'd been another couple of time travellers who'd arrived around the same time as Bets and Anne: George and Ashlea (Ash). Jon hadn't learned their stories except to hear that they'd been travelling through all sorts of different time periods and dangerous situations, that both of them could also fly yet were not Princes of the Air, and that they'd recently run into some Creatures for the first time.

The two of them had gone into great detail about how awful and disgusting the Creatures were – George in particular had been muttering about a wheelbarrow and talking rodents – and Jon had just clamped his mouth shut. He hadn't wanted to say a word about his own background, not when the others seemed so horrified by what was clearly a feral Creature or two.

But George and Ash had stayed a while, then had trundled off to their own separate times with barely a goodbye. Jon hadn't thought much of them since, except to briefly think that they'd seemed to enjoy each other's company as much as they'd enjoyed bickering…and that one of them would die of old age before the other was even born.

Time travel could be sad, too.

Just then Bets bounced up beside him, her new plain grey skirts catching his eye just before she spoke. "What takes your attention so, Jon?"

Jon hurriedly dashed his hand over the surface of the water. It had been flickering over the same scene of his birth mother again, saying all those fantastical things about Jon's own future. If Bets saw it, she was bound to ask questions, and he didn't know how to answer them. He didn't *want* to answer them. "Uh…"

"Ash!" Bets squealed suddenly, her pitch making him jolt in fright.

"What?" Jon looked down to see the image on the water had changed and now showed the familiar face of the other time-travelling girl. She was wearing white, with her dark hair loose around her shoulders, and she stood face to face with the guy, George. He was wearing black and white, kind of like an old-fashioned waiter.

Jon did a double take at the girl's white clothing, for a moment thinking she was dressed as a Prince of the Air. Then he realised that the extremely old-fashioned, lace-covered gown had nothing to do with Creatures, but meant something else entirely. "Are they...?"

"By the rood," Bets breathed. "I'd vow this is a wedding. Ash and George are getting married!" She turned to Jon excitedly, her green eyes wide and earnest. "Oh! And Anne said they did not like each other enough for such a thing, but she was wrong!"

She turned back to watch the scene avidly, and Jon watched along with her. He wasn't as attached to these two as she clearly was, but it was interesting to see the unfamiliar ceremony play out. "Are they exchanging rings?" he asked a few minutes later, squinting at the scene.

"I believe such things are customary in the future," Bets agreed, then glanced up at him shyly. (Because of course she didn't know that his own time was far, far ahead of both George and Ash's – and he didn't care to tell her.) "What are wedding ceremonies like in your home, Jon? Are they very lovely?"

"Not especially," he replied absently, still watching the scene. Someone else in a similarly old-fashioned suit was speaking now, gesturing between the two, but Jon couldn't hear what was being said. "Although I've never been to a proper wedding since it's an archaic custom. Not many people get married where I'm from." Only if they were really conservative, or if they wanted the legal bond like with the odd situation between Anni and Luke/Luca.

Bets' head shot up so fast he leaned back to avoid being head-butted. "Archaic?" she squeaked. "So your parents are not wed?"

"Oh, they are," Jon replied, wondering what she was so concerned about. "Legal reasons, you know? And it's only a legal connection, not a fancy ceremony like this one."

Bets' eyes flicked away from his, and he wondered what she wasn't saying. "So...you yourself would wed for the sake of your eventual children, yes? So they wouldn't be...*bastards*?"

Her voice had lowered towards the end of the sentence, and Jon found himself leaning in to make out what she was saying. He didn't understand *why* she was saying it – wasn't a bastard a badly behaved person? And what did that have to do with unmarried parents? But just then they were interrupted by a loud coughing sound.

Jon and Bets both looked up, and he saw Anne standing right behind them.

Anne's small hands were on her hips, and her mouth was pressed into a thin line. "Did you not hear me calling?"

Jon was still trying to work out the connection between unwed and bastards, and why Bets seemed so uncomfortable. "You were calling?"

Anne scowled, her red eyebrows drawing low over her eyes. "Indeed I was, sirrah, although I sought my sister rather than you. I now see you have held her attention instead. And what might you have been saying that required you to sit so very close?"

"Anne!" Bets blushed deep pink, although she did shuffle away from Jon – as if she had anything to feel guilty for. "You need not glare at him so, for we were merely speaking. We've been watching your two odd friends, Ashlea and George, and 'tis the strangest thing! They are together."

Anne didn't seem to take that in, instead rattling off some fantastical news about Amaranthus offering her immortality. Chaos, the girl was self-absorbed, Jon thought. And was it even possible to gain immortality? Back home he'd heard of one or two special carriers who never seemed to age, but otherwise, being human was an eventual death sentence.

But then if anyone could break the progression of life-to-death, it would be Amaranthus.

His attention returned to the conversation just in time to hear Bets say, "That would be a fine thing indeed, sister, although Amaranthus has already told me I do not have to return home."

Jon turned to stare at her in shock, feeling utterly betrayed. Amaranthus hadn't promised *him* any such thing. Why these girls and not him, huh? And why would *Anne* get offered immortality and not him?

Who said I never offered you immortality?

Amaranthus's quiet mental voice cut into Jon's roiling thoughts, stopping them short, and for a moment, making him blank out entirely. Then he managed to formulate the thought: *Are you offering…?*

It's already done, the reply came back clearly. *I'd never forget you, Jon.*

Jon couldn't speak. He just sat there in silence as the two girls chatted obliviously around him and Amaranthus spoke into his mind, downloading images and knowledge that he'd never even thought to ask about.

The moment a human connected with Amaranthus of their own free will – whether by freely entering the Mountain of Glass, or drinking the water of life that sprang from this place, or some other means out in the normal realm – their truest self began to be transformed by the everlasting light from this place. Their inner self, beyond their conscious thoughts (what some called the spirit) began to transform into something undying.

They began to transform into one of Amaranthus's People. But it wasn't until the old human form was left behind that they would really *live*. A paradox – to truly live, they'd have to die.

Meanwhile, Anne was still speaking about her own journey to becoming one of the People, and Jon realised she had no idea what it actually required.

He definitely wasn't going to tell her!

"And Amaranthus has given me tasks to perform on behalf of the Mountain, anywhere across time or space by use of the remnant gateways." Anne beamed, her small, pale face almost glowing with enthusiasm. "Oh, I am most excited! He said I may go at once if I wish. There is a gateway open at the south end of the second vineyard. I merely wished to advise you before I left."

"Oh," Bets said. "Then I do wish you the blessings of the Eternal One, dear Anne. We shall await your return with interest."

Jon shrugged half-heartedly, because his mind had just been blown. He couldn't care less what one snooty antique aristocrat did with their days, even if it *did* involve time travelling via permanent doorways through space and time.

Anne nodded at her sister's comment, then narrowed her eyes at Jon. "And you two, stay in public places!"

"Sister!" Bets looked like she was about to burst with embarrassment.

Jon had no idea why.

Immortality. He'd gained it without even realising it, and the universe seemed an entirely different, open and incredible place.

But as the days went by and Jon's mind was opened up to those new and fantastic possibilities – he didn't need to fear death! – he also found himself thinking about his friends from Frencia, the ones who'd been so kind even when he couldn't speak their language. He now knew exactly where and when he'd been, and he knew that Nadine, Francois and the others were in terrible danger. They were right in the middle of the Frencine Great Terror, the revolution that had overthrown that nation's monarchy and had killed huge numbers of their nobility.

Jon found that his new understanding of the afterlife didn't stop him from wanting his friends to live full lives. At this point, they might end up rather brutally cut short. Or maybe they already had, or *would...*

Time travel. Argh.

Jon started to practice speeches for how he'd ask Amaranthus to save them. He'd half-hoped Amaranthus would just pluck the desire out of his mind as he so often did, but not this time. It seemed Jon would have to actually ask. He wandered back and forth down the myriad halls of the inner Mountain, muttering to himself, but could never seem to find the right words.

Finally he sat down in a hallway, stretching his legs out in front of him. He'd just have to say it, he decided. It had to be done. In a way Nadine and Francois had saved him, so now he had to save them right back.

That was when Anne tripped right over his legs and fell hard on her hands and knees. "Ooh!"

Jon hadn't even seen her coming up – clearly she hadn't seen him either – but he felt guilty that she might have been hurt. It made him ruder than he should have been. "Watch out."

Anne sat up and scowled at him, slapping him hard on the leg. "Who's the one sitting in the hall like a numpty?"

A…numpty? Jon didn't know what that meant, but he could guess. He sighed. "You're right. I'm sorry I tripped you."

Her jaw dropped and her eyes widened. "Oh, my. You truly are out of sorts, for you have never before apologised for anything."

That couldn't possibly be true. "I apologise," he argued.

"Not to me."

Jon waved a hand dismissively. He didn't want to argue over his own manners (or lack of them) when Nadine and Francois might be getting guillotined right now, and finding out promptly whether their truest selves would be pulled down to the Creature cities, or freed to wherever it was that Amaranthus's People went.

He could feel Anne's gaze still fixed on him, and when she spoke again, it was with a hint of compassion. "You fear so much for your friends, then? What is their danger?"

Jon didn't think he'd ever directly told either sister about the Frencine, but he'd clearly said enough for Anne to guess the cause of his worry. "Have you ever heard of the Frencine Great Terror?"

She frowned quizzically. "Something to do with rats?"

"No! What's so terrifying about rats?!"

Anne shrugged. "Plague?"

Jon sighed, because she clearly had no idea. "Not rats, not plague. Revolution."

"Ah, yes." She nodded. "Angland shall have one of those, although after my lifetime. I believe we shall execute our king, briefly attempt a republic, then reinstate a much-weakened monarchy. Is that what is happening in Frencia?"

"You know your own country's future?" Surely that wasn't safe. Although Jon had to admit, he'd find out what he could if he had the chance too.

"There were history books in Ash's time," Anne argued, clearly referring to the time she'd spent in the twenty-first century. "Was I not to read them? Besides, I did not learn anything about my own future."

"Revolution," Jon explained slowly, "is somewhat different when one is living it. They're killing all the Frencine upper class, Anne. Locking them up in their castles, and then chopping off their heads one by one. *That's* what Amaranthus pulled me out of, and that's why I'm worried about my friends." Of course he hadn't understood that was what was happening outside of the quietness of Chamborde, but now he did. Now he knew everything.

"Oh." Anne was silent for a long while, her face screwing up into a series of unhappy expressions. "Why did Amaranthus not take all of them away?" she asked finally. "Why only you?"

Jon shrugged again, feeling utterly weary and defeated. "Because he took me from my own time in the first place, I suppose. We mustn't think that time travel is the usual solution to problems, because it isn't. You, me, Bets – we're exceptions, not the rule. And who knows how much time has passed outside the Mountain? They might all be dead now." He hoped they weren't…but they might be.

"Or they might not!" Anne retorted. "Have you ever gone back to see?"

"Of course not," he said a little defensively. He'd thought about them enough, especially since seeing the pool version of his time there, but until recently hadn't focused on going back to visit at all. "I only arrived here a few weeks ago, barely before you did. And I haven't been given permission to gallivant around the gateways as you have."

"But were you instructed *not* to use them?" she challenged.

Jon was silent for a while. Anne, Ash and George had described the remnant gateways that shimmered like heated air above an underground vent, but Jon had always struggled to spot them when they blended in with the scenery. And while Amaranthus had never told him *not* to use them, was that the same as permission?

"No," he admitted, "but I wouldn't know which one to use. I don't see them like you seem to, Anne, maybe because I never used the Eternity Stone like you did. How would we find it? Where would we *take* them?"

She seemed to ponder the question for a few moments. "Verily, there are gateways everywhere," she answered finally. "And if you recall where you first arrived here, we ought to be able to find the right gateway. I can test it first, see if 'tis the right one."

Oh, it sounded like such a good idea, but... "How would you know if it was? You wouldn't know my Frencia from Iron Age Briton." Jon himself only knew because as a child he'd loved historical VR programmes.

"Then we shall go together, and we shall find a way to take your friends to safety."

He really, *really* wanted to go, but this kind of time travel sounded like it could also go horribly wrong. "But Amaranthus-"

Anne rolled her eyes. "He *lives* for such deeds, Jon. He'd never say aught. We shall start with finding the point in which you entered. You do recall it, do you not?"

"Of course I do." Jon sat up, straightening his shoulders. He couldn't let some tiny, snooty redhead take control of his adventure. He clearly remembered how he'd come through onto the top of the Mountain of Glass – the inner mountain, that was – from the temple-room back in Chamborde castle.

"Well, come along, then. We shall save your noble froggy friends, never doubt that!"

"Froggy?!" What did those cute little amphibians have to do with Nadine and the others? But Jon got up anyway and followed her along the hall.

"I heard George say it once," Anne explained as they moved through a doorway out into the garden. "It refers to the Frencine diet of frogs, I believe."

"*I* never ate frogs!" Jon said indignantly. "Although there were some extremely small chicken legs…"

Oh. Maybe he had eaten frogs after all.

They hadn't been half bad.

Anne patted him on the arm, but there was a clear hint of glee in her expression. "As I said. We shall save your froggy friends, never you mind."

Erus city-state, 3004 AD

Luca hummed as he studied the VR screen that displayed a rather gothic scene of a woman chained in a dark, dungeon-like room. Her white flight suit was stained and a little tattered, and her dark hair straggled over her olive-skinned, classically beautiful face. She wriggled as if she could get herself up off the dirty floor, but couldn't do more than move her shoulders and neck.

That was the point of the paralytic dart he'd drugged her with – via drone, and a perfect shot at that, since she'd been mid-air at the time. While his own real body was trapped in the borderlands, he'd got rather good at manipulating this human one instead. Then it had been a simple case of labelling this woman as a dissenter in the city records, and he'd been able to bring her straight to this place without a spot of trouble.

"Don't bother trying to move," Luca called through the speakers. "You'll just wear yourself out." He paused. "On second thought, move as much as you like. It's quite entertaining to watch."

Especially since he'd gone to the trouble of tipping dark

paint and dye on this floor, knowing his new visitors would be wearing white. Gerak's Princes of the Air were so predictable – gorgeous, violent, single-minded brunettes who wore their flight suits without fail.

The woman scowled. "Who is that? Why did you shoot me? I'll have you know I'm Gerak's senior Prince of the Air in Erus, and I'll have you punished to the full extent of the law for what you've done!"

Now that was terribly, wonderfully fun, so Luca took the time to laugh as loudly and obnoxiously as he could manage. "Oh, *dear*. I didn't even change my voice, but you clearly don't recognise me. It's Chairman Luca DeMannard, and I captured you on the Tiger's orders. The Tiger is also known as Audaline, also known as Auda, and also known as Erus's new and terrifying patron Creature." The woman's face had paled with every word, and he asked with slow, deliberate emphasis, "So *how* were you going to have me punished, exactly?"

The woman straightened her shoulders, her lips tightening. "Why does the Tiger want me? I'm pledged to Gerak."

Luca wouldn't mind knowing the same thing, since that was why he'd brought her here first instead of sending her straight off to the Tiger.

"You're a carrier, actually," he corrected. He glanced down at the long list of facts he'd gained about this woman before he'd easily tracked her down. "Seyen 'Sashy' Johannis, age thirty-seven, carrier for Gerak since the age of eighteen. Gifted with flight, of course, and…hmm, 'the ability to find objects of power'. That must be useful, since it seems you've been running errands for your Creature for decades." He leaned into the screen, not that she could see him. "Did you not notice something about your Creature bond change in the last week or two?"

Seyen scowled. "Sure, the link's seemed a little different. But what's that supposed to mean? I've been given my task to complete, and I was right in the middle of doing it when you shot me down, you fiend. And your housekeeping is terrible."

"No need to be rude," Luca said lightly. "But you should probably know that the Tiger has claimed Gerak's power, including all pledges and carriers. Hence you being called in."

There was a brief silence. "But…I haven't heard the Tiger's call," Seyen said finally. "Gerak would talk in my head.

Sometimes take over my body for a while. But it's been…quiet since he gave me the task."

"I expect you'll need to repledge to the Tiger too, hence the visit," Luca said dismissively. Or the Tiger would kill her. Who knew? "But before that…what exactly had Gerak set you to do?"

Seyen's eyes narrowed, and he knew she was debating whether to answer.

"You can tell me," Luca added silkily, "or the Tiger. It's up to you."

She ducked her head. "He heard about a particular object of power, one so rare as to be mythical. Supposedly it was chipped from the very bedrock of the Other realm when the realms were split millennia ago. The Creatures can't use it, but he's thought of a way-"

"Yes, yes," Luca waved a hand dismissively – but of course she couldn't see that either. "Half of the best objects of power fit that criteria. What is it *called*?"

There was a pause, then she finally answered, "The Eternity Stone."

Luca sucked in a startled breath along with a startled laugh, then choked on the combination. When he'd finally recovered, he said through tears of laughter, "Don't say another word. I'm coming to you."

Leaving the apartment wasn't convenient, but Luca got into his vehicle as quickly as he could and activated all the tech to keep out listening drones or bugs, plus the alter-power wards to keep out any listening Creatures. The dungeon/prisoner control room was right at the other side of the city, and it would take him a good half hour to get there even at top speed, even using all of his council driving privileges, plus a couple of illegal ones. But it would be worth it.

The Eternity Stone. Chaos and perdition – that was a name Luca hadn't heard in some time. The thing was legendary in some circles, meaning that many of those who even knew what it was didn't believe it existed. An object of power that prevented a human from ageing, that gave them endless freedom to move across time and space? That basically gave a human the power of (gasp!) the immortal enemy's timeless People?

The Stone had supposedly shown up regularly in ancient

times, judging by the many folk tales that described ancient gods or goddesses as wearing a black, hourglass-shaped pendant.

Luca would have dismissed those as just stories, except that his own mother Lilith had emphatically told him that the Eternity Stone existed. She'd mentioned it just once, when she'd accidentally drained one of her boytoy conduits and had been melancholy over the waste.

See, Lilith hadn't always needed to link herself to humans so that they could siphon or drain other humans' alter-power on her behalf. For most of her excessively long life, she'd taken what she wanted from any human stupid enough to let her (and most males were that stupid, since she could make herself appear very appealing). A sort of energy vampire, one could say.

But then about four hundred years earlier, when this very region had only been a small rural town full of doorways to the Other realm, she'd literally stumbled across the Stone. As a Halfling, Lilith hadn't been able to travel through time, but she'd used it to move from place to place faster than the blink of an eye. Apparently the Stone had ruined her ability to siphon small amounts of life force/alter-power and she'd ended up violently taking *all* the life force from her victi- *donors*, but knowing her, she wouldn't have cared.

Luca wasn't entirely sure what had happened after that since she'd become vague and unhappy about finishing the story. But it seemed that she'd got into some kind of firefight with the local police force along with some agents of that same immortal enemy, and she'd barely escaped with her life. While her looks (ha!) had quickly recovered, she was never again able to gather power directly.

Hence the boytoy conduits she always used these days. With some help from the Tiger she could now transfer her old abilities to *them*, and in turn, they gathered power on her behalf. But it meant that Lilith, who'd always been a servant to the Tiger, was now more of a slave.

But that wasn't his problem. Right now, what was holding Luca's attention was the fact that Seyen Johannis, AKA Gerak's senior carrier, not only knew where the Stone was rumoured to be, but could use it herself. Hence he could use her to use it…and so forth.

Luca finally reached a complex of multi-storied warehouses

at the edge of the city limits. He docked his vehicle in a small, unnoticeable bay, taking the time to fold it to its smallest setting before leaving it to charge under a VR cover that would make it practically invisible. Then he hurried through not one but three doors sealed with old-fashioned metal locks, the sort that exploded if the wrong people tried to open them. Then down a set of actual stairs (no liftpods here – the tech could be traced) and *then* through a double-sealed door…and into the dungeon.

It was an ancient meat locker, kept at a balmy four degrees Celsius, which of course wouldn't bother an alter-powered carrier like his current guest. Speaking of which, she was clearly still paralysed, and clearly unhappy at her position on the ground.

"So nice of you to come by," Seyen said sarcastically. "Maybe after you've let me go, you could run a cleaning drone or twenty over this place. It's disgusting."

"And maybe after I've killed you, I could leave your body here as a warning to the next person," Luca said mildly, leaning back against the now closed door. "How does that sound?"

She clamped her mouth shut, and he continued, "Or, you could tell me everything you know about the Eternity Stone, and we could make a nice friendly deal that leaves both of us happy. How about that?"

Seyen nodded emphatically. "I'll tell you whatever you want to know, but you need to first swear you'll let me go. That you won't harm me or send me to the Tiger without my explicit and free agreement."

"I swear," Luca said easily.

"A *binding* oath. In blood."

Ugh. She was clearly smarter than Gerak's other Princes, one of whom was a vapid girl with a penchant for spike heels, and the other of whom currently had two broken legs.

"Very well," Luca said testily, because he didn't like binding himself to anyone for any reason. But he quickly cut himself, then her, and made the markings that would prevent either of them from breaking their word. A quick burst of alter-power, and it was done. "Now tell me."

And she did. She rattled through Gerak's instructions, and how he'd heard a rumour of a rumour that the Stone was in the borderlands to the northeast of the city, and then after weeks of searching, she'd confirmed it was true. She'd expected to find it today, then deliver it to a place Gerak had instructed.

Luca listened in silence with his hands behind his back, his mind whirring through all the ways he could best take advantage of this situation. "You have no idea what it does, do you?"

"No…"

He told her, and he saw the realization dawn on her face that she'd almost given away something of unimaginable value. "And it can't enter the Other realm," she echoed, her green eyes wide. "The Creatures can't use it."

"The moment a human uses it, they break almost all Creature connections and ties," Luca told her. "Or so I hear. I'll never be able to use it myself."

Seyen watched him with narrowed eyes. "So you don't want to become the greatest human who ever lived? Hard to believe from someone as narcissistic and violent as you."

"Sounds like you're describing yourself. And no, I don't want to be the greatest *human*, because I'm a Halfling. A half-Halfling, to be precise." He straightened his already immaculate suit jacket, gesturing down at himself. "Luke DeMannard has generously provided his body as a sort of carrier, but in this moment, I'm definitely in the driver's seat."

She nodded. A lot of Creatures would occasionally take over control of their carriers, but for the most part, it was just a human with a funny Creature hat, so to speak. But then Luca's arrangement between Halfling and carrier wasn't at all typical. "But what I want is none of your business," he continued. "Here's the deal. You get the Stone, then bring Jayel Jonnamin DeLuca straight to this spot, one hour from now. I'll need some time to set up. Then you need to leave this time period immediately."

"Where should I go?"

"Wherever you like. Go to a tropical island and eat coconuts, or go to ancient Grecia or Reme and pretend to be a goddess, I really don't care. But don't ever come back here to this time, and don't *ever* tell the Creatures that I was involved in this – past or present. Is that clear?"

Seyen agreed, but Luca added to the binding oath since he couldn't risk being found out on this one. If the Creatures discovered he was trying to work around them, he'd be in trouble. As it was, he'd have to provide the Tiger with the two younger Princes of the Air and call it a day. He also added a nasty little curse, in case Seyen decided to break her word and fail to retrieve Jon. Hopefully it should last even across time and space. It would stop her from flying again (assuming the time travel didn't deal with that) and it would also deal an even worse blow.

"So if you decide to cheat me and don't bring me the boy, your face will melt like hot wax," Luca explained conversationally as he marked the curse into her hairline. "Fair?"

She paled again – showing that he'd chosen the right deterrent by aiming for her looks – but agreed. "How am I supposed to find him? How can I bring him back? You want him alive, right? I've got this soul-drinker…"

Luca glared. "Obviously I want him alive. You can knock him out, but he'd better be in one piece and fully operational. The Stone should allow you to bring him directly, but as for how to find him…" He pulled out a small bag that he'd kept for some time, just in case. "Here's a collection of his fingernail clippings, hair and skin particles from the cleanser unit. Use a basic finding spell – apparently you're good at those."

Seyen grimaced as he tossed the bag to land on her unmoving legs. "Ugh. Fine. Now let me out so I can find the Eternity Stone, will you?"

"Sure." Luca bent down and stuck a tiny syringe right into the skin of her clavicle. She didn't even flinch. "Give it ten minutes and you'll be frolicking like a spring lamb."

Then he got out of there. Ten minutes was also enough time to get some distance between them – since the antidote also had some serious laxative qualities.

And that, Luca thought, was why one should never wear white.

The Mountain of Glass, time irrelevant

Jon led Anne confidently to the top of the inner mountain, right next to the viewing pool he so often watched. "This is the place," he declared. "This is where Amaranthus brought me through."

He'd thought it would be straightforward, but Anne put her hands on her hips and squinted around the small yet scenic space. "I see four gateways. Do you recall what view you beheld upon arriving?"

It had been all dark, of course. But then when the light was finally switched on… "Green. Lots of green." Which meant it really could be any of the gateways, since this place was surrounded by green.

Anne sighed heavily. "Very well. What did it look like, the place you left?"

He tried to visualise the place he'd left. The chapel/temple room…wait, no. It had been just *off* that room. "A hall with a marble floor, and paintings with gilded frames on the walls. Dark blue velvet curtains."

"That should be simple enough to find," Anne said decisively. She grabbed Jon's hand, then promptly vanished into thin air, dragging him after her.

Jon didn't even have time to react. His whole body tingled briefly, then suddenly he was standing at the bottom of a rocky ravine with cold water running over his boots. "What-"

"Z'wounds, 'tis the wrong one," Anne exclaimed. She stepped backwards, dragging him with her. There was another tingle and the water vanished, and they were right back on the inner mountain. "We shall try again."

"Wait," he began, but she'd already moved through the next spot, and her grip on his hand was like iron.

Now forest was all around them, with sunlight shimmering faintly through the high canopy. It was clearly the wrong place…but Chaos, it was glorious. Jon didn't know the last time he'd been surrounded by such verdant natural beauty – if he ever had.

So when Anne moved as if to return to the Mountain, he dug in his feet. "Where are we? This place is beautiful."

"'Tis, rather," Anne allowed. But two seconds later she tugged on his hand. "Come. I know not what kind of people and animals would be around here, and 'tis not the right location."

Jon reluctantly allowed her to pull him back to the Mountain, and then just as she moved towards the third gateway, he dug in his heels again. All this sudden movement was making his head spin. "Do you really move so quickly?!"

"Of course," she answered, sounding surprised. "What sense is there in delaying?"

He tried to explain. "Don't you need to, I don't know,

prepare mentally?"

Anne just stared at him blankly until he finally shrugged. "Oh, alright then. Let's go."

Third time lucky. They stepped through the gateway (that he still couldn't see) and it was immediately clear they were in the right place: a narrow hall with a marble floor. The rows of uncomfortable seats were just three steps away, with a partial wall separating this hall from the main area of the temple-room.

"This is it," Jon said in relief. "This is Chamborde castle."

15

A Strange Detour

Jon had certainly returned to Chamborde castle, and far more easily than he could have imagined. But something seemed out of place.

"You said there were curtains and paintings," Anne pointed out. "I see nothing of the sort."

Neither did he. "It's changed since I was last here. The revolutionaries must have taken them." Or Nadine could have sold them, he supposed, which was the far better option. If the revolutionaries had been *here*, then his friends were in great danger. But how much time had passed?

"Your garb has not changed, though," Anne said. "Mine has." She gestured down at her clothing which had gone from a rich fabric rather like the missing curtains, to a much duller brown dress over a billowing white shirt. She sighed, clearly unhappy about the change.

Maybe some other time Jon would appreciate the subtle alter-power at work, but for today, they were just clothes. "I suppose we'll have to find out how much time has gone by, and if they're dead or alive."

Chaos, it was the last thing he wanted to do, but the question had been preying on his mind for so long. He began to stride down the hall towards the doorway out to the main castle, and Anne skipped to keep up. "Did you hear a noise as we were leaving the Mountain?" she asked.

"No, not at all."

They walked in silence through the door, then into another narrower hall, then into a wide space fully built of clean white

"

marble. In the centre of the otherwise empty room was an open staircase with ornate bannisters of the same white marble. It seemed to spin around and around on itself, like a strand of DNA.

"Clever, isn't it," Jon muttered. "Two staircases winding around each other, and never meeting."

Anne gave him a long look. "What has you so sour? We are here, are we not?"

"We're here, yes. But I've no idea how much time has passed – and I haven't seen a single soul." The place shouldn't be so empty.

But even as he thought that, a young girl swept into the open space. She wore very full skirts in the usual style of this place, with a tiny waistline and a tall, elaborately curled grey wig to complement her powdered and painted face. "Shon-Loo-ee!" she exclaimed, her eyes widening. "Ooo-eyteeay voo?"

Jon brightened. He didn't understand half of what she'd said, but he'd recognised his 'name'…and he knew who she was. One of Nadine's friends, or maybe a younger relative. Who knew? "Bonshoor, Sohfee-Onge," he said in his best Frencine (which really wasn't that good).

Then there was a long silence where the girl smiled at him brightly, and he smiled back, but was unable to ask her what he needed to know.

But then Sohfee-Onge reached forward and looped her arm around his. She rattled off something in Frencine – he recognised the word 'comtesse' which always meant Nadine – then she led him away, with Anne following behind.

They made their way through the castle interior, which seemed to be missing most of its paintings and curtains and indeed, furnishings of any kind. Jon even saw where a large painting must have been removed, since there was a distinct square of brighter wallpaper.

But then they reached one of the larger parlours, and Jon could hear that it was full of people even before they went inside.

Everyone was in there, all chattering away at high speed. Jon blinked at the sight. When he'd last seen them, he'd thought they were beautifully dressed in a really antique sort of way. But now they seemed kind of…grubby. He figured it must be because he'd come straight from the Mountain of Glass, where everything was supernaturally clean, fresh, and alive.

Everyone turned to stare at the new arrivals, then began talking at an even higher pitch for several moments until Nadine got to her feet and silenced everyone with a single exclamation. There was a high-speed exchange between Nadine and Sohfee-Onge with gestures towards Jon. Then they all looked at him, as if he could explain anything.

He wouldn't mind a few explanations himself! How long *had* he been gone?

Things could have been quite difficult from that point, but then Anne proved herself to be useful for more than just finding remnant gateways. It turned out she could also speak any language, which included Frencine circa 1793.

"But how could you have lived in this place," she asked him in his native Mesianth, "and not speak the native tongue? You called these people your friends-"

"They *are* my friends," Jon cut in. "They took me in, looked after me in one of the darkest times in my life, and I owe them everything. But I didn't choose to come here, just as you and Bets didn't choose to leave your own time, and I'll do the little I can to help. Even if they don't understand me."

Anne studied him briefly, then nodded. "Very well. I shall be your spokesperson, and we shall save your friends."

But convincing everyone else turned out to be a challenge. Even with his limited understanding, Jon could see the expressions of disbelief on so many faces...all except Nadine's. Although he didn't see Francois anywhere. The man had taken off a week or two before Jon left this place – Jon didn't know where too – but perhaps he'd never returned.

"I thought it might go this way," he explained to Anne. "Only Nadine and her lover ever believed that I'd been brought here by alter-power, and he disappeared weeks ago. The others all thought I was being paid to play a part."

"Who's Nadine?"

"The comtesse d'Auran," he replied distractedly, still scanning the room for that missing face. "My betrothed." His time in the Mountain had clarified that much at least – that he had been playing a particular role while he'd been here. No wonder the Frencine had looked at him strangely whenever he'd come across Nadine and Francois acting affectionate.

Anne's jaw dropped. "Betrothed?!"

"Oh, come now, I did tell you I was betrothed."

Anne was silent for long enough that he stopped to look at her. Was that an expression of real shock? He quickly explained, "It's not a real betrothal. I did just tell you that she has a lover, didn't I?"

And where *was* Francois? And where were all the curtains?! *How long had he been gone?!*

Two days, Jon eventually found out. To Nadine and the others he'd been gone only two days, although he'd swear that he'd been in the Mountain for weeks, maybe even a couple of months.

After much nagging and awkward conversation, Anne finally translated enough to explain that Francois had gone off to arrange passage to Angland, or something similar, but hadn't been seen since. Nadine seemed distinctly worried by that, but even more by the tales of unrest and executions that had come from the nation's capital. After Jon had left, she'd felt they were no longer protected here either.

"Does she think you a celestial, Jon?" Anne asked in disbelief.

Then he had to explain that yes, he'd shown up suddenly out of thin air, so it seemed Nadine did think he was some sort of heavenly being.

But even though of course Jon was just a human being, Nadine had influenced the others enough that they'd decided to leave. Just the day before, they'd quietly traded the last of the castle valuables in exchange for passage north to a coastal town where they intended to set sail. They'd be leaving with almost nothing but the clothes on their backs, and there was no guarantee they'd even make it to safety.

Ouch.

Once Anne heard their plans, she'd decided they shouldn't take such a risky route. No, instead she thought they should go through a series of remnant gateways until they arrived in a similar time period, but somewhere safer. She'd even found a new gateway conveniently located in a nearby hall, and she was convinced Amaranthus had left it for them. She just needed to check it out.

"Do check it first," Jon agreed. "But don't look for a similar time. We need the *same* time."

Anne just waved a hand dismissively and disappeared through the gateway, leaving Jon alone in the empty hall, and feeling quite useless. For someone who was supposed to perform great deeds, he must be a late bloomer.

But he wasn't alone for long. Almost on cue, as soon as Anne vanished another woman appeared. This one was slightly older – perhaps twenty or so – and quite stunningly beautiful.

Madame Roelle was rumoured to be the mistress of a royal, if he'd understood correctly. He didn't know what brought the dark-haired, green-eyed lady out to this castle in its quiet valley, but she was always on the edge of things, not quite included by the others, yet seeming not at all bothered by her isolation.

Jon had only seen her once or twice, and he didn't like her much. There was something predatory about her, although she couldn't be more than a couple of years older than him.

Today she wore her black hair unpowdered, and a single black jewel hung around her white neck. Her gown was blood-red, matching her smiling lips. She was taller and more strongly built than the other women here, her features perfect in a way that reminded him of the genetically engineered people of his own time rather than the slightly irregular features of the Frencine locals.

Madame Roelle smiled at him and said something in Frencine. And because he was polite, he smiled back awkwardly and replied in the same language. "No Frencine. Sorry."

"I said," she repeated in fluent Mesianth, "we missed you these past few weeks. Where did you go?"

"I thought it was only…two days…" And then Jon's jaw dropped as he realised how she'd spoken. "Chaos. Are you another time traveller, or do you have a gift with languages?"

"Both, of course." She smiled at him cheekily. "But you didn't answer my question. Where did you go two days ago? You simply disappeared."

He didn't want to tell this woman that. Just because she was a traveller didn't mean she was trustworthy. He'd heard enough tales from other travellers in the Garden to know that, as well as his own experience back home.

"Who are you?" he asked instead. "Are you really the king's mistress?"

"That weak-blooded boy? I think not. But I see that you

haven't heard. The king was executed last week, and we've only just received word. There's no doubt that if Chamborde wasn't so isolated the nobles here would already be in the same position."

Jon's heart sank. The king had been executed – the others here would be desperate with fear. "The revolutionaries want to destroy the upper class," he said in dismay. He'd picked up as much from his time in the Mountain of Glass, added to vague memories of historical VR sessions when he'd been a child.

"You know, it's not just the nobles being killed," she continued in a confidential tone. "It's anyone who says or does the wrong thing. There are peasants being executed for hoarding. *Hoarding*, would you believe it? And I hear that the comtesse's common-law husband Francois was supposed to find a way for this lot to escape to Angland – you may have missed that, what with your unfortunate language barrier – but no one's heard from him at all. One would almost think he'd died." Madame Roelle gave a careless shrug. "But that's life, isn't it? And you still didn't answer my question, Jean-Louis."

"You didn't answer mine," he countered.

The two of them stood there, staring almost eye to eye – she was a tall woman – and then she sighed as though giving in. "Very well. I shall tell you…" She ran her hand gently up the side of his face. There was a sudden intense pain, and then he couldn't move. There was something around his neck, something growing tighter and tighter…

"I'm learning," Madame Roelle whispered into his ear even as he silently choked, "that the more mysterious the circumstances, the more likely you'll flood me with alter-power when you die. Nothing personal, you understand."

The edges of Jon's vision began to blur, and he knew he was passing out. Surely when you died you should be able to struggle more, to make an effort? But she was killing him as easily as one would swat a buzzing fly...

Suddenly the world was brilliant white and silver, and someone was screaming. Then the tightness around his neck loosened and Madame Roelle's lovely face so close to his began to change; smooth skin bulging with warty lumps, green eyes turning milky, hair fading away as she *screamed-*

Then she grasped that black jewel at her neck and winked out of sight, leaving Jon blinking from the bright light and with a dreadfully sore throat. There was the faint smell of burning, and Anne's worried voice in his ear. But she was babbling and he couldn't understand a word of it, even as her small hands patted his throat as though she could heal it.

"In Mesianth," he choked out.

But Anne kept babbling unintelligibly, and finally he was able to see enough that it wasn't Anne at all. It was her younger sister; very similar in appearance, but with dark hair and green eyes rather like Madame Roelle's, except filled with worry rather than murderous intent.

"Bets," he managed to say. How had she got here? And what had she done to Madame Roelle?

Somewhere, sometime

Seyen grabbed at her throat, gasping and twitching from the remembered pain. It hadn't been physical pain, but more the sense that her whole body was coming apart in some terrifying way. And now it had stopped, but she could feel…could feel that her face wasn't what it should be.

Her hairline burned, and as she reached up to it with trembling fingers, she remembered the curse that Luca DeMannard had laid on her. Or his Creature had, more like.

What had he said, that if she failed to bring the boy back to him then her face would melt like hot wax? What a horrendous thought. But in the same breath, he'd told her that the moment she used the Eternity Stone to move through time, she'd be free of the Creatures…and him, more or less.

Seyen lowered her hand away from her ruined face, feeling icy cold all of a sudden. When she'd seen the boy after all this searching and had felt the strong alter-power emanating from him, she'd held her soul-drinker and had thought: *what if I don't go back? What if I just kill the boy?*

She hadn't thought Luca could keep the curse going all this way across time. She'd risked everything on it, in fact – and she'd failed.

Argh…he'd also cursed her to lose her flight ability. Seyen took a moment to try to lift off the ground, but felt as heavy as lead. She knew she'd miss that ability, although not the utter dread that came with it.

But where in frozen Hades had that silver fire come from? Seyen shivered, clutching her impossibly powerful necklace closer to herself, and for the first time noticed where she was. In a landscape of pure white with blue shadows, the pale colour stretching out to the distant horizon. A land of ice and snow, and her crimson skirts stood out like a blood stain against the colourless surroundings. There wasn't a person in sight, nor a hint of civilisation.

Good.

Seyen looked down at the shell-like soul-drinker she held in her free hand. Its covering of fine, delicate spellwork was scuffed, and she had no doubt that it would no longer behave exactly as planned. Like a broken VR programme, it was now useless to her. She threw it aside in disgust.

But she knew it wasn't over. Apparently she held the most powerful object in history – and although her face was ruined enough that she didn't dare to look at her reflection, that wouldn't matter for long. She was free of the Creatures.

Free of the Creatures!

Now all she had to do was find a way to recover her power and her looks, and the whole of history would be hers. After all, it wasn't as if Luca could curse her twice. She'd just have to make sure she never returned to any period anywhere near her home time. Ancient eras only – where the Creatures were hidden behind the barrier to the Other, and where the local humans were stupid and superstitious.

Maybe she'd find a nice beach somewhere, after she'd fixed herself up, Seyen mused. Or maybe she'd set herself up as a goddess. Or a queen. Or maybe even both – all it would take was a few more objects of power, and who was more qualified to find such things than herself?

And even though today had been an utterly terrible, ruinous sort of day, Seyen Johannis found herself smiling.

The Tapestry Room, the Mountain of Glass

And so the Eternity Stone began its journey through human history. Strange to think that it began its journey at the end of time – and went backwards – when every mortal to come across it would imagine the exact opposite.

But then mortals tended to be linear thinkers, Amaranthus mused. It was because most of them were trapped within their own timelines, unaware that life could be any different.

He stood alone in front of his vast tapestry, but his attention was on one tiny thread. Black and stained with Creature influence even though there was no longer a direct link, Seyen Johannis's life thread had pulled well away from its place at the very end of the tapestry, and was beginning what would be a monumental journey…at least by human standards.

But Amaranthus just noted the points where her thread would intersect with many others, and carefully wove in the threads of his own People who would be nearby. She'd make her own choices – humans always did – but he'd also give her every chance to make better ones. What she did, was up to her.

Although, he noted, if she was so very determined to collect objects of power, he'd make sure she found the non-lethal ones. So he quietly made a few short movements, rearranging the threads so that the right person would find the soul-drinker she'd just discarded, then moved on.

The Mountain of Glass

It was the most incredible thing, Jon thought later as he sat at the top of the Mountain, outside the viewing pool. Bets had shown up out of nowhere, dressed in a fantastically ornate black and white gown, and babbling a completely unintelligble language.

So, it turned out they did *not* speak the same language while outside the Mountain of Glass. Oh…and someone had just tried to kill him. A Mesianth-speaker, although he didn't know what he'd done to offend them so much.

Anyhow, Anne had shown up from mid-air, having found a route that would lead them all to a safer location in the same time period (or so she said). And there hadn't been an answer as to what had just happened, but it was hardly the time to ask.

So Jon had rubbed at his neck and had done as Anne had asked. They'd led Nadine and Sofee-Onge and a dozen other Frencine nobles (and a dog) through several gateways – through the home of that other time-traveller, Ash – and then to a dirty, grey waterfront city that apparently the Frencine were quite happy to be in. Lunden? Some strange name.

Francois was still missing, of course, so Anne had trotted off through a completely different gateway in order to find him. Jon wasn't sure about the wisdom of that, so he'd just retraced his steps along with Bets until they were back in the Mountain, and able to speak to each other again.

Chaos. What a day..

...And why were people always trying to kill him?!

"What are you thinking about that has you frowning so?"

Jon looked up from where he'd been examining his booted foot, still clad in whatever Nadine had given him when he'd first time-travelled. He smiled up at Bets, who stood hands on hips in front of him, panting a little from the walk since she couldn't fly.

"Just thinking about our trip to the Frencine castle, and how that woman almost killed me," he told her. "She'd been speaking Mesianth, and I wonder if maybe she was from my time, too."

Bets wrinkled her little nose. "The evil queen Seyen Johannis? Did you recognise her from your home?"

"No, but..." Jon wanted to ask more about the 'evil queen' thing, but realised he'd almost said too much. He'd never before told Bets about Erus city-state, because he didn't want her to know about the kind of world it was, how involved the Creatures were...and what kind of miserable, isolated person he'd been. He wanted her to keep her rosy view of him, because it made him feel like maybe, maybe he could be that better person.

"...I didn't recognise her," he finished. "I was just curious since I couldn't even talk to you then, but she didn't have a problem with my language."

Bets seemed to think on that for a while, then shrugged. "Tis most irritating that you and I could not understand each other outside the Mountain, but many other people have a gift with tongues. My sister Anne can speak any language." Her eyes widened. "Mayhap I shall ask for a similar gift, if Amaranthus were to be so generous."

Bets chattered on, and Jon tried to put his mind away from Erus and the Creatures. It was hard, though. Every time he saw his own reflection – or caught a glimpse of his own skin – he'd see that influence.

He was still too pale, and that just represented the power that the White Prince somehow still had over him.

Bets didn't know that, either. She was really sweet, and he was pretty sure she had a soft spot for him. It went both ways, to be honest, but he didn't dare show her his real self.

There was no way she'd understand.

Erus, 3004 AD

"I completely understand," Elspeth said earnestly. "I'm no child, and I've seen much of the world, and much of history. 'Tis full of wicked people, in truth, and I do not blame you for your wariness. I might be a friend – but then I might be a vile, canker-blossom'd fiend instead."

There was no reply, but then she hadn't expected one from her reflection in the education Centre's bathroom mirror.

Elspeth made a face at her shining expression – she did so love the beautiful mirrors and sparkling clean conveniences here – then sighed, for 'twas a conversation she was yet to have with Tarie. She still needed to explain that she was not truly a harmless stolker, but in fact a guardian.

And Tarie did indeed need a guardian. Far too early this morning Elspeth had woken to find Tarie conversing in the foyer of her building with two of those beastly thugs from Centre – the big angry one who'd almost killed Jon when Elspeth had first arrived, and the golden-haired one who always had a sneaky smirky on his sharp-featured face. Elspeth liked him not at all, but then she liked few of the people who'd bothered to speak to Tarie in the time since Elspeth had been her guardian.

They hadn't done Tarie any harm except to deprive her of

sleep, and Elspeth too since she'd been watching unseen from nearby. But just because those two hadn't behaved like villains, did not mean the true villain wasn't out there, watching and waiting for their chance.

Mayhap Elspeth should have continued to pursue the sound of music back at the museum until she found her target. Too late now.

Feeling a little blue – and weary – she left the bathroom and moved quietly into the busy halls of the Centre. Nobody seemed to see her, but nobody ran into her, either. She shuffled along towards the room where she'd last seen Tarie. 'Twas some kind of history lesson, but all the 'history' took place after Elspeth's own time. More of a future lesson for her, mayhap. She'd wondered briefly if she ought to avoid knowledge of such things, but then dismissed the idea. Unless she was to return to Tudar Angland and set herself up as a seer, who would care?

But when Elspeth stepped back into the classroom, 'twas to find Tarie sitting alone in her seat near the back. The other seats were now empty. She sat with her arms outstretched, resting on the table in front of her, and her blank expression was fixed on the now empty screen.

She looked as though she'd fallen asleep with her eyes open.

Elspeth took a seat nearby, just out of sight, and waited.

And waited, and waited. But Tarie never moved. Except for the faint rise and fall of her chest, and an occasional blink, she may as well have been a statue.

Elspeth shuffled closer, studying the other girl in confusion. Something wasn't right…and there was something small and red growing up out of the table top. "Tarie?"

"She can't hear you."

Elspeth jumped at the deep, rough voice, turning to see the big, dark-haired brute who'd tormented Jon. Rokal stood not ten feet away, looking almost as bad as he had this morning. His white suit was clean and his hair somewhat tidier, but he still looked…damaged.

By the rood. He also appeared to be looking right at her.

She stared at him, unable to keep the scowl from her face even as she realised he truly was looking at her, Elspeth, rather than Tarie.

The silence dragged on for several moments until Rokal

broke it. "You can talk, right?"

"I do have the power of speech," Elspeth replied, lifting her chin. "Why do you say Tarie cannot hear me?"

He gestured towards the still-seated girl. "She's in VR. You can tell by the way her eyes are flickering."

How could this brute see *her*? And… "How can she be in VR?" Elspeth blurted out. "This lesson is not meant to have such things." The very room was not set up for individual VR – she'd been watching long enough to know.

He shrugged. "Ask her."

"I cannot, for you say she cannot hear me!"

"Then you'll have to wait, because it's rude to drag people out of VR," Rokal countered. His gaze flickered over her, but it seemed curious rather than cruel. "Even though she probably shouldn't be in there right now. She's not even standing on a VR panel."

Elspeth sniffed. "What happens if there's an emergency, a fire or some such thing? One must be able to awake others in such a situation."

The young man studied her, his eyes narrowed. "One must," he agreed in an odd tone. He slid into the seat next to Tarie, then leaned in and said sharply, "*Knock knock.*"

Then he leaned back and waited. Elspeth waited too, but after a good minute had passed with no response, she raised her eyebrows. "What was that?"

"It's supposed to tell her someone wants to talk to her, but I guess she doesn't want to talk back. How badly do you need to speak to her?"

Elspeth didn't really need to speak to Tarie. "The more burning question is, why do *you* want to speak to her, Rokal?"

Rokal blinked at her. "My name is Max, and I asked you first." His eyes narrowed. "I've seen you before, haven't I?"

Yes, in the borderlands museum where she'd inadvertently (very well, somewhat advertently) set him on fire. Not because she'd thought he was any direct danger to Tarie, but because he was truly dreadful, and she'd hoped to reduce the Creature influence on him. So when he'd got into the path of the cleansing flame, she had not tried to avoid him. "Er…no?"

"Yes, I'm sure I have," he persisted, leaning forward and setting one hand on the table next to Tarie. "Are you a student?

Where-"

Silvery flame shot from Elspeth's hand and poured over Rokal's...Max's. But instead of running up his arm – and therefore giving her a chance to flee or steal Tarie away – it simply fizzled on his skin. He squinted down at it. "What's this?"

By the saints, he could see that too! But before Elspeth could respond, the tiny, sputtering flame on his hand sparked and jumped across to Tarie's brown arm where it rested against the tabletop. The small flame briefly became a palm-sized inferno, centred somewhere around her elbow.

Elspeth probably ought to have done something about it, but she found herself staring along with the brute as something tiny and spiked fell off Tarie's skin to land on the tabletop. 'Twas blackened from the flame, which had turned to an almost purple hue, then died out.

"Uh oh," Rokal/Max said, staring at the thing.

Elspeth knew not what 'twas, except that the cleansing flame had targeted it – and Tarie still had not awoken. "What is this?" she asked, echoing his earlier question.

He paused, turning to look around the room as if afraid of being watched. "I'll tell you," he said quietly, "but not in here."

"I shan't leave Tarie behind!" Elspeth snapped. "I am her...friend, and I will look after her."

"I'll take her." Rokal/Max moved forward, bending down as if he'd pick Tarie up.

On instinct, Elspeth's hands lit up with that same silvery flame. He froze, his eyes fixed on her hands.

He didn't burn.

The quiet thought cut through Elspeth's panic and even a little through her anger. The cleansing flame hadn't burned Rokal/Max today, even though it had made him scream a few days earlier at the museum. That meant there was now nothing to burn. Nothing Creature-based, anyway.

Furthermore, he definitely had not seen her back at the museum, although he saw her today. She recalled how he'd run straight past her. So something had indeed changed.

Elspeth slowly lowered her hands. "I like you not at all," she told him bluntly. "You may remove her to somewhere else – but do not leave my sight."

He nodded brusquely then bent to pick Tarie up. Even

though the girl was half his size – she had not yet regrown to her previous height – he let out a grunt of exertion. "Oof. She's heavier than she looks."

"Verily she is," Elspeth agreed aggressively. That was a compliment, yes?

And even though it felt so wrong to have her enemy touching the one she guarded, she followed him as he carried the board-stiff Tarie out of the room.

16
Whiter than Snow

The Mountain of Glass, time irrelevant

Jon stood at the top of the inner mountain, watching the images flashing in the viewing pool again. They'd been different lately. Instead of showing his past or that of his friends, he saw…an event. Something happening in his future, in Erus, that sent a shockwave rippling through the city and the Other realm. Or *would* send a shockwave…et cetera.

He still didn't know exactly what was going to happen, but he knew it was to do with why the Creatures hated him.

And worse still – obviously – he had to go back to the future to do it.

That was why when the lights seemed to dim around Jon, he wasn't surprised to see he'd moved locations. Now he seemed to be in a darkened room, but this time he could just make out the walls of the room far in the distance, like some kind of black and white pattern just visible in the dimness. He could see Amaranthus too, not far away.

But still he asked aloud. "Did you need me for something?"

In the next moment Amaranthus was right next to him- oh, nope, Jon realised he'd moved instead.

It's time, his host said.

And even though Jon knew the answer to that too, he still asked. Maybe it was a delaying tactic. "Time for what?"

Time to go home.

Even though Jon had known it was coming, hearing the words – in his head – hit him like a blow. He found himself trembling. "Oh…are you sure?"

Amaranthus looked at him, his dark eyes solemn and wise. *Is there a problem?*

A problem? Why would there be a problem?! "You could tell me what it is that I'm meant to do," Jon burst out, his words spilling out too fast as he jittered in place. "You say I'm protected, but you could give me a little more info since it doesn't *feel* like I'm protected and I've had a lot of bad things happen. You could…" …send someone else instead, please. Let him stay here forever.

There was a long silence, so long that Jon's shoulders slumped in defeat. "I'm scared," he said, finally admitting the truth. "I'm always scared, even before I pledged to the White Prince. Scared that something terrible will happen, or that nothing at all will happen, and that everything's pointless. I feel like…I feel like fear rules me, and I can't see how I can do whatever I need to do, or even live a decent life when I'm scared all the time."

Perhaps Jon had said something Amaranthus had been waiting to hear, because Amaranthus smiled. "Fear incapacitates," he said aloud. "It's one of the main tactics the Creatures use to stop my people doing what I've asked them to, and from fulfilling their hopes and dreams. But…"

He led Jon closer to what he now saw was an enormous wall – some kind of sewing thing, made of all these teeny tiny threads all woven together in a tangled mess. "…when you know where you fit, how valued and visible you are, fear has no true power."

Then he took Jon's hand and lifted it up to a tiny white thread peeking out of a patch of black. *This is you. See?*

Jon didn't see at first, no. But the longer he touched that thread – a thread he realised represented his own life with all the others it intersected with – the more he saw the truth of what Amaranthus had said.

He wasn't overlooked. He wasn't forgotten. He was accepted and valued by the people who mattered – and the one who mattered most of all, who was standing right here next to him.

He had a purpose, and he was going to achieve it.

And the colour…the white that stained his skin didn't even matter. It wasn't about the outward marks of his previous bad choices. When it came to his life's thread, his old stained self had been washed whiter than snow. There wasn't even a hint of Creature influence or long-term damage, not anymore.

Now if only he could feel that way inside. "I'm still nervous," Jon admitted. "But I'll go. Can I say goodbye to a few people first? And…uh, can I have a weapon please?"

Amaranthus looked at him. *You want a shining sword and a shield? Something that will make you invulnerable so you can take out the enemy from a mile away?*

Yes, that sounded rather nice.

Don't forget that you're as protected as you've always been, and you haven't even begun to achieve what you are going to achieve. But let me tell you about authority and the value of knowing someone's true name…

Jon leaned in eagerly, feeling as if he was about to have the secrets of the universe revealed to him.

When you know a Creature's true name, you know their true nature. And when you know their true nature and you hold my authority…you can send them any way you like.

Jon frowned, furrowing his brow. "Uh…" he said aloud. "Do I hold your authority?"

You will.

"OK…thanks." He supposed.

Shortly after that Jon found himself back in the garden, bug-eyed and noticeably tense. Funny how he could in theory have everything he needed, and still feel overwhelmed.

But at least he could say goodbye to Bets first.

But some hours after *that,* he'd wandered around what felt like the entire garden without finding the girl. He didn't even have enough energy to feel annoyed about it – after all, the longer he took to say goodbye, the more delayed his return would be.

Time to go home.

Ugh.

"Hello, Jon! Are you full of excitement to see all your old friends?"

The voice was young, female and cheerful, and for a moment he straightened, thinking he'd found Bets. But when he turned, it was to see Bets' redheaded sister instead. He scowled. "Was that sarcasm?"

"Most certainly not!" Anne replied brightly. "Would I use sarcasm?"

Before he could agree that yes, she would, she carried on,

"So mayhap there are troublesome elements to your return. But indeed, you *shall* enjoy seeing your old friends, for you are not the same as you were before. Besides, you shall have one of us within reach at all times, even if you do not see us."

For a moment Jon thought of Bets, but immediately dismissed the idea. She was small and sweet and helpless, no matter how she thought of herself, or that she now had some 'fire' gift that only she could see. Would such a thing help her against even one carrier determined to pull her into a Creature temple? Unlikely. For her own safety, Bets must *never* go to his time, he swore to himself.

But to Anne he replied, "Is that so? Thank you, I guess. But I'm actually looking for…"

"Elspeth?" Having pronounced Bets' impossible-to-say full name, Anne waved a hand vaguely to her left. "Head to your favourite peach tree, and you shall find her soon enough."

"Thanks." Jon gave the redhead a wary look over his shoulder, then headed over to the spot she'd mentioned. Anne had changed significantly since he'd first met her; even more so than he had himself. He'd changed on the outside, but she'd changed on the inside ever since becoming immortal. She was now much, much easier to get on with. Mostly.

Jon located the peach tree that had somehow become his and Bets' 'favourite' to sit under, then plopped down in the grass in its shade, trying to think of the right words to say when she arrived. How did you tell a friend that you'd probably never see them again?

But he'd been there less than a minute when he saw her wander into sight as if she didn't have a care in the world. She wore a simple cream-coloured tunic typical of this location, with a loose, long skirt similar to her own home time, but it somehow looked wonderful with her dark brown hair and light green eyes.

She'd never even seen him fly, he realised. She never would.

"Where have you been?" he asked, his mood dropping even lower at the thought of not seeing her again. "I went looking, and finally had to ask your sister. I couldn't find you anywhere."

Bets just blinked at him, her mouth opening as if she wanted to speak, but then closing again. She didn't answer, so he got up and walked over to her. This close, it was clear how small she was – she barely reached his shoulder.

"I have to go home, Bets, and soon," he said, his chest aching a little. "It's...well, I can't say, but I have to go. But I didn't want to go without saying goodbye."

Her face fell noticeably. "Simplicity said you'd gone back to where you came from."

"You mean the inner mountain? I went back to talk to Amaranthus about something, then when I returned, you'd gone. Where did *you* go?"

Bets got this funny look on her face, but Jon couldn't place why. After a long silence she replied, "Oh, here and there. When do you leave?"

"Um...now." Unfortunately.

"Oh." Her eyes glimmered a little as if with unshed tears, and she ducked her head. "Then I wish you luck, my friend. You do not need any...assistance?"

"Amaranthus has that covered. There are a few people back home that will help with what needs helping with... I think." Jon sighed, wishing once more that he didn't have to return, or that he wasn't *him*. "Bets..."

"Yes?" She looked up at him wide-eyed.

What could he say? *You're so sweet, Bets, but if you knew what I was really like, you wouldn't like me at all. You'd be happy I was gone. If you knew where I was really from...*

"Thank you," he said stiltedly." You've been a good friend."

Should he hug her? He should hug her, right? Jon leaned forward to do just that, but stopped himself at the last moment. He wasn't in the habit of hugging friends, and she'd never indicated that she'd want him to do so. He quickly stood and casually scrubbed a hand through his hair. "So, I guess that's goodbye."

"Goodbye," she echoed.

Ugh. So awkward. But with nothing more to say, Jon quickly turned and strode towards the gateway that Amaranthus had just created specially to send him home. Something about the original remnant gateway having just been removed? Who knew. Who *cared*.

He was going back to Erus Province, 3004 AD. Ready or not.

The gateway back home looked rather like the one he'd first arrived through: an orange-lit crevice in the rock. But unlike that entry gateway, this one was vertical and was set in the high rock wall that surrounded the Garden.

Jon stood at a distance, trying to gather enough courage to step through. *I don't live here,* he reminded himself. *I always had to go home eventually. This was a…holiday.*

A surprise holiday with an abrupt ending. He realised he didn't know how much time had passed since he'd left Erus. He'd have to come up with an excuse for his absence. Huh. 'Other realm' would probably be enough-

Phomph. As if it had grown tired of waiting, the gateway suddenly sent out a wave of warm, orange light that enveloped Jon. For a moment he felt like he was inside a hot, dry cloud, then it faded away and left a faint chill behind, leaving him blinking in the dark.

Dark. Oh, Chaos. He was back.

Jon took in a long, deep breath, looking around warily with his hands outstretched, ready to move. He could barely make out his surroundings, but he knew it must be the Other realm back home. Nowhere else did he get that odd fuzzy, covered sort of feeling, mixed with a mild sense of dread. Surely it was the Power Performance temple he'd come in through, but he couldn't even feel the ground underfoot…

A moment later Jon realised that there *was* no ground underfoot – because he was in the air. High, high, high up in the air.

He squeaked in surprise, flailing his arms and legs in reaction, then managed to calm down when the usual fear didn't come flooding in. He had to double-check that the ground was far beneath him, but…

"I'm flying," he breathed, "and I'm not afraid."

He really had changed!

Jon stretched out his arms as a superhero would, shooting to the left, then the right, then as high as he could manage in this almost pitch-black environment. But then the euphoria wore off, and he realised that while he could now fly freely, he was still in a Creature temple, or in the dangerous part of the Other that was well outside the Mountain of Glass.

He focused his attention on finding the exit. Since he could hardly see the ground, he had to drop rather lower. But soon enough he spotted a faint line running below him, and closer up it became clear that it was the path. But he hadn't followed it for long before he came up to a large shape looming against the darkest grey sky. It was a building.

Jon blinked at it, feeling a growing sense of familiarity. Then realisation dawned.

Although he was in the Other realm, this wasn't the Power Performance temple at all.

It was the White Prince's temple.

The marked boy had returned to their atmosphere as quietly as he'd left. He might have gone unnoticed except that various Creatures were looking out for his return, and his mark glowed so brightly he could be sensed from miles away.

All the better to avoid him.

In the darkest wilds of the Other, the White Prince felt the connection with his lone Prince of the Air reappear. It was just the tiniest, faintest thread of power – not enough to influence through any longer, but enough to build on if he wanted to do so.

He clenched and unclenched his bony hands thoughtfully as chaotic thoughts ran through his head, clashing and echoing until they formed an idea.

The next step.

Erus city-state

He's back.

Luca glanced at the text that appeared on his wrist, careful not to let his expression change in reaction. Who knew who'd be watching? The message had come from his mother of course, since she was the only other person who was as invested in Jayel Jonnamin's whereabouts as he was. There were plenty of interested Creatures in the Other realm, but no one else out here in the normal realm.

Luca sat in silence, uncertain of how to feel about that since he'd clearly instructed Gerak's Prince of the Air to fetch the boy, and the woman had clearly failed since the appointed hour had come and gone without any sign of him. As for Seyen Johannis, there'd been not a glimpse of her either in the last few days. Luca liked to think that if she'd failed him then his curse would have removed her looks and her flight ability in one go, even across time and space.

But *had* she failed? Maybe she was responsible for Jayel's return, but just to the wrong location and time? Such things did happen.

He didn't know what to think.

Finally, Luca sent a thoughtful reply. *Does he look different? More…enemy?*

The response came at once. *Bright as the sun. The Creatures won't go near him, but don't forget what the Tiger ordered you to do.*

Of course he wouldn't forget! But if no one else would go near the boy, Luca was hardly likely to go rushing off in their place, was he? *Let's see how things play out,* he suggested. *We've got bigger things occupying our attention now anyway.*

Lilith's reply came after a delay that meant she was either distracted or irritated by what he'd said. Judging by her words, it was probably the second option. *You're young, son. Don't misjudge what is important and what isn't.*

Only among immortals was eighty-five considered young. This body he used was only half that, but almost middle-aged. Luca set his communicator to 'absent', then turned to focus on what possibly wasn't more important, but was rather something he could control today.

Rehearsing his speech for the quiet takeover of Memrys city-state. The Tiger had disarmed Gerak some time earlier – literally, it appeared – so at this point, merging the governments of the two city-states was just a formality.

Elspeth followed Rokal/Max out of the Centre, her lips tight and her gaze firmly fixed on the board-stiff Tarie. Although it seemed against everything Elspeth had expected of him, she had allowed the big brute to carry Tarie out of the Centre to her own tiny vehicle.

But it quickly became clear he would never fit inside that vehicle, and they sorely needed to have a conversation about Tarie's condition, so Elspeth graciously allowed him to carry her for the brisk twenty-minute walk back to their apartment. After all, he already knew where Tarie lived.

"Floor forty-two," Elspeth ordered, her tone less imperious than it had been back at the Centre. As they'd walked here, and Rokal/Max had silently done everything she'd requested, she'd begun to regret her earlier sharpness. All they'd done so far was exchange names, though.

"You won't be able to get into her apartment if she's unconscious," he pointed out as they piled into the tiny lifting room. "The scanner locks are set that way to stop forced entries."

"We shall go to my quarters instead."

He raised his eyebrows. "I thought there were only two apartments on each floor. Tarie's and…Jon's."

Elspeth gave him a suspicious look. "I vow you know far too much about everyone's living quarters." She'd heard as much from this morning's early conversation. But still, 'twas with a little satisfaction that she led Rokal/Max out of the lifting room, down the hall to her own, overlooked door. "In here."

He carried Tarie in and set her on the largest couch, then looked around with clear interest. "I didn't even know this room was here."

"Of course you did not," Elspeth said with a dismissive wave of her hand. "But I did not bring you here to discuss my lodgings. Tell me, why will Tarie not awake? And what was that wicked little spiked dart in her arm?"

Rokal/Max sat down on the couch next to Tarie, causing it to sink in the middle. Tarie's prone body slumped against his shoulder, and he gently pushed her back upright. "I'll tell you, if you tell me what you did to me. I know you did *something*, because I don't feel the same."

Elspeth gulped. In truth she'd done him a favour, so he ought not to be angry...surely? "Very well," she replied demurely, seating herself on the opposite side of the room. "But you first. You said you know what ails Tarie, but couldn't explain at Centre."

He didn't even argue. "Tarie's been shot with a VR dart. It's a direct access point to a preprogrammed VR session, but they're illegal because of course no one chooses to shoot themselves like that...and because depending on how they're set up, it could be really hard for the person to escape. The dart substance is really toxic too. Even a few specks in water makes people susceptible to mind control."

"Escape... Mind control..." Elspeth looked at the girl in question, a pang of dismay twisting her belly as she tried to make sense of his words. She'd watched many people use VR, but as she'd never used it herself, she lacked complete understanding. "Do you mean escape from the...VR session?"

Rokal/Max gave her a long look – but then of course she had not yet explained who she was, nor where she had come from. "How much do you know about VR?"

"Er...'tis like a vivid dream or vision that you enter apurpose," she hedged, "but one that others may share with you." She nodded, feeling quite pleased with her summary. Mayhap he would not think her a stranger to these lands after all. "Carry on."

His dark eyebrows shot right up. "That's accurate enough, I suppose. Most of the time VR sessions have a set finishing point. Usually you just need to think about leaving to get out, or say an exit word like 'evacuate'. But sessions that have strong security might need you to leave by an actual doorway inside the programme. And at worst, you get sessions where there are no exit words or exit locations. You're just stuck till someone lets you out."

He paused, glancing across at Tarie who still sat stock-still next to him on the couch. "Scammers use things like this to get money. They make people think they're in real life and steal their details, or people can be held hostage until they or their families pay for them to get out. In the past, terrorists have used this type of thing on groups, or politicians on their rivals. People aren't much good when they're not eating or drinking or even sleeping properly."

Elspeth followed his gaze to Tarie, her heart sinking. "So if she does not awake, she may…die?" She swallowed with an audible *gulp*. If so, 'twas fair to say she'd failed in her duties.

Rokal/Max hesitated. "She'd have to have some real enemies if she's stuck in that sort of VR session. Maybe it was just a prank. Maybe just wait and see if she comes out on her own."

But Elspeth thought of how the VR dart had burned, showing the presence of Creature influence, and she could not believe Tarie's state was anything but malicious. The dart had been removed, and still Tarie was trapped! "And if she does not?"

Again he hesitated. "There are some universal entry points to VR in case of situations like these. Like at the council offices, but they're not easy to get to. You'd have to get permission from someone high-up. Or…" He met Elspeth's eyes. "…you could go through Elsewhise."

Some time earlier

Tarie jolted awake, realising that the lecture hall around her was now empty of people. She must have fallen asleep. Hopefully no one had noticed…and hopefully the tutor wasn't offended if they had.

She moved to pick up her bag, intending to leave straightaway, but couldn't find it. The floor around her feet was also empty.

Chaos. Best case scenario, someone had taken it by mistake. Just as likely, someone had taken it for a prank. She glanced down at her wrist comm so she could report the possible theft – or at least check the time – but realised that her wrist was now bare of any ornamentation.

How in chaos had someone managed to take her comm as well as her bag?!

Muttering to herself, Tarie stomped her way out towards the exit. She'd have to report this the old-fashioned way – in person. If she was lucky, her things might have been handed in already.

Smack.

Tarie hit an unseen barrier full-force and went bouncing

backwards, almost falling over. She caught her balance and stared at the empty doorway in confusion, rubbing her arms from the shock rather than any physical pain. Then she moved forward again, but this time reached one hand out in front of her cautiously.

Her fingertips tapped against what appeared to be an invisible surface, as hard as plastimetal. It only took a few more moments to work out what had happened. Someone had really pranked her – they'd hidden the door to make it look like it was open so she'd walk right into it.

Thanks a lot, thickheads. She'd bet it was Rokal or Orla, or maybe Gavriel if he didn't feel like pretending to be nice. She *hoped* it was one of them, since she didn't want any more sort-of-enemies than she already had.

Except now she couldn't find the door's exit panel either…

Tarie swore under her breath, then when that wasn't satisfying enough, swore aloud. Or tried to: she couldn't hear her own voice.

Chaos. Chaos. *CHAOS!*

What was going on?!

Tarie spun around, studying the empty room as if it would give her a clue as to what had happened. Then the slight shimmer in the air connected with some vague memory.

Could she be…in VR?

The more she thought about it, the more it made sense. This *felt* like VR, although she surely hadn't brought herself here.

It's illegal to put someone in VR without their permission, she tried to say, but of course no sound emerged. With more force she tried to say, *EVACUATE!*

Nope.

EMERGENCY EVACUATE!

That should have been a shout, but nope. Silence.

Tarie tried using sign language for 'evacuate' as well, since signs and lip-reading were meant to work in every programme. But no matter what she did, she was still in that empty, silent lecture room, its open doorway seeming to mock her inability to move through it.

Now furious, Tarie began speaking the Words in what would have been full volume had she been able to make a sound. She slammed her hands against the door's unseen barrier, then began moving around the room, patting the walls as she did so. If she'd been tricked, then maybe the real door was somewhere nearby, just hidden from sight too.

But as she moved, something strange began to happen. The walls began to fade and change where she touched them, the flat lines turning into something shiny and rounded. The chairs and desks began to disappear around her too. She could hear the faint sound of some tune, like a music playlist had been left on 1% volume.

Then soon enough she wasn't in a classroom at all. Instead she stood on a wooden floor inside what looked like an enormous glass dome, its closed, rounded top arching above her head, just beyond the reach of her outstretched fingers.

Something thin and brown appeared on the floor beside Tarie's feet. She quickly realised it was a stick, the dry sort she'd seen in VR programmes where you pretended you were camping in the forest and you'd make campfires and roast sweetballs or chocopuffs. (Those programmes just made her hungry in real life, so they were best avoided.)

Then another stick appeared, and another, until the floor was covered in dry brown sticks piled all around her as high as her knees.

Still muttering silent Words at high speed, Tarie looked out at the shining barrier now surrounding her. She could still hear that faint music, and then a dark shadow appeared just beyond the barrier. It looked vaguely like a person, but it moved too fast for her to focus on.

Hmm. This was starting to feel like more than just a prank.

Then writing began to appear on the barrier.

Jon hovered in the air above the building where he'd pledged to the White Prince, seeing the dark outlines below him as hard evidence that something was there. Evidence of one of his greatest fears.

He was in the Other realm. In the freakin' Other, right above one of the worst possible places he could be. Dread began to creep over him, making his body tingle, but he forcibly took his mind back to the last conversation with Amaranthus.

You're as protected as you've always been, Amaranthus had said. *You haven't even begun to achieve what you're going to achieve... When you know a Creature's true name, you know their true nature. And when you know their true nature and you hold my authority...you can send them any way you like.*

You haven't come this far to be taken out now, Jon told himself fervently. *Be brave.*

Just then he recalled an odd situation that had happened earlier, before he'd pledged to the White Prince. He'd gone to see Domitian out of desperation, but the Creature had refused to appear. Until Jon had called him...

He thought back to what had happened. It really had felt like Domitian had come because Jon had asked him to, but Jon had dismissed that idea at the time. What kind of crazy person thought they could control a Creature? But even as Domitian had insulted Jon, hadn't he said something like 'let me go'?

Jon hovered in the air of the Other, his mind whirling. Yes, he remembered. Domitian *had* said that, and he'd only vanished when Jon said he didn't need him anymore.

Chaos and perdition. Now *that* was a miracle. Amaranthus had said that Jon *would* have his authority...but maybe he already had it, to a point.

Chaos. *Chaos.* Now he just needed to know the White Prince's true name, Jon thought a little wildly, and he could send that beast away too! (Cue hysterical laughter.)

But whether or not Jon had controlled Domitian, he knew that it wasn't over yet. He was going to do something important...apparently. So even though he was here in this place, with a malevolent Creature that would probably eat him if it could, he was going to be OK. He could feel that fuzzy, invisible blanket which confirmed his layer of protection was in place, so even the White Prince couldn't touch him.

Anyway, Amaranthus could have made the gate to anywhere. But it led to here, so Jon figured it was for a reason.

Jon looked around one more time, a little amazed in spite of the circumstances that he could make out anything in this darkness. To his right he could see the horizon in the distance: deepest grey sky against charcoal black ground. Back to his left was the glowing outline of the exit back to the normal realm, that would lead to that run-down, depressing temple entrance in a run-down, depressing part of Erus city. Everything near that was a little easier to see, as though the exit itself was the sole light source.

Just then a tiny flicker of light caught his eye. It was on the ground just past the White Prince's lair, like someone had dropped a lit-up wrist comm and the thing was still working. Had it been there last time?

Jon glanced at the exit once again, but his curiosity was greater than his desire to leave the Other. Next moment he was hovering right over the tiny light. This close he could see that the object was half hidden under a piece of rubble. He kicked the flat stone away, exposing a bright ring of light.

It wasn't a wrist comm. It was something else.

He held a hand over it, testing its warmth, then when it felt safe, picked the thing up. It was a thin circle of what he at first thought was metal, but then when he held it, proved to be lightweight and bendable. Its circumference was slightly larger than his outstretched fingers, like it would sit nicely on his head. It felt warm and tingly in his hand, and when he touched it, the last of his fear left. Suddenly he didn't care that he was back in his own time – not when he held this object.

The thin shape was marked with some kind of design that seemed to flow and move the closer Jon stared at it. He squinted and the shapes changed until he could see one word, repeated over and over around the circumference of the object.

AMARANTHUS-AMARANTHUS-AMARANTHUS-AMARANTHUS...

A moment later Jon realised why the object seemed so familiar. He'd seen this very circle – *circlet* – many times before, in memories and visions displayed in the viewing pool at the Mountain of Glass.

His birth mother had held it, speaking the name inscribed without realising who it represented. *Amaranthus, my son will be loved and valued. Amaranthus, my son will make a difference in Erus. Amaranthus, my son will be a world-changer... Vitally important... A history-maker.*

She hadn't seemed to lack confidence, he remembered thinking. He'd also briefly wondered what had happened to the circlet since the visions had shown her disappearing, although not what had happened to her.

Jon looked around the dark, desolate landscape once again, a weight sitting heavily in his stomach.

Maia had been here once…and then she'd gone.

At least now he knew what must have happened to her.

17

A New Pledge

Elspeth looked down at her friend who sat motionless on the couch, then at their foe turned friend. "I do not think Tarie will awake on her own," she said sombrely. "Tell me of this Elsewhise, if you will."

Rokal/Max hesitated, then looked down at Tarie too, his expression solemn. His legs were still held in those odd contraptions that meant he hovered rather than walked, and they stuck out awkwardly from the couch where he sat. "If anyone finds out I told you, I'll be in real trouble."

"You have bigger troubles than that, I trow. But I will not reveal who told me."

He nodded, breathing slowly out of his nose. Then he told her.

Elsewhise was a place on the borderlands. A walled town that existed in the Other but also somehow overlapped VR. VR was held in the mind, but it seemed that the Other realm was very close to the mind too. And if you knew how, you could walk straight from the normal realm into someone else's VR session...or into different Creature temples all over the world.

Indeed, 'twas a terrifying, incredible revelation.

"Elsewhise is strictly controlled by the Creatures," Rokal/ Max explained, "but it's also secret. Domitian didn't run it even though the entry point I always took was in Erus province, near the borderlands museum. It's run by Audaline instead."

Elspeth blinked, trying to match the name with a particular Creature, and trying to work out what seemed so familiar to her.

"Wait...a museum?" she burst out. "The one that fell down recently?" Or strictly speaking, that she'd accidentally set on fire

260

and caused to fall down.

If it hadn't wanted to be set on fire, she thought, it oughtn't to have had so many Creature conduits inside, should it?

"Yes. How did you know?" Rokal/Max frowned, his eyes narrowing. "Now I've answered your questions, you answer mine. You were at the museum, weren't you? You did something to me."

Elspeth sat back in her chair, folding her hands demurely in her lap. "I confess nothing."

"But I just answered all your questions, and I don't even know your name!"

Her lips tightened, and she shook her head, jiggling in her seat with discomfort. 'Twas *hard* to be a tight-lipped guardian! "Oooh…very well! My name is Elspeth of Covington although you may call me Bets since I expect you'll struggle with the 'th'…and I burned the evil off you. You no longer have a Creature connection."

There was a brief pause where he just stared at her and she added defensively, "You really ought to thank me, even if you do not know it-"

"Thank you," he cut in abruptly.

Elspeth closed her mouth mid-rant. "Truly?!"

"Yes. *Thank you.*" Rokal/Max shook his head, his dark eyes wide. "I don't know how you did that, and I'm sure it wasn't legal. But it's like a ton of weight has dropped off my back. I feel so empty – terrible at first, actually – but my head is clear for the first time in years. I almost feel like me again."

She studied him where he sat next to the still-frozen Tarie. He still appeared a big brute of a man next to the much smaller girl, but something in his expression and posture was very different from how it had been mere days earlier. Indeed, even if Elspeth had not known of the break in his Creature's influence, she might have suspected something was different by the way he held himself.

He looked dreadful, she had to admit. Terribly ill-groomed. But he also no longer held that cruelty and apathy in his expression that he had every other time she'd seen him...and he wished to be called by another name. Max. Mayhap she should have the good grace to call him by that new name too.

"Am I no longer pledged?" he asked. "Because I can still fly.

It might even be a bit easier now."

He looked around, then did something with his comm that made a nearby wall shimmer and change into a wide VR screen reflecting their own appearances. And there was Elspeth, small and brown-haired and with a surprisingly fierce expression...and a bright, blobby mark on her forehead. In stark contrast, his was entirely blank. Clearly, he was not pledged to beastly Gerak any longer.

Elspeth pondered the question. "Indeed I would say you are no longer pledged, although the flight gift appears to continue independently of the allegiance to the Creature. But you must repledge yourself to someone greater, or I vow you'll end up in a worse position than before."

Rokal...*Max* frowned, his shoulders hunching. "Who's greater than Gerak? Audaline?"

"There is only one," Elspeth told him decisively. "Amaranthus, the Eternal One. He'll protect you, and he never turns down a pledge, no matter one's history."

Max glanced down at Tarie again. "I might be in trouble with the Creatures if I go to anyone else."

"You'll be in trouble with the Creatures regardless," she countered. "Do you truly wish to return to Gerak?"

He shook his head. "No. No, I don't. And if you tell me your Amant...Amarantus... *Eternal One* will accept me even now, then I'll pledge to him. Where's his temple?" Elspeth's eyes widened. She hadn't expected such a prompt response. "Ah...here, I suppose." A little more confidently she added, "He does not require entrance to the Other, for he is not restricted as the Creatures are. All you need to do is pledge your allegiance to him here. He'll know."

"Uh...alright." Max shuffled a little, looking as uncomfortable as a six-foot-seven man could. Then one stammered vow later he'd pledged his allegiance to a new non-Creature 'Amarantus' (the 'th' sound clearly being difficult regardless of who was being named) and had rescinded his pledge to Gerak just for good measure. Then he turned back to the VR wall and stared at his new reflection. "Huh. The symbol looks like a shiny blob of paint."

Elspeth stood next to him, feeling child-sized next to this Goliath. But indeed, Max now sported a bright splattered mark on his forehead where his Creature symbol had once been. It was almost identical to Elspeth's own. She was a little disgruntled to note that they were similar in brightness – she thought hers really ought to be brighter what with her greater experience and so forth.

But all in all, a good day's work. Now Rokal was Max and no longer in the Creatures' pocket, she really ought to treat him like an ally, not an enemy. 'Twould be no easy feat to forget some of his recent misdeeds, though.

And there was still Tarie to deal with…

Just then the little room's outer door opened. Both Elspeth and Max turned in response, and in strolled Fylax in his human form.

"You're back!" Elspeth exclaimed in delight. "I have not seen you since-"

Fylax's shaggy white eyebrows rose and his lips curved in a smile. He nodded.

Elspeth leapt away from the reflective wall, all other thoughts forgotten. "Jon has returned!"

She ran for the door.

Jon flew home slowly, the circlet tucked safely inside a security pocket in his jacket. The slowness wasn't from fear this time, but instead to give him time to make sense of everything and to get used to being back. He'd only been gone two months, but it felt far longer.

Ironically, only five days had passed here in 3004 AD, if the date on the clocktower he just passed had been right. Not even one full week for people to miss him. *He* hadn't missed this chaotic, dirty, manmade place and most of its inhabitants.

Anni might have missed him, he acknowledged. But that just made him think of Maia again, and the fact he'd have to tell Anni about her sister's fate.

Death by Creature. Probably. It was an ugly way to go, but he felt oddly relieved at knowing what had likely happened to his birth mother. He hadn't been abandoned.

The only thing he didn't understand was why the circlet

hadn't kept Maia safe. He now knew enough about the Mountain and alter-power to know the White Prince couldn't have taken it from her. Had he tricked her into giving it up?

The idea of her suffering made Jon furious. Honestly, if he could kill a Creature, he'd do it in an instant. Malicious, vile, violent monsters. The universe would be far better without them.

But that was an impossible request because Creatures were immortal. It was just as unlikely he'd ever find out what had really happened to her, not unless he got back to the Mountain of Glass.

That, however, was possible.

By the time Jon came into the familiar streets of his neighbourhood then into his apartment's liftpod, his anger and confusion had ebbed enough for him to realise one thing. He'd needed closure about Maia's fate...and now he had it, somewhat. He just didn't know what to do next.

"Jon."

Anni wouldn't be too surprised when he told her, Jon reasoned as he reached his front door. She'd suspected foul play for years too. It would surely be good for her to know what had happened rather than just wonder...

Just then there was a light tap on his arm. *"Jon."*

Still distracted, Jon looked down to see a smiling face. Smiling at *him*. A girl who looked like Bets...but who couldn't be Bets, his mind told him, since she was *here*.

"Jon," the girl who looked like Bets said again, showing that she sounded like Bets too. But she was speaking Mesianth even as her smile faltered and she asked, "Do you not know me?"

He just stared at her, his mind finally short-circuiting and coming up blank. He wanted to smile back – because it was Bets – but...

The Bets-girl's smile vanished completely and she stepped away, lowering her hand from his sleeve. She wore a modern hooded jacket in a very dull shade of grey, loose black troushoes, and now an expression of disappointment. "My apologies," she said in a small voice. "I thought you were...someone else."

She turned as if to walk away but suddenly Jon's hand was on her shoulder, stopping her. "Wait," he said slowly, his gaze never leaving her pale face. "Why...what...how...?"

"Where and when, 'tis more the issue," she joked, but her expression was still wary. "Must I introduce myself?"

"What…*Bets!*" Jon suddenly exploded. "What are you doing here!?"

Bets – his sweet, innocent little friend from the Mountain of Glass – was *here.* Here, in his tainted, Creature-controlled home era.

This felt like the worst thing in the world…and he couldn't handle it. Not now. Not on top of his birth mother's death and the expectations that apparently rested on him.

Bets' eyes widened. "Er…visiting?"

"Are you crazy?!" he burst out. "This is the last place I want you to be! It's not safe for someone like you! There's a reason I never told you about it!" He dragged his hands through his hair, turning to pace across the hall in agitation then back again. "Bets, you have to go back to the Mountain. However you got here, you need to go straight back, for your own safety."

"But-"

"I can't believe you're even here," Jon ranted on. In this moment it felt like he'd just found a kitten in the middle of a highway. "I just said goodbye what, two hours ago? What was Amaranthus thinking, letting you come here?" He turned to stare at her accusingly. "Did you even ask if you could come or did you just waltz on in through an unguarded remnant gateway?"

There was a long silence as Bets stared up at him, her green eyes wounded and her arms wrapped around herself. "I thought you'd be pleased to see me," she said in a small voice. "I see I was wrong."

Suddenly feeling guilty, Jon's shoulders slumped. He put a hand over his eyes, his anger leaving him. It had come from panic anyway, not true anger. "I would be pleased to see you, at the Mountain. Not *here*, Bets. Here-"

He'd literally just come from the Other where his birth mother had apparently died, even though she'd been armed with what could have been an incredible weapon. And if *she* couldn't protect herself, what good could little Bets do? She was a dear friend…but she knew the friendly Jon from the Mountain, not the Pledgeless Wonder/freaky former carrier. He sure didn't want her meeting that Jon either.

The real Jon, complete with the horrible history that he was trying so hard to leave behind.

"…Here might be my birthplace," he continued carefully,

"but it is not a good place for you. For anyone, really. So you need to go back to the Mountain at once. You don't even have to tell anyone what you've done. Show me where the entrance is, and I'll come visit when I can."

He brightened at the thought. That was quite a good idea, wasn't it?

Bets was now staring at her feet, clad in those trouser-shoe combinations that were so popular here. When he stopped talking, she looked up at him. Her eyes were still wide, but her lips were set in a tight line.

"I did not come here of my own accord," she explained in a steady, rather slow manner as if talking to a child. "I was sent here by Amaranthus to guard your neighbour Tarie, who was in dire need of such care. You may also notice I am speaking your language, which implies I did not steal my way here. And while I wished to see you, I understood that the time was not right." She let out a long, slow breath. "So no, I shall not be returning to the Mountain yet."

Jon blinked at her. She *had* been speaking Mesianth…and in that moment he remembered that previously they hadn't been able to communicate outside the Mountain of Glass. Obviously. "Guard? You mean…Tarie was guarding you?"

"I mean I'm guarding her!" Bets shouted suddenly, her hands fisting at her sides. "Me! *I* am the guardian, not some foolish child who needs to be shuffled off to a safe corner lest she accidentally walk off a cliff!" She glared at him, her lips set in a straight, white-edged line. "Trust Amaranthus if you will not trust me, O great Prince of the Air."

Then she spun around and stomped down the hall, away from the liftpods.

That's a dead end, Jon thought. But he didn't speak. He was too stunned that his sweet, earnest little friend had shouted at him – he hadn't known she *could* shout. That she could be anything except sweet and earnest, in truth.

Then it dawned on him that she'd called him 'Prince of the Air'. He'd introduced himself that way when they'd first met weeks or months earlier, but hadn't mentioned it since. Either she'd remembered, or…

"Bets," he called after her, feeling cold inside. "When did you arrive in this time?"

She stopped at a blank section of wall, turning to look back at him. "Three weeks ago."

Then she stepped right into the wall and vanished.

Tarie stood inside the giant clear cage, staring in dismay at the barrier that held her in. She watched as scrolling text appeared row after row across the clear surface, the words in some unknown script.

Then she spotted her name and realised it was Mesianth after all. She was just seeing it backwards, as though it was being written from the other side of the barrier. She set herself to making sense of it…then wished she hadn't.

Let the cage's captive be cursed with insanity, it read. *Let pain fill their mind and every thought until they become worthless for anything else. Let their body be forgotten and useless until they are as good as dead.*

Well, that wasn't very nice!

It's just VR, she told herself, even as her hands clenched into fists at her sides. *VR isn't real, so nothing in here can really hurt me.*

And VR wouldn't usually lock her in, for that matter. Now she just needed to get out.

Through the barrier the dark shadow was more visible now, as if it had stopped moving once the awful curse had been scribbled in full. Its silhouette darkened against the slightly fogged barrier, then two slender, long-fingered hands appeared around chest height.

She could almost…almost make out a face, but it didn't look human. More like a twisted artist had made a figure from charcoal and hadn't bothered completing it. Or more like whoever had stuck her in this awful prank had given themselves a mask of sorts, while somehow removing her voice.

Tarie stomped up to the edge of the barrier, pushing her way through piles of crunchy dry sticks, then pointed her finger aggressively at the figure. She still remembered a bit of universal sign language from early schooling and what she didn't remember, she made up for with forceful hand movements. *This is illegal!* she told them. *Let me out of here right now!*

The shadow's hand moved on the other side of the barrier, and this time the written word was readable from her side. *No.*

She'd sort of assumed they would say that, but couldn't help herself from trying anyway.

Why are you doing this?!

The shadow's hand moved again. *Because you're too hard to kill,* the writing read. *But if I do this right, it won't matter if you're still breathing on the outside.*

Tarie froze, her heart sinking. Suddenly this didn't just seem like a vicious prank by someone at Centre. It seemed infinitely more serious, and she was horribly reminded of Gavriel's comment when she'd first started Centre. He'd told her someone was following her. She'd thought at first that it was Nesbit, then when the girl had turned out to be more of an oddity than a threat, had forgotten about it. More important things had been happening.

Slowly she signed, *Tell me you're joking.*

But instead of responding, the shadow moved away, almost out of sight. For a moment there almost seemed to be two faint shadows behind the barrier.

Then the dry sticks at her feet burst into flame.

Jon gaped as Bets vanished into the wall at the end of the hall. It looked like he'd found the remnant gateway…and it was so close!

Just then the door to 42-G slid open and Anni was standing there, her eyes wide. "Jay-Jon!" she exclaimed. "You've come to visit…and you've gone back to normal."

Come to visit, as if this wasn't his home. As if he hadn't been away for months, but rather for a few days. His throat suddenly feeling choked, Jon smiled at her. "Hi, Ma. Can I come in?"

"Of course!"

He followed her inside to the kitchen as she continued, sounding a little nervous, "This is still your home, Jay-Jon, and you're welcome here any time. I know you're a Prince of the Air now, and that your father has a much larger house-"

"Ma." Jon set a hand on her arm, slowing her down, then smiled again when she turned to look at him. "I missed you."

Anni ducked her head, her face momentarily screwing up with distress. "I missed you too, darling." There was a pause then she added, "But you could have messaged me back any time. I know you're worried about the…the *curse* thing, but surely you can get a handle on it, if you've been able to get your appearance back to normal." She gestured briefly at his face.

Jon tried to make sense of her comments as she went straight to the nutri-dispenser. "Ma, if you've messaged me, I haven't been able to answer. I lost my wrist comm in the Other on the day of the move." He paused, then decided to be open about his experience. It had practically shaped him. "Actually, I've been lost in the Other since then, sort of. I only got out just now. It feels like…it feels like it's been a lot longer than a week, and a lot has happened."

There was a long silence as his mother stood unmoving at the machine, its gentle *whirr-blurp* the only sound in the room. Finally she asked, "You weren't ignoring me?"

"No!" Jon moved to stand next to her, putting one arm around her shoulders. "I know I had been…have been, whatever…difficult. But you raised me better than that." He grimaced. "I'll have to get a new comm. I'm just surprised Luca didn't tell you that I hadn't been at his place either."

There was another silence. "Luca told me you were with him."

Jon swore under his breath. "Not unless someone has been impersonating me, and I don't think they'd get past his new house's identity scanners." And it was unlikely Luca had 'accidentally' made Anni think Jon was ignoring her.

Anni let out a long breath of relief and sat down at the breakfast bar, ignoring the cold drink now ready behind her. "Why would he do that?" But her tone was sad rather than genuinely curious, as though Luca's motives didn't need explaining. He was Luca; ergo he was an ass.

Jon sat opposite her, feeling like his mind held a whole world full of new information that he could impart, but unsure of what he should say. What he could say.

"Luca is not Luke," he said finally. "He's Luke plus whatever secretive Creature Luke pledged to. Maybe more the second than the first. You know that, right?"

"I know." She smiled up at him, a small curve of the lips that nonetheless seemed genuine. "And you're different too, aren't you? I was worried when I heard shouting in the hall, but I see that something has changed for the better."

Shouting in the hall...Bets! Jon sat bolt upright as he remembered who he'd been shouting with...at. Hard to believe he'd been distracted enough to forget that. "I ran into someone I didn't expect to see," he explained. "Someone I have to speak to. And..." He thought of the circlet tucked into his jacket, but couldn't bring himself to mention it yet. "...Do you have a spare wrist comm I can use?"

Anni slipped hers off. "Use this one. I've been using it since I've been off work, but now they've taken me back on, I get to use my work one again."

"Say what?"

She beamed, her smile lighting up her face. "A lot has happened for me too, Jay-Jon, especially in these last few days. I got my job back! It turned out my supervisor had been selling goods on the side and he'd been the one to blame me, but he must have got sloppy and got caught, because yesterday they called me back in. I've been given his position!"

"That's great, Ma," Jon said sincerely, feeling the weight of that particular guilt lift off him. Could it be a coincidence that she got it back after his link was severed...mostly severed with the White Prince? "That's the best news I've heard all day."

"And...er...well...*I'vebeenseeingourneigbourTarrenandI'vechan gedmyallegiance!*"

Jon blinked at her. "Pardon? What was that about Tarren?"

"Oh, never mind that," Anni said, but her cheeks were reddening. "Let me show you the change."

Then she took back the wrist comm and tapped at it briefly before holding it up to her face. Her skin shimmered and smoothed out under what was clearly the VR scan setting, her hair becoming a brighter shade of auburn. But instead of the triangular symbol of her Creature Sarassius, her forehead now displayed what looked like a drippy, bright gold thumbprint.

It didn't take Jon long to recognise the symbol. He'd seen it once before on Tarie, what felt like months ago, and he'd never thought he'd be lucky enough to see it on Anni. "What a wonderful coincidence," he said, beaming. He took the wrist comm and moved it to shine on his own face. "Me too."

Not long later, Jon stood at the end of his hallway. He'd walked the hall thousands of times but had rarely walked past his door, because there wasn't meant to be anything there except a blank wall. Apparently, there was also an entrance to the Other realm.

He paused where he'd seen Bets disappear, but didn't try to walk through. Instead he cautiously reached a hand up to the wall, but instead of passing through, it just hit the textured wallprint. "Bets?" he called quietly. "Are you there?"

Barely a few moments passed before the wall rippled. Then she appeared at the height of his chest...but only her face and folded arms showed through the wall. The rest of her disappeared behind it, like a glitching VR scene.

"Argh! I mean...hi." Jon took a big step backwards, trying to encourage her to move further out – since that was really disturbing – but she didn't move. Her eyes were red, he noticed.

"Have you come to scold me more?" she asked in a dull voice. "If so, I shall not listen."

He swallowed. He'd clearly misstepped earlier, and badly. "No. I came to apologise for how I reacted before. I'm *scared* for you to be here, Bets. But if Amaranthus sent you, then I have no right to say otherwise. And I shouldn't have shouted at you. I'm sorry."

She muttered something that sounded like 'Amarantus', then her eyes grew wider, some of the dullness leaving them. "No, you should not have. And he *did* send me. But 'tis not just fear for my safety that makes you unhappy I am here, is it? There is more."

Jon looked away from her knowing gaze, down to where the tips of her shoes also appeared through the textured wallprint. It looked ridiculous, but he wasn't amused. Shame warred with anger and guilt inside him. He hadn't wanted her to come here because it wasn't safe...and because he hadn't wanted her to see him at his worst. From the little she'd said, it sounded as if she already had, which made him angry. And ashamed, then angrier because he felt ashamed and didn't want to.

"I don't know how much you saw," he began haltingly. "But my life here...it hasn't been good. And I didn't want you to see that...*me.*"

So much went unsaid. He couldn't say more, it was too difficult.

But suddenly he felt two small arms tight around his middle, and Bets' dark head was tucked under his chin. She was giving him the warmest hug he'd ever received from a non-family member while she muttered something into his chest.

A sudden wash of warmth ran through Jon. She couldn't be entirely disgusted by him if she was holding him like this, right?

He slowly put his hands down on her back, finally returning the hug. "I can't hear what you're saying," he admitted. "But I hope it's not too bad?"

Bets looked up from his chest area, her green eyes fierce. "'Twas not your fault, Jon. Not at all!"

Oh. So she *had* seen something bad? But she was still holding him rather warmly...

"And you oughtn't have gone to that horrid Creature," she continued fervently, "but you did not know any better. Yet now you do, yes?"

"Yes...? Yes! I mean, I do!"

Bets put her head back against his chest. "Good," she said firmly. "And I set the brute on fire for you, you know."

"Er...what?"

Elspeth froze in the pleasant yet rather improper embrace, realising what she had admitted to. "I would not have thought you minded," she hedged. "Not after the cruelty he showed you. Anyway, 'twas not true flame, merely the cleansing flame from the Mountain."

"Rokal?" Jon asked, as if still trying to make sense of her words. He leaned his upper body away from her so he could look her in the face. "You set *Rokal* on fire? For me?"

"Of course." In hindsight she had to admit that that she'd targeted Rokal just a teeny, tiny bit at the museum, and there was a clear reason for it. Flame here, flame there...oops, that was a man... "I also tried to trip him several times as he could not see me, but 'twas not at all satisfying. As he could fly, he never fell on his face."

Jon was staring down at her as if he'd never seen her before.

"I should probably be ashamed of my behaviour," she admitted in a small voice. "Especially if you are displeased by it. But I could not bear to see you harmed in such a way without fitting recompense. You must understand."

Jon's eyes – now a solid brown rather than the lighter shade she'd first come to know him with – crinkled into what was a genuine, broad smile. She hadn't seen as such since those early days at the Mountain. "Bets, if you can overlook whatever you saw, that I can definitely overlook whatever you think you've done."

What Elspeth *thought* she'd done? She frowned a little at Jon's wording, but dismissed it. Ten minutes ago she'd thought he would never speak to her again. Now…well, 'twas much more pleasant than embracing her sister, it must be said.

Knowing she really ought to release Jon, but unwilling to do so, Elspeth leaned into his warm, firm chest and let out a happy sigh. "I thought you were far above my station," she admitted. "But now I see that in our own ways, we are equals. I am free to love you, Jon."

She felt him go tense even as she realised which words had spilled from her foolish lips.

"Eh…what?" he asked.

Her eyes widened and she frantically tried to cover her newest misstep, forcing herself to casually stand upright and put a relaxed expression on her face. "Pardon?"

"You just said…"

Elspeth widened her eyes, acting innocent. "Yes?"

Jon frowned, looking absolutely baffled. "Is there something wrong with your translation?" he asked hesitantly. "I know you're not used to speaking Mesianth." He pronounced the last sound like 't' rather than 'th' – 'twas only recently she'd seen the name of his language written down and realised it had a silent 'h'.

In that moment she couldn't read his expression as to whether he was pleased or dismayed by her profession of love. She'd blurted out the truth like a fool, but now 'twas out there she did not wish to take it back. So she lifted her chin, thinking of how Anne might have dealt with such a situation.

"Nothing is wrong with my translation," she said firmly. "I said what I meant. And even if you do not feel the same way, you will always be my friend regardless."

"Oh." But Jon was staring down at her with an unreadable expression on his face.

Just then, Elspeth remembered rather a larger problem just behind her. Literally and figuratively. "By the by, I must tell you what has happened to your neighbour Tarie…"

She quickly described the events of the day, explaining that Max had told her about the wicked VR darts and the possible ways to get around them, including this mysterious place called Elsewhise.

"Max?" Jon asked as she led him through the wall. It seemed to have created a barrier for any who had not been granted entry (or who she had not brought with her). "I don't know anyone called Max."

Elspeth froze just inside the room, realising that she hadn't told him the *other* rather important thing regarding his worst enemy, who was now his former worst enemy. But fortunately the inner room appeared to be empty except for Tarie's small, sturdy figure on the couch…her head and shoulders now covered in trailing vines. "Oh! Where did this come from?"

"The greenery?"

"Mm. Before we spoke, there was none at all." Elspeth crouched in front of Tarie, pulling away the delicate, pale green tendrils that seemed to originate at her lips, their colour tinged with red. 'Twas not blood, but rather the tint of the plant itself, which had barely any roots to speak of. But Elspeth couldn't push away the sense of unease she felt at seeing them. "I wonder…"

Elspeth let out a gentle burst of flame straight at the vines, but they did not blacken or even wither. Still, somehow the release of the flame made her feel better. She blasted a little more, then for the sake of it, cleansed Tarie's entire prone body, the couch and the leftover plate on the low table. Nothing burned, but the sense of unease left.

"An improvement," she said aloud. "But you see our problem, yes?"

The flames leapt from stick to stick, sending up a roaring wall of fire far faster than Tarie could have imagined. She stumbled backwards to the centre of the prison, her lips and tongue forming silent words at a speed driven by panic.

It was VR. Just VR, she reminded herself frantically. Nothing could hurt her in here!

But there was a reason people lived their lives in VR, she knew. Because while it wasn't really real – not really truly – it was real enough to convince your brain. Real enough to enjoy a full meal or a skilled massage.

It was also real enough to set off her pain sensors, and Tarie could feel the heat of the flame from here. Soon it would surround her, and there was nowhere to go.

Now the curse made sense, and in that moment she felt sheer terror. She looked across the leaping orange flame and straight at the shadow person, and for just a second she saw two of them again. Two shadowy outlines, both staring straight at her with those unfathomable expressions on their blank, false faces. Then the flame rose too high, too fierce, blocking her view.

But then as suddenly as the flame had begun, her vision filled with silver. A wave of something shimmering washed over her and her surroundings, and suddenly the fire was gone. Instead, the wooden floor was simply covered in the ashy remains of what might have been sticks. The slightly fogged barrier of her prison cleared, leaving faint scratches of what had been a truly nasty inscribed curse.

Was that meant to happen?

The two shadow-people were visible again, and Tarie stared at them for long enough to see their reactions. Purely by body language, she'd say they were confused…and angry. One of them moved forward and began running their hand over the barrier again, rewriting the same text as before in superspeed.

But they seemed slower than before, or perhaps it was just that this time she knew what they were doing. When the dry sticks reappeared – kindling for the fire, Tarie realised – and the flame came a moment later, she wasn't surprised. She just kept silently speaking what would have been the Words if she could have heard them – punctuated by the occasional hopeful 'Emergency evacuate!' – and then when the silver wash came a second time, she knew for sure she was protected, even in here. Whatever the shadows had wanted to do to her, they had failed.

Now if only she could get out.

But then Tarie saw that the second silver wash had done more than just put out the fire. Now, through the clearer substance of the barrier, she could plainly see who stood on the other side.

18
Enemies

Jon watched as Bets moved her small, pale hand over Tarie's darker face, a sort of shimmering, quick-moving mist trailing over her skin as she did so. This was progress, he figured, that he could now see what must be the 'cleansing flame'. He hadn't seen anything before…or maybe he just hadn't been looking hard enough.

"Why do you keep doing that?" he asked. "Nothing is burning."

"I do not know, in truth," Bets replied pensively. "But it makes me feel better."

He couldn't argue with that.

Just then a figure emerged from the door at the other side of the room. It was a hulking dark-haired young man who seemed familiar.

"Fylax, that was incredible," the young man said in an equally familiar voice, looking over his shoulder to someone who was out of sight. "A mountain inside a mountain? Incredible! And that was the best water I've ever drunk. And I don't even like water!"

Jon froze, staring at the guy. Hadn't he just gone through this weird, familiar situation with a girl who looked like Bets? Except that girl *was* Bets.

And this…this *guy* looked like a dishevelled, enthusiastic version of Jon's most hated, vile worst enemy. He even wore braces on both legs like Rokal did, although they didn't seem to be doing much at the moment.

But he was here. In a room that was surely part of the Mountain of Glass, acting like he'd just drunk water from the inner mountain. Acting like he belonged here, in a place that should have been safe for Jon. In Jon's building.

Jon's.

A buzzing sound filled Jon's ears and he couldn't focus on anything except the face of that guy – *that guy* – who looked like Rokal but couldn't be, because why would Rokal be HERE, and he was thinking of how this felt horribly familiar but way, WAY WORSE-

"Jon?" Bets said nervously from beside him. "This is…Max."

"Rokal's twin, I presume," Jon heard himself saying, his voice seeming to be coming from some distance away. "Rokal being the evil twin."

Max glanced at Bets, his smile faltering. (That in itself didn't fit with Rokal, who never smiled, Jon realised. He only smirked or sneered.) "I can leave, if you like."

"Not yet. We need your aid to free Tarie," Bets countered, but her gaze flickered between Jon and the other guy, then settled on Jon again. "I have discovered something new. My cleansing flame…can break the bond between a carrier and their Creature."

It took a few moments for Jon to realise what Bets was saying.

This *was* Rokal – apparently minus Creature.

"If that's true, then I know a fiend or two who'd benefit from your flame," he found himself saying. "It's a trick. It's got to be, because you can't trust him a fraction. He'll stab you in the back." He shot a narrow-eyed glare at the taller man. "Or drag you to the top of a flagpole."

Rokal/Max blinked at him and his lips tightened, but he didn't argue.

That…was also not like Rokal.

"Yeah, you did that," Jon persisted, moving closer to his enemy. Maybe it was their surroundings – or this guy's clear differences – or Jon's own recent history, but his usual fear had been replaced by fury. "Do you remember? Because I do. That was the day I decided I'd rather risk death than be at your mercy again."

Rokal/Max finally spoke, and his voice was different too. Rougher. "Yeah, I remember. You went to the White Prince, then came back as different as I'd been. With a new name too, and a new attitude." He glanced down at his legs, still in their hovercasts. "But it looks like we've both repledged now."

Jon stared at him. He wouldn't have dared talk like this with the usual Rokal, but this wasn't the usual. "As simple as that. We're both repledged. No apology for the years of misery you and the others caused?"

The taller guy opened his mouth then closed it again. Then he shrugged a shoulder. "I'm…sorry? I don't know why I did the things that I did."

Well, that was a weak, useless half-apology, wasn't it?

Jon would have set off again, his fury seeming like a ceaseless flood, but he felt a soft touch on his arm.

Bets. "Do not forget Tarie," she said softly. "You can have this discussion after she's safe, yes?"

It took a concerted effort to turn away from Rokal/Max and back to his neighbour, who still sat stock-still on the couch. "She's supposedly stuck in some unsanctioned VR session, right?" He glanced narrow-eyed at his enemy at the back of the room. "And it was *Max* who told you this. How do you know it's true?"

Bets gave him a look that seemed slightly irritated, but from behind her Rokal/Max said, "Take a look for yourself."

So Jon did. He tried all the tricks he knew to get someone out of VR, then a couple which were meant to forcibly pull people out in case of an emergency. None worked. He even grabbed Tarie's shoulder and shook her gently.

Jon stared down at his neighbour in resignation. He still wasn't convinced of Rokal/Max's trustworthiness, not even slightly, but he couldn't deny the obvious. Tarie really did appear to be stuck in VR. Rokal/Max *might* have had something to do with it – but considering he'd just come straight from the Mountain of Glass, it was unlikely.

But Jon still wouldn't be turning his back on the man.

"This Elsewhise place sounds dangerous," he said finally. "There must be some other way to get to Tarie. The original dart isn't working?"

Bets pointed to a tiny, blackened shape sitting on the central low table. "I killed it with fire." She cocked her head. "Must entry pieces always be in the form of darts? Recently I had an odd experience in the foyer of this very building. I'd bent down to pick up some sort of metal object from the floor, and in the next moment I found myself in quite a different location." She shrugged. "A town full of mirrors covered in red and green cloths, and people with strange symbols on their foreheads, and even a Creature or two. 'Twas the oddest thing, for I could still feel the true ground underfoot, but could see only the town. So I set the object afire at once, and soon enough I returned home."

The two men stared at her for some time. She only mentioned this *now*?

"I really ought to have known better," Bets added, sounding like her usual earnest self. "I could feel the alter-power emanating from the object well before I touched it. 'Twas curiosity, mayhap, or boredom."

"Could the object have been a dagger?" Rokal/Max asked. "I know of a few dagger entry pieces, but they're carefully watched. You can't have just anyone going into Elsewhise. Except you just described Elsewhise, and what are the chances of that?"

"Mayhap 'twas a dagger," Bets replied thoughtfully. "But in truth I cannot say, for its condition was very poor."

"It could be a coincidence," Jon offered. "But I doubt it. It's probably a set-up or an opportunity." An idea sprang to mind. "Hold up. I'll see if I can still access the foyer's video on my comm." Technically he'd borrowed it from Anni, but comms would always key themselves to whoever held them. That way, if your comm was stolen then the thief didn't get access to your personal information, only their own.

Most building occupants could see the past and present views of the shared foyer as a sort of security measure. Jon rarely bothered using it, but... "Here we go," he said triumphantly. "This is the view of our dropbox, so hopefully you were in sight of it, Bets, when you found the dagger...or whatever it was."

A moment later a slightly faded image of the foyer sprang into the air, half life-size and birds-eye view. Jon adjusted it for a better view, then scrolled through the last few weeks of footage at high speed, setting the video to search for the rather odd terms of 'picking something up off the floor'.

It turned out that a lot of people dropped things and picked them up again in that area. Some of them probably should have been abandoned, Jon decided, screwing up his nose at a child from another level who dropped their sweetpop on the ground then after retrieving it, popped it straight back in their mouth.

"Bets, I can't find you," he said in frustration, skipping randomly from scene to scene. "Can you tell me exactly when you found the dagger…er, object?"

"'Tis most likely my unnoticeability causing problems," Bets replied, her tone apologetic. "Most people do not see me in person either, unless I wish them to."

"Hey, look at that," Rokal/Max said abruptly, pointing. "There's some video missing. See how the plant wall just triples in size suddenly?"

Jon skimmed back and forth over the footage, watching as the foyer's scenic plant wall, typically full of undersized ferns and pot plants, grew incredibly lush in mere moments. Frowning, he slowed it down to only twice normal speed and replayed it. This time he noticed a familiar figure opening the dropbox next to his own apartment's.

It was Tarie. She seemed to be emptying rubbish out of the box and into the nearby waste compactor. Just after she'd moved in, Jon figured. But then she took out something small and undistinguishable from the dropbox, and for several minutes she didn't move at all. Not a fraction, except for her lips which were moving high-speed.

Jon turned up the audio to full volume but couldn't hear more than an unintelligible muttering. And in the background, the plants grew faster than anything he'd ever seen before…

Then suddenly Tarie shook her head as if coming awake. She dropped the object into the waste compactor and rushed away, out of sight of the video.

"That's interesting," Jon murmured. As finding Bets on the vid seemed to be a lost cause, he changed the search settings to focus on that area. Sure enough, that evening the trashbot trundled by to empty the foyer's waste compactor. It trundled off again with its tidy, dense block of trash, but a small, battered-looking object tumbled out to land on the floor.

"That's it!" Bets said excitedly. "I wonder if 'tis the same as Tarie touched?"

The more they watched, the more likely it looked. It also looked increasingly likely that the object was in fact an entry piece – and if so, Jon decided to take it as a stroke of luck, most likely orchestrated by Amaranthus, who did love his 'coincidences'.

They still couldn't find Bets on the recording – but they *did* find a smear of colour that flickered in and out of the vid over a period of minutes. And they *did* see what looked like a crumpled metal shape on the floor, almost hidden under the plant wall, well away from where the trashbot had dropped it. And then yet another figure bent down and picked the thing up – but this time they took it away.

"Hey," Rokal/Max said slowly. "Isn't that…"

"Luca," Jon finished flatly. "Luca has the entry piece."

"It'll be at Luca's new house," Jon said several minutes later, when the three of them had decided that chasing the entry piece was probably a better choice than trying to get into Elsewhise through the borderlands entrance. "He cleared out all his valuables when he moved out."

"Wyet says Luca keeps all his valuables in his office in the city," Rokal/Max offered. He'd been mostly quiet until now, surely well aware of Jon's disdain. "He says that Luca should have moved everything into the chairman's office now Tybalt's dead, but he still uses this other smaller live-in office. You know, the sort with a bed and facilities. So Wyet thinks that Luca must keep valuables there instead."

Jon stared at him. He called his father by his first name? A moment later Jon realised he did the exact same thing, and it wasn't a sign of closeness. "Even if it is, it'll be locked up," he pointed out. "I can't just walk in and say 'I'm Luca's son, let me into his office'. He'd have to have already granted me access, and that'll never happen."

Especially not now Jon knew exactly how the Creatures disliked him. Luke had seemed fond enough of his only child, but Luca was…such a thickhead. It *had* to be the Creature making him like that.

Bets sat on the couch next to Tarie, periodically running her hand over the girl's face and head, brushing aside any greenery that appeared. She seemed pensive, her fine brows low over her eyes. "I could go," she offered. "I can go most places, as long as a door or a window is unlocked. Most people do not notice me, as you know."

"A door or window won't be unlocked," Jon countered. He sighed, leaning back against his seat. "I've got a better chance, although not much of one."

"You're still a Prince of the Air," Rokal/Max said. He met Jon's eyes for the first time. "If you can fly, you can get away with all kinds of bad behaviour. Just ask the security to let you in and act as if you expect it."

Jon raised an eyebrow. "I know you're saying that from experience."

"Yep."

It hadn't been a question, but still. Jon had decided to have a temporary truce with this new Rokal/Max, as in he'd put aside his loathing of Rokal until a better time. Then, he'd feel free to hate away.

Jon looked once more at Tarie, who most certainly wasn't alright. "We could try the official route," he murmured. "Take her to someone who deals with this kind of mishap. Chaos, even tell her *father*."

Bets and Rokal/Max gave him identical appalled looks.

"You do know that the government is effectively run by the Creatures, yes?" Bets said in a tone that suggested he was slow in the head. "What do you think will happen to an Amaranthus-follower who's in such a vulnerable state? I'd vow we'd never see her again."

Jon raised an eyebrow. "How long have you been here again?" Because she seemed to know this place far too well.

"She's right," Rokal/Max interjected. "People like Tarie- like us now, we're better to keep quiet and keep away from anything official. Maybe there are other ways to deal with this. Maybe it'll sort itself out in time…" He frowned. "But I don't think so."

They discussed their options for a while longer before deciding on the least awful one. Jon would quietly drop by Luca's office, see if by some extreme miracle he could access that knife(ish) entry piece, then see if by some second extreme miracle, they could access Elsewhise and Tarie's VR session, *and* get her out of it.

And if they couldn't? They'd bring in Anni and Tarren, and see if their parents had any better ideas.

Jon moved towards the door, feeling a sense of peace even as he was reluctant to leave. He told himself it was because he couldn't leave Tarie and Bets alone with the new-and-weird Rokal/Max, but that didn't sit right.

It was that this little room felt a bit like the Mountain of Glass, and it felt like peace and safety.

"Wait!" Bets leapt to her feet and rushed towards him, her

hand outstretched.

Jon looked down at her dumbly. He briefly wondered if he was meant to shake her hand – or kiss it, as the Frencine did back in the eighteenth century – but then realised she was offering him something. It looked like a seashell on a looped cord, covered in a glossy brown varnish. "What's this?"

"'Tis a safekeeper," she explained. "A sort of…pocket universe, I understand. In truth I know little about it, except that it holds a clean sort of alter-power now, do you not think?"

Jon slowly took the object, and he knew exactly what she meant. Maybe before his visit to the Mountain he wouldn't have understood, but now he could feel the warm tingle of power emanating from the thing. Rather like when he entered a temple doorway, but without the sense of spine-chilling dread that came with that. "A pocket universe," he mused. That sounded vaguely familiar. He figured she'd got it from the Mountain, because where else? "How do you use it?"

"I believe you order objects into it," Bets replied, "then out again when you need them. 'Tis a way to carry the entry piece safely, if you find it." She grimaced. "Forsooth I have used it but once as a test, and I could not retrieve the object I'd wished to carry. So if you find an empty drinking cup inside, then return it to me, yes?"

Jon raised his eyebrows, thinking the safekeeper might not be worth the risk of using it. But rather than argue, he slipped its cord over his head and tucked it under his jacket…rather close to the Amaranthus circlet that he still hadn't addressed yet either.

Then, because there was really no excuse to delay, he left.

Elspeth watched Jon disappear down the hall and into the liftpods, his ever-present protector right beside him, although surely unseen. Jon hadn't given one single indication that he knew of Fylax's presence, even after his time at the Mountain. Fylax gave her a wave then blinked out of sight.

She waved back even though the Person had already gone. Then she moved back inside the room. "I wonder why Fylax hides himself from Jon?" she mused aloud. "He is Jon's protector, after all."

Max let out an amused huff. "I can guess. I'd be pretty uncomfortable if I knew *that* was following me around for my entire life."

Elspeth made a shrug of agreement. Fylax was most impressive, and somewhat daunting to the uninitiated. She herself had been startled into silence when she'd first seen his true form, and she considered herself particularly tolerant of supernatural oddities.

"I'm going to go," Max said abruptly. "To the Elsewhise entrance at the borderlands museum. I'm not convinced Jon will get what we need, and I don't think Tarie has the time to wait."

"And you think you will?" she asked.

"I've got as good a chance as any."

Which was no promise of success – but it was all they had. Elspeth nodded at him. "Take care."

Max left, and Elspeth remained next to the one she guarded, occasionally wafting a silvery wash of flame over Tarie's head.

What an odd hour that had been. 'Twas as though the whole world had changed around her – Tarie caught in a trap Elspeth never could have imagined, then the horrid brute Rokal turning out to be the rather more helpful Max, then Jon returning and being so upset at first…

Which she really ought to have expected, she now realised. 'Twas clear that Jon held much shame over his life here. She wanted to truly speak with him, to show him that she held it against him not at all.

Elspeth suddenly remembered the last words she'd blurted out – something foolish about being free to love him – and her hand stopped for a moment in its movement over Tarie's head.

Humph. Mayhap she'd said more than enough already.

But they'd had a sort of reconciliation. Not nearly enough to please her, but there should be time for that…once Tarie was well, and Jon came back.

Elspeth's eyes caught on a small dark shape still sitting on the nearby table. 'Twas the burned VR dart that had stolen Tarie's mind away. Both Elspeth and Max had touched it without ill effect, causing her to think that its power had been lost with the damage it had sustained.

But she found herself picking it up with her free hand and

studying it curiously. The pointed end of it did not look so very sharp...

Poik.

Ugh! By the rood, it still worked...

The journey to Luca's live-in office didn't take nearly long enough for Jon's liking. Soon enough Jon found himself reluctantly standing outside the central city multi-block building, the sort with air vehicle landing strips around every second floor. Obviously he didn't need an air vehicle...but he did need to get in somehow.

Jon paused outside the eightieth level's foyer that led to several office-apartments, including Luca's. *Here goes...*

But then when he stepped forward, the foyer's security door opened for him. Hmm.

Luke had given him clearance years ago, Jon reminded himself as he stepped inside. Before he'd become Luca. Maybe he'd just forgotten to update the security permissions.

Jon focused his attention on looking relaxed and as if he belonged, in case anyone was watching. He headed for Luca's door and reached out to the DNA scanner.

He recoiled as it shot a short, sharp burst of electricity at his questing finger – *ouch!* – but then the sting quickly faded and the door opened.

Obviously Jon still had clearance, but he didn't appreciate the zap. Security systems were meant to shock people who *didn't* have clearance – although on second thoughts, Luca had probably set it up that way on purpose.

But it seemed like a good sign Jon could get inside at all. Sometimes a string of coincidences could mean that Amaranthus was watching over someone, lining things up so they'd play out in the best possible way. Yeah, that must be it.

Except when was life ever that easy?

Two minutes later Jon had to admit that sometimes, life *was* easy. He'd found a battered, blackened dagger poorly hidden by a VR screen on a nearby shelf, its location obvious because of the buzzing emanations of alter-power it gave off. He briefly considered using the safekeeper Bets had given him, but then settled on his jacket's resizeable sleeve and large, thick pockets as a holder he could definitely retrieve it from.

A moment later his pocket was heavier, and he turned for the door only to find that it now shimmered with the distinctive sign of an active VR wall-screen. The blank white door flickered briefly with colour, then suddenly Luca stood in the image, life-sized and directly in front of the closed door. His blue-green eyes looked curious rather than angry, and was that humour curving his lips?

"Hello, son. Dropped by for a little chat and theft after your time away, have you?"

It was just an image. Just an image rather than the real person, but Jon couldn't help his emotional reaction anyway. Chaos, Luca was a terrible father – and he'd clearly been keeping an eye on this office. Jon stepped closer to the door, but its security light flashed red and a brief, painful shock emitted, making him jolt.

The door was locked and secured, which meant that Jon was too.

"Sure," Jon replied brusquely. Strangely he felt annoyed rather than scared, as if he'd left the last of his fear behind when he'd spoken with Bets. "Let's chat, *Father*. Why did you tell Anni I was ignoring her instead of admitting I wasn't with you?"

Luca's eyebrows rose – the arch more pronounced than Jon's, but still similar. "I could hardly admit that the chairman of Erus council had lost his own son, and a Prince of the Air at that. What would people think?"

Jon scoffed derisively. "That Princes of the Air do whatever they want, and the White Prince's carrier even more than most. Now this has been a lovely chat, but-"

The door's seal flashed red again. "You can go when we've finished speaking," Luca said evenly. "You can even take that precious object you've got stowed in your jacket – though good luck using it for anything worthwhile." He cocked his head to the side. "Or, I can contact security now and let them know my estranged, deranged offspring has abandoned all reason and is currently robbing me. What do you think?"

Jon's lips tightened. "You're probably calling them now."

"Nope. I'm really not. And you're stuck in here anyway. So…shall we chat?"

What else was there to do? Jon nodded tersely but didn't move from his place by the door. The moment it was unlocked, he was out of there. Or maybe he should just try crashing through…

A large armchair appeared in Luca's otherwise blank surroundings and he seated himself with a flourish, crossing his legs at the ankles. "I don't like you," he began without preamble. "And you don't like me either."

Jon let out a startled laugh. "Seriously? You're keeping me here for this?"

Luca shrugged.

"I liked *Luke* well enough, sure. I didn't understand him, but he was alright. And if you want the truth, then no, I don't like you at all. But you're not Luke, are you? And you've caused me harm over and over. You've *lied* to me over and over." In fact, Jon was increasingly certain that Luca wanted him dead, and wouldn't have provoked him into going to the White Prince otherwise. That had been just one murderous deed on top of years of verbal abuse and humiliation. "Luca is just a shell for whatever twisted Creature is running that body, and I know you Creatures hate me."

Luca's eyebrows rose again, and his lips curved into a smirk. "Is that so, son? I see you've gained all sorts of wisdom and knowledge in your time away…presumably in the Other realm. I also see that you've changed your allegiance to one whose very name the Creatures cannot stand."

Jon didn't confirm the statements. Luca seemed to know already. And oddly enough, Jon realised in that moment that since all the Creatures *did* hate him, it meant when Rokal had attacked him like he had, he probably had been trying to kill him.

Wonderful.

When Jon didn't respond, Luca continued, "Then you clearly know all about the immortal Creatures who are trapped in the prison of the inhospitable Other realm, banished from the source of eternal life for their treason…and eternally pissed about it." His smirk turned into a full-fledged grin – the same open, happy one Luke used to show once in a blue moon. "Sure, they hate you, oh Marked One. But what about the children of those 'twisted' Creatures, hmm? The ones born of humans. Do those

Halflings also hate you? Are they cursed, deserving of your disdain even though they committed no crime except to be born? And what of their children who can walk in both the normal and Other realms? Their children's children?" Luca's voice changed suddenly, sounding like a dozen voices speaking in harmony. *"What of the half-Halflings, son?"*

It was clearly an audio effect from whatever speakers were projecting Luca's voice, but Jon couldn't help but shudder a little at the sound. "I know Halflings aren't Creatures," he said. Not that he'd met many himself – he'd heard they were often odd-looking, and often couldn't live away from the alter-power-rich atmosphere of the borderlands. "And surely they can't have carriers like Creatures do, either. Where are you going with this?"

"I'm not Luke, no. I *am* a separate being who's running his body right now, yes," Luca said distinctly. "But I'm also not a Creature that's compelled to hate you, and I don't generally control your dear father or even overwhelm his personality. Instead I met him when he was at his lowest point. I offered him greatness, freedom from the emotional pain that crippled him, if he would give *me* the freedom to leave the borderlands occasionally by allowing me to hitch a ride, so to speak."

Luca grinned, spreading his hands out, palms up. "And Luke found he liked the freedom and confidence of being *me* so much that he wanted to do it all the time, not just occasionally."

Jon had assumed Luca would lie. He did it so much that Jon would be surprised if the man ever told the complete truth. But while Jon was wholly suspicious of almost anything Luca did, he couldn't deny one thing.

Luca wasn't like the Creatures or carriers Jon had run into since his time away, or even before then. He was different. Utterly selfish, uncaring and egomaniacal, yes, but in the way that the worst humans were. He seemed to lack that malevolence and brutality that Jon now knew Creatures wore as close as their own skins.

So maybe Luca – or whoever this Creature/Halfling was – was in fact telling the truth right now.

"You're saying that you're a Halfling," Jon clarified slowly. "Sharing a body with Luke DeMannard rather than controlling him."

"Half-Halfling, strictly speaking," Luca said. "A handsome

and impressive one descended from your own White Prince, in fact. Millennia ago he fathered the immortal Lilith with some pointless human woman, then proceeded to go absolutely mad and shut himself away from Creature society – rather like a human hermit. And more recently, Lilith, who's a bright, determined survivor just like myself, proceeded to make *me* with yet another incredibly powerful but somewhat insane Creature."

He shrugged again. "Voila. It's a travesty that I'm such a rare and talented being, yet I'm still unable to live freely in the normal realm on my own. If I did venture out of the borderlands in my real body, I daresay the humans would panic at the sight of my unique half-Halfling self, and eventually the normal atmosphere would deflate me like an old balloon. So...my real body sleeps in the borderlands, and instead I use a carrier called Luke DeMannard, who I make smarter, stronger and better in every way."

Jon stared as the man shuffled in his VR armchair, seeming to flick through settings until he was sitting on a...yes, that was a throne. A rather odd metal one made up of what Jon eventually realised were letters...spelling out 'Luca'.

Could it be true? Could Luke be a carrier for a youngish half-Halfling – an almost-Creature – instead of a true Creature? And what difference did it really make? "If I'm not talking to Luke right now," Jon asked, "then who are you, really? Why are you telling me this?"

"I'm not going to tell you my true name because it would give you a measure of control over me," Luca said matter-of-factly. He leaned forward in his letter-throne. "But I'm telling you because you don't trust me. You hate me like I'm a Creature...but you can hate me like I'm an ass and a bad father instead. I don't want you dead, Jayel Jonnamin. I'd be perfectly happy to ignore you from a distance like I've been doing for this last week."

"I haven't even been in this time period!" Jon burst out. "Of course you ignored me!"

Luca raised one perfectly arched eyebrow. "Well, that's interesting information, and it explains where you went. I'll ignore you like I ignore my other son, then. The six-year-old in Dailan province with his feckless mother."

For a moment Jon couldn't speak. He shouldn't have said that about the time travel, but... "Your *other* son?"

"Oh, didn't Anni tell you?" Luca cocked his head to the side, exaggerating a thoughtful expression. "Oh, I suppose she couldn't, since Luke never told her. *I* certainly didn't. But there was a reason that Luke suddenly wanted to marry her and have himself declared your legal father five years ago, when he was happy to be only verbally acknowledged before that.

"You know he was living off the grid in Dailan province for years, which is why he never became part of your life till you were older, yes? But you didn't know that he was involved with a pretty, rather careless woman called Cahlie. And Cahlie broke his heart when she decided to go back to her own useless husband, along with Luke's baby son. She said Luke was a loser who didn't deserve to be a father and would never amount to anything, or something equally heart-wrenching. But it was enough to send Luke into a spiral of despair that led first to a hasty but platonic marriage with Anni – then later to me."

Was that true? Luca was a liar, but it sounded dreadfully possible. Jon felt the weight of the dagger in his jacket and his mind flicked back to Tarie's state. Luca liked the sound of his own voice, but not like this. "I'm not interested in hearing any more," Jon said hollowly. "What'll it take for you to let me go?"

"Giant statues made in my honour," Luca replied promptly. "And a marching band making permanent circles around the city-state, proclaiming my glory, and fireworks spelling out my name to be sent up over the city every Monday, which I'll rename to Lucaday, since no one likes Mondays. But since you can't get me any of those things, I'll settle for a vow."

"I'm not pledging to you-"

"And I don't want your pledge of allegiance," Luca cut in. "Instead I want your promise that you'll never lift a hand against me, your not-so-dear father and his helpful half-Halfling friend. That instead you'll remember who your real enemies are in the Other realm – the White Prince and his cronies."

"Does the White Prince even have cronies?" Jon asked incredulously. If he had, surely he'd have eaten them by now. And apparently he was Luca's *grandfather*…

"Probably not." Luca shrugged. "But a Creature is a Creature. Well? Swear upon your new master's name that you won't ever attempt to harm me or my empire, and you won't send anyone else to harm me, and I'll let you go along with your dirty old knife."

Luca's *empire*? How had Erus turned into an *empire*? Feeling like he was stuck in some VR farce, Jon stuttered out, "I swear on the name of Amaranthus that I won't try to hurt you or get anyone else to hurt you...except in self-defence. And I think that's as much as you can ask."

Luca had winced at the name 'Amaranthus', but as Jon finished speaking he nodded. "Seems fair. Well, off you go, my brave spawn. Go free your friend, conquer the world or ride a bicycle, I don't care – just leave your dear old father out of it."

Then Luca's image stood and stepped aside as the door slid open. Jon warily walked through out to the small foyer, waiting for the trap to be sprung. Surely there must be one, because why else would Luca just let him go with a stupid promise? *Promises are never stupid,* a quiet thought reminded him. *Even if they never should have been made, they're still your oath for how you intend to shape the world around you.*

Right. If that was the case, then Jon's shaping of the world wouldn't involve Luca...who may or may not have been the White Prince's grandson.

And Luca had known about Tarie, Jon realised suddenly. That wasn't a great sign.

But Jon wasn't allowed to harm Luca. Except he still could send Bets to flame him up and see if it broke the carrier bond...that wouldn't classify as harming, right?"

Jon gave one last uncertain look towards the now empty apartment, then stepped out into open air.

Luca stood in the live-in office's safe room, behind closed doors and with the VR walls on full force. There was silence from inside the main room, so after a few more minutes Luca stepped out of the safe room.

Jayel Jonnamin sat half-crouched on the carpeted floor, his eyes blank and his fingers twitching as he reacted to the VR scene that ran through his head.

Quite an effective bit of security, Luca had to admit. The lock was programmed to send a miniscule VR dart into whoever tried to enter without permission, then to make the intruder think they were getting whatever they wanted. In truth, it gave Luca the chance to hide/call for security/grab a weapon as appropriate. (One of the perks of being chairman. He didn't have to obey the laws about VR darts, because who would dare accuse him of doing wrong?)

The moment Luca had heard Jon was back this morning, he'd rushed to reprogram the locks on all his doors and windows. He didn't *really* think the boy would come after him, but he'd thought it was better to be safe than sorry.

It turned out that precaution had been just right. Jon *had* come here, and Luca had brought him into a special VR scene that replicated the inside of the office. All the better to find out what Jon really wanted.

It seemed he'd wanted the entry piece – the battered old dagger that had needed quite a bit of polishing to come back to even a semi-attractive state. Luca had easily guessed what it was for, since Lilith's boytoys had just been boasting about pulling a new trick on the Memryse Word-speaker, AKA Jon's little neighbour.

Luca stared down at the boy a while longer, wondering how someone so drastically ordinary could cause such an uproar in the Other realm. The boy was too stupid to figure out why, as well. He would soon enough, but he better keep his promise. A vow made in VR was still a vow.

Then Luca quietly moved to the safe where the real dagger was kept, pulling his loose sleeves down till they formed thick gloves over his hands. (Practical *and* stylish!) The multiple security locks and their VR covers flashed and released at his approach, and he withdrew the entry piece from the safe with caution in spite of the gloves. He hadn't gone to such effort to reprogram its destination just to accidentally send himself there instead.

Besides, these entry pieces were made of a highly toxic material. Like the darts, if ground into a water supply, they could make an entire city susceptible to mind control. Not exactly what he needed right now.

Luca held the dagger out, blade first. He briefly considered just plunging it into the boy's neck – after all, hadn't the Tiger wanted him dead since his conception? – but he dismissed the thought. Better to keep the boy alive and directed at someone else. Besides, Luca couldn't shake the uncomfortable thought that someone was watching him, and that any fatal attack would go badly for him rather than the boy.

So very slowly and carefully Luca slipped the dagger into Jon's outstretched fingers. His head VR set showed the new program being activated, overriding the realistic security setting that currently showed Jon flying over an almost perfect replica of Erus city.

Luca backed away, debating whether to call for his vehicle or just retreat to the safe room again. He didn't take his eyes off the crouched figure for one moment.

But then the atmosphere in the room grew tense and rich with alter-power, enough to make Luca's blood fizz with energy in his veins. Enough to funnel excess power back to his true form where it slept in the borderlands. The alter-power grew stronger and stronger, centred around the entry piece in Jon's fingers, until-

POP.

Jon vanished from the room along with the entry piece, leaving a slight dent in the floor's memory-foam and an uncomfortable feeling in Luca's ears.

Luca wiggled a finger in one ear, grimacing as the air pressure balanced out again. He'd hoped the entry piece would act as a true gateway to move the boy's physical form, but hadn't been sure. Luckily he'd been right.

Still, he couldn't help himself from watching the empty space suspiciously as if the boy would suddenly reappear. Nothing happened, but...

Perhaps it was worth going to his other safe room, just until this was all over.

But then another alert went off on Luca's comm, showing that Gerak's male Prince of the Air had reappeared and was even entering an open, sparsely populated area. Luca raised an eyebrow as he studied the live footage. The lad was gigantic by human standards and as unlikeable as his father Wyet, broken legs notwithstanding. But what remarkable stupidity to go out on his own at such a time as this! The kid was basically asking for it.

Luca shrugged and ordered an attack drone, the sort that came equipped with darts and a net. Even if he couldn't deliver Seyen Johannis to the Tiger, he could at least get the other two.

19

Fire and Flame

Elspeth sucked in a breath as the scene around her changed. She could feel a faint throbbing in her finger where she'd touched the sharp end of the dart, and the couch was clearly underneath her. She could also feel Tarie's curly hair just under her hand, with the comforting warmth of her cleansing flame.

But what she could *see* was now different. Directly in front of her, a vast globe rose up from the ground, like a giant glass fishbowl that had been set upside-down. Inside, red and orange colours flickered alternately with silver.

And Tarie was inside too. She stood just around the curve of the globe, pressed up against the side of the glass with her hands against its barrier, her eyebrows low and angry-looking, and her mouth moving high-speed. She appeared most displeased, but Elspeth could not hear her at all.

Huzzah! Elspeth cheered. She'd made it into Tarie's VR prison! Or outside it, anyway, which was near enough.

Elspeth looked around, noting that the globe-prison's surroundings only seemed to appear when she focused on an area. There was a high, plain wall around them, rather like the globe had been set down in an empty courtyard. But when she squinted, she could see buildings beyond the wall - not the many-levelled sort from Erus city, but rather a blockier, plainer version of a small town from centuries past.

Hmm…many different centuries, as a matter of fact. The style of the buildings seemed to vary from place to place, as though they'd been created and plopped down without any consideration for consistency. Most interesting. It may well have been the same town she'd briefly visited that day outside the museum, although one could hardly say without seeing it in full...

Tarie, Elspeth reminded herself emphatically. She was here to rescue Tarie, not to ponder the mysteries of an alter-power-VR location run by Creatures.

Elspeth set her attention on the globe once more. Then she blanched as she saw that the orange and red colours inside appeared to be *fire*. And was that a mountain of twigs acting as tinder?

By the rood and all saints – how utterly dreadful!

Overcome with righteous rage, Elspeth stomped towards the globe and set her hand against the side. She could feel the cleansing fire at full-blast, though she could not see it, and that knowledge gave her some peace even as the regular fire swept through the globe's interior, rising then vanishing from moment to moment.

Then Tarie turned around and finally saw her. Her eyebrows shot up and her lips moved – it looked a bit like 'What in Hades are *you* doing here?' but surely the girl would not be so crude.

"I am here to rescue you!" Elspeth told her loudly, then when it appeared she'd been unheard, tried again. "RESCUE YOU!"

Tarie's face scrunched up and her mouth moved again. She looked back to where she'd originally been focusing, then back at Elspeth. She raised a hand...

Just then there was a change in air pressure and the closest section of the glass barrier suddenly vanished.

Elspeth brightened, moving forward towards her friend. *Never fear*, she assured her. *We shall leave at once!*

Hmm. It must be very loud in here, she mused, as she had not even heard her own words. *Good day*, she tried again. *Hello...?*

In front of her, Tarie threw her hands in the air and began gesticulating wildly. Mayhap the motions were intended to replace actual speech, but if so then Tarie was very poor at charades. Elspeth understood only one gesture – 'turn around'.

So Elspeth turned around, and she saw that the globe's side had not vanished at all. Rather it had moved outwards so that Elspeth herself was now inside the globe...with the fire, the tinder and the oddly silent Tarie.

Oh.

Never fear, Elspeth told herself, since Tarie couldn't hear her.

'Twas merely a game of the mind, and she already knew the exit code.

Evacuate.

Except that for some reason her words had no sound, and within the globe she remained. Within her mind only, of course. The real world still felt semi-solid under her, but that knowledge did not free her mind.

Tarie raised an eyebrow, setting her hands on her hips. Elspeth could understand that expression without any problems, and a sinking feeling came over her. It seemed that mayhap, in spite of her determination to be prudent, she may have been very foolish instead.

Oh, *collywobbles.*

Nesbit. Ah...Bets. Seriously? Tarie took only a few seconds to decide that the girl was harmless – but also pretty useless in this moment. She didn't know where Bets had come from, except that she now appeared to be just as trapped as Tarie herself.

Nice one.

But in this moment Tarie had much more urgent worries than her inept stalker. Like the shadowy figure whose face she'd seen very briefly but had recognized immediately. And while in dodgy VR sessions like this one, people could change their appearance however they liked, she was almost certain she'd seen the truth.

The two shadow men seemed to be conversing on the other side of the barrier. And for the first time, if she focused, she could just make out what they were saying.

"It's not working. Someone's still protecting her."

"We got the other one when we extended the barrier, didn't we? Just because we can't see them doesn't mean they're not there. Try harder."

The first shadow man slumped, seeming to sulk. Then there was a dark blur and suddenly he was gone, leaving behind the second shadow, the one Tarie had recognized. The one who'd been so close, hiding behind a smile all this time.

You once said that you could move fast enough to blur my vision, she signed. *But you undersold yourself. You can move faster than the naked eye can track, can't you?*

The shadow man cocked his head to the side, clearly following along.

But when he didn't answer she persisted, adding, *I know that the music was you too. I don't know how, but it was some indication that you were nearby, doing…something. I could feel it too; feel the air going too dry all around me, and I'd get short of breath. It felt wrong, but I couldn't pinpoint why.* She felt both vindicated and betrayed to realise she hadn't been imagining those odd feelings.

There was a pause, then the shadowy figure blurred and changed until it was a familiar, handsome golden-haired young man. His cheekbones were sharper here in VR, giving him an almost hungry look, and his eyes were filled with hatred.

She'd recognized him. Even though the prison's sound barrier silenced her, there was no doubt. So Gavriel dropped the disguise, and lowered the sound barrier just a little. Just one way.

"I guess there's no point pretending when you know who I am," he spat, finally letting himself express the distaste he'd felt the moment he'd seen her; the moment he'd heard Lilith – the powerful Halfling he was pledged to – whisper in his ear and confirm exactly why he felt so uncomfortable in the girl's presence. "And while talk won't save you, allow me to explain something. You're a *Way-follower*, Tariana Filat. I didn't need to see it scratched on your trash-heap of a vehicle to recognize that, even without the mark on your forehead or hearing you babble that language straight from the Mountain."

Tarie's dark eyes widened, and her lips tightened. She gestured furiously, *But I never hurt you! I never hurt anyone!*

He laughed derisively. Stupid girl – she really had no idea, or she wouldn't have restrained herself these past few weeks. Speaking the Words was as effective as speaking out a spell or sending a spray of painful enemy alter-power into the atmosphere. It planted a seed of whatever his master's enemy wanted to create, and it always worked against his people's goals.

In fact, the first time Tarie had spoken the Words in front of him, she'd actually struck him silent – the power reaching into him, then travelling through the connection to Lilith, and silencing the both of them.

What an insult! She'd had to die after that…but it was easier said than done. Even with the gifts he'd gained from Lilith (and had given up so much for), he still hadn't been able to get Tarie. He could move faster than the eye could see; could drain the energy straight from a target and send it down his connection to Lilith. Most of the time he just siphoned a little energy from the people around him. If he went too far and accidentally siphoned it all, it was easy enough to call those deaths heart attacks or overdoses, and he'd thought Tarie would be just as easy. But it seemed that Tarie only felt 'short of breath', before a cloud of painful silver flame knocked him away from her, over and over.

And Tarie had spotted him once, too. He'd quickly made up some nonsense about her having a stalker – which was of course true, because it was *him* – and that seemed to deflect her attention for a while. But he still hadn't been able to harm her. He'd even tried running a cafeteria cart at her at full speed, but it hadn't even made a dent!

He'd failed, over and over. Gavriel had started to genuinely fear that Lilith would give up on him, would send him the way of her other rejected young men. She'd take back the power she'd given them, and he understood that process was fatal.

But then he'd had the idea to attack the girl's mind instead of her body. VR darts were easy enough to come by if you knew the right people, and very hard to defend against. And this should have worked – had *almost* worked, except for whoever was interfering – so it was lucky that they had a backup plan.

But Tarie was clearly waiting for a response to her statement about never hurting anyone, so he said, "Word-speakers are always marked for execution." Then his lip curled and he leaned in against the clear barrier, feeling the warmth of the fire he and the other man had so carefully designed, and which kept going out in spite of their clear instructions. "You might keep your sanity, girl, but it won't matter for long. We've sent a little surprise to your apartment, and we'll get rid of your whole filthy family in one go. And no one will even care."

Tarie's eyes narrowed. *I'm not in my apartment,* she signed. *I know that much. Thickhead.*

"You *are* in your apartment," Gavriel spat, furious at her disrespect, "because I saw Rokal carry you there. You looked catatonic, so it's no surprise you didn't notice." He sneered, adding maliciously, "Best be more careful who you're unconscious around. Rokal has a reputation, so who knows what he did while you were unaware?"

There was a long silence – not that she'd been making any sound, anyway – then he saw the moment she decided not to believe him.

"I lied about his mother so you'd feel sorry for him," Gavriel added quickly. "She's not dead, and he's not a broken soul as a result. He's just a vicious brute, through and through."

But even though that had been true, Tarie didn't seem to believe him. She made a rude gesture and turned her back on him.

In that moment, Gavriel was so enraged; felt so *impotent* that he would have shot her if he'd had opportunity.

But just then Lilith's other current pledgee returned. Basir was a few years older than Gavriel and was straight out of prison, with the haircut to prove it. Gavriel figured Lilith kept him for his loyalty and viciousness rather than his brains, but Gavriel thought he was a waste of space.

"Lilith wants you," Basir announced. "Now."

Gavriel cringed internally. That wasn't a protestation of desire – because his master really, really wasn't the sort. In fact, it was probably a bad sign.

But he couldn't say no. "I'll be right back."

And then they'd make certain that the fire worked.

Jon shot out over the city, heading back towards 42 Eastern Way with his collection of precious objects stuck inside his jacket. The conversation with Luca played over and over in his head. It had been an amazingly frank discussion and it might have even been true, but he couldn't shake the feeling that something wasn't quite right.

The sooner he could get home, the better.

Jon ducked between two towering buildings whose multiple levels crossed over each other like poorly set-out children's blocks, then turned to skim under a covered pathway that led between the two buildings. As he did so, he almost scraped against the metal of the nearest building.

Then he noticed something. The metal held a faint shimmer that would usually mean a VR wall. But who would put VR underneath an archway that only fliers would ever see?

Jon slowed, taking a second look at the building's surface. There was definitely something off about it, he decided. He cautiously set his hand against it. It looked normal enough, and felt a little cool, just as he'd expected.

No, wait. It hadn't felt cool until he'd *expected* it to…

Chaos.

He spun around mid-air, noting that any time he focused, that same faint shimmer was visible. This definitely wasn't right. If he didn't know better, he'd say he was in VR.

Just then he felt a tingle and a faint pressure against his fingertips. He looked down to see a familiar battered dagger appear in his hand, right out of thin air.

He barely had the chance to wonder how it had got out of his jacket when the atmosphere around him changed with a gut-wrenching twist. It felt like a giant grabbed him by the tunic and shook him, and suddenly his vision was gone. He slammed down onto a rocky surface, letting out a cry of shock as pain radiated down his side. But it was just an ache rather than any indicator of true injury, and as soon as the darkness had come, a strong, blanketed feeling had also come over him.

He was in the Other.

What the…?

Max had never flown so fast in his life. Now that his binding to Gerak had been replaced with this light, sweet new pledge, he felt so free. So quick. So clear-headed.

Flying just high enough to avoid insects and delivery drones, he'd well and truly left the city limits behind. The densely packed suburbs and central city filled the air if he cared to glance behind him, but most of his attention was on what lay ahead.

It was all so green out here. He wondered if he'd noticed that before. He could see the thin trail of that train track far below, snaking its way from the edge of the central city right out across plains and around villages, then straight out into the distance.

Max couldn't see the borderlands from up here, but he hadn't expected to. They'd sneak up on a person – one moment he'd seem to be in just another stretch of forest, and the next thing, gravity would seem to triple and pull him out of the air, mere moments before he'd find himself in a place that was neither normal nor Other.

He'd accidentally made his way into the Other right after the fire incident at the museum; furious and confused. He'd been lucky enough not to come across any Creatures, especially now he knew what they were really like. And he'd managed to wander out in much the same way, having lost a couple of days of his life.

Tarie had helped him then, he remembered. He'd help her now.

Down below, the long, thin shape of the train emerged from a tunnel in a hillside. It stopped at a building complex standing all on its own, and there seemed to be people funnelling from the building, through an enclosed clear tunnel, and onto the train.

Max squinted, trying to see more clearly since from this height they were almost the size of ants. Surely all of these people weren't going to the museum. Surely it hadn't been fixed already.

He looked up ahead again, following the line of the train track as it led deeper and deeper into the hazy blue distance. But then he noticed something new. It didn't only curve away to the right, to where he knew the borderlands museum (and its Elsewhise entrance) to be.

It split and also curved to the left, then vanished into a hazy grey patch that didn't sit right with its surroundings.

Max blinked at it for a moment, then swore under his breath. He had so many vague and patchy memories from his years as a carrier, but he knew what that meant. The tracks led straight into the borderlands, and most likely into the Other realm.

He glanced back to where the train had begun to move again, fast enough that it would soon outpace him, and wondered what the Creatures wanted with a bunch of humans. Surely nothing good.

His attention was so fixed on the train and its possible destination that he didn't notice the shimmering patch of air to his left, not till he heard a faint *whsp* sound. There was a slight pain in his neck, and then numbness began to spread from that area.

Max had just enough time to realise he'd been shot by a dart from a drone – and to think *seriously? HIM TOO?!* – before the sound around him faded away, and-

In a VR programme back in the city, Luca lowered his virtual rifle with a smile of satisfaction. The attack drone he'd sent was completely controlled from here in VR, but just for fun, he'd set the programme to resemble an old-fashioned hunting expedition, with himself in beige-coloured shirt, trousers and round hat. He'd even added a thick, curling moustache for the occasion.

Good shot, he congratulated himself. Now, for the net.

It was time to bag his trophy.

The Other realm

It didn't take Jon long to connect the battered dagger in his hand with his sudden change of location. It was an entry piece. He didn't understand what had happened, but it was clear he'd been tricked.

However, this kind of entry piece was meant to lead to Elsewhise, he reminded himself. Unless Rokal/Max had lied about what entry pieces did. *That* was looking pretty likely too.

And this – this was undoubtedly the Other realm, or an excellent VR replica. Except he could feel the fuzzy protective layer from Amaranthus, and that had never been replicated in VR.

Feeling a little more confident in spite of his surroundings, Jon pushed himself to a seated position and squinted into the darkness. He could just make out faint dark grey shapes within the deeper black, but he had no idea what they were.

He needed some light.

As if on cue, Jon realised that the faint light enabling him to see just a fraction was actually coming from under his jacket. He hastily felt around and pulled out the Amaranthus circlet. It was warm in his hand, and it glowed with a comfortable, steady light. He raised it into the air and lit up his surroundings.

Five seconds later Jon's brain had made sense of the different shapes and textures around him, and he was half-wishing he'd never used the light. He swallowed audibly, trying not to tremble. It wasn't…it wasn't good.

He was inside a room with a high ceiling. He could faintly see the outline of a high, rounded window, and the shape of this place distinctly reminded him of the White Prince's temple, if only seen from the inside.

Once when Jon was a boy he'd been wandering the lower districts of the city, feeling bored and curious. He'd sat down at the side of an overgrown public gardenette, edged in large, battered bricks. One of the bricks had fallen on its side and he'd reached out to push it back into place without even thinking about it.

Underneath the brick had been a mass of white web, thicker than any spiderweb he'd ever seen, shaped like blankets rather than the delicate lace of most webs. And inside that blanket web had been the biggest, fattest spider he'd ever seen, squatting and beastly in its well-built home.

He'd gasped and let the brick fall, then had run in the opposite direction, shaking himself convulsively as if the creature might have hitched a ride. It hadn't…he didn't think…but he'd learned his lesson that day about picking up things in gardens. There was a reason humanity paved over dirt with thick layers of concrete, and it was probably spelled S-P-I-D-E-R.

But that was then. Now, Jon crouched on the cold stone floor of what was basically a giant brick inhabited by what was surely the most colossal spider in existence, judging by the size of the webs. Curtains of white draped across the walls, and in layers up to the ceiling, almost obscuring the stone behind them. And within those layers were suspiciously humanlike shapes, wrapped like ancient mummies in bandages.

Eep. The only upside was that he hadn't yet seen a spider…

Scrape. Scritch-scritch-scritch.

Jon leapt to his feet, his heart pounding as he held the circlet outstretched, swinging it from side to side so nothing could sneak up behind him. He heard a clatter which made him leap again…then realised he'd dropped the dagger entry piece onto the hard floor. It had skidded to land under a heavy veil of spiderweb, right up against one of those mummy-like bundles.

Chaoschaoschaos he needed a weapon – or a flamethrower!

But he'd settle for an immediate exit. Now if only he could find it…

Jon stepped back, turning as he did so. But he was too slow to see his foot land on a thick chunk of white webbing, and suddenly he was enveloped in it, pulled up into the air with sticky padding pressing against every part of him.

The circlet was gone from his hand, and the darkness was now absolute. But he could still *hear* that faint *scritch-scritch-scritch* sound…

He couldn't even scream.

The VR prison

Elspeth sat in the safety of her little room, tucked out of sight from anyone except those she wished to have visit. She could still feel the real furniture underneath her legs and fingertips. But within her mind, she was very much trapped within this globe of silence. 'Twas much like her earlier experience with the entry piece knife, where she somehow inhabited two realms at the same time.

Here in VR, the orange flames sprang up on the far side of the globe, leaping from glowing twigs into a roaring wall that could be felt even from here. Meanwhile, Tarie continued her game of furious charades with the person on the other side of the barrier. It seemed that the responsibility for escape fell upon Elspeth herself.

By the rood, this was *not* enjoyable.

Muttering to herself – and sweating from the rising heat – Elspeth raised her hands and called forth her cleansing flame. She would indeed fight fire with fire, and then those villains would be sorry! Once she discovered who they were, of course.

But while in the real world Elspeth could feel the tingle of her gift working against her palms, here in her mind's prison, she saw nothing but pale, bare skin. Her own fire had not made it past the barrier.

Oh…dear.

'Twas tempting to panic in that moment, but Elspeth quickly reminded herself of her first experience with this place. She had not been able to see her flame then either, but it had surely existed. She merely had to focus and remember the truth, and not let her surroundings overwhelm her-

A flame licked at her shoe and she stomped at it furiously. It seemed to weaken for barely a moment before promptly rushing up the loose leg of her trousers. Not just her trousers – *all* of her clothing.

Elspeth screamed and slapped at it, but it just leapt to the long sleeves of her tunic, then rushed up those too. It left a sharp, burning pain in its wake –*'twas hot!*

Argh!!!

Tarie rushed over to Bets with a gasp of dismay as the girl went up like a bundle of straw in a fire. She was screaming and threw herself down, but there was just more flame around her too, since all the tinder had caught.

Where was the silver flame that had helped before?! Tarie thought in panic. *Why was this happening?!*

She tried to beat the flame off Bets, but now she'd caught fire too, and it didn't seem to matter how fast she mouthed the Words. The flame spread like lightning, and an incredible heat came with it.

Suddenly there was no room for logical thought; nor the use of her own gift. Her vision filled with orange and her mind filled with *heat-pain-panic*…and behind that, the absolute shock that somehow, this terrible thing was happening.

Amaranthus…the Eternal One…the non-Creature that she followed…if he had even a nanogram of power or care, then he needed to *HELP!*

Basir DeCasimir smirked as he strengthened the insanity curse on the flaming globe, carving the lines deeper and deeper into its surface. Chaos, he could almost feel the heat himself, and it was taking literally all the energy he had to enforce it on the two prisoners.

He couldn't even see them any longer in the inferno. But he was winning. He was *obviously* winning.

Lilith would be so proud of him…and Gavriel would be so jealous.

The Other realm

In the Other realm, Jon couldn't move an inch. Suffocatingly thick fuzz pressed in against his face, his arms, holding him in an absolute grip. It was cold – no, warm – and the intense darkness was broken up into shades of deep grey. He could just make out something moving towards him, something big. Something inhuman, with long, weirdly jointed legs.

Then the White Prince spoke. *"You betrayed me,"* he hissed, his voice seeming to amplify through the thick webs enveloping Jon. *"You lied to me. You did not challenge Audaline. You took from me and did not repay."*

Jon began to shake from head to toe even in his muffled wrapping. The White Prince was terrifying enough from a distance, and that was when Jon hadn't known what the Creature really was. Now he did know; he knew how much malice the thing contained, and he was helpless to save himself.

This shouldn't be happening! He shouldn't be inside the White Prince's temple!

In the darkness, the faint shape loomed over Jon. It seemed to glow, revealing sharply outlined wings with jagged edges and empty struts. Too many long, long legs rose up on either side of the wings, and the White Prince's pale face seemed almost like a skull with deep, hollow dark eyes. A true monster.

Jon let out a long, low whimper.

That pale, dark-eyed face drew closer until it filled his vision. Chaos, it had *teeth*…

"You're a thief, Jayel Jonnamin DeLuca. Do you know what I do to thieves?"

No…but it looked like Jon was about to find out.

Amaranthus…HELP!

20
The Mind Trap

The VR prison

Tarie curled up in the inferno, her whole attention focused on the *heat-pain-fire-panic* that consumed her. It didn't stop. It didn't stop. It didn't…

…until suddenly she realised that she could think again. The flames were as intense as they'd always been, but somehow she became aware of a third person in there with them. She couldn't see them, couldn't hear them talk, but it felt like they touched her on the shoulder before vanishing again.

And then through the fire Tarie could make out Bets' sobbing, rocking form. She reached out as far as she could manage and just brushed her fingertips over the girl's ankle.

Somehow, in the midst of the pain and chaos, Elspeth felt a faint touch on her ankle. Just the lightest touch, but it sent a jolt of coolness through her body. Everything still hurt, but she was able to formulate one important thought. The only one she could.

Amaranthus!

At first there seemed to be no change. But Elspeth gradually became aware again of life beyond the fire's scorching heat. Of her side pressed up against the crisp, bumpy shape of the tinder still underneath her – of that light touch on her ankle. Of the *real* world, in which she sat safely on a solid yet giving surface. Of Tarie's *real* hair under her hand…of the *real* cleansing, soothing flame arising from her palm.

It hurt, oh how everything hurt, but a gentle peace seemed to overlay her confusion. Her mind was somewhat free of the trap – 'twas once again her own, just enough to form clear thoughts, although not to move, nor even to open her burning eyes.

My gift, she cried out within her mind, directing the thought strongly towards Amaranthus. *Why has it failed to enter this place?*

There was a brief pause, then an image entered her head. 'Twas of her globe-prison as she had first seen it; a completely sealed space in which the fire raged and fell. She had been able to use her own soothing flame from outside, moving even through the barrier. But not from in here…

Suddenly revelation dawned – the globe-prison surely prevented the use of any gifts inside it. 'Twas both simple and terrible.

Elspeth rolled onto her back, ignoring the pain as she pondered the dilemma. 'Twas a trap of the mind that held them here, convinced that they were unable to leave, and that they were in the most dreadful pain. How did one convince one's own mind that 'twas mistaken?

There must be a way, she thought fiercely. There was *always* a way. After all, had not her own sister Anne once been in such a situation? A snake pit, or some such thing, which Anne had eventually escaped from once she understood 'twas mere illusion…but only after staying an entire night in such frightful circumstances.

Finally Elspeth dared to open her eyes. Orange and red filled her vision as before, but this time she squinted until she could make out the edge of the prison, and what appeared to be a faint dark shadow.

The villain!

The Other realm

Jon was going to be eaten by a crazed Creature. It was going to happen, he realised in panic, even as the fuzz of his web wrapping seemed to overwhelm him with warmth, completely in contrast to the situation.

Oh Chaos, he was going to go the same way as his birth mother. Killed by a truly terrifying, bestial Creature without the wits to control humans rather than destroy them. He'd probably end up a desiccated pile in some Creature latrine – if Creatures used latrines.

This was not a heroic ending!

Jon began to struggle frantically in his bindings as the White Prince's silhouette loomed over him. So when his fingers touched on something thin and hard, his only thought was that it could be a weapon. He tried to swing it, to cut the web…

…and suddenly he was on the ground. *Oof.*

But even the fall had seemed muffled, padded.

Jon's mouth certainly wasn't, though. "Amaranthus!" he blurted out, unable to stop the cry for help.

A beam of light shot out from whatever was in his hand, momentarily cutting through the darkness and illuminating the building's interior. But instead of making Jon blink at the change, he felt like he saw *everything* in that moment before darkness returned.

Where was the White Prince?!

He looked down at his hand, squinting at what was surely the outline of the Amaranthus circlet. *Thank you!*

But the danger wasn't over yet. Jon could still hear faint sounds of movement that surely weren't his own, and when the White Prince spoke again, he'd been expecting it yet still jolted in shock anyway.

"Jayel Jonnamin." The voice rang out, soft and almost hissing, with that distinctively *Other* tone to it. **"You broke your promise to me."**

It seemed the White Prince wanted to talk rather than attack. Fine! Jon spun around, looking for the source of the voice. He liked the first option too! "What promise?"

"You pledged to be my eyes and ears, my hands and feet in the normal realm," the White Prince whispered. His voice seemed to be coming from multiple directions, but he was still unseen. **"I gave you power and respect. You still use my gift of flight, yet you've turned your back on me. You retrieved the curse-breaker, but did not face Audaline. How terribly disloyal."**

Jon swallowed, feeling the hairs standing on end over his whole body. There were so many things wrong with what the Creature had said, but he couldn't pinpoint any of them because he was so shaky with fear. Curse-breaker? Was the White Prince referring to the circlet? And what was the defence against Creatures again?

And he'd taken back that promise about being the White Prince's carrier, damn it!

But the terror blocked out everything except Jon's immediate surroundings. He felt so small, so helpless, like his doom was surely moments away. What could an unarmed nobody like him do against an immortal Creature?

Jon held up the circlet in shaking hands, and a glint of light caught on the scrolling text.

Amaranthus.

Maybe he wasn't entirely unarmed after all.

The VR prison

Elspeth sat crouched in the middle of an inferno, her mind and body almost entirely overwhelmed by pain.

But not entirely. She still held just enough clarity to see the dark smudge of the villain standing outside their prison, and to feel the tingle of her cleansing flame in her real hand in the real world.

If 'twill not work inside this prison, she thought, *then I shall go outside of it.*

Using all of her energy, Elspeth imagined the silvery flame rushing up the outside of the glass globe, directly towards the villain.

And somehow, even through the roaring of fire in her ears, she heard a scream.

Hurrah!

The normal realm

In the real world, Luca leaned back in his safe room's chair, letting it tip until his head touched the ground, then slowly bounced back up to level. Tip…bounce. Tip…bounce.

"Would you stop that?!"

"Ah, Mother. Your dulcet tones lose nothing over this VR connection compared to real life." Luca's words were sarcastic, but he still sat upright as ordered.

The small room had the necessities to live in for up to a week – food, a closed-away bathroom, and three video/VR walls. So while he was still locked away in his live-in office's safe room, through VR he was also sharing space with Lilith, who was based in her own lavish apartments in the borderlands.

Unusually, her side showed real life rather than a constructed VR scene. Right now, she sat in a living room with her two current boy-carriers. The one with short dark hair sat slumped in a chair with his eyes closed, twitching a little at whatever VR scene his mind played out. The blond one seemed a bit smarter, since he leaned forward in his seat, his full attention on his master. He definitely looked a little anxious, though.

"I've got one week," Lilith finished telling the blond. "Which means you have three days, Gavriel. Is that understood?"

"Of course, Master. Anything for you."

Lapdog. Luca wondered again how his mother managed to attract these obsequious boys into her service. She always ended up with young, good-looking ones, and she'd leave them both far stronger and far weaker than how they'd begun, and in complete servitude to her. They'd give up any hope of fathering children (should that have been a desire) and they'd end up funnelling power to Lilith for as long as they survived.

But that must be Lilith's greatest talent, besides her innate immortality and her ability to change her appearance. She could convince men that she'd give them everything they ever dreamed of. Her follow-through wasn't good, but they still seemed to fall for it.

Speaking of which… "The stupid one's ears are smoking," Luca pointed out helpfully. "Maybe he's thinking too hard."

Lilith and Gavriel both turned to the seated young man,

who indeed was steaming a little, like one of those humorous VR settings Luca occasionally liked to use. Lilith cursed as the boy began to spasm. Gavriel stepped towards him, but she grabbed his arm.

"Don't touch Basir," she ordered. "Something's happening to my connection."

The blond's eyes widened, then his lips tightened into a straight, angry line. "It's the fire thing, isn't it? It's what happened to Rokky."

Ah. How enlightening. Luca sat up straighter, studying the scene with more interest. He'd known well what had happened to the second of Gerak's carriers – because obviously the boy was no longer attached to Gerak at all. It was a lesson to anyone who used conduits or carriers to avoid this newest enemy weapon, which was quite clever, even if used by the wrong side.

"Aren't you going to try to stop it?" Luca asked mildly. "It doesn't look comfortable."

"It *isn't*," Lilith snapped. "And I can't stop it. Basir has to choose to exit Elsewhise – he's not locked in."

"Dangerous," Luca mused through a half-smile. Leaving that one to decide anything on his own was not a smart idea.

He caught Gavriel's eye briefly and saw a spark of spite in his expression. Gavriel obviously wouldn't be trying to rescue his fellow conduit/carrier.

Meanwhile, the stupid one – Basir – kept thrashing, throwing his arms and legs around as if trying to shake off whatever assailed him. He rolled out of his chair then onto the floor, turning until he hit the nearest wall, right underneath Lilith's array of mounted valuables. Those included a couple of expensive entry pieces, including a polished metal one almost identical to the one Luca had given to Jon. He already knew they were real rather than VR, and he wondered idly how well they were mounted on the wall.

But because there was nothing better to do, he leaned back in his chair and watched the drama unfolding from across the city.

The Other realm

Jon held up the circlet with shaking hands, abruptly aware of what it was, and how his birth mother had once used it. He didn't understand exactly what it did, just that it had power.

Maybe it *was* a curse-breaker.

"Amaranthus," he breathed, half a plea for help, half a statement of intent. If the circlet held any power, he needed it *now*.

Suddenly a bolt of light shot from the circlet to strike the nearest wall. A huge, webbed curtain fell heavily to the ground, sending up a cloud of dust.

Jon blinked, seeing stars from the brightness against the surrounding dark. He…he hadn't been expected that.

There was a long silence; so long that he wondered if he'd somehow scared away the Creature. Could he be so lucky?

"Traitor," the White Prince hissed.

Chaos. No, Jon clearly wasn't that lucky.

"Your little lights don't bother me," the Creature continued, his voice echoing around the room so its origin was impossible to pinpoint. *"Lay down your weapon, vow to do my bidding, and I may just allow you to live."*

Jon caught sight of a shadow from the corner of his eye, and he turned towards it, holding the circlet at arm's length as he shielded his eyes with his other arm. "Amaranthus!"

This time the burst of light was as explosive as a lightning bolt. He didn't see where it hit, but the feeling of being blanketed in warm fuzziness grew even stronger.

"Failure!" Now the White Prince sounded like he was right behind Jon. *"Weak, stupid, pointless child. I'll sharpen my teeth on your bo-"*

"Amaranthus!" Jon shouted as he spun around, holding the circlet outstretched like a weapon. "Amaranthus! Amaranthus, Amaranthus, Amaranthus, Amaranthus!"

With each word, light burst out of the circlet, striking the White Prince's temple over and over and bringing the massive, heavy layers of web crashing to the floor. Jon stopped caring where he aimed, deciding he was going to bring this place to the ground. Creatures were immortal, but he was going to wreck this one's day if it was the last thing he did.

"…AMARANTHUS!!!"

A truly massive burst of light shot out of the circlet, exploding outwards to hit every single wall. The last remaining webs crumbled and fell to the ground, clearly visible in the now constant light. Jon held his breath as some of the piles of webbing seemed to move a little…or were they just settling into place? He couldn't see anyone else in here. Even the human-shaped mummy forms had disappeared, if they'd ever really been here.

"And I take back my promise!" he shouted, then his panting breaths were the only sound to break the thick, eerie silence.

Until…

"Missed me," the White Prince whispered.

The VR prison

Filled with new purpose, Elspeth set her mind to funnelling the cleansing flame to one specific place just outside the globe.

At first nothing changed within the globe – 'twas as dreadful and fiery as ever – but then bit by bit, the fire began to reduce. Through the glass barrier she could clearly make out a silvery form, flickering in and out of sight as though 'twas made of mist.

Then two shadowy, gnarled hands pressed against the outside of the barrier. Purple light emitted from their overlong fingers, carving glowing shapes ever deeper into the prison's barrier. It appeared that although Elspeth had caught the villain with her flame, they were intent on strengthening the prison nonetheless.

But Elspeth was determined to triumph. She clambered to her feet even as the fire within her prison reduced to embers, then slapped her hands against the barrier just below the villain's, almost matching them. Then she focused on spreading and intensifying her silver flame.

You shall not win, she vowed, even though she still could not hear her own words. *You shall not win, oh wicked enemy of ours.*

As if encouraged by her determination, she watched as her silver flame licked up the outside of the globe, wrapping around a now-distinct tarlike figure. The deep symbols and text on the globe's barrier glowed a brighter purple as if the villain too put all their energy into the battle, even as they themselves were consumed.

Elspeth could feel their fire burning low at her feet, a painful but dismissible heat. She could not make out facial features, but she'd vow that the villain looked not at all like the one she'd previously faced. That had been a woman with silvery-white hair and yellow eyes. This…this was a tar-faced fiend.

Give up, she thought fiercely, imagining the cleansing flame separating them from their own Creature-bought power. *GIVE UP!*

The pressure inside the globe built up until Elspeth's ears began to ache. Her vision was filled with silver and purple, and 'twas all she could see until-

POP!

The villain abruptly vanished, as did the last of the warmth around her feet. Suddenly the air around her felt different. "By the rood," she breathed. And this time – thank the Eternal one – she heard her own voice.

She had defeated the villain. *She had overcome!* "We won!" she cheered.

A moment later she heard Tarie say, "Emergency evacuate! EVACUATE!"

Elspeth turned to look at her. The other girl was sitting on the ground, her dark eyes wide and her curly hair dishevelled. "The escape code still doesn't work," Tarie said redundantly. She huffed out a heavy sigh and got to her feet. "Oh, well. I don't know what you did, but we're still inside this place, and the curse is still active. So thanks for whatever that was – but any ideas for escaping?"

Then Elspeth saw that indeed, the symbols or text etched in the globe's side still glowed purple, even though the tinder had vanished from around their feet.

They were still in danger, she realised in dismay.

They had to find a way out.

Missed me, the Creature had said.

This wasn't a game! And in spite of the faint, now ongoing light cast by the circlet, Jon couldn't see the White Prince at all. It should have made him terrified, but instead he was suddenly furious.

He shouted into the darkness, "What do you want from me?! Was it not enough for you to kill my birth mother; do you have to target me as well? Why would you try to send me against Audaline? Is this the curse-breaker or not? And if it is, why did you send me to Audaline when you had it the whole time? And why does every Creature always try to send me to *another* Creature, when they refuse to take my pledge themselves?!"

His words didn't even echo; absorbed immediately into the dull, muffling surroundings. He knew it was stupid to ask such questions of a depraved immortal Creature, but he'd said them now, and he found he wanted to know the answers.

"Your mother…?"

Jon still held the circlet at arms' length, a weapon ready to go, but he couldn't pinpoint the voice's source. "She had this circlet. Then seventeen years ago, she came here and disappeared. Then I found it here. So if you didn't kill her…"

There was a long silence, long enough that Jon found himself tensing up, waiting for a sudden attack.

But then the White Prince said with a soft, sinister chuckle, **"Oh, she was just another body in a long line of them. But her death will seem merciful compared to your own. Beg for mercy, little boy; repledge yourself and I might just-"**

Jon had heard enough. "Amaranthus!" Chiding himself for expecting any worthwhile answers from a Creature, he sent off another round of light bolts, channelling his pain and anger into bringing down every last visible web.

Finally he stopped, panting as he looked around at the destruction. The more light he shot, the more the webs shrivelled and disappeared. The walls were clear now, and the piles of thick webbing were reducing. It seemed their contents were too.

But he still couldn't see a Creature.

It suddenly occurred to Jon that in the normal realm, hearing a voice didn't mean someone was nearby. It just meant there was a speaker of some kind, maybe even playing a recording.

Why should the Other realm be any different? Maybe the White Prince wasn't even here. Maybe he never had been – and maybe the shadowy form that Jon had seen and had been so terrified of was just an illusion.

Even as Jon thought that, he caught a glimpse of something moving out of the corner of his eye. He spun, aiming the circlet but not yet shooting. With his view directly through the circlet's centre – almost like a telescope or the sights of an old weapon – he suddenly saw what he'd missed before.

A small, shrivelled Creature, hunched in the corner of the room, and almost blending in with the grubby, pale webbing surrounding it.

The normal realm

Luca watched with interest from the safety of his locked room as Basir twitched and spasmed on the floor, banging repeatedly into the wall and making the rack of decorative-yet-functional entry pieces rattle above him.

"He's really hanging in there," Luca commented. "Blondie, maybe you should go back into the programme and give him a hand."

Gavriel gave him an evil glare across the VR connection. He stood some distance away from his fellow conduit/carrier, with his arms folded and his lips tight. "I can't fight this weapon," he snapped. "Once it's got you, you have to run and try again later."

"Fail again later…" Luca goaded, since that was exactly what had happened. He'd been watching that drama unfold with interest too – from the moment a new Word-speaker moved into the apartment across from his, Lilith had marked them for execution. Tiger's orders, of course. Word-speakers were a dangerous breed, although Luca wasn't sure exactly why they were any worse than anyone else attached to their enemy. And while Basir, Gavriel and Lilith had never identified what (or who) had been targeting them with the silver fire, it appeared that mystery was now solved.

It was another little girl, and one they'd caught in the same VR prison carefully crafted to trap the Word-speaker. From what

Luca had picked up from Gavriel and Lilith's conversation, the girl flashed in and out of sight, but seemed to be trapped and powerless nonetheless.

Until now, obviously.

Basir gave one last almighty spasm as a faint silver mist seemed to cover his body, then suddenly his eyes popped open. He swore passionately and at length, then looked up at Lilith with a despairing expression. "I failed you, Master. I built up the curse and almost destroyed the enemies, but then they fought back. I could not hold on long enough."

"If you'd held on any longer, the carrier bond would have broken entirely," she said sharply. "Then I would have had to remake it, and you would not have liked that."

"Maybe with Gavriel's help..." Basir glared at the other young man. There was no love lost there.

Lilith waved a hand dismissively, which Basir clearly took as approval. He staggered to his feet, narrowly missing getting a blade entry piece to the back of the head, then turned to study the rack. A moment later he touched the shiniest entry piece, the one like a silver knife. His eyes glazed over again (not much of a change, Luca thought) and he went still.

Gavriel sighed inaudibly then moved to follow, but Lilith put a hand on his arm. Whatever she told him must have been via their mental connection, but Luca could work it out for himself.

If it all went wrong, Lilith didn't want to lose both of them at once.

Good help was so hard to come by.

The VR prison

Tarie stood next to her unlikely rescuer with her hands on her hips. They both stared at the enormous clear barrier that kept them in. Even though Tarie had been...not in a good place mentally...she still knew exactly what that writing said.

Bets shuffled her small feet, crunching the dry tinder underfoot. It was blackened a little, rather like the globe itself, and every last hint of heat had abruptly left it. But even though it ought to have burned up a dozen times over, it was still *there*.

"What do you think the symbols say?" she asked finally.

Tarie raised an eyebrow, but didn't comment on the girl's illiteracy. She was plain strange, but she was also clearly not the one Tarie needed to watch out for. "It's a curse," she explained. "To drive the target insane."

Bets' green eyes widened to almost comic proportions. "How truly wicked," she said in a hushed tone. "But I'd vow it almost worked. I was entirely incapable of thought for some time." She shivered.

Tarie couldn't help shivering in sympathy. She was grateful not to be a trembling wreck right now, but it seemed that as soon as the pain had gone, most of the trauma had gone with it. But only most. "Do your fancy abilities extend to breaking open this kind of cage?" she asked, giving the barrier an experimental push with both hands.

But it proved to be now far thinner than it had been before, and it crumpled under her fingers like a damaged piece of plastic sheeting. She gasped and pulled her hands away, but the thin, fragile barrier moved with her. The glowing text of the curse was a mere handspan above her fingers. "Ugh! Get it off!"

"I shall help!" Bets grabbed onto the now-stretched barrier, which had crumpled entirely inwards as if made of melting plastic. She tugged it away from Tarie and bathed it in some kind of silvery mist, but it stayed glued to Tarie's hands even as it pulled away from the ground – the barrier no longer complete. "Oh look, a hole! We may escape!"

Not if Tarie was dragging the curse along with her! She shook both hands frantically and spoke the Words at high speed, feeling tremendous relief at actually hearing them again, and held her arms outstretched as if she could distance the foul text from her body.

Elspeth tried to help, but the barrier was too strongly attached to Tarie. It tore and shrivelled until it didn't cover them at all; until it was the size of a bed sheet; then until it was as small as one of Tarie's tunics. But the remaining fragment was still firmly attached to both hands, and the curse itself shrunk and grew denser and darker, the text still reversed from her point of view.

"Stupid thing!" Tarie exclaimed. "This is the worst VR

programme I've ever been in, bar none. If only we could evac-" She suddenly realised that with the barrier removed, the usual VR functions might have returned too. "Evacuate! *Emergency* evacuate!"

But to her immense disappointment, nothing changed a jot. Just like last time.

"'Tis most likely forbidden to leave in such a way," Bets said apologetically. "Max told me as much, since he said 'twas a VR dart that brought you to this place against your will. So let us find the exit, as surely such a thing cannot follow us out of this cursed VR programme. Once we are free, we shall be free indeed."

Tarie made an unhappy sound but had to agree. She didn't know who Max was, but she understood the comment about VR darts. Those were illegal tech – but if you were trying to *kill* a person, that was just as illegal.

So she stopped her panicked flailing for long enough to see the incompleteness of the place around them. It was a very plain, commercial-style town, the sort you'd only ever see in VR. In real life, almost all buildings were many levels high due to rules around city limits. But here, the plain flat ground stretched out to a plain, high wall that seemed to surround them from every side.

Tarie spun around, her arms still outstretched and with the crumpled, glowing curse attached. "What, are we supposed to-"

Fly out, she was going to say. But suddenly there was a tall, charcoal grey figure right in front of her. It must be Gavriel. His rough features were unrecognisable even now that she knew who to look for, but she understood the expression of rage and horror on his ropy, tarlike skin. His mouth was open far too wide for any human being, and a faint purple glow emanated from the depths of his throat.

He looked down at his chest, and she looked with him to see that her hands were *inside* his chest. Right to the wrist; curse and all. It was remarkably like that violent VR game they'd once played, yet with far, far higher stakes.

"Déjà vu," she blurted out. "Last man standing."

Tar-Gavriel's mouth opened even wider than should be possible…then he exploded into a shower of dry, ashy particles.

Tarie and Bets were left in an otherwise empty courtyard as the ash dissipated into the air, taking even the curse with it.

The normal realm

Luca watched as Basir twitched in his place underneath the rack of entry pieces, his hand still lightly touching the silver blade he'd used to re-enter Elsewhise and the carefully created prison. Suddenly he went rigid and his eyes widened. His mouth opened in a wordless groan. "Aaaaahhhhhhhhhh…"

"*Now* is your connection to him broken, Mother?" Luca asked curiously. It was hard to tell from this distance. He could see all sorts of things via VR, but couldn't sense alter-power.

"Yes, but it's worse than that," Lilith said through tight lips. She took a step back from Basir, who was now flailing against the wall. He'd let go of the entry piece and began banging his head against the patterned wallpaper, making the rack above him tremble with each blow. "The insanity curse has turned against him instead."

Huh. Luca was about to ask how to remove that kind of curse – it was a useful thing to know, not that he was definitely planning to recreate such a thing – when the rack of weapon-shaped entry pieces proved itself to be poorly made, and the entire thing fell off its fixing...

...Right onto Basir, who was still mindlessly banging his head against the wall. There was a sound like '*urk*' and he suddenly went still.

Ugh. Clearly, making entry pieces in the shape of blades wasn't the best idea Lilith had ever had.

Into the shocked silence Luca said, "Your other boy could have stopped that." It was well known that Lilith's boys could move faster than the blink of an eye when they wanted to – an old ability of hers that she'd long lost use of, and could only pass on to her carriers.

Lilith gave Gavriel a cool glance, but didn't reprimand him. "Basir was lost the moment the curse took hold," she said flatly. "This way, we just have to clean up the mess." She indicated to Gavriel. "Deal with it, then go do what I told you. You're doing the work of two, now."

"One and a half," Luca suggested. "Basir never was playing with a full deck of cards."

Gavriel shot a smirk towards Luca, but his mood seemed grim. "I still need to check on the delivery I sent to 42-F, now we know the insanity curse failed. We can't let the Word-speaker get away."

Lilith looked down at her deceased dark-haired carrier then raised an incredulous eyebrow at the blond. "You don't say."

"I will complete my mission," Gavriel continued more passionately. "I won't let you down."

She sighed, setting her arm around his neck. "My dear boy, this is your last chance to get rid of the Word-speaker. If you don't succeed today…"

Luca perked up. Would she kill this one too?

"…then you'll have to leave them be for a while. Your new mission takes precedence, is that clear? While I can't believe I'm saying this, there are far, far more important things to deal with than one little Way-follower."

Gavriel looked dumbstruck, but Luca just shrugged. She had a point. There wasn't time for personal vendettas, since the whole world was about to turn upside-down.

21

Truth from Lies

The Other realm

There *was* a Creature in here. Jon almost dropped the circlet in surprise, but managed to hang onto it. Through the centre of the circlet it was like he could see what was really there; what had previously been hidden.

But this Creature clearly wasn't the White Prince. Instead, it was one of the smallest Jon had ever seen, only the size of a child. It was also shrivelled like an ancient alien from a sci-fi VR program. It hissed at him, revealing a toothless mouth, but didn't retreat.

There was nowhere to retreat to, Jon realised. The door must be behind him, but he didn't dare to turn his back on the Creature to confirm.

"Would you now attack my servant?" the White Prince crooned, his voice as ever seeming to come from everywhere and nowhere. *"You cannot harm even the weakest Creature, for they are still immortal, as you never will be. If you wish for death enough that you'd challenge me in person, then I will show you exactly how desperately weak, pathetic and inferior you truly are."*

Ugh. The White Prince seemed like a broken VR track at this point. But it was clear to Jon that he *did* have cronies after all; case in point. So much for him eating all competition…but then this small Creature was hardly competition.

Jon didn't even have the heart to try to shoot it with the circlet's light. He shuffled to the side, leaving a clear path to the door. "Leave," he told the little Creature. "I won't stop you."

The White Prince laughed in the background. The little

Creature just hissed, but didn't move.

Jon lost it then. He'd had a very stressful day – a very stressful year, in fact – and he didn't appreciate being laughed at by someone who couldn't actually hurt him, judging by the thick protective layer he could still feel. And now he was no longer overwhelmed by fear, he remembered exactly what Amaranthus had told him.

When you know a Creature's true name, you know their true nature. And when you know their true nature and you hold my authority…you can send them any way you like.

And Jon had the Amaranthus circlet, right in his hands. How much more could he 'hold' Amaranthus's authority?

"I need your name, is that it?" he snapped at the Creature. "Your true name. Well then. Amaranthus, *show me.*"

His view within the circle of metal blurred and changed, and the circlet did too. Suddenly it seemed to be a metal rope, looping from what was in his hand over to the Creature, then acting as chains around its neck, and the saggy sticks that were its wrists and ankles. Blunt, crude text ran all along the metal chain, forming as he watched. *SHAM-SHAKR'N-LESHEKER-LYGARI-FIBBER-*

"Fibber?" Jon exclaimed in disbelief. That was…a really, really stupid name for something that had been alive longer than human history.

The White Prince's voice picked up speed. *"It won't work. You'll fail as you've always failed. Better not to even try. Worthless. You're worthless and everyone knows it-"*

Jon raised his voice to drown out the unseen White Prince. Half-laughing and feeling like he'd ingested joyfruit again, he declared, "Alright, Fibber. By the power vested in me by this Amaranthus circlet, I order you to go as far from this place as a Creature can possibly go, and never come back."

It had been a joke, really. An adrenaline-fueled nonsensical statement. But it just proved that he should watch his words in the Other realm, because next thing there was a *bang* and the faint smell of burning, and the little Creature came rushing at him faster than he could blink. Jon couldn't react – couldn't even lift a hand to defend himself – but then suddenly it disappeared into his chest.

Jon looked down at himself in horror and saw a faint

luminescent outline under his jacket. It looked like his heart was glowing, but then the light dimmed.

Had the Creature gone *inside* him?!

Overcome by panic, Jon ripped off his jacket then scrambled at his shirt, ripping it open. He actually would have clawed at his chest too – as if he could pull out the Creature that seemed to have gone inside him – when suddenly a small, glossy brown shape came swinging out on a cord.

Jon blinked at it as recognition dawned. It was the safekeeper Bets had gifted him today: the pocket universe. The one that was probably broken, she'd said, since she couldn't get things out of it again.

He finally understood what had happened, and felt weak with relief. He'd told the Creature to '*go as far from this place as a Creature can possibly go'*. He'd thought it was attacking him, but instead it had been pulled inside the safekeeper he'd been wearing.

Because the farthest from this place a Creature could possibly go…was probably to the alternate universe accessed through this very object.

Jon very slowly and carefully removed the shell safekeeper pendant, making sure to hold the circlet tight in his other hand. He wasn't going to panic, he told himself. He wasn't upset that he had been inadvertently wearing a Creature like a necklace-

YUUUCCKKK, actually he was *sooo* upset because that was Chaos-damned disgusting! Jon shuddered, throwing the safekeeper at the far end of the room. It bounced off the stone wall and back towards him, and on instinct he held up the circlet once again. "Amaranthus!"

The safekeeper exploded into a fizzy little cloud of sparks, which quickly faded into nothing. The Creature didn't reappear, and it occurred to Jon that he'd probably given it a permanent home in whatever place that safekeeper led to.

Good riddance. He shuddered again reflexively, but even seeing the thing vanish had made him feel incredibly light all of a sudden, like something oppressive had vanished from the atmosphere.

At least the stupid White Prince had shut up, he thought viciously. He held up the circlet again, this time wary of any surprise Creature cronies. His initial desire to flee was gone. But while it seemed that the White Prince wasn't in here, Jon couldn't shake the feeling he was missing something.

"What am I not seeing?" he groaned aloud. He held up the circlet and tried again. "Amaranthus, show me what's really here."

The sense of being blanketed increased as Jon lifted the circlet to his line of sight, then turned and studied the room. There was something fuzzy just to his right, but when he followed it, it seemed to move as well. Then the same happened when he turned to his left. He wasn't afraid, precisely, just curious.

Then Jon lifted the circlet over his head and craned his neck to study the ceiling.

But he couldn't see the ceiling. Instead, through the circlet a massive face stared down at him, covered in shaggy white fur. Its eyebrows were shaggier still, almost covering its small bright eyes. They were so big they could have doubled as generous fur wraps for a large-framed lady. It looked like a friendly yeti, and nothing at all like the White Prince. *"Hey,"* it rumbled.

Jon dropped the circlet with a startled cry. The giant white beast vanished, but the sense of being blanketed in fur did not.

Fur. Jon suddenly realised that he always felt wrapped in a furry, warm, fuzzy protective layer when he was in the Other realm – but no one else seemed to have the same experience.

Possibly, he thought, because they were not hanging out with a colossal yeti-gorilla-thing.

Fighting the urge to laugh hysterically or run screaming, Jon carefully picked up the circlet again. He lifted it to his face, then very slowly and carefully craned his neck again, looking directly above him.

Yep. The big, shaggy white being was still there. Its face moved in what might have been a smile, but how could you tell when its head was the size of a kitchen table? Jon nodded faintly, then scanned his way down the tree trunk-sized arms that ran directly on either side of Jon's body, ending in massive fists which were like boulders.

Ohhhh. This was undoubtedly a Person from the Mountain of Glass, but unlike anyone Jon had ever imagined. He took a step forward, meaning to turn to get a better view, but the Person moved with him, knuckling on their massive arms and fists, rather like an enormous gorilla. The movement caused a faint tickling sensation along Jon's own arms even through his jacket.

"Do you do this a lot?" Jon asked faintly.

The Person's eyebrows rose and fell. It (he?) nodded.

A Person of few words, clearly. But so many odd things made sense now. Amaranthus had said he was protected, but Jon hadn't thought to ask *how*. "I thought you were a sort of force," he said apologetically to the yeti-gorilla. "A protective layer keeping the Creatures away from me."

OK, now that was definitely a smile. Then the Person lifted one colossal fist, stretched it out all the way across the room – the entire building – and knocked down the last, small remaining piece of web.

The message was clear. Those fists were Jon's protective layer.

That was why the Creatures never came near him, he realised in dawning amazement. It wasn't just his Amaranthus mark, left by his birth mother's use of the circlet. It was this guy.

Domitian hadn't dared to come near him. The *White Prince* hadn't dared to touch him! He'd just thrown Jon a creepy, metallic-tasting fruit (OK, it was clearly an organ. An organ, alright?) which Jon had eaten like a fool.

But they hadn't truly tried to touch him, because how could they get past Boulder Fists here?!

"My mind is blown," Jon told the Person – his guardian. "Utterly, utterly blown. Do you have a name?"

The guardian shrugged. *Fylax.*

Bets had mentioned a Fylax, Jon was certain of it. So he was clearly protected outside the Other as well as inside…although imperfectly. He'd been hurt enough, Jon remembered, and had almost died when Rokal had hung him from the flagpole. If not for that old guy coming from nowhere and helping him down…

Jon's thoughts stilled. The old guy with the shaggy white eyebrows, stronger than he should have been. That must be his guardian's human form. How many times had Fylax kept Jon alive and he hadn't even known it?

"Thank you," he said meekly, then again with more passion. *"Thank you."*

You're welcome. Fylax bumped Jon very gently with one fist, but it was enough to send him flying into the other fist. Then he gently righted Jon. *Don't you have something to do?*

Jon jolted himself. He'd actually forgotten that he was inside a Creature temple, looking for one of the most vicious and crazy Creatures in the Other.

Now he wasn't even scared, because he knew exactly what he hadn't seen all this time.

Elsewhise

There was nothing like a near-death experience to create a friendship, Elspeth thought. It had not taken her long to explain her presence here to Tarie, and not much longer to find the exit from the courtyard that had contained the prison. An archway had promptly appeared as soon as they'd voiced the need for one. Now Elspeth walked along the town's narrow streets with one arm linked through Tarie's, for they dared not risk being separated.

And this place *was* Elsewhise; she was certain of it – 'twas indeed the place she had visited once before, if only in her mind. Now they only had to find the true exit which would free their minds entirely.

But 'twas not so difficult, in truth. Elspeth would vow that the exit was right around the next corner…or mayhap the next one after that. This place could not be so very large, and Elspeth felt as though the more she focused, the more easily she would find what she wanted. This was a supernatural town that existed partly in the mind, partly in reality – so it appeared 'twas also shaped by the mind.

But she could not help but think 'twould be easier to focus if only Tarie would stop talking. The other girl had begun slowly, but now 'twas as though she had a river of words within her, desperate to spill out.

"And then my sister was beaten and we knew we had to leave Memrys. Erus was supposed to be safer, but it's not. Someone tried to kill me from my first day!" Tarie paused, but 'twas clearly only to gather breath as she continued. "I know I can be blunt sometimes, but surely I'm not that offensive."

"My intentions are good, but even I manage to offend

people," Elspeth said absentmindedly. She closed her eyes, focusing on her desire to leave, and the exit seemed to glow in her mind's eye, almost as though she had a rope connecting her to it. "I do believe I am becoming more tactful, but 'tis what comes of speaking your mind without first considering the consequences."

Elspeth stepped forward without opening her eyes, then decided 'twas a foolish choice and opened them again. But as they turned the next corner, an archway appeared up ahead. 'Twas the sort with rounded sides and a gently pointed tip. It stood on its own at the end of a smoothly paved path, and through it, the path continued as well-trod dirt.

Success! This *must* be the exit, for as they moved towards it, Elspeth felt as though the real world grew more and more solid round her. 'Twas as though she could blink and again find herself entirely in her little room, sitting on a comfortable couch next to Tarie, rather than in an odd little town at the edge of the borderlands.

Or more likely, if she was to walk through the archway then her mind would be entirely freed from this particular illusion/VR programme.

Now if only she could be certain Tarie would be freed in the same manner.

Next to her, Tarie sucked in a breath sharply. "You've got to see this, Bets."

"Yes, 'tis the exit, I am certain of it."

Tarie jiggled her arm where they were linked together. "Not the archway. Over *here.*"

Elspeth turned to her left, and for a moment her mind blanked. The path, which she'd sworn was within a town, was in fact running along the edge of a high, vast, dry-looking valley. And the valley was filled with these most enormous feline statues, each as big as one of the apartment blocks in Erus city. Bigger even, mayhap.

"Ooh. I have visited this place before," she said with some excitement. "The day I burned down the muse-*er…*"

But Tarie didn't seem to have noticed her misstep. "Look, the statues are disappearing," she breathed. "Where could they be going?"

Elspeth's eyes widened as she saw that indeed, the colossal forms were winking out of sight one by one. 'Twas a surreal sight, like something from a dream rather than reality. But she had no doubt that this *was* a sort of reality. "Something tells me we shall find out," she muttered.

Dragging her eyes away from the intimidating scene, she turned back to the archway. "Come now, Tarie. We've been fortunate thus far, but we must get our minds to safety before anyone notices we're here."

The other girl let herself be pulled towards the archway. Then closing her eyes again, Elspeth focused on that space and stepped through.

The Other realm

Jon circled the room once more, his giant fuzzy shadow moving with him every step of the way. But even through the circlet he couldn't find the White Prince. The Creature mustn't be here, he decided. Surely he just had the Other equivalent of good security cameras and had been speaking to him from a distance.

Besides, the White Prince hadn't said anything in a while. It could be a good time for Jon to go.

A finger as thick as Jon's leg tapped him on the shoulder, then pointed to the corner of the room where the little Creature had been hiding. Jon took a few steps in that direction, even though he'd already looked there. But this time, when he lowered the circlet he saw something new.

What he'd previously taken for shadowy rubble was in fact a tangle of fine black sticks...no, a decorative window frame with the glass missing? Jon kicked at the delicate-looking shapes and one of them crumbled into dust. But with that gone, he now clearly saw what the remaining object was.

A single wing as if from a giant butterfly; just the strutted framing without anything filling the gap. A useless wing, if it was such a thing.

A wing Jon had last seen on the White Prince, when he'd seen him through the Mountain of Glass's viewing pool. He'd learned about the price of stealing power as the Creatures had done, and he'd understood that the useless wings were the wages for taking what wasn't theirs. But had he even seen the White Prince's true form at all, or just one that the White Prince liked to project?

Jon stared down at the broken wing, lying exactly where that hissing little Creature had been. The one he'd taken for the White Prince's crony or servant. The White Prince had seemed to agree…but he'd also gone suspiciously silent the moment Jon had accidentally used that safekeeper.

The Amaranthus circlet had shown him *exactly* what was there, Jon realised. No terrifying monster about to devour him. Just a hissing little fibber, depending on lies to keep people too scared to flee – to scared to see it for what it really was.

Weak.

Jon turned to Fylax, desperate to confirm his suspicions. "Is that…the White Prince?"

It was.

"Was? How can a Creature ever be referred to in the past tense?"

Fylax opened his fingers in a starburst shape and pointed to the other side of the room, where the safekeeper had exploded. *Gone.*

"Gone? You mean, trapped somewhere else?"

No. Destroyed.

Jon's eyes bugged. "Can he come back?"

No. Destroyed, Fylax repeated, his tone gentle but insistent.

Ohhhh. It turned out that immortal Creatures…weren't entirely immortal after all. Jon cleared his throat, but his voice still came out as a squeak. "Has this…happened before?"

No. Fylax gave him a gentle tap on the back, which pushed him almost all the way to the exit.

Jon took that as a sign they were leaving. He turned and started walking backwards, talking to the Person who loped over him as they moved. "No, I mean has *any* Creature been, er, destroyed in any way. Had its wings fall off and turn to dust-"

No.

"So I'm the only person who's ever destroyed a Creature? Not that I'm claiming to have done it, just that I was holding the circlet…"

Yes.

Unreal. A Creature had been removed from the universe,

Jon marvelled…and *he'd* done it. Not by his own particular talents to be sure, but he'd still done it. Him. Jayel Jonnamin DeLuca.

A thought suddenly occurred. "Hey, can the Creatures see the future? Did they know I was going to do this?"

Their vision of the future is limited. They knew that a Creature would be destroyed by your hand, but they didn't know which Creature.

Had Jon thought his mind was blown before? Now it had gone supernova; all bright lights and sparkles and echoing sounds.

Well, he thought numbly. That explained why no Creature would take his pledge. If he knew someone had been fated to…kill him…he'd avoid them like the plague. So they'd all been keeping their distance when they weren't trying to have him killed in anticipation of what he was going to do.

Wow.

WOW.

Not so much of a failure anymore, was he?

And it explained why the White Prince had tried to send Jon to Audaline. The part about the curse-breaker had clearly been nonsense, just a way to get Jon to challenge the White Prince's enemy. Jon could only think that since the White Prince had tried to send him to the Power Performance temple, the Creatures must be more easily accessible in that place than he'd realised.

But in spite of that slightly scary realisation, when Jon reached the exit doorway from the Other realm, he stepped through it with his heart light and full of wonder.

He'd destroyed a Creature.

Ahhhh!!!

One moment Elspeth was stepping through the stone archway; the next she was opening her eyes to a veil of green. She sat up, pushing trailing vines off her face and body.

Next to her, a pile of greenery stirred and fell away, revealing Tarie's curly dark hair and cranky expression. "Chaos," she muttered. "I feel terrible."

"'Tis mostly likely the after-effects of the dart," Elspeth suggested, although in truth she had no idea. She felt quite good herself, puffed up with success and pleasure at overcoming such a dreadful challenge. "By the rood, I'd vow you are tall again."

Tarie sat up fully, which indeed did put her a good head taller than Elspeth, even sitting. She looked down at her sleeves with a grimace, then tugged at the material until it stretched to cover the bare skin of her wrists. "Where am I?"

"In a secret room just down the hall from your own apartment door. 'Tis hidden from any eyes but those who are meant to see it."

Tarie frowned. "At Eastern Way? But surely *you* didn't bring me here."

"You were your smaller self," Elspeth explained, looking the girl over. "I daresay you've grown while in that prison – what a clever trick! But as for how you got here, Max carried you." She hurried to add, "I was with him every step of the way, and I assure you all was quite above board."

"Max...?"

Oh. Had they not had this conversation yet? "Er...'tis an amusing tale, in truth. You recall how Rokal was behaving oddly after that day at the museum when I set him- Well, 'twas because his connection with his Creature Gerak was burned right away," Elspeth explained with forced joviality. "And he wished to be called Max and seemed quite a different person, so naturally I helped him to repledge to Amaranthus. After that, I felt quite obliged to trust him." And she really ought to somehow tell both Max and Jon to return, for their efforts were no longer required.

Tarie had been watching open-mouthed as Elspeth spoke, but suddenly her expression changed to horror. She leapt up and raced for the door.

Forsooth, surely the tale had not been *that* bad?

Rokal *had* carried her here. Bets was now confirming Gavriel's story, even though the girl didn't seem to realise it. And if Gavriel had been honest about that, Tarie realised, then he might have been telling the truth about sending 'a little surprise' to her home as well.

And she was here. Chaos, Lydia and their father would be home soon too!

This apartment only had one door. Tarie pushed through it easily and found herself in the hall just outside her own apartment. She raced past 42-G with its expensive plating, then barely paused for 42-F's door to open before rushing inside.

She almost ran into her father and Lydia who were hovering in the hall as if they'd just got home, hanging up their coats.

"Why hello there," Tarren said with a laugh. "What's got you in such a hurry?"

"You're all tall again," Lydia added wide-eyed. "Let me get the recorder!"

"Delivery!" Tarie burst out. "Has there been a drone delivery? Or was there anything at all in the foyer dropbox?"

Both looked baffled by her urgency. "Nothing in the dropbox downstairs," her father began. "But I haven't checked the drone-"

Tarie didn't have time to hear the rest. She ran for the other side of the apartment, straight to the slot in the wall that connected with the drone delivery box. Its light was flashing off which implied it was empty, but she didn't dare risk trusting it.

She slapped a hand against the wall slot and it opened, revealing an *almost* empty box. Except inside it was a tiny round shape, only the size of her fingernail. But *that* was glowing; turning from yellow to red and-

"GET DOWN!" Tarie shouted. She threw herself over the delivery box's open lid and-

BANG.

Jon was flying up to the top of his apartment building, headed for his own balcony, when the wall exploded in front of him.

The bright burst sent powerful waves rippling in every direction, tearing a hole in the building and scattering debris. Jon ducked, covering his head and neck with his arms until the danger receded.

Chaos. The Creatures didn't wait to retaliate, did they?

But a moment later he saw it hadn't been his balcony. Instead it had been his neighbour's...Tarie's.

With his ears ringing from the blast, Jon slowly flew closer until he could see everything. The explosion had completely taken

out Tarie's clear balcony barrier, as well as the balcony roof, floor, and part of the walls on either side. He could see straight into the debris-filled living area.

"Tarie?" he called, cautiously letting himself through the broken gap. "Is anyone there?"

A coughing sound caught his attention. Across the room, a young girl with Tarie's colouring lifted her head from behind the couch. She didn't look harmed, just shocked. Then Tarren stuck his head through the doorway, his own eyes also round with shock.

"By the rood," Jon breathed, borrowing a saying from Bets. "What happened here?"

Both Lydia and Tarren slowly looked up, staring above his head.

Jon looked up too, half-expecting to see Fylax in his fluffy glory, even though the Person had been invisible since they'd left the White Prince's temple. But instead, above him was Tarie's small, sturdy figure – hanging over the ceiling beam.

"Don't just stare," she said irritably. "Get me down!"

Jon got Tarie down as requested. Then Bets caught up to them, seeming to be blaming herself for not stopping the explosion even though Tarie was fine and Bets surely would have been blown to bits.

Then Anni came to see what had taken out a part of her balcony and had stayed, as upset as the rest of them.

Then the Public Safety drones showed up to check what had happened, and they had to file a report. Possibly the stupidest report ever.

"My older daughter grew extremely tall," Tarren had said awkwardly, "which seemed to make her extremely strong too. Then she found some sort of explosive in our drone delivery box. But somehow the force bounced off her and went outwards, so it only destroyed our balcony rather than the apartment. And…er…she's short again."

Yeah, that was basically it. Alter-power made for some odd tales, and it seemed Tarie's power had begun working in odd ways since she'd arrived in Erus. Making her grow in size and strength when she didn't use it – like pumping up a balloon full of air – then returning to normal size once all that strength and power was used up in some unnatural feat of strength.

The drones left, then everyone went to stay in Anni and Jon's home which at least had most of its walls. Tarie and Bets had burst out with the tale of how they'd escaped from a VR prison built by Gavriel (!) of all people. Tarie also seemed quite put out by some lie Gavriel had told her about Rokal's mother being murdered (rather than simply living in luxury somewhere near the Baltane Sea) which appeared to have been a sympathy ploy, but was hardly the worst thing Gavriel had done to Tarie.

"Chaos," Tarie muttered. "I forgot to put in the report that Gavriel sent the bomb. He told me in VR that he'd done it, you know."

"But if it was an illegal VR session, it won't be recorded," Lydia pointed out. "We won't be able to prove anything."

There was a glum silence.

"We'll have to move again," Tarren said, his whole posture defeated. "The sooner, the better. We can't wait for this fiend to try again."

Jon couldn't argue with that. And the Filats weren't the only ones who'd got on the wrong side of Creatures or carriers. He'd have to have that conversation with Anni tonight, and they'd make their own decisions.

"But you exploded Gavriel," Bets pointed out brightly. "Into ash, when you struck him with the curse."

Everyone stared at Tarie – some with horror, others with raised eyebrows.

"In VR," Tarie clarified. "I doubt he's really dead, even if it *was* him and not the other one." She sighed. "We should be so lucky."

That of course led to a lot more talk about how Tarie had been caught up in VR in the first place; how Jon had always despised Gavriel; and who on earth Bets was anyway. Bets had described herself as 'an Amaranthus-follower and a friend of Jon's', and the others had seemed to accept that. Anni had just looked pleased that Jon had a friend.

With all the explaining going on, it seemed a good enough time for Jon to summarize his own last week's (or months') adventures. He didn't mention the time travel, but mentioned what had happened when he'd gone to Luca's place along with ending up in the Other realm at the White Prince's temple.

In the horrified silence he added awkwardly, "Oh, and Bets, you won't be getting that safekeeper back, I'm sorry. I...er...accidentally put the White Prince in it...then exploded it into dust."

And yes, he was proud of the shocked hush that followed his statement. He added for good measure, "Fylax says the White Prince is as good as dead."

Jon didn't know if the others believed him, but Bets squeezed his hand and looked up at him with shining eyes. "I vowed you'd do something special," she said. "And now you have."

Jon blinked at her, feeling inordinately pleased by her words and her faith in him. "But why did you think that?" he asked quietly. "No one else did."

Bets seemed to ponder the question. "Amaranthus once told me that I had an inbuilt ability to see through illusion. So with you, mayhap I saw what was truly there." She shrugged and added cheekily, "It did not hurt that you were as handsome as a prince."

Jon's heart squeezed, and in that moment he wouldn't have chosen anyone else to be sitting beside him. He wanted to say more, but was suddenly reminded that they had company, and it wasn't the time for lengthy heart-to-hearts. He decided to talk to her properly the moment they had some free time (and no one was trying to kill them).

"Right," Tarie announced loudly. She sat on the floor where she'd been for the last half hour, with her hair a bit mad from the force of the explosion and her eyes a little unfocused. She held a full drink in one hand, and there was a bit of greenery stuck in her collar. "So let's address the real issue. Like Da said, we'll never be safe as long as we stay here, because someone's trying to kill us. Me. Us."

"We need to go to the authorities," Anni exclaimed. "It's not right that you'd have to leave!" She lifted a hand to her forehead where Jon knew her new mark rested unseen. "*We'll* have to leave, if the authorities don't help."

"The authorities like Luca?" Jon asked dryly. Never mind Luca's promise that they could dislike each other politely from a distance, like normal families. That had been broken the moment Luca sent Jon to the White Prince, and Jon had no doubt that Luca would drop them all in a volcano if he could get away with it.

"Obviously not," Tarie answered. "But what do you do when someone tries to murder you?"

Bets put up her free hand, since the other was still tightly holding Jon's. He didn't feel inclined to let it go. "I typically leave the location," she declared. "And the time period too, if I can."

"The time period?!" a couple of them echoed in unison.

"Are you saying you travel through time?" Tarren asked with one eyebrow raised. He looked very much like his daughter in that moment.

Bets nodded a little warily as if aware she may have said too much, then shot a glance at Jon. "Jon did too. 'Tis how we met."

Suddenly all eyes were on Jon again.

"Time travel?" Anni exclaimed. Her expression suggested she wanted to believe him, but wasn't sure if she could.

Jon opened his mouth to deny it out of habit – because only crazy people claimed they travelled through time – then realised that half the people around him had equally crazy lives and experiences. What was a little time travel compared to spontaneously growing and shrinking, or setting things on fire with your hands?

"You know how people can lose time in the Other realm?" he tried to explain. "Go in for what feels like a few hours, but come out and find that weeks have passed?"

Some of the others nodded.

"It's like that," Jon continued, "but with Amaranthus, it's not quite so…random. So yes, I travelled through time. And a bit more, which I'll tell you about when we aren't planning to flee for our lives."

The others seemed to accept that, and Bets said, "What about Rokal-Max? Is he not still searching for a way to rescue Tarie even now? We should warn him of what happened here."

Jon made a scoffing noise under his breath. The idea of inviting his former worst enemy to flee the city-state with them seemed a bit much when he hadn't even received a proper apology, but he knew it was the right thing to do. "I suppose we can't leave him unaware of the danger," he said. "Not now that he'll be a target himself."

"He's not answering his comm," Tarie replied, holding up her own piece. "I'll try again later."

Then Tarie's little sister spoke up. "Never mind that. Look at this!" Lydia had been silent till now, but she lifted up her wrist comm, displaying a good-sized holographic view of the Erus city centre and the Big Three's temples. Those were now just the Big One's temples, with that huge statue of creepy Audaline in her swirling robes and striped skin stretching over their roofs.

Even as they watched, the statue changed piece by piece. It grew until it was double the size; at least as tall as Jon's own apartment building if not taller; and it now resembled an enormous seated cat. Sharp teeth, shining gems set in its striped sides…and a head that turned to reveal one blue eye, one yellow.

"Oh dear," Bets squeaked. "That's horribly familiar."

"Get this," Lydia continued. "They're saying that Audaline is revealing herself – *itself* as some Creature called the Tiger. And it says that every single city-state now has one of these statues, and that every citizen has to come to the statue and pledge their allegiance within five days." She looked up at the others, her eyes wide and horrified. "It says that if you don't, then you're a traitor and you'll be…dealt with. What do you think they mean by that?"

"How about we don't hang around to find out?" Jon croaked. "Anyone got any cash? A vehicle?" It was rare to use cash, but most people kept a small supply in case the power went out. Jon had never bothered to, since that hadn't happened in his lifetime.

"I've got a vehicle!" Tarren said. "A good solid one, right Tarie?"

Tarie just groaned and set her face in her hands.

Jon's earlier euphoria was gone. While whatever had happened with the White Prince was significant, it was nothing compared to this. They might have to leave their homes permanently, because there was no way any of them would be going near that Creature statue.

The door sensor chimed, breaking the heavy silence. "Hello?" a young woman's voice called, echoing through the speakers. "Anni, are you home?"

Jon looked across at his mother, who was sitting snugly against Tarren. His arm was around her shoulders in a rather friendly manner – but Jon didn't have the energy to complain about it. Good for them.

"Will you check who it is?" Anni asked Jon quietly. "Set the door to 'away' if you don't recognise them."

Jon moved to get up, but just then he heard the door open.

A moment later a girl stuck her head into the room. She looked to be in her late teens; lean with long, straight auburn hair, fair skin and delicate features. "Oh. You've got company. Sorry to interrupt, but I really need to pick up Jayel. I didn't mean to leave him so long, but I think I was stuck in the Other realm...long story."

Pick up Jayel? Jon frowned, turning to look at his mother.

But Anni had frozen on the couch, her golden-brown skin draining into a pale, sallow shade. *"Maia?"* she whispered.

The girl's eyebrows shot up. "Anni. Wow...you really, *really* need a good sleep. And maybe a spa...and some makeup. You look *tired!* I guess my boy kept you up at night?"

In the dead silence Jon could hear his own heartbeat pounding in his head. It couldn't be. It just couldn't.

The others in the room looked like toys with bobbing heads as they turned from the girl – to Jon – to Anni – then back to the girl. Only Lydia didn't seem to understand that something was wrong.

Then the girl – Maia – turned to Jon. Her young face held impatience and some curiosity, and she cocked her head as she studied him. "Hello there. You know, you really remind me of this guy I...*knew*, Luke DeMannard. Are you related?"

Jon forced himself to nod, but he couldn't speak.

Anni got up off the couch and walked over to the girl. She took her hands, staring into her face. "Maia...*where have you been?!"*

Maia half-smiled, pushing her sister away a little and glancing awkwardly at the others in the room. "I wasn't gone that long, surely? Come on, where's my little Jay-Jon? He must've been missing me, and I can't wait to see him."

In unison everyone turned to stare at Jon. But he just kept staring at the girl...who was his birth mother...who wasn't dead...

...and who thought he was still a baby.

"Maia," Anni said carefully. "You've been gone for seventeen years. Jayel is..." She turned to look at Jon where he was still half-crouched on the floor.

Maia slowly turned towards Jon too, and her expression of horror and confusion must have echoed his own. "*No*," she breathed, and he mouthed the word along with her.

This couldn't be happening.

Epilogue

In the centre of Erus's temple district, streams of people came to pay their respects to the Tiger statue. They disappeared into doors at its base, then reappeared some time later from different doors on the other side.

Or most of them did, anyway. But now they wore dazed expressions as well as a tiny little mark right in the middle of their foreheads, shaped rather like a simple, squiggly-legged starfish. The new physical mark served as a tracker, proof of loyalty…and a means of control.

Luca watched sullenly from the nearby council office along with his mother Lilith. He'd had to get a Tiger mark as well to show his own allegiance. He'd managed to get it on his hand rather than his actual head, but he resented the intrusion. He was a Creature – mostly – and this was his body, damn it! Or Luke's, anyway. While Luca's true body still lay safe and sleeping in the borderlands, Luca would have to put up with the desperately unwelcome mark.

"And after I destroyed the White Prince for him, too," he said sulkily. "That was hard work, and dangerous. The boy could have killed *me!* And I sent him one of Gerak's old Princes of the Air too, not that he cares. So much for being allowed to rule on my own."

"Hush," Lilith said sharply from where she sat next to him, also overlooking the scene. Her mark was bold and black on her forehead, but Luca happened to know that was a fake. Her real mark was tiny and hidden in her hairline. Perks of being one of the Tiger's semi-trusted people. "You are still the governor of Greater Erus, are you not? With your Memrys and Dailan just as you always wanted. Stop complaining about the Tiger and focus on thriving. He may be your father, but he has no parental affection for you…or anyone. Support his reign and you too will be supported."

Yes, that was right. Luca's parents were Lilith, daughter of the White Prince and currently the world's oldest Halfling, and the Tiger, the Other's original leader. Now the normal realm's official leader.

But as Lilith had said, the Tiger held no fatherly feelings for Luca. He only cared about what Luca could do for him. And now Luca was as bound as any of these fools, unable to exercise his true independence and power over this state.

He looked past the statue to the glimmers of the Reamas river he could just see in the distance. He'd wanted so badly to bomb the Dailan side – to prove a point and because it would be amusing – but now he'd have to get the Tiger's permission to do so.

Hades. This was no fun.

Lilith stood abruptly. "I'm being called. You watch yourself, Legion – I won't always be here to do it for you."

Luca – or Legion the half-Halfling – was eighty-five years old. He did not need his *mother* watching over him...or watching him.

But because Luca was angry, not stupid, he kept his mouth shut. There had to be some way around this situation.

Long may the Tiger reign.

Not if he could do anything about it.

But while the humans pledged themselves en masse, down on the border between the Other and normal realms, something even more significant was taking place underground.

In a deep cave he'd visited many a time, the Tiger stood at the very edge of the Other realm, as far as its invisible barrier would allow him to go. Streams of power filtered into him from hundreds of thousands of new, more solid tattooed pledges, making his manlike form larger and stronger than ever before. The stripes and spots on his skin gleamed where his armour exposed it.

But his full, rather terrifying attention was fixed on a trio of humans directly on the other side of the barrier. They wore red cloaks, had marked foreheads, and were currently crouched around two sturdy, locked cases. He watched avidly as they carefully opened the first one, then withdrew a small wooden box, slightly battered by age. Then the second case was opened, and a human pulled out a tiny leather flask, the sort that hadn't been used in many centuries.

The spirit's blood. It was the last, missing piece of the Anima Chest, which for the Tiger was the most important object of power in the universe. He'd been searching for it for as long as he'd known it existed.

The red-cloaked humans moved as if to open the wooden chest, but he lifted a hand. *"Not you."* After what had happened the last time he'd tried to use the Anima Chest – exactly four hundred and six years earlier – he wouldn't risk this going wrong.

Then finally a new figure strode into view on the normal side of the barrier. Lilith wore a shiny, pretty face and body like a human would wear a coat, but the Tiger could clearly see straight through it to her real face. (Which by Creature standards was perfectly adequate.) She seemed a lot smaller than when he'd last seen her, but that was just an impression caused by the way he'd doubled in size.

"As the only free user of both realms, you are the one person I will allow to do this for me," he said coldly. *"But if you betray me, there will be no place you can run."*

He felt the flicker of her heartrate go up, but her expression didn't change. "Master, I have no need for the Anima Chest's power, and there is no one I fear more than you."

It was the right answer. But still, the Tiger pressed himself against the barrier as Lilith opened the chest directly on the other side, within inches of him. Inside were three neatly cut compartments, fizzing with alter-power. Two were already occupied with a fresh-looking flower and a mottled brown rock. The other was the right size for the missing flask, and Lilith barely paused before setting it in place.

For a moment nothing happened. The chest didn't look any different either, but suddenly he could feel a warmth where it pressed against the base of the barrier, right by his clawed foot.

And then when Lilith lifted the chest as high as she could reach, pressing it against the barrier, he pressed his hand against the other side…and grasped the box.

Then, almost bursting with triumph at this long-awaited moment, the Tiger stepped through the barrier into the normal realm.

Mountain of Glass, time very relevant

Amaranthus stood in his tapestry room, studying one of the long, darkest grey threads that ran around the edge of the entire room. Here, at the very end of the tapestry, it had suddenly moved away from its safe place at the border and abruptly into the middle amongst all the tiny threads signifying human lives. And everything it touched, it tainted.

Amaranthus didn't need to touch the thread to know who it was. He certainly didn't stop to think about his next move. For while the Creatures had an imperfect, limited view of the future, his was as complete as it had ever been.

Then he moved to the centre of the round room. Here, a fountain sprang from the centre of a gleaming black rock – the heartstone – then ran out to cover first the Mountain of Glass, then make its way as a river into the normal realm. Not just a river, *the* River.

Amaranthus set his hand against the stone's slick surface. Then connecting his mind with everyone who the River touched – from the immortal People to his human friends – he said, *"The countdown has started. Whatever you do next, make it count."*

Not quite the end...

The entire series will be concluded with book 7, *City of Light.*

Dear Reader,

Wow. Now I've released the second-to-last book in the series, I feel like I'm finally getting to the point where *everything* matters. It's a lot easier to write about low-key villains (i.e. those who seek world domination) as opposed to those who've actually achieved it (and are immortal psychopaths). Suddenly my favourite characters are in terrible danger, and there's only one way the final book can go.

They all have to die.

Just kidding, just kidding. But I have to tie up some seriously messy storylines, and I'm determined to do it well in *City of Light*.

As for *Whiter than Snow*: I've written and rewritten versions of this novel since 2014, but the story that you've just read is very different from its earlier versions. That's partly because I wrote the entire series in one go, before publishing any of them. Of course that meant that any changes to the earlier books had a flow-on effect to the sequels. Jon shows up regularly from book two, so by the time I reached *Whiter than Snow*, I ended up deleting the manuscript entirely then rewriting it from scratch. Let me tell you, this is a horrible way to write a series AND I WILL NEVER DO IT AGAIN.

Still, I'm happy with how things came together in the end. I always saw Jon's story as set solidly in this future time period, which meant I had to skim over his time in the past a little. I didn't mind, since as a reader, I don't like rereading storylines anyway. As a writer, I wouldn't do that to you either.

A few fun facts: Nadine's Chateau Chambord is a real castle in the Loire Valley, France. I was lucky enough to visit it as a teenager and it really stuck with me, so I tried to make specific details fit with the story. Any historical or architectural inaccuracies are because it's an alternate universe. (And also because it can be really hard to find out those tiny details. That's why I write fantasy, not history books.)

Tarie's supernatural 'Words' are a slightly warped mix of existing languages. For example, when she first accidentally speaks the Words in front of Rokal, Orla and Gavriel, she actually (unknowingly) says 'Be quiet, Creature, and go away' in a mix of French, Greek and Hebrew. (You may have noticed that Gavriel was the only one who actually shut up – this was due to his higher link to his own master. More to come on this.)

Besides being a necessary culmination of all the hints I put in books 2-5, multiple storylines in this novel also came from dreams. Tarie, her gift that grows things and her accidental run-ins with various baddies in VR; some elements of the White Prince and Jon's early, negative experiences flying; the Tiger's red-cloaked followers with their wiggly starfish-shaped marks; the VR battles that the classmates undertook; the many temples and doorways into the Other; Luke/Luca's bad attitude and assassination of his predecessor, and a couple of others I'll no doubt recall too late to mention.

I also shot myself in the foot when I decided Jon couldn't pronounce 'th' because of his native language (e.g. Bets rather than Beth). But I hadn't noticed that I'd also called Jon's native language 'Mesian**th**'. (And never mind our major character Amaran**th**us!) And these were in published novels, so it was too late to change those details.

Oops. So to fill that smallish plot hole, I had to quickly change the Erus pronunciation to 'Mesiant' with a silent H. Of course Elspeth had to be the one to point this out, because the locals wouldn't think to mention it in their narration.

Hopefully most readers also noticed the brief origin story of the villain from the series' first book, *The Eternity*

Stone. Yes, Seyen Johannis was always meant to come from Jon's time period, which is why she uses terms like 'Chaos', same as Jon and Tarie. She also has a soul-drinker in that book – not the same one as in this book, which was utterly destroyed by Jon using the circlet.

A few dedicated readers may have also noticed that this book's entry pieces and illegal VR darts are made of 'a highly toxic substance that can make people susceptible to mind control' when dissolved in water. This is the exact substance used in *The Eternity Stone* to control the people of Iversley, via their town water source. (Now you know.)

One final point re. why the Eternity Stone itself appears in *Whiter than Snow*, even though it was returned to its point of origin in book five, *The Hidden Door*. This is because it travels through time (duh). When the Rift happened and the Eternity Stone sprang into existence, it first appeared into our timeline in the late 2900s, right before Seyen found it. She's the one who takes it back in time and later loses it, setting it on its journey throughout history. So of course she wouldn't know that the only reason she knew about the Stone was because she took it into her own past, thus making sure the Creatures etc knew it existed so they could tell her to get it once they managed to pinpoint its location…

Understandably, this is a bit too complex to include in the actual book. So only my very favourite readers – the ones who make a point of reading the afterword – will ever find out this important information.

And with that subtle flattery, if you liked Whiter than Snow, please leave a review at your favourite retailer or Goodreads. Reviews really help to improve author visibility, as well as letting readers know what to expect.

City of Light

It's the end of the world as they know it.

Jon has finally come to terms with his life and destiny. He's even managed to make a couple of friends, including the incredible growing Tarie and fiery, time-travelling Bets. But then his birth mother Maia shows at the door, unaware that she's jumped through time and has been missing for seventeen years rather than a single afternoon.

That's a problem. But it's not even his biggest problem right now…

Meanwhile, Jon's sort-of-father/enemy Luca has offered Maia a lifeline – to find a powerful object that's rumoured to turn back time - and she'll pay any price to reclaim her past. But he has his own agenda, one that sets him against the most powerful Creature in the world.

Because seemingly overnight, the many governing Creatures have been overthrown. Now the world is under the control of just one Creature: the powerful and ancient Tiger who will crush anyone he cannot control. And there's no one he hates more than Amaranthus – the very being that Jon and the others have pledged to.

The one safeguard had always been that the Creatures could not leave the Other realm. But now that's no longer the case. The barrier between realms has been broken, and the world will never be the same again.

But Amaranthus also has his own plans that involve Jon, Bets and the others. The only question is, will they live long enough to achieve them?